THE
CYDONIA OBJECTIVE

A MORPHEUS INITIATIVE THRILLER

DAVID SAKMYSTER

Cover by Yocla Designs

Visit David Sakmyster on the World Wide Web at:
www.sakmyster.com

For Isabella.

May your imagination forever be as boundless as your thirst for wisdom

"Soon did the sons of Noah and their sons build a great tower in the city of Babel, which they would by magic raise unto Heaven, that they might see the throne of God. But God came down to see the tower they did build, and was displeased. He confounded their tongues, and scattered them across the earth. Even did he close the minds of men to magic, that they would not work as one any longer."

–Hermetic Arcanum

"The Mars we had found was just a big moon with a thin atmosphere and no life. There were no Martians, no canals, no water, no plants, no surface characteristics that even faintly resembled Earth's."

–Bruce Murray, JPL Director 1976-1982

PROLOGUE

Nuremburg, Germany—April 30, 1945

The three American tanks rumbled through the devastation, drove around Panzer tanks decimated from the early morning Allied air strike, and crunched over the wreckage without slowing down. Buildings were still smoldering, entire housing blocks flattened. Locals moved about the wreckage, calling for loved ones and searching for valuables. Dogs barked, children ran fleeing from the invading tanks, and a pall of thick black smoke hung suspended between the jagged rooftops and the steel-gray sky.

The tanks continued along their determined course, following narrowed streets, heading for the southwestern corner of the city, speeding there, in fact. Despite the lack of any sort of resistance, they seemed to be on an urgent mission to get somewhere fast.

The objective soon became clear: a small church with one needle-like steeple. St. Katherine's was a prime example of gothic architecture with yawning archways and romantic columns. Badly burnt, but otherwise structurally undamaged in the attack, it stood resolute, but defenseless.

The tanks slowed, then diverged to cover three sides of the church. Hatches opened and green-clad soldiers rushed out, climbed down the sides and hurried to set up a perimeter. They took up positions, aiming at the doors, the windows, looking for snipers.

From the center tank, two more individuals emerged. The first: a large grey-haired soldier with a cigar trapped between his lips, one that he promptly lit as soon as he touched the ground. He was helped down by what looked to be his aide: a smaller, bookish man with spectacles and a thick crop of sweaty red hair.

One of the soldiers stood up from his kneeling position and shouted back, "Church secure, General Patton, Sir! Do we move in?"

Patton drew in a huge breath of cigar smoke, let it sit in his lungs, then expelled it slowly. He stared at the church without blinking. A long, slow stare. Then he spoke quietly to his aide: "You're sure it's here?"

The red-haired man thought for a moment before responding. At least, it seemed he was thinking. His eyes closed, his head lowered, and his put his fist to his forehead. Sweat broke out along his temples, and he started to tremble. Patton pulled his attention from the church to study the man with rapt admiration.

Finally, the red-haired man nodded and opened his eyes. "A specially constructed vault below the foundation. Reinforced walls and steel doors that you will need to blow up to get inside. It's inside the vault, in a crate, hidden among the church ornaments and other stolen relics."

Patton smiled. "Guards?"

"Two just outside the door to the vault room. One inside, guarding a golden box near the back. Inside is a false relic. Don't be fooled."

His smile widening, Patton strode forward; he waved to his soldiers and pointed to the front door. As the men raced ahead, Patton slowed, then turned back. The red-haired man still stood in place, hugging his arms, shaking slightly as the wind blew smoke trails around him. A plane roared overhead, and he winced with the sound. He met Patton's gaze and his dry lips parted.

"You'll keep it safe?"

Patton drew another breath from the cigar and thought before answering. "Better than Hitler did, the egomaniac. To think, he actually let it out of his grasp. And look what happened."

The red-haired man nodded. "So it's true? They're advancing on his bunker in Berlin?"

Patton shrugged. "I don't need your skills to see that the coward will probably take his own life before we get there. It's over. The Reich is finished, and—"

"And America? Will it take its place?"

Patton's expression formed a look of annoyance at the question. "America will be what it's meant to be." He pointed to the church. "When we reclaim what Hitler stole from that museum in Austria, we'll be unstoppable. But power is just a means to an end. Eisenhower no doubt will order that we return the relic to its rightful owner, like all the other stolen artifacts we reclaim from these Nazi bastards."

"But you won't let him do that, will you?" The red-haired man's lips curled in a tight smile. "And don't bother answering, I've seen it already."

"Ah, then I suppose I must insist you keep that little vision to yourself." Patton grinned back at him, even as gunshots sounded from inside the church: a short, brief exchange, and then quiet resumed as the church's defenders met their quick ends. "So, if I might ask, what else have you seen?"

The red-haired man closed his eyes for a moment, as if recapturing a series of fond memories. "You are going to trick your commander. Your artists will create a perfect forgery, and you will let General Eisenhower return *that* to the Austrian government. Meanwhile, you are going to place the true artifact somewhere that makes perfect sense. Not only *hidden in plain sight*, but keeping it where it can wielded by the most important symbol of everything America stands for as the preeminent world power."

General Patton blinked at the man for several seconds, chewing on the end of the diminishing cigar until the ashes fell, joining others from Nuremberg's burning skyline. Then, he nodded once more.

"You have surpassed all my expectations, Jordan Crowe. I thank you. And your nation thanks you."

The red-haired man closed his eyes. And after Patton turned and at long last strode into the church to claim his prize, Crowe spoke, directing his words into the rising wind: "Hide it well, General."

He sighed and closed his eyes, the lids flickering with a far off vision.

"Hide it well, so that it may still be there when it's truly needed."

BOOK ONE
Reunions

1.

Cairo, Egypt—Present Day

As the limo violently swerved to avoid something in the road, Orlando Natch held the laptop in his weak grasp, still woozy from blood loss after being attacked by ravenous eels in the mauso-leum of Genghis Khan.

But despite everything he'd gone through, he felt rejuvenated, as if his ascent from the depths of that tomb and his multiple brushes with death had transformed him like a veritable Phoenix from its own ashes. Less than twelve hours earlier, that adventure already seemed like a lifetime ago, something that had happened to someone else, someone much braver, more deserving to be here with the beautiful young woman sitting beside him.

Phoebe Crowe continued staring at the laptop screen, even as she flinched at the sound of something striking the limo's front windshield. The image on the screen—*the planet Mars*, the red, dusty soil photographed from the Viking Orbiter in 1976, one of over fifty-thousand pictures taken during its mission—depicted a mesa-dotted region known as 'Cydonia', home to a certain famously controversial image.

A face.

A trick of light and shadow, most scientists believed, despite other equally incongruous structures nearby—things that looked suspiciously like pyramids, walled enclosures, and geometrically-precise markers aligned in relation to the mile-long, symmetrical 'face'.

Another object struck the windshield, and Phoebe looked up, annoyed.

Cairo's roads were dusty and decrepit in places, and the bumpy ride from the pyramids toward the airport was jarring, with pebbles flying and--

"Oh crap!" Orlando shrieked, just as the driver grunted and his head snapped back, spraying blood into the back seat. Above the steering wheel, the windshield had a neat hole in it, with cracks spreading out, reaching toward the other impact point where another bullet had glanced off.

The limo turned sharply as the driver slumped sideways and dragged the wheel in his dying grasp. Phoebe screamed, and Orlando reached for her as an oncoming bus slammed into the driver's side. A moment of tortured metallic screaming, and the limo banked up on its side, then flipped over.

The rest of the windows fractured, and as Phoebe rolled onto the roof with Orlando on top of her, she saw something out the back window. A black Hummer screeched to a halt, turning sideways.

And a man leaned out the window, taking aim at them with a grenade launcher.

Phoebe cursed, held Orlando tight and tried to drag him up to the front, hoping to get out the main windshield. *Never make it*, she thought, wincing, bracing herself. Any second now–

The ground rocked, the limo shook, and she closed her eyes, hoping she'd feel no pain. The explosion came, except… it sounded less intense than she would have thought. Like it was at a distance. And–

"I don't believe it." Orlando pulled her up and dragged her over the seats, over the dead driver and out the shattered windshield. Onto a street littered with crashed cars, the overturned bus, and people filing out, shell-shocked. Phoebe stood and looked back toward the Hummer and saw what was left of it on its side with flames roaring through the shattered windows.

Bewildered, she glanced around just as two more dark forms leapt from a nearby alleyway and raised sleek guns she recognized as MP5s, the kind those commandos had when they'd captured the Morpheus team down in the mausoleum.

"Oh, that's just not fair," Orlando said, raising his hands even as the men took aim. Phoebe flinched as the shots rang out—and both men spun around, the backs of their heads simultaneously exploding. Two thin red beams descended from the sky and swept over their inert bodies, before darting over to Orlando and Phoebe.

Dust and wind kicked up, her hair blew back and then forward over her eyes, and Orlando shielded his face as he looked up.

"Helicopter."

A rope ladder descended and a voice yelled from above, *"Climb up!"*

Pushed by Orlando, Phoebe reached for the second rung and started climbing. Halfway up, expecting more shots to come from darkened alleys or apartment windows or rooftop shadows, she paused, tensing.

Three shots from above got her back into action. These people knew what they were doing, she thought grimly. *I really hope they're the good guys.*

Near the top, she called down to Orlando, who was still struggling at the bottom, trying to hold his laptop and climb at the same time. Finally giving it up, he let it drop with a mournful groan, whimpered as it shattered, then scampered up after her.

In the helicopter, two men with helmets and rifles slung over their shoulders hauled her up while another with an RPG at his side started pulling up the ladder with Orlando still on it.

"GO!" one of them yelled to the pilot. The helicopter ascended and rushed ahead, even as the man with the RPG swiveled, aimed and fired two more shots at rooftop targets.

Orlando tumbled inside and clutched at Phoebe with an intensity that only surprised her because of how strong she found herself returning his hug.

The closest man shut the door, then took off his helmet, revealing a leathery face, a thick head of silvery hair, and pale blue eyes that blinked slowly as he considered his cargo.

"So you two are the ones causing all this fuss."

Orlando glanced out the window, bidding farewell to his lost laptop. "Who, us?"

Phoebe was shaking her head, still bewildered. "The driver was taking us to the airport. We were told our part was done, that we'd be allowed to leave. It doesn't make sense. Why would they have attacked us?"

Their rescuer sighed. "The limo was bugged. And so is your house back in New York. You would have been monitored. Everything you said, they'd follow. They would have hacked your computers, your phones…"

"I knew it," Orlando said. "I was right!"

Phoebe stared at him. "About…?"

The man with the gun nodded. "We tapped into their signal and heard what they heard. Heard you talking. They gave the order to take you out as soon as you mentioned the name of– "

"Mars!" Orlando shook his head. "Son of a bitch. What does it have to do with any of this? The Face? All that crazy stuff NASA's been ridiculing for years…?"

"Let's not get ahead of ourselves," the man said. "First things first." He held out a hand. "Edgerrin Temple, and the others here are what we like to call our Retrieval Unit."

"Whose retrieval unit?" Phoebe asked, shouting to be heard over the engine.

The man smiled. "We're not out of the woods yet." He pointed to a row of seats on the wall. "You might want to strap your-selves in."

As Phoebe moved into her seat, she peered out the window, seeing the looming Egyptian landmarks coming back into view, and she grinned. "We're going back for my brother!"

"Actually, no."

"*What?* We can't leave him there."

"We can. They'll be all right."

Orlando finished with his seat belt. "How do you know that?"

Temple smiled as he put a phone to his ear. "We're not without our own talents."

Phoebe gave Orlando a look. She caught his hand, squeezed it. They both nodded together and closed their eyes.

"Hey!" Temple slammed the butt of his rifle against the floor. "No psychic-stuff now. Stay with me!"

Phoebe glared at him. "Caleb's down there, trapped under the Sphinx. With–
"

"Alexander, yes we know. And your half-brother Xavier Montross."

"Who the hell do you work for?" Phoebe asked directly. "And no more games. We've been double-crossed by the CIA, the FBI, the Keepers, and some other crazy religious group. Which one are you?"

Temple's blue eyes remained radiant and sympathetic. "None of the above, I assure you, but for now, just look."

As they circled around the Great Pyramid, Phoebe and Orlando were handed high-powered binoculars. Temple pointed down to the forepaws of the Great Sphinx, where a group of figures were standing, some of them glancing up.

Phoebe focused on one figure in particular, the one apparently in charge, barking orders, moving armed men and jeeps into a perimeter, signaling others to descend below. The figure paused, then looked up.

Phoebe said, "Damn. It's Nina."

"That bitch," Orlando quipped. "Figures."

"Confirmed," Temple said into his phone, and then promptly tapped the pilot on the shoulder. The helicopter banked sharply, then took off.

"What was that all about?" Phoebe asked. "What's confirmed?"

Temple smiled. "The Dove's vision."

"The what?" Orlando rubbed his eyes. "This sucks! Seri-ously, tell us or I'm remote-viewing you clowns as soon as you turn your back."

Temple shrugged. "You might not see much."

"Why's that?" Phoebe asked. "We're good at this, as you must know if you've been tracking us."

"Yes," he said, "you're good. But we've got a Shield."

Phoebe and Orlando glanced at each other. "A what?"

"Tell me something," said Temple as they flew higher, leaving the city far below and heading out over the desert. "Did you ever try to view something, maybe like a religious something... like, I don't know, the Crucifixion, or the birth of Jesus? Maybe Joseph Smith and his meeting with the angels? Mohammed's desert vision? Any of that?"

Phoebe paled, her mouth opened. "Yes, of course. What remote-viewer with any skill wouldn't try to get a glimpse into that kind of thing?"

Orlando glanced at her sharply. "You have?"

She nodded slowly, meeting his confused stare.

Orlando shrunk a little. "I mean, I assumed you just…"

"Didn't care?" Phoebe raised her voice over the engines. "These are the most important world beliefs, the driving forces behind civilization, wars and everything for thousands of years. Billions of people believe one thing or another—and are willing to kill for those beliefs—all based on ancient events that supposedly happened but can never be verified. If we can go back and see those things first-hand, we can *know*. Actually, truly know. Forget the debate between science and faith." Her eyes glassed over, swelling with a wall of pain. "Of course I looked. *Tried* to look."

"But…" Orlando leaned tentatively holding her hands.

"Let me guess," Temple said. "You saw nothing."

"Not exactly nothing," Phoebe replied, a little bitterness in her voice. "More like-"

"A soft blue light. A hazy fog?" Temple's smile widened.

Phoebe stared at him. "Yes. How did you know?"

"Because such things—certain things like that are being *shielded.*"

"How can that be?" Orlando asked. "And by whom?"

Temple continued grinning at them like a schoolboy with a naughty secret. He held up a finger. "Shielding, we've found, is something that's either being consciously enacted and continuously enforced—as it is in our case to cover ourselves, through great effort. Or in cases like these critical faith-based concerns, it may part of a collective will, that enough people, many of them with unknown psychic talents, are directing their thoughts so much on the present unknowable, unprovable *faith*, that they have managed to retroactively go back and shield the actual events in an impenetrable veil."

Orlando merely blinked at him, as if he had sprouted a second head with a gibberish vocabulary.

"I don't buy it," Phoebe said.

Temple shrugged. "Doesn't matter. It is what it is. Our own RV members have experienced the same denial as you have, almost as if something…" he waved his arms. "…out there doesn't want the truth to be known. Some of our members have even gone so far as to suggest certain nefarious elements have shielded these ultimate answers, so as to perpetuate the multitude of religious beliefs."

"Why would they do that?" Orlando asked as he held his stomach while the helicopter lurched and dipped again.

"Why not?" said Temple. "If these other forces wanted humans to remain deadlocked, ever at each others' throats, never advancing in harmony, never speaking the same tongues…"

Phoebe nodded. "Like the Tower of Babel story. Scatter the people, keep them at odds through different tongues and beliefs. My brother Caleb's always on about that theory too."

"Yep," said Orlando. "Except he thinks we all had these abilities long ago, and that language wasn't necessarily the spoken one, that instead we all had some kind of telepathy and clairvoyance and everything, and the tower symbolized our progress."

"Until the gods came and knocked it down and 'confused our tongues'," Phoebe said.

Temple shrugged. "Whatever the case is, we're working on it. Among other things, and… we need you."

Phoebe glanced at him suspiciously. "That's why you rescued us? Because what? You want us to join you, work for you? Doing what?"

"Doing what you're doing. We've been following you, secretly cheering on The Morpheus Initiative."

Orlando struggled to follow all this. His head was pounding and his throat was parched. "What the hell for? And why, if you've got psychics, didn't you come to us before? We could have used you."

"You were doing fine on your own. And if you found out about us, you would have also found out about *them*. And that would have derailed your search for the relics."

Orlando shook his head. "Relics, plural? Do you mean the keys? The other tablets?"

Temple shook his head. "Nope. There are only two relics of power that our enemies seek. One is the Emerald Tablet, which they now possess."

Phoebe leaned closer. "And the other?"

Temple sighed. "For that, I'll let you use your powers. On the plane ride back to America. We'll have time for that, and for planning. They don't know exactly where it is, but I'm guessing you two can succeed where they failed. Ask the right questions, and find it. And give us the chance to stop them."

"But, Caleb and..."

"They have their own path to take. One that will intersect with ours in time."

Orlando frowned. "And you know this by... what this 'Dove' said?"

"Exactly. Now, enough talk, we're approaching the airport."

Orlando's stomach lurched as they descended, but he was determined to sound like he was in control, despite not once feeling that way since the limo had overturned. "Wait, tell us this at least. Who the hell are you guys?"

Temple stood and bent forward to answer. "Years ago, Phoebe, you and your brother did us a great favor, ridding our organization of its corrupt leader. Since then, I've taken his place, done what we've needed to do, what we were able to do with limited resources in response to grave threats—so many that we've countered and continue to monitor. I hesitate to tell you, because we were responsible for what was done to your father, and what happened to your mother, but I promise you, now we're more alike than you know."

"I had a feeling," Orlando said, "even though it was before my time."

Phoebe gulped, her heart catching in her throat. "You're-"

Temple nodded. *"Stargate."*

2.

Nina Osseni delivered the last instructions to the squad of men at her command, then looked up toward the flickering lights of the helicopter several hundred feet over their heads. "Is that one of ours?"

"No ma'am," said the lead agent. "Air support pulled back after you landed. Should we open fire?"

She narrowed her eyes. Directly under the craft now, she took a deep breath. Let her body relax, her mind unhinge for just a moment...

And then she was there, in the cockpit, looking backward.

Ah. Phoebe. Orlando. There you are. And who's that with you?

She snapped out of it just as quickly. "Never mind," she called over to the agent. "You have your orders. Discontinue the terrorist threat, but keep this area secure. Say that there's still concern for a bomb or something. And keep everyone out until Mason Calderon gets here."

With my boys, she thought, suppressing a rising excitement, finding herself tempted to peer into their lives. Now that she knew they were there. Now that she knew what questions to ask.

I'm a mother...

Twins.

She could hardly wait to see how they had turned out.

Back under the Sphinx, Nina stood before the obsidian door, the one that had slammed down on the hapless Commander Marcos, crushing him in half. His gruesome body still lay there, his left leg and arm splayed out, half in and half out of the mysterious chamber.

Her men had already removed the other body—that of Robert Gregory. One-time keeper and leader of the Marduk Cult. Commander Marcos had shot him in the head after his failed bid to pass beyond the Obsidian Door. Mason Calderon had suspected it wasn't Robert who was fated to enter the lost chamber. The prophecy called for one of three brothers to be the one to find the way inside and claim the contents of the iron box—the translation of the great Emerald Tablet, now in a pack over Nina's shoulder.

She could feel the Tablet's power, vibrating up her arm, calling out to her and to the keys beyond this door. Keys made from the same material as the Tablet, keys that had been secured by great conquerors in history. Cyrus the Great, then Alexander, then passed on to Genghis Khan who had entombed himself with two of the keys, protecting them from the likes of Robert Gregory and Mason Calderon. Until The Morpheus Initiative members found their way down into that nearly impregnable tomb, bypassed the Khan's defenses and took the keys.

But now they were trapped behind the door under the Pyramids. Caleb, Alexander and Xavier. Trapped... but not without their own resources. Nina had glimpses of other things beyond this door: a long passageway through the darkness, converging with a shaft under the Great Pyramid. Some kind of path used in an ancient initiation ceremony. And beyond that: further labyrinths, multi-level chambers, grottos, winding staircases leading nowhere, tunnels ending in deadly traps and rooms where one false step would lead to eternal imprisonment behind walls of stone.

She smiled, knowing that the three of them would have their hands full, but given their experience, most recently with Genghis Khan's elaborate tomb defenses, and earlier, with the diabolical traps under the Pharos Lighthouse, they would survive.

Only two questions remained: Where would they emerge, and could Nina's agents be ready to capture them?

Being Xavier Montross's companion and aide for over two years, Nina knew first-hand the man's resourcefulness, and his uncanny ability to foresee danger to himself—and avoid it. She didn't relish the task at hand, but at the same time, Mason Calderon had made it clear: capture of Caleb and the others was secondary to the main objective. They had to acquire the tablets of translation. And she was reasonably sure Caleb hadn't been able to open the iron box, despite the keys.

No, the tablets were still there, in the room beyond the door. Waiting for her and her boys. She would get those tablets. Soon. But that didn't mean she couldn't try to tie up loose ends at the same time.

There was still the little matter of revenge. Despite the revelation that he was the father of her twins, it didn't change the fact that Caleb had left her to rot. So many years in a coma under the old Stargate facility, where doctors had tended to her and even delivered her babies all while she was unconscious and possibly deliberately drugged to remain in that coma.

Caleb could have found her. Should have. If he hadn't been swept away by another woman. Lydia Gregory, Robert's sister. Another Keeper. Another traitor. She had died—good riddance—after Xavier stole the Emerald Tablet and set off Caleb's defenses under his own lighthouse basement in Sodus Bay. Lydia had been caught in the inferno, incinerated while Xavier escaped.

Nina still felt the smug satisfaction of that retribution, but now… She was a mother. And things were different. Did she still want to kill Caleb? She couldn't imagine what he was feeling now, realizing the impotency of his own powers. To think, he hadn't even considered that Nina was alive, much less pregnant with his boys. She almost giggled with the thought of how his mind must be in turmoil. His place in the world upturned. His responsibilities in flux.

Let him stew, she thought.

And then she realized she had time before Calderon got here. Before she could see her own flesh and blood.

Time.

Time to peek in on Caleb. And on her boys. And possibly, if the visions allowed—her new master.

She took a seat, cross-legged on the cold granite floor beside the dead body of Commander Marcos. Prepared her breathing, relaxing herself until feeling a tingling sensation rushing from the base of her spine outward toward her fingers. And then she reached for the dead man's hand, finding and needing a connection to something, his lingering force. Willing from the dead flesh a host of memories, experiences and more.

There was so much to see.

Commander Marcos looks *away from the mirror, finished with admiring his chiseled features. Turns to the wizened older man in the shadows. Notes the same rugged confidence, the silvery-gray hair slicked back over a lupine face with deep-set blue eyes.*

Mason Calderon rises and steadies himself against a sudden shifting of the floor. They are on the sea, rocking with the waves. Calderon leans on a long cane with a gold handle featuring a scaled dragon speared through the throat with a lance. "Soon, my friend. We will be home at last. Rid of this world..." He looks down at his body. "And these... ornaments. For good."

Marcos bows, then fixes his attention on the head of Mason's cane, the golden staff. "Then do we still need the other item, the relic the twins are seeking?"

Mason takes his time in answering. "We only need to be certain of its whereabouts—and then protect it from falling into our enemy's hands. Until we are done. After the translation—after the formula has been obtained and fed to our brothers in Alaska—then it no longer matters what our enemies have. They'll be powerless to prevent our ascension."

Nodding, Marcos walks to the only other visible object in the shadowy room. A window. And beyond: waves. Dark water with turbulent crests, and farther away—the glinting lights of a massive city, a skyline punctuated by immense towers and bridges.

And the shadowy form of a single backlit behemoth. An immense statue holding aloft a massive torch...

Nina's mind moves on.

Two infants swaddled and brought humbly before the man she recognizes as George Waxman, who peers at them with concerned but distant consideration. "These ones will have great power," he says. "Twins are always stronger psychically, but these—sons of two powerful clairvoyants..." He makes a clicking voice with his tongue. "Keep them here, under observation. When they grow older, I will decide what to do with them."

The scene shifts, *and two young boys, maybe five years old, race big wheels across the polished floors of a great mansion. Blond-haired, both of them wearing matching blue suits, they race around great marble pillars, laughing and screeching until the huge doors burst open.*

Mason Calderon stands there, hands on his hips. Dressed in a tuxedo. "Isaac. Jacob. Stop at once. It's time. Come, we must meet the others."

They both turn and brake at the same time, skidding to within feet of their guardian.

Isaac looks to Jacob. "Does he mean us, brother?"

"I think so, brother. Step to it!"

Calderon scowls. "I'm not playing, boys. Now!"

"Sounds serious," says Isaac, backing up, then pedaling forward leisurely before stopping at Calderon's feet, and then retreating again.

His brother mirrors his actions. "I should say we better do as he says. Righto?"

"You bet!"

Calderon shakes his head with growing annoyance. "Boys, please. Today is a big day. I need you to show them what you can do. Show these men and women why I've invested so much time in your development."

"'Invested', he says." Isaac grins to his brother.

Jacob nods. "Sounds like livestock, we do."

"Pork bellies, us!"

"Cow hides! Porcupine skins!"

"Boys!"

"What should we speak about, father?" Isaac stops now. He stands up and crosses his arms. His brother joins him.

"Tell them what we sees, should we?"

"Righto," Isaac says. "Tell them what we likes to draw? The dead things? The bloody things?"

Mason Calderon sighs. "They will ask you questions. You will answer truthfully."

"Questions," Jacob says, looking at his brother. "Always questions."

"Gotta know the right ones to ask," Isaac explains. "Bigtime smartee pants questions, righto, father?"

Calderon nods. "Righto, boys. Now come."

"I'd like very much to talk about the Dragon." Jacob says it. Quietly, looking down.

"The dragon?" Calderon leans forward, his voice catching, eyes sparkling with sudden interest.. "How long have you been seeing... this dragon?"

"Long," Jacob says. "Long time. Him too." He points to Isaac.

"Dragon caught in a net. Dragon stabbed with spear."

"Dragon go boom!" Jacob whispers, eyes wide.

Mason stands up tall.

"Fine, boys. In fact, more than fine. Tell them that." He smiles. "Yes, I think they'll like that very much. The dragon. The spear..."

Isaac and Jacob look at each other and grin.

"Righto."

Later...

Older, a little bigger. The boys, stepping away from their snow-mobiles. Taking off their helmets, revealing long blond curls. Shoulders broadening, arms thick, already tall for their age.

They stand over the twitching body of a magnificent stag. The deer grunts, lets out a mournful whine, then kicks helplessly at blood spattered snow.

Isaac removes the scoped rifle strapped on his back, the same one that had felled this creature minutes ago.

"Hardly sporting, brother," Jacob says, hands on his hips. "Did you really need a scope?"

"Didn't use it, you know. Never even saw the creature until I pulled the trigger."

"Oh, you saw it all right. Just with your other eyes."

"Righto." He aims for the deer's head. Fires. Smiles, never once blinking or looking away from the gore blasting outward from between the antlers.

"So much for a souvenir for father Calderon's wall."

Isaac shrugs. "He has enough. Besides, this is only practice. Isn't that what he told us? Practice for when we meet mother."

Jacob nods, glancing off to the weakened sun dancing between the trees, drooping toward the horizon. A chill wind blows through the dead forest. "Practice."

"The time is coming soon, brother."

"I wonder..."

"Yes?"

"What he's like."

"Our younger?" Isaac giggles.

Sensing the mood shift, Jacob joins in. "Our brother from another mother."

"I bet he's a tool."

"We're all tools, brother. But us, we're tools for the right side."

"Righto. The winning side." Isaac slings the rifle over his shoulder and heads for the snowmobile.

"Leave the carcass?" Jacob asks, lingering at the corpse.

"The flesh is nothing." Isaac closes his eyes and takes a deep breath, and his eyelids flicker as if he's seeing a vast panorama played out behind them. "Before we're done, every living thing on this planet will be like this..."

Jacob nods, his smile matching his brother's. He heads to the snowmobile, and together they drive off, leisurely weaving between the crooked trees, racing toward the spreading darkness.

Nina sighs, trembling. She's about to let go and pull back from the visions, when one more rushes up at her like a wave and then drags her down into a maelstrom of furious images:

Caleb Crowe, hanging onto his son Alexander's hand, follows after Xavier Montross, pursuing the red haired man leading the way through the passageways. They pause right before the entrance to a circular chamber with a low chamber that fills suddenly erupts with spring-loaded spikes, skewering the air before them.

Montross then leads them around the perimeter toward an upward sloping shaft where again he holds back a restraining arm—and then abruptly pushes Caleb and Alexander into a recessed nook in the hall, just as an immense block comes rumbling down the shaft and slams past where they had just been standing.

Later: Alexander leads them over a chasm, across a series of stepping stones, choosing only those with certain hieroglyphics.

Then: they come to a chamber with a central pillar and a doorway carved into its base. They gather around the shaft, shining their lights on the images, painted mural-like onto its surface. And they stare, uncomprehending, until Caleb points to something and says-

3.

"Here..." Caleb Crowe's voice was weak, half-choked with the thin air in the passageways under the Great Pyramid—or wherever they were after nearly seven hours of wandering this labyrinth. They had walked for miles. Winding passageways hewn from the bedrock, doubling back and forth, descending for hundreds of feet in places, then rising again. There were arched bridges spanning over yawning crevasses, and sections where they climbed spirals staircases around tower-like spires thrusting out of the impenetrable darkness below. It always seemed they heard sounds of distant splashing, as if from waves lapping against the foundations.

At first, Caleb had been surprised and relieved at the lack of water. He remembered reading essays on the geological makeup of the Giza plateau, and the speculation that even if there were tunnels or chambers below the pyramids, they would likely be full of water due to their proximity to the Nile and its annual flooding. But apparently the builders had constructed these chambers to resist seepage, or they had drainage tunnels out of sight.

His interest in geology, however, quickly waned as they proceeded deeper and deeper into the labyrinth, pausing only to remote-view the way, each of them occasionally getting glimpses of the ancient past, of robed men and women solemnly proceeding along these very paths. Just snatches of visions, unable to see the purpose to these chambers, or the destination of its early travelers. But they had seen other things: passageways where the floors would have given way or where sliding walls would have imprisoned them after a false step. Rooms where the ceiling was supported on gears that would release and flatten anyone who stepped inside.

They bypassed all of these traps, avoiding death at every turn.

And now, after climbing a steep staircase, they had arrived at the top of what seemed like an enormous rounded pillar. The lights couldn't probe anything above or below, and there was only one bridgeway leading away into the gloom. In the center of the floor there stood a huge block, inscribed with hieroglyphics and carved images. Caleb stared at it for a thoughtful moment. "This is... I don't understand this at all. Why should this symbol be here?"

"What is it, Dad?" Alexander had his flashlight highlighting the image of a baboon holding aloft a disc, flanked by royal serpents. The rest of the mural, painted around the immense block, depicted what appeared to be a scene of metallurgy: an ibis-faced man holding a hammer and a long spear, thrusting the lance into a cauldron. On a nearby table, a rectangular sheet of what seemed to be a book, except it was dyed a deep hue of green. The same god-man was bent over it with a quill, inscribing words of power.

"Down here, this section I get." Caleb pointed. "Here's Thoth as a smith. Creating, in this panel, a spear-head. In the other, a tablet. A book."

"The Emerald Tablet." Alexander said it reverently, fearful of speaking about it in this ancient place—with what might be its first-ever depiction.

But then Alexander saw that Caleb had shifted his flashlight higher, to where the symbol of a god holding two staffs stood in profile, a sphere on his head. Above him, an inverted triangle, and at the top, a coiled serpent caught in a net, its head pinned to the triangle with a long spear.

Xavier Montross had circled around the pillar, giving it little attention, instead eyeing the darkness all around them, as if imagining it concealed a multitude of monstrosities, guardians ready to descend upon them.

"We don't have much time," Montross said. "Can we skip the sightseeing?"

Caleb shook his head. "This is important."

"Yes, yes," Montross said, finally taking an interest in the carvings. "Our friends, the dragon and the lance."

"Marduk and Tiamat," Alexander said, remembering what they had been talking about earlier. "The war god killing the dragon-goddess. Stealing her

Tablet of Destiny thing."

"Yes," Caleb said, "but it's astounding that it's being depicted here, in this ancient passageway beneath the Giza complex. And at a place of seemingly great importance." He glanced back toward the stairs, ruminating on the series of tests and challenges, the deadly traps and diabolical puzzles they had managed to solve only with the aid of their psychic abilities, glimpsing the past and seeing the way ahead.

He shook his head with wonderment. "This is the crucial lesson. This is what the acolytes were meant to understand, this is the reward for everything we've just gone through."

Montross made a snickering sound. "Bit of a letdown, if you ask me. Risk-reward ratio way out of balance. It's a nice picture and all, but-"

"But it's everything,' Caleb said calmly. He pointed at the god-figure below the triangle. "That's Ra. Marduk, if you will. But the placement of his symbol, below an inverted triangle, implies to me something about *creation.*"

"But," Alexander said, "Marduk wasn't created after the dragon died, he killed the dragon!"

"True..." Caleb continued staring at the pillar, and his flashlight beam trembled. "But instead of implying that he, personally, was created by the incident, what if it means something else?"

"Like what?" Montross was still glancing around nervously as if expecting something horrific to come slithering down the air shaft and drop on them at any moment. Or the walls to close in or the ceiling to collapse.

Caleb rubbed his chin in thought. "The symbol for Marduk, there with the two scepters, can also mean something literal. Something astronomical. The planet..."

Montross whipped his head around. His eyes went wide. "Mars." He approached, showing real interest now. "Yes, yes. This, taken a certain way, matches my vision. Your visions too, Caleb. Cosmic history wrapped up in myth. The epic disaster. A conflict that destroyed a planet-sized body out beyond Mars, leaving the current asteroid belt."

"And something else," Caleb whispered, pointing again to the triangle. "It's almost as if this is saying that conflict created Mars itself, and yet..."

"That's not right," Montross said. "The myth could even read that Mars the planet acted as Marduk and influenced Tiamat into some kind of collision, if you believe cosmic catastrophic proponents like Immanuel Velikovsky. But it may have been something else, and its destruction may have created—what, a civilization on Mars?"

"Or its moons," Caleb said thoughtfully. "Depending on how long ago we're talking, we know Mars had abundant water—oceans and polar ice—millennia ago. But also, its moons—Phobos and Deimos—are highly unusual, with irregular orbits, perplexing lunar craters and other inconsistencies. As recent as the '60s, some scientists seriously considered the conclusion that they were hollow. Artificial."

Montross smiled suddenly, pointing to the two scepters of Marduk. "Phobos and Deimos. Translation from the Greek: *Fear* and *terror*." He sighed. "Whatever this is telling us, can we contemplate it later? Nina's got to be after us by now, and we're no closer to getting out of here."

Alexander shifted awkwardly, glancing at the dark passage behind them. "What about going back? Finding the upward shaft and climbing up to the Great Pyramid? I think I saw a way in there."

"And then what?" Montross snapped. "Just waltz out the main door? They'd be on us in seconds."

"We could wait it out? Hide inside the pyramid somewhere."

Caleb shook his head. "Not with Nina out there. And especially not if her... kids show up."

"You mean *your* kids," Montross said with a lopsided grin. Then he added, "So it seems I'm blessed with even more nephews, huh?"

Caleb looked away. Reached for Alexander and squeezed his shoulders reassuringly. "I don't know what to think about them yet. But I've gotten some visions, and I'm... worried."

Alexander nodded. "I've been seeing them too. For a long time, I think. Without knowing who they were or why I was seeing them. I wonder, were they glimpsing me too?"

"Probably," Caleb said. "If they're as good as you."

"Again," Montross said, his voice rising. "Can we proceed? I say we move on ahead, scout out where this infernal labyrinth winds up. There has to be another exit."

"Tell that to the minotaur," Alexander said.

Caleb glanced toward the darkness. "This may be it, and there's no other way out. The path of the initiate was from the Sphinx to the Great Pyramid. Everything else is mere confusion and more tests of the candidate's resolve."

Montross stared at the shadows ahead of them. "No. There's something else. Another way out. I've seen it. Come along, I know the way."

Caleb lingered for a moment, glancing one more time at the dragon, focusing on the spear embedded in its skull. He reached out and before he knew he was doing it, he touched the image. Traced the dragon's scales, then after a slight hesitation, put his finger on the raised markings of the lance.

Nothing happened. With a sigh, a mixture of relief and regret, he was about to start after his son and his brother when a question suddenly popped into his head, and the resulting psychic trigger knocked him flat.

Where is that spear now?

The Theban Legion, *six thousand strong, stands at the ready in a rocky valley between snow-capped peaks, with a sprawling mountain range at their backs. A light snow falls from a hazy, dark mass of clouds obscuring any sign of the late afternoon sun. Heads high, eyes skyward, the legion stands defiant, motionless until their leader steps forward to meet the regal figure leading a larger force of centurions toward them. The thundering steeds strain to break into a rout and plunge into the midst of the legionnaires.*

But one horseman raises a hand and the entire force comes to a stop. Garbed in a purple cloak, with a crown of gold on his head, he leads his horse ahead, directly into the path of the approaching Theban legionary.

The commander of the Theban Legion removes his helmet, revealing a dark-skinned face, a bald head, and shining eyes. He holds a spear in his left hand, sets its base into the cold earth, and then lowers his head and bows.

"My Lord Maximian. You grace us with this unexpected visit. We have just come from Gaul, and have put down the revolt with all speed and success. And minimal loss of life. All glory to Rome."

Maximian nods indifferently. Glances around at the men, at the state of their armor, their bandaged wounds. "I hear stories, Maurice. Stories, stories.

Always stories, all the way across the empire they come, flying like diseased crows, bearing ill news."

Maurice lowers his eyes. "What news, my lord?"

"Don't play games, commander. You know why I've come. Why I've had to personally make this trip..." He waves his arm around the mountainous land. "...to deal with a wayward commander and a legion that refuses orders."

The centurions at the emperor's back jitter nervously, hands tightening on their weapons. Tense, eyes scanning the legionnaires with a mix of fear and respect.

The legionnaires make no move, but only return the stares.

"My Lord," says Maurice. "There is but one order I have had my men refuse."

"And why is that, might I ask?" Maximian fixes him with a dull stare, then punctuates it with a yawn. "Wait, don't tell me. You and most of your men have already shifted your beliefs to that of this new cult. This 'Christianity'. And so, when I tell you to visit violence on any who refuse my divine right of rule, to these... cultists who bend a knee only to their martyred savior, you refuse. You side with them over your emperor. You call yourself loyal, yet you feel it is your right to disobey."

"My Lord, never. We have always succeeded in our missions. We have found... other ways of enforcing your rule. Without resorting to violence upon your otherwise loyal subjects."

Maximian rears his horse, and it stomps its forelegs down around Maurice. "Loyal!? Tell me how they are loyal when they bow to another? Tell me too, commander, how are you loyal when you likewise refuse? If I tell you now, march back into Gaul and slaughter every one of these defiant Christians, what will your answer be?"

"My Lord, please. We are your strongest legion, your most able fighters. Feared among your enemies. Even..." He looks beyond the Emperor, at the trembling centurions. "Even among your own private armies."

Maximian waves his hand as if shooing off a cloud of bugs. "Yes, yes. And that is the only reason I haven't slaughtered you on the spot. But I must ask, what good is a commander, an entire legion, no matter their battle prowess, if they cannot follow orders?"

"Lord Maximian, please." Maurice takes his hand off the lance—and for just a moment the spear point catches in a sudden shaft of brilliance as a break forms in the dense clouds and the sun bursts through. An incredibly smooth silver surface, ringed in gold, with a thin sliver of wood set in an indentation in the center of the spear-point.

Maximian shields his eyes. And Maurice stares directly into the fierce glow—and lets his hand drop away. He lowers his head. "If that is what you ask, then I refuse." He faces his men. "I cannot order you, my soldiers to do the same. I will bear responsibility alone for dis-obedience." He turns back to Maximian. "And I alone will suffer the consequences."

Maximian, still squinting against the glare, has nothing to say. He seems to be agonizing over the intensity of the light.

But then Maurice steps back, out of arm's reach of the spear, and drops to his knees.

And the sun disappears, hungrily devoured once more by the churning dark clouds. The light goes out, and the spear point shimmers another moment with a residual brightness, then dulls.

Maximian blinks, then leans forward on his horse, composing himself. He raises his voice, and addresses the standing legion. "If your commander refuses my order, who will follow it?"

No one speaks. The snow continues to fall, collecting on their bare heads, on their bloodied, scarred shoulders.

"The penalty for disobedience is death." Maximian moves his horse around Maurice, riding in front of the first line of legionnaires. Studying each one's face. He rides down the line, then back. "And the sentence will be carried out here. On this rock, today! Who will step forward and command the legion? Who will march back into Gaul and do as I ask?"

Maurice lifts his eyes to the spear, and it's as if he still stares into the brilliance of the sun. Tears collect, roll down his cheeks.

And as one unit, the legionnaires set down their weapons.

Drop to their knees.

Lower their heads and clasp their hands together in prayer.

Maximian stops pacing. Stares at them, at the entire force. Rides back to Maurice. "We have determined their loyalty." He glowers at the commander, fury rising in his blood. "Very well." He raises a fist, rushes back and grasps the spear, yanking it from the earth and setting it across his lap. He rides into the midst of his centurions. And yells:

"Kill them all!"

He continues riding against the onrushing force, galloping away as fast as his steed can carry him over the rocky terrain. Far into the hills and rocky trails, far enough to escape the sounds of slaughter.

Until he hears the sound of returning hoof beats, Emperor Maximian stares at his prize, the lance and the spear point that seem to pull at his thoughts, influence his emotions and stir up even greater dreams of power, dominance and subjugation.

Caleb interrupts the vision. Tries to peer back further. Willing his mind to track the spear. *Where was it before Maurice…?*

A series of glimpses, fast and appearing intercut with the darkness, lightning-quick:

A figure on a hilltop before a series of thatch shacks, brandishing a scintillating spear point atop a different-looking staff, thicker, whiter, made of Birch wood. He yells out a command in Spanish, and descends upon a force of invading Roman warriors.

Irish moors, low fog over an ice-packed shore. And an assembly of warriors in fur cloaks and wooden shields. Men of huge stature, led by a hulking brute of scarred man with a misshapen head, and but one eye… Facing him and this immense force is a loose confederation of young men and even women, barely armored, woefully under matched—yet surging with confidence, following a blond youth with a spear held high—its point seething with reflected brilliance, bathing the leader with a fiery aura and causing ripples of panic in the mass of giants ahead.

Further back:

Something brilliant streaks from the night sky, dashing against the barren cliff side, startling the inhabitants of mud and clay huts, who rush into the desert. One man races to the glowing impact site, tools in his hands, shouting to his brothers. They gather around the crater, looking down to the glowing, spherical rock, tinged with cracks of emerald, pulsing and giving off intense heat.

The man's eyes widen. They all drop to their knees and bow their heads.

"When it cools," he says. "Bring it up to my workshop. God has spoken to me in my dreams. Told me this was coming. Given me instructions. Shown me what I must create."

His brothers nod, and the mason trembles with excitement, his hands tingling with power, anticipating what will take years to mold.

"His will be done."

Too much. Caleb tried to pull back. Dimly aware that Alexander and Xavier were around him, carefully monitoring his condition but fearful of waking him.

Come on. Refine the question. He focused, thought carefully.

Where did Commander Maurice get it?

A blast hit him, bright and intense:

A centurion, this one wrapping a cloak about himself as he races alone on a horse across a craggy terrain. Pouring rain, raging winds. The same spear, strapped to his back as he rides, heading toward a familiar circle of giant stones on the moors.

Caleb groaned. *Before that, show me...*

Another blast of light. *A shadowy image of a heat-riddled city, a crowd of jeering, shouting men in rags. More Roman shoulders pushing the crowd back, making room for...*

A blast of BLUE, like a broken reel of film giving way to a blank screen. It jitters, and for a moment Caleb sees a hillside at twilight. *The same Roman soldier seen previously on the moors, dragging the spear point behind him. The point, covered in oddly-translucent crimson blood, leaving a trail in the sand. Behind him, up the hill...*

The briefest image of crosses...

And then the blue screen again. Fiercely blue like a cloudless sky over the ocean.

And then he's—

Lurching up into his brother's supporting arms. Brought to his feet now, against the central pillar.

Alexander moved into view, his face pale by the flashlight glow. Worry crossed his features. "Dad? You okay? Looks like you saw a ghost."

Caleb straightened, wiped the sweat from his forehead and nodded. "A couple, I think."

"What were you looking for?" Montross asked. "Not the way out, I take it?"

"No, figured you had that covered. I was checking on our friend, The Spear."

"And—?"

Caleb rubbed his eyes, then pushed off the pillar after giving it one more glance.

"Now I know what it really is."

4.

Cairo Airport

"Where are we going?" Phoebe asked, boarding the Cessna-14, a plane she knew was capable of travelling long distances without refueling. She glanced backwards, to the darkened stretch of Cairo Airport's runway, half-expecting to see armored vehicles racing after them or sleek ninjas bursting out of the shadows.

Commander Temple took her by the elbow and gently led her up the stairs to join Orlando inside. "Ultimately back to our base, but first we've got another passenger to pick up."

Phoebe followed him inside to a luxurious cabin, where Orlando was already sitting in a huge white leather chair, tapping the armrests and grinning as he looked around. Two 40-inch flat screen TVs were built into the wall in front of the seats, a bar rested on the left side and two couches faced each other behind the three rows of seats. Orlando whistled. "Now this is more like it. You guys sure know how to spend the taxpayers' money."

As a crewman hauled up the ladder and sealed the door, Phoebe took the seat beside Orlando. "So, we're going to rescue someone else?" A note of hope flickered in her voice. Maybe they'd found Alexander or her brother?

Temple signaled the captain, then shut the cabin door and sat in a chair beside them. "Yes, and I'm sorry for this, but it's not going to be without danger."

Orlando groaned and held his bandaged neck. "Just tell me there aren't any eels."

Smiling, Temple said, "No eels. We're going someplace a lot dryer."

Phoebe lowered her eyes. "Why can't we just go somewhere safe, let you pick up this person, then meet us? Seriously, Orlando's hurt, and we haven't slept in days."

"Sorry." Temple shook his head as the engines breathed into life and the plane rattled. "But this is urgent. And for this mission, well... We kind of need you."

"Oh great." Orlando rolled his eyes at Phoebe. "Another psychic gig. We know the drill: all the risk, none of the reward."

"Your talents..." Temple began.

Orlando held up a hand. "Yeah, yeah. We know. If you ask me though, freakin' *Spiderman* ruined it for all of us after the whole 'with great power comes great responsibility' mantra."

"We're not superheroes," Phoebe contradicted. "Let someone else go."

Temple shook his head. "This is part of the deal in rescuing you. Plus, the Dove saw that you'd be instrumental in helping us. Indispensable, in fact."

"All right, I'll bite," Orlando said. "What's the objective? Who's the target?"

Smiling, Temple leaned back. "Her name," he said, "is The Hummingbird."

The plane lurched, rocked to the side, then ascended. After the rocky take off, Orlando turned to the commander. "Great, another bird." He scratched under his thick hair. "Doves, hummingbirds..." He glanced at Phoebe. "*Crowes.*"

She jabbed him. "Okay, who is this hummingbird person, and more importantly, where is she?"

Temple opened a briefcase by his seat and pulled out a red folder, sealed with a string. He held it up. "Exactly where she is, you'll have to tell us. But the general vicinity is here..." He pressed a button on his seat's armrest, and the TV screen in front of them lit up. Displayed there was a map.

It took Phoebe a couple seconds to recognize the outlines, but it wasn't hard. She'd seen it on the news enough lately. "Afghanistan?"

"Uh oh," Orlando said, straightening up. "Seriously, I didn't sign on for this.

Would've joined the army if I wanted to sweat it out in a desert battling Taliban, avoiding roadside bombs and rabid scorpions. Thanks but no freakin' thanks."

Temple pressed a couple keys and the image zoomed in to a location north of the center of the country, about a hundred miles west of Kabul. A site marked by rocky hills, huge cliffs and rugged peaks.

"Bamian," he said, pointing to the screen as he got up and fixed himself a drink. Ice. Gin. "Know anything about it?"

Phoebe nodded, her eyes darkening. "For centuries it was a major tourist site and pilgrimage location. And before that, a thriving city. Part of the ancient Silk Road trade route. Home to the two colossal Buddhas, carved by monks in the seventh cen-tury right into niches in the sandstone mountainside. One was like, a hundred and sixty feet tall, larger even than the Statue of Liberty, and the other one was over a hundred and twenty feet."

Temple returned to his seat. Pressed another button, and the screen shifted to a bright view of the mountainside and the enormous niche housing a standing, faceless Buddha.

"You said 'was'?" Orlando asked. "Are they…?"

Temple took a sip, then pressed the key again. The same niche now, but inside it was only rubble. "In 2001, just several months before 9-11, Mullah Muhammad Omar ordered that these emblems of the infidels be destroyed. That was after they also raided the Kabul Museum and destroyed countless priceless artifacts from the region."

"That should've been our cue of more to come from those whackos," Orlando said.

Phoebe swallowed hard, staring at the image. "The statues survived for over a thousand years, even managed to escape destruction when our old buddy Genghis Khan invaded. One of his grandsons had been killed on a raid here, shot by an arrow from the well-fortified guard posts on the ridges. Genghis was pissed, and personally saw to the city's complete destruction."

"Yet he left the Buddhas?"

Phoebe nodded. "Maybe he respected them—or the original builders—too much to risk that sacrilege."

Orlando sighed. "Something the Taliban could care less about."

After taking another swig, Temple said to Phoebe, "And I'm guessing that you know about the legends."

"Always legends," Orlando said, groaning. He eyed the bar and licked his lips.

Temple noticed his glance. "Help yourself. Self-serve around here."

Phoebe shifted and leaned forward, still staring at the picture. "Well, when it comes to ancient history I guess I take after my brother and my dad a bit. But you're right. There are myths about this place, namely that those statues were here long before the Buddhist monks arrived."

Orlando slowly got to his feet and headed to the bar as Phoebe continued: "Legends claim they were built as 'imperishable witnesses', reminders left in the mountain by survivors of the great flood."

Orlando chose an old bottle of scotch after reading the label and whistling. "Let me guess. Atlanteans?"

Phoebe shrugged. "That's what some believe. That they migrated here after the sinking of the island, that they built a network of caves within the mountain and under it. And the seventh-century monks only found the Buddhas already here, and used the existing caves as their homes, painting beautiful murals and designs—and also I recall, smoothing out the faces on the statues—and covering their nakedness in plaster robes."

Orlando returned, sat and raised his glass to the screen. "Well, so much for the 'imperishable witnesses.'"

Phoebe turned to face Temple. "Why are we really going to Bamian?"

Temple turned off the TV. "I told you, for the Hummingbird."

"And," Orlando asked, wincing after a swig. "Where is she? Oh wait, you're just going to say that it's up to us to answer that question."

"Exactly," Temple said. "But I'm glad you're not uninformed about the caves and tunnels. Because we know this much from our source: that she's down there under all that bedrock and sandstone. Somewhere in the very network of miles and miles of caves and tunnels in which we believe many of the terrorists are hiding, waiting us out and coordinating their attacks."

Orlando finished his drink. "And you want us to...?"

"I didn't say you two need to go down there," Temple replied. "You have the unique ability to keep yourselves out of harm's way and still get the job done. Just find her for us. Tell us exactly where they're keeping her. And then we'll go in and get her."

"Wait." Phoebe faced them. "You said you had other remote-viewers on your team. The Dove, for one. Why not use them? Why us?"

Temple lowered his head. "We've tried, but... there's been difficulty."

"Like what?" Orlando asked, swishing the ice around in his glass. He glanced out the window at the expanse of moonlight speckling the shrouded desert below.

"They're using the Hummingbird's talents. Blocking us."

Phoebe's eyes widened. "She's a shield?"

Temple slowly nodded. "A very powerful one. They have another, as well. We don't know too much about this one, except that he's Al Qaeda too. A top-level member. Highly-trained, and ruthless. His shielding skills and the Hummingbird's extend to technological surveillance as well."

"Meaning," said Orlando, "that you haven't been able to spy on them? Not with satellites or psychics? No wonder we can't find any of these terrorist cells."

Temple rubbed his hands together. "Two shields are needed to be effective. One can't stay awake and in control of the shield twenty-four-seven. But it's in those times when the Hummingbird is asleep and the other one is, shall we say, not in complete focus, that we've been able to get as far as we have. We know their approximate location. At least as of last night. And so, we were dispatched. First to get you, then to get her. We've got a small window of time. It has to be now. Before they move again."

Orlando refilled his glass, then set it down, seeing Phoebe's reproachful look. "Yes, but again, I don't see how we're going to narrow this down for you. If the shields or whatever are working..."

Temple held up a hand, then set his head back, resting against the seat pillow. He fitted a sleep mask over his eyes. "You'll do fine."

"How?" Phoebe asked, almost exasperated.

Turning to his side, Temple said, "Because you two are the best. You'll find her because you know what questions to ask. Questions that will get you past the shield."

Orlando snatched up his glass again as he headed back to his seat. "What do you mean, get past it?"

Temple smiled. "There's more than one way to skin a cat. I trust that you'll find it."

"But-" Phoebe started, then gave up as the commander fit headphones over his ears and promptly dozed off.

Orlando shook his head. "And we don't get to sleep?" He shifted uncomfortably, frowned then looked on the seat below him. He picked up the red folder, sighed, then handed it to Phoebe.

"Guess we've got our homework assignment."

Phoebe nodded reluctantly. "Let's get to work."

5.

Cairo Museum of Antiquities

"You're sure they're coming this way?"

Mason Calderon leaned on his dragon-headed cane as the commandos barred the entrance doors behind him. The sun was just coming up over the high-rises and the bustling traffic began in earnest outside, while inside his team spread out through the exhibits.

The two boys put down their skateboards, set their feet on them simultaneously and grinned back at Calderon. "Oh yes," said Isaac. "Our brother will be here soon."

Calderon felt other eyes upon him, shivered for a moment fearing someone distant might be observing him, but then faced the glass case to his left, where a four-thousand year old bust of Pharaoh Ramses II, cast in limestone, stared back at him. Calderon felt those eyes boring into his soul from across the millennia, cold granite eyes that sought him out—possibly, he thought—as an equal. A fellow seeker after immortality, a king, a divinity forced to exist among lesser beings.

A smile crept on his face, a thin mimicry of Ramses' expression. Destiny was in his corner, and a long line of worthy predecessors awaited his ascension.

He watched the boys skateboard in and out of shadows and cones of light, gracefully moving among the ancient artifacts, past friezes, mummies, trinkets and weapons, rolling towards sarcophagi and shelves of canopic jars.

"This way, Sir." One of the commandos led him ahead, as two followed at the rear, leaving another pair guarding the main doors against unwanted intrusion. Outside, the administrator and curators were being briefed about another possible bomb threat, and escorted to a safe perimeter.

Calderon followed the commandos and the boys through the halls, past treasures remarkable and commonplace to the eras from which they were plucked. He thought about the power the boys had, the same one shared by their parents, by Xavier Montross and the others in the Morpheus Initiative. Certainly an entire wing of this museum could be filled with the bones of psychics who claimed to share their ability. Other mystics and prophets who could see the past, and some of them even the future. The woman who glimpsed the opening of Thoth's box by three brothers must have received some vision and spoke of it in a prophecy that had eventually reached Pharaoh's ears.

Calderon continued into a stairwell where below, the boys' voices echoed cheerily. They were carrying their skateboards, laughing as they tapped the boards against the stairs. Still, he thought, a shame he hadn't been born with the gift. To be chosen for such a task, selected by Destiny, and yet not given all the tools and weapons he should have… How he rued that missing aspect, and yet… Perhaps it was a blessing. It kept him single-minded, without the distraction of curiosity and the power to quench it.

He knew what was required of him. Knew what they needed to complete the weapon. The Tablet of Destiny. It was so much more than that fool Caleb could imagine. He'd had it for seven years and didn't even begin to gleam its secrets. Oh, for sure its latent power would have stimulated Caleb's mind—and his son's, and anyone who came near to it; but to really understand its power, its true destructive capabilities…

Calderon was ready. Robert Gregory and the other Keepers had an inkling of what the tablet really was. And so did George Waxman, Stargate's head man and the originator behind the Morpheus Initiative. In his quest for psychic candidates for the government, he had tested one man who had seen it for what it truly was: a threat to all life on this planet. And, Calderon mused, *any other planet or satellite we might choose to target.* Good thing Caleb was such a believer in the preservation of knowledge. He would never consider destroying such a find, regardless of what Waxman feared could happen. And so he kept it, believing himself a better Keeper than his other new friends, including his wife.

But he was wrong, and the time was coming. The time of

release. Marduk's vision, nearly achieved. It was so easy to set the gears in motion to retrieve the tablet. Robert Gregory, as the Keepers' leader, desperately wanted the most prized element from the lost Alexandrian Library. And all Calderon had to do was keep fanning the flames, leaking out information about who had it, and how he might get it.

Of course, to get by Caleb's defenses, they needed a psychic, someone just as powerful to see the way. And Xavier Montross had been only too willing. Gregory and Montross did all the work, but it was Calderon who had pulled the strings.

And now here they were. Tablet in hand. Translation almost in place. But even without that, the contents of that locked box under the Sphinx, they had what they needed. The Tablet. The ancient piece of technology, an interface between mind and machine.

The weapon was built and ready. Waiting for this final piece, the instructions and codes to harness the power of the universe.

All that remained was to eliminate any threat to its deployment. And that meant the threat to the Tablet itself. The one artifact that could destroy it.

He had to act fast. Their enemies—their real enemies—wouldn't be idle for much longer. Not if they too, could *see*.

Calderon watched the boys eagerly glide ahead, deeper and deeper into the museum's secrets. Now they were nearing a restricted door in the back, which Calderon knew led to a private stairwell that would take them to a basement below the storage sublevels.

"It's down here, father!" Isaac yelled back, grinning.

Jacob waved his hand. "They're coming, hurry!"

Were they sure? Calderon hadn't relied on their talents yet, hadn't had the necessity. The boys were young, green and untested. The visit to the Statue of Liberty proved that they weren't ready. They were powerful, to be sure, but just not focused. A wasted trip. And he hadn't had the time then to help guide them. But if all went well here, if they could capture or kill Crowe and Montross, even eliminate the Morpheus Initiative, then Lady Liberty could keep her secrets for all he cared.

Three mercenaries, HK-45s out in front, filed around him and moved ahead of the boys. They opened the door, and Calderon tapped his cane once, hearing it echo metallically off the walls and amidst the relics, then he followed them inside and down into the subterranean chambers to await their quarry.

Xavier Montross pushed the center stone on the wall. He really didn't need to remote view this part. He knew this was the door, the exit that in ancient times had led out a half-mile beyond the Khepre Pyramid, where the initiates could exit into a well, then ascend to the desert and see the monuments from a different vantage point. Caleb would've said it had something to do with mental perspective and a sense of spiritual evolution, but Xavier could care less.

This part was easy. In his flashlight beam, the light dimming already from four hours of continuous use, he could see three rectangular blocks set in the wall to the right of a large, smooth block. The door. And here, it was too obvious. Two of the blocks had the hieroglyphics facing right, as was typical. The middle one had the characters facing left. While he couldn't translate these scripts specifically, he didn't need to. Push the right one, the door opens. Push one of the other two and…

All right, he thought. *Didn't get this far by being impulsive. Better just be safe and take a look…*

He closed his eyes, spread out his arms and concentrated. On the door, willing to be shown a time when it didn't open, when in fact someone had gotten it wrong. *Show me.*

He teetered unsteadily. A vibration traveled up his spine, tingling the base of his neck. Pushing through his skull to the center of his forehead. His mouth opened and he let out a gasp.

A nervous young bald man with a wavering hand reaches for the middle stone. Pushes it with confidence, smiling–

-right up to the point the block he's standing on drops. Only a few inches—but it's enough. Something sharp whisks across, driven with incredible force. The youth screams in agony, slides backwards and lands, lifting his legs to look in horror at the stumps where his feet used to be…

Enough!

Xavier pulled himself back, snapped his mind out of the vision. He'd seen too many of these sights, experienced so much pain and death. As if he'd been there himself. But whether it was one soul or an entire world's population, death was death. Brutal, remorseless. Uncaring.

Steadying himself, he looked at the stones again. And realized his mistake.

The middle one, while different, was really just a mirror image of the top one. They were one and the same, copies just written in reverse.

The bottom one…

Montross leaned forward. Pushed it—and felt his feet tensing, ready to jump at the slightest movement. Not that he'd have the chance.

But then the wall ahead shook, dust fell from the ceiling, and a thin sliver of light appeared at the left, steadily growing as the block pulled aside.

Light? Xavier squinted. He turned off his flashlight. The stone slid farther. *Run back,* he thought, and had a flash of a cluttered room, something like a storage area, with crates and boxes pulled back from the wall, from the open wooden door on the other side. Just a glimpse, before the four men in black suits raised their weapons at him and surged through the opening.

Back in the shadows, around the last corner of this point of the labyrinth, Xavier crouched. On his knees. *I'm not going to die,* he thought. *I would have seen it.* And then he cursed himself. Too often this gift of foresight about his death led him to a false sense of security. He failed to fully scout out other more uncomfortable situations.

But he was far from without resources.

Calderon walked through his mercenaries as they encircled the red-haired man who had emerged, squinting, from the doorway.

"Ah, Xavier Montross. We meet at last." Calderon cocked his head. Something was odd. Montross was too calm. He'd just emerged from what should have been a stiflingly hot, oppressive and dank labyrinth, and yet he wasn't even sweating. His hair was perfect, no dirt on his face, nothing to tell of any ordeal. Like he had just awoke from a peaceful nap.

Isaac scampered between two of the soldiers, approaching Montross from behind. Jacob, meanwhile, had taken an interest in the doorway. The open section of flimsy drywall that had concealed the sandstone entrance beyond it.

"Jacob." Calderon called to the boy. "Wait." He moved closer to Montross, easing between two of the guns. "We don't know what's down there."

"I do," said Isaac. With a sneer, he kicked out with a swipe that should have bent in the back of Xavier's right leg—but his foot passed right through and Isaac tumbled, off balance and with a cry of shock.

Montross' image gave a wink—and then disappeared. Furious, Calderon gripped the head of his cane like a sword hilt. "Inside—now! Get him, he can't be far!"

Or could he? This was it, Calderon thought. One of the gifts bestowed by the Emerald Tablet, a power he needed, and one only he fully understood. Its implications were all-encompassing, not just on a personal level, but what it could do if interfaced with the right technology, such as what they had built up in Alaska.

If Montross had practiced, if had deciphered the Tablet and perfected the skills, he could be anywhere.

But he wasn't, Calderon realized. The door had been physi-cally opened from the other side. He was close.

Worth a shot, Montross thought as he breathed his consciousness back into his body, just as air would fill his lungs. He had just enough time to start to run back the way he had come, intending to get far enough to trip one of the traps he had avoided on the way here. But it was too late.

They were on him. Pinning him to the wall. Hands behind his back, secured with plastic bonds. Then hauled back out, into the light, surrounded by crates, dust, and two boys.

"Ah, my newly discovered nephews." Despite his predicament, Montross found it wasn't that hard to smile, and to mean it. "You actually look a bit like your father, but those green eyes of yours—all Nina."

"Well, Xavier…" said a voice he had heard many times, but only in visions. In dark, smoke-filled rooms, and once on a massive glacier under the midnight sky, observing the Northern Lights over a sleeping radar facility.

"This time in the flesh." Mason Calderon leaned forward, both hands on his cane. His skin was lustrous, shining in the lights as if he'd applied a liberal dose of makeup before a stage performance. His eyes were hooded but sharp, moving rapidly, taking in everything about his captive. Thin white hair was slicked back from his high forehead, except for a lone curved strand that fell across his face like a scimitar blade.

Montross stood up straight. "Well, you got me. Not too much effort for you, I hope. But, sorry to say, I'm all you're getting. The other birds have flown the coop."

One of the boys moved around so he could stand by his brother. They both glared up at Montross with an oddly similar glints in their eyes. One had slightly finer hair, more chestnut than his brother's walnut-colored tangle of curls. "We can still get them, father."

"No Jacob," Calderon replied. "Not without trusting this man here to guide us."

"We can do it," the other boy insisted.

"We can see as well as he can."

Montross gave a little chuckle, but he had to admire the kids' guts. Definitely a potent mix of their parents' qualities.

Calderon shook his head. "Sorry boys. Besides, I believe Montross here did what he set out to do. He bought Caleb and Alexander time to head back and get out the main entrance, hoping to fool us here." He smirked. "Good thing Nina will be there, waiting."

Montross shrugged. "Maybe they're not coming out. Lots to do down there. While traipsing through history's looking glass, I saw all kinds of ceremonies, people living for years in those ventilated chambers, tunnels that connected to faraway exits, ports along the Nile and farther."

Calderon sighed. "And I doubt I even need to ask, but I assume you do not have the keys on you?"

Montross laughed. "Wishful thinking, but of course not." He nodded over his shoulder. "They're back in there."

Calderon cocked his head, and Montross knew the man was weighing his words, deciding how much stock to put in Montross' answer. But at this point, he didn't care.

Montross took a deep breath. "So, Senator Calderon. You've got the Emerald Tablet. Or at least, my former associate does. And you believe she's now in your employ because of these..." Montross raised his chin toward the defiant boys, who were glaring at him with twin looks of menace. "...these lovely angels. But you don't have the translation. Nor the keys to get into that box."

"We will, soon." Calderon twirled the cane in his fingers, tracing the golden scales of the dragon, letting his index finger glide across the length of the spear thrust through its skull. "Although it's not essential. From what you've just shown us, you've confirmed that proximity to the Emerald Tablet alone can get me what I need."

"Yeah," Montross said, "but my mind's better tuned toward it, or am I wrong and you're actually a psychic yourself?"

Calderon flinched. His eyes narrowed. The twins looked at each other.

Isaac grunted. "But we are, aren't we 'Dad'?"

"Righto," Jacob chimed in. "We can do it, can't we? Give us the tablet-thing. We'll show you."

"Boys, don't get ahead of yourselves." Calderon never took his eyes off of Montross. "You may be right, Xavier. Which is why Nina will soon have these boys in that chamber. We'll get the box, then go after Caleb and Alexander. There's no way for them to escape, we'll find them and those keys. Once the translation is in my possession and the Tablet's secrets are mine, I'm certain that I will be able to duplicate your abilities. And much more. Its arcane instructions, I'm told, will fully reactivate what time and evolution have blocked." He fondled the dragon's wings, then smiled. "But more importantly, I will have what I need to complete our facil-ity's true purpose."

"Don't count those chickens yet," Montross said quietly. "There's the little matter of the Morpheus Initiative in your way."

"Oh, I don't think they'll be in my way much longer. Last I checked, Phoebe and Orlando had their car destroyed outside of Cairo. And your brother and nephew..." He shrugged. "Only a matter of time. There's no escape. I may have Nina give them the opportunity to join us in this momentous occasion, but I doubt Caleb's visions could actually extend so far as to see the greatness of what we're doing."

"Which is what, exactly?" Montross asked, his wrists struggling against the sharp bonds. "Besides wiping out everyone on the planet?"

Calderon smiled. "Not everyone." He tapped his cane against the floor. "It's heartening to know that despite your powers, you can't see it all."

I haven't asked the right questions, Montross thought. That was something, at least. To know there might be more, another way to save themselves.

Calderon turned and walked confidently up the stairs. The soldiers jabbed Montross along, and as he followed, Jacob and Isaac moved so they ascended on either side of him. Both looked up at him with an unnerving curiosity, like executioners taking perverse pleasure in watching the condemned on his final climb to the scaffold.

Montross tried to ignore them. At the top, as he emerged into the museum's westernmost wing, he took a moment to get his bearings. He thought about remote viewing the next passage of time, trying to glimpse what lay in store. But instead he got a flash of something else:

Mason Calderon standing on a dizzying metal platform, pale blue electric sparks in his hair, his cane raised high. Like a modern-day Merlin, calling down elemental spirits. The sky itself turns a magnificent swirl of orange and hardened emerald, folding and twisting like a multicolored tapestry, everything churning and exploding over snow-capped mountains.

Suddenly, Calderon's face appeared in his sight, jarring the vision. "What are you seeing?"

Montross had gone pale. His lips trembled. "I think... it was the beginning."

"Of what?"

"The end of the world."

Calderon nodded, with a light dazzling in the darkest centers of his pupils. "I may not be psychic, but that's one vision I've seen as well. Many, many times..."

6.

"This is crap," Orlando said with a groan about thirty minutes later. He thumbed through the papers, the small-print, the few photographs of the region, the caves seen from a distance, some satellite maps, and a blurred-out picture of a little girl working in the fields with what may have been her parents.

"I agree." Phoebe snatched up the last photograph, unclipped it from the folder's edge. "This here, this is all we need. The other stuff will only cloud our thoughts. Focus on her, and let's get this over with."

"But there's a lot of that 'other stuff' in here. If this is true, Jesus. She's only ten! The daughter of an American missionary and a Bamian native woman. Watched her mother butchered before her eyes."

"Stop," Phoebe insisted. She closed the folder, tossed it on the floor. And with a scornful glance at their sleeping companion, she reached into her pack and pulled out a scrapbook. Two pencils. Offered one to Orlando and ripped out a sheet of paper.

"I'll use… damn. No laptop."

"Sorry to bring you back to the Middle Ages, but just grab a damn pencil." She took a deep breath, leaned back and grasped her pencil lightly between her finger and her thumb. In a moment, as Orlando watched, her eyes rolled back, her mouth opened and her arm shook.

Orlando sighed. "All right then. Don't wait for me."

First: a full vision of Blue. Deep and tranquil like the depths of the Caribbean. Close, and yet impossible to grasp, like the sky.

Phoebe struggled. Pulled back. Sent her questions away from the depths, toward more solid ground. Toward the past...

Blue again. But this time, the pure infinite blue of the Afghanistan sky. Down to the great cliffs of the Kohebaba range. A rock wall pockmarked with caves, ridges and steep grooves beside an immense hollowed out niche. Its smaller twin far to the right.

Pull back...

The fields. Dust and sand. A few straggly juniper bushes. A goat here and there. In the blistering sun, a crowd of villagers stand in the center of a loose scattering of adobe shacks. A lone rusty well sits untended and unused at the edge of the village, and scrawny buzzards perch on its rotting boards.

Riding horses, three men carrying AK-47s are keeping the villagers together in a group. Forcing them to remain. To watch.

A mujahedeen fighter, all in black astride a white horse, unravels the sash from his face. A single eye glares at the villagers; the other—the left, is hidden behind a black patch with jewels embedded in the cloth. He raises his gun and shouts toward the cliff wall, addressing the seemingly empty caves. "Bring her out!"

The walls are silent. The largest niche, holding only the rubble now of the largest statue ever built, trembles slightly as if the earth had just rumbled.

The man known as The Eye shouts again. "Bring her out, infidels! Or the will of Allah will fall upon your friends." He makes a motion with his left hand, a nonchalant waving in the direction of a bewildered young man standing by himself.

Another fighter on horseback rides up behind the youth and with a ululating cry, brings down a scimitar, silencing the boy's sudden cry of fright. A spray of blood across the sand, and the other villagers erupt in shrieks and cries.

"NOW!" the Eye shouts again to the hills. In a moment, he points to another villager, a huddled old woman.

But then, motion in one of the caves. A man and a woman emerge, heads bowed. Dressed in tattered clothes.

The Eye holds up a hand restraining his men. Gallops ahead a short distance. "Show me the girl!"

The man's shoulders slump as he steps away from the woman, letting a small girl walk into the sunlight. Blinking, shielding her eyes, she walks to the edge. Trying to appear brave, she raises her dirty face to the sky and spreads her arms as if they're tiny wings.

And the villagers murmur to themselves. Some drop to their knees, others whimper.

"Enough!" hisses the Eye. He motions to his men. "Bring her down." And as they gallop toward the base of the giant niche in the cave-riddled mountainside, he stares at the girl, not more than seven or eight. And he finds it difficult to look at her, despite the grime and dust covering her face and hair, her shredded clothes.

She's glowing, reflecting the painful brilliance of the sun.

But in minutes, the three of them are down, herded like wayward sheep into the clearing.

The Eye dismounts and stands before them.

"You gave me a good chase, girl." She refuses to look up at him. Her eyes— bright blue like the sky—stare only over at the headless young man at the edge of the clearing. Her father squeezes her hand tight and her mother clasps her other hand.

The Eye considers the three of them, then tells the girl, "You have the look and the stink of your American father about you."

"Leave her alone," the father says, daring a tone of defiance. "We don't know why she can do what she does, but it's not evil. It's not-"

"I know that, infidel." The Eye grins, and taps his jeweled eye patch. "She is a gift from Allah. A gift I was meant to find. And use."

"No, please-" the mother starts, and tries to pull her daughter back.

At a motion from the Eye, one of his men yanks the woman away. He pushes her to her knees and pulls out the same bloody scimitar that had just seen action.

"No!" her husband yells, but he too is restrained, dragged away from the girl until she stands there, arms splayed, hands empty.

"You're my gift," the Eye says. *"But you must understand that I have to ensure your compliance. I leave the choice to you, Hummingbird. Your mother or your father. Which would you have stay in this world?"*

She turns to him, and now meets his cold one-eyed stare.

"No," the father yells. *"You can't make her choose. Take me, kill me."* He struggles, almost frees himself but then the butt of a rifle slams into his back and pins him to the rocky sand.

"Choose," the Eye repeats, stepping closer so his hulking shadow envelops the girl. His robes flow and whip in the rising winds and sand devils blow around them both.

"Please don't..." the mother whimpers.

The girl looks over to her, a cry on her lips. "Mother-"

"Good enough for me," the Eye says, and nods to his man. The woman's head scarf is tugged back. Her neck exposed and then torn in a jagged, swift cut as the blade digs deep. Flesh and muscle parting, blood escaping. Her eyes go cold with surprise and then... acceptance.

The Hummingbird turns away, an unvoiced cry in her throat.

The father whimpers his breath into the rocks.

And the girl focuses not on the object of her hatred, but on a lone boy standing in the crowd. A grime-faced curly-haired boy her own age. A boy trembling with fear, but whose eyes hold such emotion. He struggles against the clutches of his parents, who hold him back from running to the girl...

-His one friend.

The Hummingbird shakes her head slightly at him as if to say, 'not now'.

"It is done," the Eye says matter-of-factly. He points to the girl's father. "Break his legs, bind him and bring him with us." Then he kneels down, takes the girl's chin in his hands and uses a dirty thumb to wipe a tear from her eyes. "You'll do as I say from now on. You keep us safe, and your father lives. These villagers live. Fail me, and they all join your mother."

With a flourish, his black robes whipping around, he scoops up the Hummingbird, sets her on his horse and climbs in the saddle behind her. With a joyous shout, he races toward the cliffs.

"And now, my sweet. You will help us navigate the tunnels, and when we have found a place of safety deep within the mountains, my brethren will join

us, and our work can truly begin."

Into the cavern, darkness covering them. A seeping of blue forms around the edges of the vision. Closing over the sparkling reality of everything in the center. The white of the horse's mane, the thickness of the leather harness, the saddle, and the shaking little hands that hug the horse's neck, drawing comfort from petting the magnificent beast.

"You will sleep," the Eye says, "only when I let you. When I am in slumber you must cloud our presence—in the past, the present and the future—as I know you can do. Just as you hid yourself and your parents from me for months. You will do all this, and your father will live." *He strokes her hair as the veil of blue encircles the entirety of the vision. And his last words follow Phoebe out of it...*

"The Eye and the Hummingbird. You and I, child. We will be unstoppable."

Complete BLUE.

Phoebe pulled back. Twitching, eyelids fluttering. Dimly aware of the plane descending, the pressure tightening in her eyes. *Stay in it,* she thought. *Focus... retreat, find something...*

Back in the clearing. The villagers disbanding, returning to the fields. Tending to the dead. Saying prayers and moving on.

Except for one.

The curly-haired boy.

He slips away from his parents as they go to mourn and prepare the funerals. Scrambles toward the wall of caves, the place that holds such mystery for him, even though for others the caves are used merely for shelter, for makeshift homes.

He follows the tracks of the one-eyed man. Enters the cavern and quickly makes his way after them. Descending deep into the mountainside. Coming to a branching trail, narrowing passageways.

He follows the light ahead, dimming. But he sticks to the shadows and creeps along.

Blinking, Phoebe stirred and opened her eyes. Yawned and popped her ears.

Gotcha, she thought. *The boy is the key.*

And then she noticed Orlando, eyelids moving rapidly. His hand, wielding the pencil, was a blur of motion, creating a series of lines and diagrams, twisting trails through a maze.

"You're seeing it too," she whispered, but Orlando kept drawing. His lips were dry, cracked, and his face slick with sweat. Phoebe couldn't help but smile. His face, so scrunched up tight, muscles in his neck taught. His curly unkempt hair falling over his face. Before she knew it, she found herself touching his hair, brushing it with her fingers as he dreamt.

"Sweet and productive dreams, my prince."

Orlando zeroed in on the boy at once. At first he was but a shadow, a darker silhouette, like a jellyfish bobbing in the blue depths. But the motion was there, pulling at the remote-vision.

Ask the right question, get the right answer. Orlando smiled as he dropped deeper into the trance, willing himself to see it—to follow someone outside of the shield, someone else who tracked the girl. *Come on, come to focus. Ah, there you are.*

The boy, returning to the caves at night. With a knapsack full of an assortment of dried meats and a few nuts, a dirty bottle of water, an oil lamp, and a blanket. He stopped before the great sandstone cliff and gazed up at the hollow niche. He had been born after the statues' destruction, but he often came here in the starlight and used his imagination, dreaming up a magnificent protector, a wise and living god to care for the village. And especially for *Nadjee*, the one they called the Hummingbird.

He moved forward into the cave and retraced his steps from earlier. He had played in these caves all his life, searching out their deepest regions, following miles of twisting passageways, until the rebel Taliban took up residence in some of the outlying tunnels and set up traps and mines. His older cousin, Jalik, had lost a foot in one of the subterranean passages last winter and then his parents had forbade any further play or exploration within the sacred mountain.

But this was different.

He scampered inside

And Orlando followed. Unconsciously sketching the map, diagramming the layout of branching corridors, dead-end caverns and places where the boy noted spring-mines or stepped over wire-triggered explosives.

On and on he moved, cautiously, reverently as if he made his way through the winding intestines of some immense, slumbering deity.

He slowed at one point, glancing to his left into a deep shadowy recess. The darkness blurred and the boy retreated, his back against a wall.

A haze of bright blue pierced out from the shadows—an instant before obscuring the figure of a man in white robes. A kindly face, a bald head and a long beard. A hand reaching out...

What the hell? Orlando thought, grimacing in a migraine-like vise of pain.

But then it was gone—the blue *fading, fading, replaced by the dim orange glow of the oil lamp off the dusty rock cavern walls. The boy, moving again. He glances back, toward that alcove and the murky shadows. Shakes his head, then continues.*

And Orlando resumes his sketching.

After another twenty minutes of winding passages, twists and turns, the boy slows. Extinguishes his lamp, and eases toward the faint glow at the end of the descending passage.

He creeps to the edge, where he hears soft voices.

It's the girl's voice, and the boy smiles, almost chokes on his gratitude for her safety. But then he hears her words...

"Don't hurt him, please don't..."

"Sorry, little one." The Eye's voice. "He's managed to track us, and can't be allowed to live."

"No, please no, please!"

The boy freezes, then scampers back.

But he's too slow.

Armed men turn the corner and descend upon him.

The last thing he—and Orlando—hears is the swishing of blades. Quick. Painless.

Then darkness.

Temple shook him, and when Orlando opened his eyes—streaming with tears—he forced himself to focus on Phoebe to help ground his dislocation.

"You're back," she said. "Back. Just relax. Take a deep breath."

"They killed him," he whispered. "Just a boy, they..."

Phoebe gripped his wrist. "The boy following the Hummingbird?"

Orlando nodded gravely. "Just killed him right there."

Temple took the pages off Orlando's shaking hands. "This it? The way to her?"

"Yeah. I saw it all so clearly. But I'd say you have to move fast. I'm not sure how they knew the kid was coming, but if they can see him, maybe they're sensing us too."

"Maybe not," Temple said, as he used his PDA to snap digital pictures of the pages. He tapped a few keys, and the image appeared on the main screen, the pages merged. "Let's hope not at least. But with this diagram, hopefully we can get in and get her out, quick."

"There was something else," Orlando said, getting up. He touched the screen. "At this point, there was something strange. Everything got all blue again, but I swear I saw some kind of bald monk coming out of a hidden recess and touching the boy. Almost as if he knew..."

"What?" Phoebe stared hard at him.

"Knew maybe that the child was going to die. Not sure what he did, but..."

"Blue," whispered Phoebe. "So this monk guy, he was a shield too. One of the terrorists?"

Temple shook his head. "Bald's not their style."

"Then who?"

"Not sure," he said. "But anyway, we're landing."

"Okay," Orlando said, breathing more relaxed now. "So me and Phoebe can just hang out in the plane while you guys go get her, right?"

Temple smiled devilishly. "And miss out on all the fun? I have a feeling we're going to need your skills even more down in those tunnels."

"Come on!" Orlando said.

Phoebe grasped Orlando's hand, and when he saw her face he sighed. "Fine, I feel like I'm kind of vested in this now. And besides, I want to see that one-eyed son of a bitch pay."

7.

After they left Xavier, Caleb led Alexander along the side passage he had viewed before saying goodbye to his half-brother.

"We'll see him again," Alexander said, his voice hushed in the gloom of the narrowing passageway. Caleb felt a cool breeze brushing across his face from ahead, and knew somewhere up there was an opening to a deeper chasm, some abyss that tapped into the water table far below, with caverns and small tunnels leading to the surface, most of them too small for humans to fit through, but which provided enough ventilation to breathe. At one point, he had seen a glimpse—in the far past, or more recently, he wasn't sure—of a line of robed figures carrying torches, descending along a narrow ledge towards a sunless sea. A dock, and Egyptian-styled boats moored against the port, waiting to take passengers to some mythical destination.

"I hope you're right," Caleb said, shining his light ahead, and keeping his free hand on Alexander's shoulder, keeping him close. He couldn't lose Alexander again. Not after finding him, not after what the boy had been through. How he'd been forced to grow up in a hurry. He thought of Genghis Khan's tomb, and what Alexander had needed to do.

"Son…"

"Dad, don't worry. I'm fine."

"You know what I want to talk about. Now that Xavier's not here, I-"

Alexander looked up at him, and the shadows draped over his face, covering his eyes. "Which thing do you want to talk about? The fact that I have two brothers I didn't know of, that I saw Mom die, or that I… killed a man?"

Caleb stopped moving, turned toward him and dropped to a knee. He lowered the light and in the soft reddish glow off the confining sandstone walls, he looked into Alexander's eyes, even as his own were welling with tears.

"I'm so sorry. About all this. Your mother…"

Alexander suddenly lunged forward and threw his arms around Caleb's neck, crushing him in a desperate hug. And Caleb realized he hadn't had a moment to grieve. Neither of them. Not since a week ago when this all began, when the fire took Lydia, and Alexander and the Tablet both were snatched from his lighthouse.

They held each other for a long time, neither saying a word until the light started to dim; Alexander pulled away, wiping the dust and the tears from his face. "Come on Dad, we've got to help him."

Caleb nodded. "You're okay?"

Alexander tried to smile. "No. But hey, we're *Keepers*, right? Comes with the job."

"It's why they pay us the big bucks." Caleb stood, rubbing Alexander's hair. "But soon, we'll talk. About her. About Xavier and those twins. About everything."

"How are you, Dad?"

"What?"

"Well, you just found out your old girlfriend's still alive. And she's pissed at you, and you've both got twins you didn't know you had. Doesn't that change things?"

"It does. And I can't… Can't even imagine what Nina's going through now. To know they took her children, kept them from her."

"From you too."

Caleb squeezed the flashlight tighter. "But that's it. I don't know what they did to them. How they were raised. What they're like."

"I think I do," Alexander said. "I've seen them a lot. Thought they were just part of my imagination. Imaginary friends to help when I was lonely. But these playmates, they were always mean to me, even in my dreams. They're not nice."

Caleb lowered his head. "I know. But they're young. They haven't been with their real parents yet."

Alexander started walking down the shadowy corridor. "Well," he said, "you better hope you get to make an impression before they meet their mom. Then, it's all over."

"Where are we?"

Alexander shined his light around like a light saber, trying to ward off the darkness. He couldn't tell how large this chamber was, but it had to be huge. Couldn't see the walls anymore, and the ceiling—if there was one, was way up high, beyond the reach of his beam that just faded into the hungry darkness. There was something in the center of the room, another massive block or pillar of some kind. Caleb was shining a light at it, inside a square-shaped opening in which there was something that looked like a chair. Carvings and symbols far stranger than mere hieroglyphics adorned the sides.

Caleb moved forward into the structure. He turned and gently sat in the stone chair.

"Dad, wait."

"It's ok. It's not trapped." Caleb looked around, and Alexander had the impression that his dad was sitting in a cockpit of sorts. Except there was nothing else in there except a slot, a groove in the arm of the chair, by his right hand.

"Its... different," Caleb said. "I believe we're directly under the main pyramid. And this..." He looked up, then shined his light up there, and Alexander understood. The interior of the pillar, or shaft, was hollow.

"What do you see?"

"Nothing. It just goes up straight." He turned off his flash-light, closed his eyes. "Hold on, I'm getting something, seeing more of it..."

Alexander closed his eyes, reached out into the darkness as if to pluck his father's vision like a piece of fruit. Absently, he switched off his own flashlight. And now in complete darkness, a new light sparked behind his eyes.

*A **man** sits where Caleb had been. This one is dressed in full Egyptian* *splendor. Colorful breastplate, long golden skirt. Bracelets, necklaces. A crown with two asps in its center. Except he's glowing, with arching tendrils of electricity or plasma pinwheeling over his body and arcing about the interior of the shaft.*

Clutched in both hands is a familiar item:

The Emerald Tablet.

Then there's a sound, a grunting, then a low moan as the Pharaoh sets the edge of the Tablet against the slot in the chair, and eases it down. There's a massive sound, a piercing pitch that compliments a deep rumbling vibration.

The chamber fills with light—hot, intense white light, energy great enough to tear flesh and bone apart and pulverize every cell, and yet... The king is unscathed. Still sitting calmly, head back, mouth open. It's as if he's directing the energy. Focusing it, sending it up. Up the shaft, and out.

A *flash* and Alexander's mind is outside-

-the great Pyramid. Alone on a lush, grassy plain. Dawn, and the sun is just emerging over a thick forest in the east, past the width of the Nile. There is a deep, lush jungle where the other two pyramids should be, and the causeway leading up to the Sphinx has been neatly landscaped, the trees and bushes pared back from the great marble stones. And the Sphinx itself—different. Its head is larger, leonine, and proportional to the immense body; it faces the rising sun, and its eyes hungrily follow the dawn.

But then the golden capstone above the smooth, reflective walls of the Great Pyramid begins to glow. Brighter and brighter. Turning from gold to silver, blindingly bright.

And then a beam stabs out, straight up and out, thrusting into the azure-violet sky...

...arcing toward a single pinpoint of reddish-white light. A faint star.

A planet.

"Mars!" Alexander whispered as he came back to the present. Caleb's light was back on. His father rubbed his eyes, and cautiously traced the slot with his index finger. "Did you see it?"

"I... saw something. A man where you're sitting. Putting the tablet in there, and then directing some kind of light beam out the top of the pyramid, toward what I think was Mars."

Caleb cocked his head, looked sharply at Alexander. "You really...?"

"Didn't you see it too? You've got to believe me. It was a long time ago, had to be. Only this pyramid and the Sphinx were there, but Egypt wasn't a desert. There was a jungle, and-"

"I believe you." Caleb leaned forward, rubbing his head. "I don't want to believe you, but I do. There have been a lot of crackpot theories about this site, this pyramid. I never gave much thought to some of the more outlandish ones, like that the Great Pyramid was an ancient power source, or a weapon used by extraterrestrial 'gods' in their own petty wars. But now..."

"But now it doesn't seem so... crackpotty."

Caleb smiled. "Nice word, Alexander. No it doesn't, but I didn't see all that. I saw something else, I was focused on the man."

"The Pharaoh guy? What about him?"

"It seemed," Caleb said, "he wasn't really there."

Alexander blinked, trying to recall what he'd seen. The man sitting there, holding the tablet. All that heat and power passing into him, through him. "Oh."

"Yeah," Caleb said. "I think that was just his projection, what-ever it is Montross learned how to do."

"And Grandpa."

Caleb nodded. "But somehow, while in that out of body phase, he could still touch the Emerald Tablet. Move it, insert it."

"Like I was able to move the lever under the Sphinx!" Alexander's eyes shined with the memory.

Caleb nodded as he shined the light into the groove, trying to see anything down there. "And that's the key, I think. To what the Emerald Tablet can do. It interfaces with consciousness, or our souls, or something. One and the same and phased together with the spirit, the Tablet's full power can be consciously controlled, wielded."

Alexander whistled. "So what did I see them attacking?"

"I can't say, yet. But I don't think it helps us now. This... place. This facility is dormant. I can feel it. Even if we brought the Tablet down here, I think they—whoever they were—Thoth's enemies maybe, dismantled the core. Maybe it was in some ancient war, something that turned this lush land into a desert. Whatever it was, this facility, this pyramid, is nothing now but a tomb. Our tomb, unless we can get out."

"Perhaps," said a new voice. "I can be of assistance."

Alexander spun around, fumbling with his light. Shining it this way and that, finally zeroing in on the presence: back at the passage entrance that led into this chamber. A lone figure stood there.

It took him a moment to see that it was a woman. Someone in a long gray cloak. Actually, he realized, a *sari*. Draped over her shoulder and wrapped around her body. She had short hair, white, and her face was beautiful despite its age.

"Easy," Caleb whispered. "I think I know her, but how-?"

"-Did I find you?" The woman approached, her own flashlight aimed down, a large maglite beam glinting off the solid floor and making it seem like she walked on a star. "I got a call from your very concerned sister."

"Phoebe!"

"She was fine when I talked to her. In a helicopter, heading towards some mission for your American friends."

"What friends?" Alexander was rubbing his head, shining his light from the newcomer to his father.

"Not important now," said the woman as she took a moment to shine her light on the central apparatus, following the shaft upwards to where her more powerful light caught it merging with the precipitous ceiling. "I can't believe it. This really exists."

"Who are you?" Alexander asked, but then his eyes adjusted, and he saw her more clearly, not as a ghostly goddess of the abyss, but as flesh and blood. He had seen her before, on rare occasions when all the Keepers would gather. When Lydia and Uncle Robert would send him off to play (or learn) in the upper levels of the Alexandrian Library while they met and decided the fate of the recovered scrolls. "You're-"

"Rashi Singh." Caleb stood and bowed to her. "Keeper, this was too dangerous, you coming down here. And how did you even bypass the guards up there?"

There was a gleam in her dark eyes as she spoke. "Herodotus. The lost chapters.

Deliberately cut from his *Histories*, preserved and sent away, according to his notes, because the priests at Thebes demanded that what he had seen below the Pyramids be kept secret."

"I must not have seen that scroll," Caleb said excitedly.

"You were too busy," Rashi replied, "apparently with your own secrets."

Caleb let that slide. "So Herodotus was down here. He had spoken of legends about a labyrinth."

"Hints, myths. The priests allowed such talk."

"So the lost chapter had a map?"

Rashi pulled out an iPhone and turned it so Caleb and Alexander could see the screen, where there was a scanned image, a hand-drawn pyramid, and a series of tunnels and chambers sketched beneath it. "It did, one that showed several other exits, including the one at the Cairo Museum."

"Uncle Montross!" Alexander perked up.

"I believe he's been captured," Rashi said quietly. "But you knew that already. I assumed he was your decoy, and you hoped to find one of the other exits."

"That was the plan," Caleb said. "But first, this..." He motioned to the central chamber. "Did Herodotus mention what this was?"

Rashi shook her head and raised the phone, scrolling over on the screen. "It's drawn here, and Herodotus relates in his scrolls that he has heard only half-whispered legends, rumors that it might have been a place of defense, a way for the king to send his divine wrath against any adversary, anywhere on the earth. Or in the sky."

"A weapon," Alexander whispered.

The Keeper stared at the chamber, moving closer and stooping so she could look inside. "Herodotus claims even the priests had lost all wisdom about its true function, and any clues had now been transformed into unrelated ritual and half-remembered purpose."

Caleb nodded. "Then we're done here. I assume you got in through the more distant entrance point. From what I had RV'd, it was northwest of the city, not far from the Nile."

"Yes. But come along quickly. Before they brave the traps to search for you.

And before they once again try to RV you—and perhaps see us."

Alexander shifted. "Maybe they've already done it and they're waiting by the exit like they were at the museum."

"Maybe," Caleb said. "But hopefully they didn't ask the right questions and only got that hit for Xavier. But you're right, they'll be trying again soon. I just hope Nina's preoccupied and her kids… I mean our kids… aren't that focused."

"We'll have to take that risk," Rashi said. "Now come on, I have a boat and a crew standing by to take you."

"To where?" Alexander asked, giving one last look to the chamber, imagining himself in there, sitting at the controls, with godlike power dancing from his finger tips.

The Keeper smiled. "I have a feeling you're going to need our help once more. We're going to Alexandria."

8.

They landed at the Bamian airstrip, one and a half miles from the town, and an armored convoy waited for them. A contingent of NATO forces, Marines and CIA operatives, almost forty men, armed to the teeth, gathered in their vehicles and took off as soon as Temple herded Orlando and Phoebe into the third jeep and gave the order.

Looking pale as he slipped into a flak jacket two sizes too large for him, Orlando tried to sound jovial. "Just like Saigon, eh Phoebe?"

"Knock it off with the *Die Hard* quotes," she snapped as Temple helped her into her vest. "You weren't even in diapers, much less junior high."

"Yeah, knock it off. We're losing the element of surprise." Temple pointed through the front windshield. The huge sandstone cliffs loomed ahead, pale blue in the pre-dawn shadows. Venus kissed the peak's crown, then Phoebe watched the morning star disappear in the sand and dust from the lead jeep's spitting tires. And then the first glint of the sun's rays touched the upper edges of the mountains.

Phoebe craned her neck to see better. The western niche in the cliff was achingly empty. And far to its right, the other one, smaller but just as lonely. Already plans were being made by several archaeological preservation societies to rebuild the statues, but the region still wasn't safe. Not yet.

She looked ahead grimly and found her heart racing as they came to a sliding stop in a cloud of dust. To her left and right, the other members of the convoy were leaping out of their vehicles, rushing toward a cave entrance.

"Let's go," Temple said, slipping on a helmet and fixing Phoebe's, switching on the maglite at its center.

Orlando held up his bare hands. "Where's my gun?"

"You're just an observer," Temple said, kicking open the door and leading them out. "If we get to the point where you need to shoot something, we're already dead."

Orlando coughed as he jumped out with Phoebe, and the dust and the already stinging heat knocked him back. He staggered, but then Phoebe's hand caught his, and he was running along with her and six NATO troops—or Marines—he couldn't tell. Weapons drawn, scanning the cliff side, aiming at the darkened caves. Back at the lonely village tenements a few huddled forms appeared, watching with mild interest.

Somewhere a rooster crowed, and up above, a pair of eagles circled hungrily.

Phoebe paused, steadied herself and stared up at the giant cliff wall, the imposing deeply carved-out niche. And she closed her eyes. "Wait, I just want to see if I can-"

"Not now," Temple barked. "Satisfy your curiosity later."

"But, I can see who really built them!"

"Later." He dragged her forward. "The Hummingbird's running out of time."

Orlando followed Phoebe's wistful glance to the empty niche and the rubble of the once-proud statue. Then he chased after them. "I sure hope they haven't RV'd us coming."

As they entered the first cave and took up positions, lining the initial cavern and the first part of the descending passage, Temple said: "Not likely, but we're on our guard. Hopefully the fact that you only recently RV'd the boy and got us our approach plan, that changed the future sufficiently."

"I thought this Eye dude was just a shield," Orlando said.

Temple shook his head. "He's what we'd call a well-rounded bastard. RV skills just like yours. He was searching for the Hummingbird, and we believe she knew it. She and her family were originally from Kabul, but they fled. Came here while she shielded their movements. Found a cave and tried to stay awake and hidden as long as she could. Probably had her parents try to keep her alert and focused. Coffee beans, whatever, but in the end she couldn't last. Dozed off and the Eye zeroed in on her."

He pulled out an iPhone and Phoebe recognized Orlando's map on it. A few others in the team had the same thing. Temple raised a fist, pointing ahead, and the lead team of four moved off silently, approaching the first of many mined-passageways Orlando had seen.

"Here we go," Temple whispered, and pushed them on ahead after the others had all descended into the depths of the ancient mountainside.

"We'll pause at two-minute intervals," he said. "And give you two a chance to look ahead and see if anything's changed."

"On it already," Phoebe responded, touching her forehead under the helmet. "Multi-tasking."

"That's my girl."

Orlando glared at him.

"Easy," Phoebe whispered, reaching back to grasp his fingers.

He smiled. "Sorry. Without your big brother around, I have to protect you."

"Oh? And what about you? Last I recall, you were the one getting your ass kicked by eels and needed me to save you."

"Fight about who loves who more later," Temple hissed as they rounded a corner. He raised the phone, spoke something into his microphone, and two more soldiers rounded the right-most corner and doubled back, standing guard.

"Through obstacle three," came a voice over Temple's headset. He ordered the team ahead, pushing them on. And then they were moving faster through a section relatively free of mines and traps. Orlando let go of Phoebe's hand to adjust the light on his visor, and he ducked in several places as the cavern ceiling dipped. Seeing it in this viewpoint, from a higher angle than when he remote-viewed the village boy, left him disoriented.

A few more twisting turns, a short, steep descent, then a sharp turn, and suddenly they all stopped as the lead members went to work disarming another trap.

Temple turned around. "Okay, you two are up. Try RVing–" His eyes went wide. "Where's Phoebe?"

Orlando spun, reaching out into the shadows. His light probed the walls, the corners. He darted back and turned the corner.

But she was gone.

As part of her multi-tasking, Phoebe was viewing the path ahead, and specifically trying to hone in on the Hummingbird. Hoping maybe the girl was still asleep, without her shield, but it wasn't working.

Nothing but a wall of blue greeted her when she thought about the child. A repelling force like a shockwave, more powerful than she'd ever felt before, like she'd been slapped away from snooping where she didn't belong. She groaned, slipped behind the last tier of squad members who kept moving, following their PDAs.

Hugging a wall and catching her breath, Phoebe finally shook her head and tried to follow the dark shadows and the flickering beams of light up ahead. But it seemed they'd sped up, the corridor lengthened, and no matter how fast she tried to move, she couldn't close the distance. They rounded a corner and she was alone.

Panicked now, she moved faster, scuttling after them, holding out her hands, brushing the rough walls with her fingertips. Reaching a dead end, she turned her head left and then right, shining the feeble beam in each direction, stabbing into the endless gloom of both passageways.

She held her breath.

Listened.

And heard only scrapes and scuffles sounding from each hallway.

She turned back around, but the way she thought she had come from was now blocked by a solid wall of sandstone. She desperately wished Temple had fitted them with radios like the other team members, but now there was nothing to do but stay here and wait. She couldn't call out and risk alerting the enemy.

Maybe she could RV the way. And for a second, she thought first about her brother, wondering how Caleb and Alexander were faring.

A glimpse—a flash of light in the gloom, and she saw them: *following a woman in a gray flowing sari across a stretch of desert, toward a waiting boat on the Nile.*

Smiling, she turned her attention to the corridor on her left, and as she was about to project her thoughts in that direction, her light caught the flash of something white darting out of view. Her breath caught in her throat and she staggered forward, mouth open. Still not daring to call out, she rushed ahead then skidded to a stop, suddenly terrified of setting off fish wire traps or buried mines.

Was this a trick?

I saw a face, she thought. Someone all in white, there for a moment, gone the next. Still fearing a trick, she moved cautiously. A few more steps, then she stopped. Flicked off her headlamp. *Don't want to give anyone a target.*

Then she tried to peer ahead in her mind.

And once again she winced, reeling immediately from a wall of blue.

A sound up ahead like a throaty chuckling.

"Who's there?" she called out.

Laughter again. Cruel and mocking.

This time, behind her.

She backed up. Flattened against the wall and crouched. Again she reached out with her mind, trying to see, but there was nothing in either direction, nothing but that awful blue, closing in around her on all sides like a sphere. Shrinking.

And then the laughter again. And footfalls approaching.

"Come out, come out..."

Oh god, it's the Eye.

"I've got you now, another bird for my cage."

A light sprang on, just feet away, the beam extending—

"I've got-"

-then freezing. Dust motes suspended.

"...you..." The word slowed, stretched and faded with a series of echoes as the light dimmed.

And Phoebe realized she was falling backwards, through the wall that now wasn't a wall. A veil of blackness sucked her in, then resealed where she had been crouching just as time seemed to hiccup, then snap back into place.

"...now!" She heard the Eye speaking, but it sounded like it came from a great distance.

The darkness around her trembled.

Fists pounded on the other side of the wall and a defiant grunting reached her ears.

Dazed, she turned around and saw that she stood on a great precipice overlooking an impossible sight.

A glimpse only, lasting maybe four or five seconds. A time in which she took in an incredible vista, a chasm stretching miles across and just as deep, jagged cliffs encircling and enshrining a valley in the shadowy depths. The gloom was punctuated only by an array of lights—some sort of oddly purple phosphorescence—clinging to unnatural towers of rock or crystal, shimmering domes and palatial hillside gardens. The sound of underground streams reached her ears, the plunking of rocks into a cool lake. A fresh breeze rushed across her hair, cooling her skin, blowing back her dusty hair.

But then the image faded, the darkness closed in around her, and all that remained was a man in a white robe, with a gray beard down to his waist.

He smiled at her and said, "We have watched you for a long time, Phoebe Crowe. Welcome to a place no outsider has ever seen, except in the embrace of dreams that never linger for long upon waking. Welcome..." He spread his arms wide and the darkness behind him unclouded for just a moment, revealing the subterranean city in all its glowing splendor.

"...to Shamballa."

Orlando wanted to race back through the tunnels looking for her, calling her name, but Temple hauled him back. He waved to two of his men and sent them back, hissing at them that they should have watched her.

"Now kid, we have to move on. We're losing the element of surprise here."

"But-"

Temple pulled on his arm and then they were rounding another bend, and then—according to the map, there should be one more looping passage, a quick descent and then the approach to the chamber where the Hummingbird and her father were being kept. "Come on," he said. "We're almost there."

But then a flash of red, a rush of heat, and six men leading their team up ahead disappeared in a blast of fire, rocks and collapsing sandstone. Screams and shouts. The others rushed ahead to help their buried comrades. Temple was yelling, pulling them back, barking that it was a trap, they'd been seen-

And then Orlando's ears stopped ringing long enough to hear the mocking laughter at his back, accompanying the knife pressed against his throat.

The Eye dragged Orlando back, using his body as a shield as the Americans turned their weapons toward him, but the com-mander held up a hand to hold their fire.

"Let the mountain claim you!" the Eye yelled as he backed around a corner with his captive. He nodded to one his men, who paused long enough to ensure the forces were following—then pressed a button on a remote.

Orlando whimpered as another explosion rocked the tunnel, this time spitting out dust and rocky debris right past them.

The Eye nodded, satisfied, then continued hauling Orlando off, towards a passage they had skipped on the way down. "Your friends are dead. Or at the least, buried and running out of air. You're alone now."

Orlando grunted, choking for breath around the crushing grip of the big arm around his throat. But he managed to get a word out. "Phoebe?"

"Ah, the other bird has flown." The Eye's voice faltered. "Somewhere out of my reach, but only for the moment. Somewhere... never mind." His eye blinked and lines of concern formed on his brow, then smoothed away. "But I have you now, and soon your song will join the Hummingbird's."

"I'm not helping you do anything." Orlando forced his mouth to work. "You've got no leverage. Can't threaten my elderly relatives to make me comply, so why don't you just suck it, dickhead?"

In the flickering dark, the jeweled eye patch glinted and the lone eye narrowed into a feline slit that regarded him like a helpless, wounded mole. "I know you, Orlando Natch. I've spied you ever since your plane approached. Saw who you are, what you are." His smile broadened and sickly yellow and brown teeth emerged from cracked lips. Orlando winced against the smell.

"Shouldn't go snooping, you know."

"Shut up and move, Mr. Natch. You'll help, or when I find your precious girlfriend, and I will find her, I'll make you wish you had."

Orlando winced as something prodded his ribs, and then he stumbled forward, lurching to remain in balance. For a fleeting second he thought he could make a break for it, but then he was shoved ahead, flanked by four other foul-smelling soldiers, and marched toward the Hummingbird.

Her real name was Aria. And her father—Brian Greenmeyer, formerly of St. Louis, except for the past fifteen years ostensibly trying to spread the Word of God to the impoverished Afghan villagers—was in fact a deep-cover CIA agent. So deep he even fell in love, married and fathered a girl of exceptional talents. And found himself devoted to a people whose peaceful and practical existence in the face of such harsh conditions had led him to be the perfect agent. He still gave out the occasional report on Taliban and Al Qaeda activities, and ran courier information and gathered what intelligence he could from unsavory types that nonetheless trusted him, but his foremost mission in the past seven years had been to protect his daughter. To protect Aria.

Protect her from both the radical Muslims who would either kill her or use her for their own protection, and from the U.S. government. Brian knew about the   history   of   the   military's involvement with psychics, and how they had often been treated as strategic assets, not as people.

He wouldn't let that happen to her. But his options had run out. He had contacted Commander Temple, his old friend, weeks ago, after he had learned that the Eye was closing in on them in Kabul. Told Temple they were going into hiding—but for how long?

And now, his legs were broken and useless. Barely given enough food and water to stay conscious. He could scarcely think, and every minute he was awake, he could only writhe in agony in his chains, unable even to reach the cage where they'd imprisoned Aria.

The Hummingbird.

He smiled. The name fit. Some of her friends back in Kabul called her that because she liked to dart around, flapping her arms, and seemed to move faster than any kid should. Brian met her big blue eyes and he couldn't help but smile, even as his heart cracked inside.

"I'm sorry, honey. I know I said I'd protect you."

"Don't worry, father. You did it. Brought the good guys here. They're coming for me."

Good guys? He shrugged. "Not so sure about that, baby, but I do think they're better than who's got us now."

"They are. And they've brought others with them. Two people, like me. They'll help me, you'll see. But first, it's time." She brought her hands up, two fingers outstretched on each, and pressed them to her temples under the tangled strands of auburn.

"Time?"

"To leave the Eye without his protection. Time to drop the shield."

"But-"

"It's so she can find me. Get ready, father."

He pulled himself up to his elbows, wincing in agony, gasping. Turned his body so he could drag himself to the wall of this tiny cul-de-sac. He glanced around the room, his mind clearing suddenly with a rush of adrenalin. He saw the oil lamp. A bunch of old rags. The water jug and bowl for their toilets. And his boots, there in the corner. Long laces still on them.

Perhaps he could rig a trap, trip the guards on their return, break the lamp and set one on fire, but then-

He was still useless to move, would never make it out, much less crawl to Aria's cage to free her. But if someone else was coming, someone who could help...

"Sit tight, honey. Just try to see. Tell me who's coming first. Everything you can see, every detail."

The Hummingbird nodded rapidly as her fingers grasped the bars of her cage. And she closed her eyes and smiled.

"The Eye... he's almost here..."

"**Open your eyes**," the old man whispered. Which Phoebe thought was odd, since her eyes were already open. But she tried to obey him anyway. It seemed the right thing to do, the friendly thing for one who had just saved her life.

Her eyes opened, and she had the sudden impression that everything before this instant had been a dream, one that would quickly fade.

One second Phoebe had the impression of standing in thin air, over the precipice looking down at the fabled city below her dangling feet and thinking: *this can't be real;* and the next, she was floating in space over a cratered lunar surface. The cold vastness of the void at her back, winking stars in all directions. Below...

Striated lines, deep gouges in the pock-marked gray-blue surface. A deep impact crater so deep it seemed it must reach the center and punch through.

Phobos, said the old man's voice in her head.

And the moon turned, revolved as if in a sped-up move-frame, and a bright red glow filled her eyes, and she turned and caught her breath, dazzled at the immense, seething crimson planet looming into view. And below, directly below her feet now, lined up with the Phobos crater...

A familiar section of the planet, just north of the equator. Her mind's eye expanded and the view enlarged and there, looking back at her—

The Face.

And more... emerging from the red sands... Enormous hands, a chest thrust outward. Two legs, the toes of massive feet. An entire statue shaking free of its dusty prison. The head was tilted back so the face was thrust toward the heavens, the eyes looking up. One arm was at its side, the other reaching, reaching... up... to her...

And then the stars rushed by, filled her view and she hurtled through space, across the millions of miles to another glowing rock, familiar sphere. The Moon's lunar surface suspended over the green, blue and white hues of Earth.

See, came a command from somewhere close. Her consciousness rushed over the bright cratered surface, over to the wall of darkness, to the opposite side,   the   shrouded   hemispheres, toward a crater with a flashing light, a strobe of some kind.

A beacon.

See...

And then a flash of *blue*, and everything faded.

A hand on her forehead, gently pushing her back. Back. Her feet moving on her own.

Her eyes blinking furiously, each involuntary motion elicited a vision and formed a montage. The tomb in Belize. The fall, the wheelchair... The laboratory and the unraveled Herculaneum scrolls... the vault door under the Pharos opening at her command... running on the hill with Alexander, her legs healed... the descent into the Khan's mausoleum... reaching for Orlando, kissing his lips for the first time...

And then...

A frozen wilderness guarded by enormous ice-capped mountains, with a dazzling aurora overhead.

"You have a great destiny ahead of you, Phoebe Crowe. Much work to do, much sacrifice, but equal joy." The pressure released from her forehead.

"But-"

"Go now."

Phoebe blinked. "Wait!" She stood in an alcove with three exits—and what looked so out of place she didn't realize what it was at first—a door. A plain white door with a brass handle. The city was gone, the chasm, the hollowed-out valley. If it ever existed. "Was it real? Shamballa? What you showed me?"

The man, backing away toward the shadows in the central exiting tunnel, merely smiled. "I showed you nothing. I only freed your mind for a minute, long enough for your questions to seek some answers. You saw what you needed to see."

"But who are you? Can't you help us?"

He sadly shook his head. "On the contrary, it is you who must help us. You who are still blissfully ignorant, only you can end our suffering."

"What suffering?"

"Existence without amnesia."

"Huh?"

"Go now, that door will save your friends. It is all I can do. Go, and remember this one thing. The *Custodians* are not what they seem."

Phoebe approached the door. Pulled the old ornate brass handle, glancing behind as she did so. The old man was gone, and she stood in an enclosed cavern, her light dancing across the low-hanging ceiling formations, the rugged walls and rocky floor. One exit at the back.

Suddenly the door flew open, releasing a flood of rocks and debris. And then she heard scrambling. Muffled voices. She shined her flashlight through the door and saw arms and legs, a head. A man pushing through the cave-in.

Temple coughed up a mouthful of sandstone. Staring at the surrounding cavern, weakly shining his flashlight in the direction of the exit. "Just in time. How did you find us?"

"Not now," Phoebe said. "Get your men out, and come find me."

Temple started frantically digging. "Did you see-?"

Phoebe's eyes blinked and her focus shifted. "I can see her. The Hummingbird. She's released her shield. I have to go. Now." And then she was off, leaving the commander to double his efforts and free his men, hoping she knew what she was doing.

Orlando moved on ahead, feeling like a human shield. Wrists tied behind his back, he found it harder to walk the rough stones and navigate the dark caverns than he had imagined, especially without using his hands for balance. And the lights from his back were jolting, shifting back and forth, bouncing off the walls, then disappearing, making him feel like he was suffering a seizure, with light and dark spots alternating in his brain. The air was stifling, the oxygen thinning.

Video games never captured this part of dungeon trekking, he thought, coughing and choking on dust that seemed to just resettle in his lungs and esophagus. Something jabbed him in the lower back and he stumbled ahead.

He glanced back into the jumble of lights, the two turban-headed fighters directly behind him, and at the rear—the taller one with the patch. Gathering his balance   and   his   courage, Orlando tried to smile. "So, are we there yet?"

"Shut up," the Eye snapped. "It's just around the corner. Farrakh, you go first."

A hand pulled Orlando back, slowed him down, and then the other man squeezed past. He turned the corner, descended a small, slick trail, and then Orlando could see a light ahead. A dim glow from an opening, a wider aperture. But then the man's back was in the way.

Orlando closed his eyes for a second and willed a glimpse of the next chamber. And it came at once:

A cage, like for a dog. Metal bars, a bowl in the corner. But it was empty. The door open. Farrakh rushes in, shouting and slips on something slick coating the floor...

He opened his eyes and was about to call out, but instead, he dug in his feet and stopped moving forward. Someone crunched into him and drove him into the wall with a curse, but then the fighter kept running by. There was a shout, a slick, wet sound and a grunt.

Twisting, Orlando turned and inched backward—right into the glowering form of The Eye—who caught his throat in his huge hand. "You saw something?"

But just then a burst of light from the cave, a rush of heat—and a pair of bloodcurdling screams. The Eye swore a local curse, shoved Orlando back, then ran headlong toward the fire. Two flaming, lurching men in robes flailed out into the hallway, and the Eye burst through them, knocking each aside like bowling pins as he leapt over the pool of ignited oil.

Brian Greenmeyer had improvised the best he could, the best anyone could have, having only been able to crawl. But as he was setting up a tripwire made of shoelaces and a coating of oil on the ground below, the young woman appeared.

She was alone, which was surprising. Greenmeyer kept looking past her down the cavern hallway, expecting and hoping to see his old friend, Temple. But the woman stepped by, went right to the cage and knelt in front of Aria.

Their hands touched. "I'm Phoebe," she said, reaching through the bars and stroking Aria's hair, gingerly touching her face.

"I've seen you," Aria whispered, eyes wide. "But hurry, he's coming. The key..."

"I know," Phoebe said, scrambling to her feet and reaching up to the top of the cage, way out of Greenmeyer's reach. She found it, dropped back down and unlocked the padlock.

Aria burst out, scrambled to her father and threw her arms around him. "You can come with us."

But he shook his head. "No time." He looked back at the corridor. "I hear them, hurry."

"No," Phoebe said, glancing around the cul-de-sac, her eyes settling on a blanket and a collection of bags and boxes near the shadowy reaches in the back. "I have a better idea."

Once everything and everyone was in its place, Greenmeyer scuttled back, holding the sole lamp, cranking its flame inside the glass as high as it would go. It still had a half-full canister of oil, more than enough to ignite and scatter to burn the coating he spilled on the floor.

He heard the footfalls. Then the rushing feet. One of the guards he remembered as Farrakh tripped over the lace and skidded face-first on the oil. He got to his feet, slick and bloody, yelling that the cage door was open, then he turned and saw Greenmeyer just as the lamp was flung to the floor.

Greenmeyer rolled away as the glass shattered, the flames erupted and Farrakh screamed. The whole front of his body ignited, then his dry robes, and then his turban—and he was a walking, flailing inferno that turned just as his partner came barreling in too fast and collided with him. They both rolled through the flames, then got up howling, throwing themselves against the walls, seeking anywhere to roll and put out the flames.

Greenmeyer choked on the smell of burnt flesh. And he hoped his daughter was staying low, covered under the blankets. Not looking...

Then another shape burst past the burning bodies and jumped over the flames. The lone eye sought him out, and a snarling face turned to a mask of rage. The AK-47 was thrust into his face. A boot against his neck. *"Where is she?"*

Greenmeyer gagged. Smoke stung at his eyes. "Gone. Rescued..."

The boot rose—then fell, smashing against the side of his face. The room dimmed and he thought he heard a choking sound. *Stay awake... buy her time...* "Can't... you see...?"

Another snarl. "Her damn shield's on you fool. I will find her. And then I'll haul her back by her hair and make her watch as I skin you alive, then burn your limbs off one by one. The agony you caused my men is nothing compared to what you'll face."

"Quit talking then." Greenmeyer forced a smile. "Get to it, or else my little girl will outrun you."

The Eye kicked him in the ribs, and then again in the side of his head, before he ran back out. The room dimmed and as unconsciousness swirled around him, Greenmeyer relaxed and gave in, confident that The Eye had taken the bait.

Orlando had a small head start, but he knew it wouldn't last. The light from the burning corpses was fading, and the flashlight strapped to his head had cracked. Its weak bulb struggled to light a few feet ahead, like the glow from a cell phone screen. So he paused, closed his eyes and tried to RV the way.

Crashing footsteps behind him. A curse, and a shout.

Damn it! He had seen a tiny glimpse—a greenish-hued, fast-motion exodus of his mind's eye through the caverns ahead: straight, then right, then left and-

He was off, running. Trusting his vision.

A light at his back. The Eye rushing after him like a crazed rhinoceros. Orlando raced ahead, started to turn right but jarred into the edge of the cave wall. Grunted, spun, then found the opening and sped up through it. Skidded to a halt. His wrists burned, his shoulders were in agony and he just wished he had time to try that maneuver he saw in the movies where handcuffed heroes were somehow able to step back through their bound arms and at least bring their wrists up front so they could use their hands.

But he kept running in the dark. Bouncing off the walls, jarring his head on a low-hanging section at one point. Stars pinwheeled in his vision, but he kept moving. Skidded to a stop, backed up and took the turn he missed.

Rushing right at him—a bobbing flashlight in the hands of his pursuer. The lone eye locked on him, full of rage. Orlando sped up, attacking the darkness with abandon. Still trusting his vision. Trusting that-

Whoa! He jumped, leapt as far as he could, suddenly recalling that near-instantaneous out of body trek through this section, and seeing now that there was a mine, showing up bright red in his vision. A circular mine set in the center of the passage, about a foot and a half wide. A pressure-sensitive trigger plate.

Orlando leapt it awkwardly, crashed onto his knees and rolled. And kept rolling into the darkness.

He got up and looked back to the approaching light. Hunched his shoulders and ducked his head.

Step on it you sonofa-

But the light just intensified and the thudding footsteps stopped and skidded. The Eye stood right over him. The gun pointing down.

Lucky bastard, Orlando thought, looking up into the glare and offering an exhausted smile. "Got me." He closed his eyes, ready for a gunshot to the head or at least a punch that would shatter his fragile jaw, knock out his teeth and mess with his almost-good-looks to the point Phoebe would probably never gaze longingly at him again. *If we ever even make it out of here.*

But instead, he heard an unfamiliar voice.

"Hey ugly! Back here!"

Surprisingly, it sounded like it belonged to a little girl.

Phoebe and Aria made their stand at the entrance to the upward sloping tunnel. "I've seen this," the Hummingbird said calmly. They had followed the Eye back out, after Aria had first kissed her father's face, almost sobbing but happy he was still breathing. "Let's end this," Phoebe said, taking Aria's hand and leading her out.

They moved quietly but quickly, following the Eye's bludgeoning track after Orlando.

"We'll save him," Aria whispered, sensing Phoebe's urgency once she realized who that was up there, fleeing blindly into the dark. Once the Eye had glanced back, but the darkness—and her mental shield—had protected them from his sight. He turned one corner, then another.

Phoebe quickened the pace, almost pulling Aria off her feet. What was she thinking? They had no weapons. As much as she had hoped to take the weapons off the charred dead men, the guns were partially melted, and way too hot to touch. So they moved ahead, armed with nothing but optimism.

"Hey ugly!" Aria shouted just as they turned the corner and saw the Eye standing over Orlando. "Back here!"

Phoebe put her hand around Aria's mouth, but it didn't matter. The Eye had seen. He shined his light on them, catching and blinding them both.

"Ahhhh," came the echoing sound. "My lost birds. Thought you could fly to freedom?"

Aria pushed Phoebe's hand away. "I'll never be caged again."

"Think not?" The voice approaching. The light, brighter.

"I've seen it," she said defiantly, holding up her arms, wing-like. "You can't catch me."

"Aria-" Phoebe hissed, trying to pull her back. But then she realized it was too late.

He came barreling toward them, charging like a madman, his lone eye gleaming with hate.

Aria smiled as she turned, pulling Phoebe around with her and ducking.

The Eye saw the move and had a sudden flash. A vision. Too late, he couldn't stop or change his forward momentum—which took him right onto the pressure plate. The mine flattened under his right foot. His left dug in, halting his motion, but he was already falling forward, sliding off the plate.

"This isn't over." He dropped to a knee, his back leg twisted at a nearly impossible angle, still exerting just enough pressure on the trap to stave off detonation. He closed his eye.

Behind him, Orlando had stood up, and was backing away after a glance assured him of Phoebe's safety.

"It's over for you," Aria called back. "And soon for your friends."

The Eye chuckled. "I have many friends. You may get those here, but the others—the masters I truly serve..." His laughter continued as he sighed and moved his foot off the trap.

"There will be nowhere to hide."

The explosion rocked the cavern and sent chunks of flesh and bone in all direction.

Orlando ducked just in time and kept his head down, hoping the whole roof wouldn't collapse with the blast.

Finally he stood and looked back, but could barely make anything out. The explosion had taken out the flashlight as well.

"Phoebs?"

"Here," came the echoing response. "We're ok. Follow my voice."

"And watch where you step," came the girl's voice.

Orlando moved ahead. "Yuch. I'm so taking a shower after this is over."

Just then, several flashlight beams converged on Phoebe and Aria. Shouts and screams. In Arabic from the left, English from the right.

Phoebe pushed Aria ahead, toward Orlando and into the branching tunnel just as gunshots erupted. Rushing forward, Orlando met them both and Phoebe threw her arms around him and pushed him against the wall. The gunfire continued. Men screamed and screamed and then...

Silence.

Lights filled the hallway.

Phoebe pressed her lips against Orlando's ear. "It's okay, I think..."

"Hi there," said the little girl, stepping back into the corridor and waving into the light. "My dad said you've been looking for me."

The lights dimmed, moved away, and Orlando saw a half-dozen men, their khakis torn and filthy, some limping and nursing wounds, but alive. Temple lowered his light.

"That I have, little one, that I have." He looked at Phoebe and Orlando, then at the mess in the center of the tunnel. "Good work, you two. Now come on, let's get this one's father, and then get out of here."

Aria reached back and took Phoebe's hand and Orlando's arm and walked between them. She looked up at them both, smiling. "We're going to the snow mountain where the wizards live."

Phoebe and Orlando glanced at each other, then shrugged.

Temple shook his head in wonder. "Damn, she's good. Glad she's going to be on our team."

9.

Egypt

Nina strapped the MP5 submachine gun over her shoulder as she climbed the ancient steps out of the Sphinx's lower chamber. She headed back outside, into the winds and the sound of the helicopter engine. She ascended and moved into the semicircle of soldiers awaiting Senator Calderon and his guests.

As the seconds dragged on and the door still didn't open, she was surprised to feel so calm. Here it was, finally she was going to meet her boys. Her children. After all those years apart. All that time, did they even know she was alive and sedated? Did they visit? Did they care, or did Calderon shape their minds to one single purpose, stoking their egos and building them up as... what were they to him? Messiahs, or merely tools to his own ascension?

She clenched her teeth and fought a renewed pain from the shoulder wound she'd received back on the Mongolian steppes. She'd have to get the dressings changed and have that looked at soon, but so far she'd been running on adrenaline, purpose fueling her every step of the way. She'd come too far, and now she had a new purpose. A responsibility.

Suddenly she was very jealous, bitter at Calderon for depriving her of the chance to mold these children, to shape them into the future leaders the way she would have wanted. And what about Caleb? She struggled with that the most. Two hours ago she would have gladly stuck a knife in his heart and twisted it slowly. He had left her, presumed she was dead and left her without so much as an RV attempt to check on her. But if he had seen her, lying there helpless in a coma, would he have even come to her aid?

Maybe, she thought, if he had seen she was pregnant.

But none of that mattered now.

Now, the door was opening. Two small forms leapt out in unison. They both set flashy skateboards on the paveway and pushed off together, gliding toward her.

They executed a sharp inward turns, skidded to a stop several feet away, then kicked up their boards into their hands.

The one on the left stretched out his arms. "Hello, mother."

The other one, his head lowered in slight show of respect, said: "It's good to see you. And for real this time."

"Catch up later, boys." Mason Calderon walked behind them, twirling his cane. "Let's get down there and get what we came for." He beamed at Nina. "Good to finally meet in person, Ms. Osseni. May I please have it?"

She nodded, drawn to something about him. The power in his shoulders and in his walk, the dazzling hint in his eyes revealing his utter belief in himself. Without hesitation she lowered the satchel, zipped it open and held it out for him. For some reason she thought she should bow her head, as if offering a grand gift to her king.

He reached inside and reverently took hold of the Emerald Tablet. Pulled it out with trembling hands. It was glowing, brighter now, dazzling in his eyes, swallowing up their blackness, substituting a throbbing green aura. He wobbled and Nina thought he might collapse under the thing's power. But then it seemed to rejuvenate him. His mouth opened, almost in an ecstatic silent cry. "At last..."

And then he was walking past her without another look, and the boys were in his place.

Nina's eyes darted back and forth. One child to the other. Both so similar and yet she also saw them with other senses. She saw their differences, little nuances. And she knew, from her glimpses into their pasts, which was which. Jacob on the right: a streak of something... different in him. So different than the cold-heartedness they both chose to portray. A little smoother, Jacob was, his edges not as sharp as Isaac's. His thoughts more deliberate, his words more carefully chosen. He... he was the reader, when occasion allowed. He did it in secret, when Isaac was asleep. Jacob... *he's more like Caleb, I can see it...*

Isaac... Nina smiled at him, and the boy grinned back, taking the attention as a selfish compliment proving he had been singled out over his brother. Competitive from the start. Isaac was definitely hers. She continued smiling, thinking about the contrast that no one else could see.

"Move," Calderon said, nodding to her and to the troops. "I'm back in charge. Let's get what we came here for and get out. I don't like all the attention that's coming our way." Beyond the perimeter, news vans struggled to get close enough to see, but were kept back by more Egyptian troops. Bright lights stabbed out, away from the Sphinx so no one could get a clear look at what they'd found.

The boys hurried past Nina, and each grabbed a hand as they passed, turning her around and bringing her with them. She clasped their hands, and she was surprised at how normal this felt. How good. Like it was just another day, and they'd been together all this time.

On her way down, she glanced back and saw two guards leading a red-haired man out of the helicopter, moving him along towards them.

Ah, Xavier. Coming to join the party. I wonder...

But that was when she felt the surge, jolting up her arms from where she held her children. As if they were each live wires, and she was caught in the middle, unable to let go as the currents ripped through her psyche.

It was as if there was a split screen in her mind. On the right, from Isaac came a flood of unrelenting visions, bombarding her with their brazen ferocity:

A younger boy with a mop of curly brown hair stands over a writhing frog, its legs and lower torso flattened. A streak of gore leading to the skateboard a few feet away. The boy has a screwdriver in hand, angling its sharp tip toward the frog's blinking eyes...

Another shift and he's a bit older, sitting before a large screen, sipping lemonade while watching scenes of desert warfare: anonymous planes bombarding villages, cluster bombs decimating ground forces, sniper rounds exploding soldiers one after another... Isaac giggling, eating popcorn.

On the seat beside him, Jacob is watching, no less rapt, but seems to wince at every scene of escalating violence. In the shadows near the back, a man stands leaning on a golden-tipped cane.

All this Nina saw in only a few seconds, but what she found herself focusing on was the left-most panel, the one showing only a single image…

Jacob, perhaps only four, lingering by the bedside of a patient, a woman strapped to a table in a familiar room. He looks back at a departing figure on a skateboard and when he's sure he's alone, he reaches out. And takes the patient's hand in his.

The boys let go simultaneously, in their enthusiasm for seeing the door at last. The door under the Sphinx, the one that only they could open. *If,* Nina thought, staggering a little after the release, *they could duplicate what Alexander had been able to do.*

She was dizzy, lightheaded. Her arms felt like jelly rolls.

"And how are the little rugrats?" came the voice at her back. She turned slowly to see Montross standing on the last step. His hair was a crimson mess, tangles and strands across his face. His shirt covered with sandstone dust, sweat and dirt, yet he looked radiant. A beaming smile, twinkle in his eye as if despite everything, despite being bound and in the enemy's camp, he was right where he wanted to be.

I wouldn't doubt it, she thought. Nor would she let her guard down. She had new allegiances now, and owed this man nothing more. In fact…

"You knew," she hissed. "You must have."

Montross let his smile falter. "I didn't. I never asked those kinds of questions, and didn't know I needed you until several years after they had taken your boys. I was too busy hiding from Waxman. Hiding, exploring… Researching all this. The Tablet, what it can do." He cocked his head, looked around her to where Calderon had the boys probing the wall. Isaac seemed morbidly distracted by the blood smears on the floor. The remains of Robert Gregory and Marcos.

"I don't know if I believe you," Nina said, keeping her eyes on Montross. She thought about the long journey they both shared. The plans devised late into the evenings. The shared visions, often in bed together, where she returned his thrusts by penetrating his mind, reveling in his visions—those that she could access. She had found it surprisingly difficult to get past some of his defenses, to see the things that truly drove him. Hints of attachment beyond what he had felt for his mother and his foster father, who were taken from him at such a young age. Nina knew there was another woman, someone he was protecting. Someone he might even...love? And that knowledge had both intrigued and infuriated her. That she couldn't see who it was. That he still had his secrets.

Montross shrugged. "It doesn't matter at this point. I only hope they know what they're doing."

"And do you?"

"Me?" He glanced down at himself. "What am I doing? Nothing, I'm just a captive, my fate at the whim of your new master." He blinked and glanced over at Calderon. "He *is* your master now, isn't he?"

She fumed. He knew that would get to her, still knew how to push her buttons. "I   have   no   master.   I   choose   the   best   team for my talents."

"Not always successful at that, right?   Could've done better than Waxman."

"Or you?"

"I thought we made a pretty decent team."

Nina smirked. "Just be quiet and let my boys work."

"Got it!" Calderon whooped a second before the grinding sound thundered inside the chamber. The wall was rising.

Jacob tottered, appearing dizzy. But Isaac ducked and rolled under the door, taking advantage of his brother's condition to get inside first. Nina headed toward Jacob, going to check on him. She reached out, but Calderon grabbed her wrist forcefully and brought her with him into the room, illuminated by the bright spotlights set up down here from when Robert Gregory made his attempt at access.

Nina looked back. Jacob was still doubled over from the effort, and Nina realized he was the one that had solved the puzzle and opened the door. And Isaac had just taken the credit. He felt her attention, glanced up and met her eyes and for a moment there was a hint of need. But then he blinked away all the emotion and the coldness set back in as he stood up. He squared his shoulders and quickly moved inside.

"The keys?" Calderon asked hopefully.

Isaac was checking the box, looking at it from all sides. Poking the center piece that held the three triangular slots. He shook his head. "Our dear brother has taken them."

"Thought as much," Calderon said. He let go of Nina's wrist, but gave her a slight push toward Montross. "Xavier, my friend. It's time to be useful. I'd ask you to willingly tell us what you know, but I'd never trust you."

Montross clucked his tongue against the roof of his mouth, then laughed. "Are you saying we just can't be friends?"

"Not today. Nina?" Calderon pointed with his cane, giving her a target. "Do your thing. Find out what Montross knows about the keys, and where the boy is hiding. We're going in after them, and I don't want any surprises."

Her head down, Nina approached, refusing to make eye contact. When she finally did, reaching for Xavier's face, planning to start with a gentle caress that would shuffle his memories and visions, causing what she needed to drop into her thoughts, he said in a low voice:

"Your master bids, and you obey…"

Her intensity shocked even herself. Maybe it was knowing that she had spectators and she didn't want to disappoint, didn't want to show weakness, especially in front of her boys. Or maybe Montross had just gotten under her skin, and she was striking back tenfold.

Either way, she went at his mind, hard. Dug in deep, forcing herself upon his psyche, taking every inch he reluctantly surrendered, every fleeting glimpse he failed to protect, snatching at the images like a multi-armed Hindu goddess. A hundred eyes, all peering into separate nooks, places Xavier could never blockade, not all at once under such an onslaught.

She saw things, so many, all at once. Too much to process now. She saw a woman on the edge of some monument in the Grand Canyon, with Xavier holding her hand as they watched the sunset paint glorious hues upon the striated cliffs. She saw a warehouse full of shelves a hundred feet high, with locked compartments guarding things of such antiquity… and Montross sneaking out, darting from the shadows with something spherical and shiny in his grasp, a thief in the dark.

And then she saw them: *Caleb and Alexander, rushing through a shadowy maze of passageways. Hurrying, following someone in a gray cloak.* Her vision fast-forwarded, piggy-backing onto Xavier's spark of prescience.

And now they're outside, climbing out of a well onto the desert sands. In the distance, a motorboat revving up. Dark figures on board, holding guns and watching the skies, looking southeast, toward the distant peaks of the three pyramids. Fast forward again:

A giant half-dome of glass, sparkling in the sun, surrounded by high-rises and minarets.

Nina let go, backed away, gasping for breath. Wiping the sweat from her brow, she turned away from Montross, who wouldn't look at her. "Senator," she whispered. "They're not down there anymore."

"Where-?"

She blinked, standing up straight and focusing on Montross. He shook his head, but she continued anyway.

"They're heading to Alexandria. To the library."

Calderon nodded. "Ah, our friends the Keepers." He started twirling his cane in his fingers, slowly, focusing on the dragon.

"Stepfather?" Isaac asked quietly. "Are we going there?"

"Oh we are, my boy." And he smiled broadly. "I'm through playing cat and mouse with them. There's no longer any point to the chase. Not when we have a way to end this once and for all."

Isaac was rubbing his hands together, and even Jacob seemed excited.

"It's time," Calderon said, "for the new library to meet the fate of the old."

10.

Over Pakistan

"One more unscheduled stop, I swear." Colonel Temple emerged from the pilot's cabin and faced his passengers. Phoebe sat beside Aria, who was sound asleep but turning fretfully, her eyelids fluttering. Orlando sat on the other side, as if they were the girl's protective parents, and for a few minutes before takeoff, he actually let himself imagine such a fantasy—that he and Phoebe were living out normal lives. Maybe returning from Disneyworld with a tuckered out daughter.

But then the plane banked away from the sandstone cliffs and Aria looked back on her father, sedated and asleep, hooked to an IV and sprawled out on the back three seats. Orlando met Phoebe's eyes, which for a moment were clouded with fear and adrift in loss, before she managed to find strength in him and draw it to herself.

She reached over and held his hand and tried to smile. "So, where are you taking me on our next date?"

Drifting off, Aria managed a giggle. "I like you two."

"We like you," Orlando said. "Even if we don't understand how you do what you do."

Her eyes were the bluest he'd ever seen, but the pupils were so large, threatening to spill over into the blue. It was as if she had been drugged. *And maybe she has*, he thought. He knew Colonel Temple needed her fresh and alert when they got back to the Stargate base, and her powers weren't really needed here, as long as they were a swiftly moving target at fifty thousand feet. They were safe. So maybe he did give her a little help in order to sleep.

"I just do it," she said. "It just happens. Natural, like if I threw a rock at you. If you couldn't dodge it, what would you do?"

Orlando looked at Phoebe, then back at the girl. He shrugged. "Try to block it or hide behind my arms?"

Aria nodded. "Just like that. Reflex. Except instead of raising my arms, I raise this... thing. This layer, like a blanket, except it's really wide and long and stretches pretty far back in time too."

"Neat," Phoebe whispered. "But you look exhausted. Your dad's stable now, he's resting. You should do the same."

Aria yawned, closed her eyes and smiled. And then she was out.

Even Temple's entrance didn't wake her. "Don't worry," he said. "We don't need her for this."

"For what?" Orlando asked, straining to see out the window. His ears had just popped with their descent. "We haven't been flying for more than an hour. Where are we?"

"Over part of Pakistan."

"Ugh," Phoebe said with a groan. "Please tell me we're not making another extraction or going into another cave."

Temple shook his head. "This one's simple. We land, you get out and you give me your impression of the site."

"What site?" Orlando asked. And he started wracking his brain for possibilities. What was in the mountains of Pakistan that they needed to see? What, besides another terrorist cell, or a cache of weapons or something?

"Just something I have my team members probe to test their talents."

"Another test?" Phoebe asked. "Really? After all we just did?"

Temple folded his arms over his chest. "Okay, it's not a test. I just want to see if you two can give me more information than those other psychics. Please, it's important." He took a seat in front of them, strapping himself in.

"Important for whom?" Orlando muttered. He grabbed hold of the armrests, preparing for a bumpy landing.

"For you," Temple replied. "Because this... you just have to see. I don't have your gifts, but I'm told it's quite... earth shattering."

"Mohenjo-Daro," Temple said after he had led them from the small landing strip to the edge of a hill overlooking a vast plain and a sprawling view of ancient red brick walls, ledges and boundaries, a few silo-like towers, arches and perfectly aligned streets. "The Mound of the Dead, as it's translated."

Orlando whistled. "I know this place."

"Thought you might," said Temple.

"Figures," Phoebe said, rubbing the sleeve of her blouse across her forehead, dabbing the sweat. The sun was just descending, but painfully intense, baking the ancient ruins below. "It's an old city, right? Archaeologists found it, and yeah it's pretty cool. So why are we here?"

"We're here to take a peek," Orlando guessed. He cracked his knuckles, stretched his arms and gave a little jog in place, as if warming up before a race.

"Yes, a peek." Temple waved his arm over the view. "Mohenjo-Daro was re-discovered in the 1920's. They believed it was built in 2600 BC and that it served as one of the centers of the Indus Valley civilization, of which very little is known. An incredible degree of sophistication went into the planning and design of this city. Urban sanitation systems like we wouldn't see again for two thousand years."

"Always a good thing, but probably no plumbers union back then." Orlando grinned, then shrugged at Phoebe.

"Precise geographical and astronomical layouts of the streets and buildings, and despite the best efforts of the world's leading linguists, a written script that has never been successfully translated. A mature language that appeared in these two cities as well as several thousand other sites across the area—for which they can find no evolution or development. It seems to have just appeared."

"Yeah, yeah," Orlando said. "Get on with the real juicy morsels. You know, tell her what's really crazy about this place." He glanced at Phoebe. "I tried to get your brother to let us make Mohenjo-Daro an objective that we should scout out during our downtime. But he thought it wasn't worth our effort."

"Doesn't sound like him. He must've been preoccupied." Phoebe kept staring at the city, and in the hazy sun the ancient buildings began to shimmer and wobble. She was feeling the tug of a vision.

Temple coughed. "I can understand Caleb's reluctance. But I must also now tell you in complete sincerity that what I'm about to say is above top secret, and-"

"Yeah, we know. Tell no one..." Orlando raised his hands in a gesture of being terrified. "...or else you'll have to kill us."

"Oh, I won't kill you," Temple said with a smirk. "But someone else assuredly will. Now, listen Phoebe, since I gather Orlando has already been briefed by Wikipedia or Conspiracies-R-Us..."

"Hey!"

"But this site, and its sister city not far from here, called Harrapan, are much, much older than 2600 BC."

"How old?"

"Undetermined. The problem with you psychics is that while you can see the past, you never manage to glimpse a newspaper or something with the date on it." He grinned. "Just kidding. But the problem of dating remains unsolvable. Best we can do is look to the geographic landmarks—or in some rare cases, we've had luck with the remote viewer coming out of the vision and drawing what the night sky looked like."

"Ah," Orlando said, clapping. "Plug the constellations into a computer program and let it match up the orientation with the patterns of stellar drift and the Earth's precession and wobble, and-"

"All right, all right." Phoebe rubbed her temples. "So did you do any of that with this site?"

Temple nodded. "But I'm not divulging that information yet, as uncorroborated as it is. I don't want to taint your impressions. Bad enough you already have a guess as to the target, and Orlando has his... theories. I need you to try to see for yourself."

"The target is Mohenjo-Daro," Phoebe said, nodding and taking a deep breath, focusing on the city.

"The target," Temple corrected, "is *the event.*"

"What event?" she asked.

Orlando let out a big sigh. "What he means, what he's getting at but won't tell you, is that the government's not stupid." He glared at Temple. "He knows what the scientists and the so-called quack archaeologists found. The skeletons flattened in the streets. Huddled in their homes, holding hands as they met their doom."

"Flattened?"

"Devastated. The walls bear evidence of extreme heat and exposure to an unknown source of energy. Something that left a radiation signature across this whole place. A signature not seen again until Hiroshima and Nagasaki."

Phoebe frowned at him. "Conspiracies-R-Us?"

"Try, *The Mahabarata*. The old Vedic epic and holy book… there's a whole battle scene in there that describes the gods raining these kinds of arsenals down upon their foes. I recall one of the verses went something like: '...*a single projectile, charged with all the power of the universe/ as bright as the thousand suns / a column of smoke and flame rose in all its splendor.'* Then something about reducing the people to ashes, corpses burning, hair and nails falling out. Descriptions that sounded way too much like nuclear fallout."

Temple grinned. "You've said too much, Orlando. Let her work with an unclouded mind. Phoebe, just try to see what happened here. What did them in?"

"Why?" she asked. "If you guys apparently know it all? What's the point?"

"Because," he said. "We need to know exactly what we're up against, and we need you to understand that what we're doing isn't because we're power-hungry elitists who want to jealously guard the truth from the pitiful masses."

"That's a relief."

"That's the truth," Temple said. "We have much bigger problems. Because whatever did this, whatever happened here, it's going to happen again if we don't get that Tablet back."

She saw it on the way down the hill. Just a few steps from the first wall of red brick, the dust already kicked up by her shoes. Maybe it was the smell, the proximity to the ancient stone. The sudden feeling of *belonging* here. Being one of with Mohenjo-Daro's population. Seeing it-

-*for the first time… The sound, the bustling throbbing sound. A perfect cadence of voice and motion. People, such a mass of people. Bright colors, hats, silken scarves, elegant robes and practical coverings. Commoner and royalty, it seemed, merge as one in the streets and... flee.*

Out of the city. Not a mob, but not so orderly as to be a ceremonious event. They're scared. Carrying some possessions, boxes, bags. A little girl carrying a dragon-shaped doll...

A rumbling in the earth.

Screams, people turning.

Something in the center of the city draws their attention. A tower, of sorts. Pyramid-shaped, glowing at its tip. The rumbling continues, intensifies—and a gathering light at the tip of the pyramid appears. Brighter and brighter, until the crowd moves slowly away, as if mesmerized by the sight, yet terrified of what might happen next.

There are things in the sky. Lights moving bright against the blue background, multi-colored orbs and flattened disc-shaped brilliances. They seem to be at war with each other. Some are spinning, dissolving, falling in snowflake-like patterns across the sky and over the mountains.

And the light from the pyramid turns darker, a deep indigo hue that in the blink of an eye blasts upward with a force that shatters the outer layer of stones from the pyramid and flattens nearby homes. Now there's a beam of light, pure nearly blinding light stabbing through the sky—and beyond. The air shimmers, people cover their eyes.

And as if in reply to this city's offensive, something comes down from the sky. Nothing entirely visible, but this nothing lands with an impact like a god's fist striking the ground. The earth trembles, the walls and buildings shake. But then the aftershocks, like concentric circles of energy, descend one upon the other, in widening diameters until the whole city, the entire plain is caught in its frequency.

A frequency that shatters living beings, flattening them like insects underfoot. The crowds, as one, are gone. Everyone still in the main center of the city—just pulverized. Whatever this force is, it spares the bricks, the earth, the structures, but leaves them smoking, simmering.

Everyone's gone except those who had just made it out of range. Stumbling away into a ravine, looking back in horror, back toward the beam from the pyramid. The beam that's flickering now. Fizzling, its power used up.

Amid the wailing, screaming and desperation, a last, lone look up at the sky...

And the tiny light, tinged in the approaching dusk with a light reddish hue. The only object in the sky above the pyramid. The only available target...

"What... the hell..." Phoebe clutched at Orlando's shirt, meeting his eyes with such lingering horror, "...was *that?*"

Orlando shook his head. "I didn't get enough. Just saw, I don't know, like I was in some structure, and I had a tablet. It might have been the same one you guys found. I was sitting in some throne-like contraption, and all these strange symbols and I don't know, equations or something, were whirling about my head. And it seemed they were directing this device, this coiled apparatus that had colored electricity sparkling from it, and-"

"Jeez," Phoebe backed away from him. "Where were you?"

He shrugged.

"Probably," said Temple, "you could find out with another vision. But not now. I think Phoebe saw what we needed her to see. Now, before we head back. There's one more target."

"Come on, man. Phoebe's been through enough. Let her rest."

"I'm fine." She smoothed back her hair, stood up straight and turned back to the city's ruins, looking over the ancient walls, seeing for a moment the former glory of Mohenjo-Daro, and again feeling the crushing loss, the doom that was so decisively brought to them.

"I saw them! I don't know, it seemed like it was a war. In the skies, with lights attacking each other. But I think the people here, they got off a shot from some tremendous weapon. Maybe the same thing that hit them a moment later."

"A shot to where?" Temple leaned in, focused.

"Dumb question," Orlando said. "If they launched a missile, it would go up straight, then follow the curvature of the earth as it approached its target."

"Let her finish."

Phoebe raised a finger to the sky. "It wasn't a missile or anything like that. It was a beam of light. So I'm guessing it went straight. The only thing I saw up there was a tiny light. Maybe it was a ship."

Temple was nodding, but looking at her closely.

"...or maybe it wasn't. It looked like a star. Or a planet. And... it was reddish-colored."

Orlando closed his eyes. "Mars." He shook his head and stepped in front of Phoebe, facing Temple. "You know more about this than you're telling us. Come on, spill it."

"Not here. And anyway, you need to see one more thing. Final pop quiz, if you like. Before you join us."

Orlando let his shoulders sag, but his fists were clenched. "You're really pissing me off."

"I can live with that. Now here goes. It's a trick that seems to work well with the other recruits. Kind of like free association. I'll give you the target, you give me the first thing that comes to you, the first thing you see."

Phoebe sighed. "Sure, let's get it over with."

"Okay," Temple said, taking a step back. He lifted his face to the sun and closed his eyes. "Here's the target: *Seven-seventeen AM, central Siberia. June 30th, 1908.*"

Phoebe heard Orlando make a choking sound, but it was lost in a tremendous roar, a deafening explosion of sound and fury. *She stood on a muddy hill looking down toward a river. But in a miles-long stretch of terrain, the forest was decimated: trees flattened, others blackened, the ground churned up, smoking. A huge swath cut through the wilderness.*

And then: it was as if the viewing reversed. A rumbling, which rose and rose to such horrific volume and intensity until it swallowed up the world, the trees rising, filling, turning green just after an immense light retracts into a glowing wave of energy, rippling backwards and up at an oblique angle into the sky...

Orlando was doubled over. "Tunguska," he whispered. "Another target Caleb should have put on the list."

"What was it?" Phoebe asked, her lips now parched.

"No one's really sure," Orlando said, after it was apparent Temple wasn't going to speak. "At the time, they thought it was a meteor. But after several scientific teams got there and searched, they found no impact crater and no evidence of meteorite elements. But something sure hit that area with a force like a meteor."

"Good enough for me," Temple said. "You passed the quiz. Now back in the plane and let's get to work."

"So we're in?" Phoebe voiced. "Past the bullshit?   No more secrets, no more games?"

"Or freakin' quizzes?" Orlando added.

Temple grinned. "No more quizzes. But as for the secrets… In time I'll let you in. Don't want to blow your minds all at once. Then you'd be no good to me. Or your friends."

"Our friends," Orlando whispered. "How are they?"

"You can find out soon. Get on the plane and let's head back to our facility."

"But…" Phoebe looked back to the ruins, silent and desolate. "But this city was so ancient. And Tunguska was only a hundred years ago. What's going on?"

"They're both related."

"And Mars?"

"We'll get to that." He stepped back into the plane. Orlando met Phoebe's eyes, and saw all her confidence fleeing. Saw her teetering on the edge of exhaustion, overcome by the weight of such visions and responsibility.

He felt the same things, but right now he feared something far more personal. If he didn't get her out of this, she might never come back. So he did the only thing he could think of.

He took her hand, pulled her close. And kissed the dust from her lips.

11.

Alexandria

Caleb hadn't been back here, to the modern library, for almost five months. The last time, he and Alexander had spent a couple days in the city, visiting all the tourist spots and sailing in the harbor, where Caleb had pointed out the place where he had nearly drowned that fateful day he had his first vision of the Pharos. They visited Qaitbey's Fortress, and Caleb had a difficult time keeping Alexander from finding the secret lever that would open the door to the sub-chambers... and the great seal guarding a now-empty vault. The boy wanted to see, and Caleb couldn't blame him. Someday, he promised, they'd come back when it was safe, when they wouldn't get caught.

He had vowed that they would do it together, with Lydia. The next time all three were in Alexandria together. The next time...

Caleb had to stop and hold onto a pillar as a rush of images burst into his skull. Like she was still there, still waiting.

"Let's take him," Lydia says while propped up on her elbow on the bed beside him. "Tomorrow. He's ready!"

"Isn't one vault enough? He's got enough to do here."

"What are you worried about? The danger down there..."

"Is still real. It's not like the traps don't work anymore."

"He just wants to see. He's proud of you. Proud of us—what we did. It's something before his time, and he feels left out."

"Well, he wasn't. He was a big part of it. If it wasn't for him..."

"You and I would not have been apart. And you might not have found the

way in with me holding you back."

Her eyes are so profoundly large, green like the Emerald Tablet, so deeply resonant and magnetic. It's as if she knows he's lied to her. Knows he's hidden it away, told her it was lost. Should he tell her? Is now the time?

He opens his mouth, but she's leaning in. Her lips against his, silencing his voice. She pulls back, only for an instant. "Just think about it. We're running out of time. A boy's only a boy for so long."

Caleb caught his breath and looked up to see Alexander and Rashi staring at him, both concerned. They stood between a gap between two enormous rows of shelves. Books as far as he could see in any direction.

"I'm okay. Just had a moment."

Alexander moved forward. "Was it Mom?"

Caleb smiled. "Yeah… just, I haven't been here since…"

A flash, an explosion of fire. A charred body, spinning around, and facing him, two green orbs in a blackened skull boring down at him, recriminating…

"Dad?" His hand on Caleb's shoulder, Alexander pulled him up. His grip was strong, firmer than Caleb had ever remembered. *It's already too late. He's not a boy anymore. And it's my fault.* "I'm sorry," he whispered.

And Alexander shook his head. "No reason to be."

"I did to you what my mother did to me. She stole my childhood, and I never forgave her for it, not until the end."

Alexander rolled his eyes. "I'm still a kid. I'm—what's the word? *Resilient.* After we stop the bad guys and save the world, I'm still going to want to watch cartoons and play that 3D PlayStation you're going to buy me for Christmas."

A laugh mingled with a choking sob as Caleb stood up and hugged his son under the watchful gaze of the Keeper, Rashi. When they were ready, they made their way through the stacks and the shelves, the seemingly endless texts, volumes and tomes. While they walked, he took a moment to gaze fondly on all these works, and looked up at the sunlight-kissed levels above, all those treasures preserved here, hopefully for a long time to come.

At last, they made it to the elevator and accessed the locked sublevel. As the doors closed, Caleb glanced away from his son, out the doors and saw-

In the center of the library, on the marble floor in a shaft of light, Lydia stood alone, head bowed in silence.

The once metal-walled hallway was now decorated with ancient artwork: Sumerian friezes, Babylonian bas-reliefs, Egyptian murals... Caleb had walked this hallway more than a hundred times, and each time he felt as if he were coming home.

Into the vault, Rashi joined several other Keepers: two men and a woman busy at work at their stations. Hideki Matusi, bone-thin, yet regally elegant in a way Caleb always associated with ancient scholars, stood over a glass table, lit from below, as she analyzed scroll fragments with a microscope. She took a break from translating the ancient texts and came down to greet them.

She nodded sympathetically to Caleb. "We mourn for Lydia. But the work must continue, as she would have wanted it."

Caleb looked down at his shoes, choked up.

But then Hideki smiled at Alexander. "Ah, the precocious child returns."

"Hello Hideki!" Alexander waved, beaming at her. "Can't wait to help out again."

"Yes, yes, so long as you promise not to spill chocolate milk on any more priceless fifth-century BC papyri."

"I promise."

"I mean it."

Caleb found it surprisingly comforting to laugh, to be dis-tracted from the finality of loss. "She means it, Alexander. And so do I. Socrates would have been *pissed.*"

Rashi took a seat at the conference table, the very same one used by Nolan Gregory years ago when he had confined the Keepers down here for their protection. That day was the last great crisis for the Keepers. But now, they had lost two key members in the past week. One to tragedy, the other to greed. With Lydia and Robert gone, the Keepers needed a leader, and despite the regard they all held for Caleb, they knew he couldn't step into the role held by his wife. Not under these circumstances.

Rashi took the reins, and she'd moved quickly but deliberately. They had to be extra careful, but they still needed to replenish their ranks. Hideki had a son, fifteen, who unfortunately showed no promise, or interest. Alexander was almost ready and could soon fill one of the gaps, but Rashi felt deep regret that she had never succeeded in bringing a child into the world. There was always adoption, but for some reason, she couldn't bring herself to that stage where she would have to admit it was physically impossible for herself.

But now, she had a new focus. Leadership.

Their enemies were closing in. What Caleb had discovered, what Robert Gregory was a part of... it stretched back to the dawn of human history, to the very origins of civilization. A conflict, dormant for millennia, about to be rekindled.

"If what we've discovered in these texts is true, then we have no time to waste. No time to grieve. No time at all."

Hideki joined them at the table.

"All these scrolls..." She looked around at the hermetically sealed cabinets, the honeycombed alcoves, filled with the contents of the vanished Alexandrian Library, the most esoteric texts, some so ancient they had yet to decipher the language. "Everything you found, Caleb. And yet..."

"And yet," said Rashi, leveling her gaze at him, "the one thing that could have helped us most prepare for this moment..."

"You kept from us," Hideki finished.

Caleb swallowed and looked in turn at the Keepers. He met their stares of recrimination. "I can't apologize. I didn't trust you, it's true, but..."

"You were right not to," Rashi said, raising a hand. "We are not condemning. We're merely stating fact, preparing the setting, so to speak. The foundation for what we must do next. We are not judges."

"How could we be," Hideki said, "when one of our own, our very leader, was corrupted?"

Rashi leaned in. "If you had not kept the Tablet from us, Robert would have had it, and he would have used it."

"That," Caleb said in a low voice, "is what I need to understand. How would he have used it? What are they planning? Xavier Montross *saw* something. And I did too."

Rashi nodded. "I can guess. Destruction. You saw it on a scale unimaginable."

Caleb felt Alexander's eyes on him. Large, almond-shaped, glassy. A hint of jade, like his mother's. "The Tablet itself is undecipherable. I got nowhere with it, and honestly I didn't want to try. It was enough that it fell to me to protect it. But now... Now I wish I had tried a little harder. Maybe I'd know what it is we need to do."

Rashi kept her head down, contemplating the lines on her hands, between her knuckles. "We'll tell you what we know, but after this you must rejoin your sister. And the others like yourself."

Alexander perked up. "More remote-viewers?"

"Soon," Caleb said. He had seen it, too—brief glimpses of well-trained men escorting Phoebe and Orlando through caves in the desert, then onto a plane, heading back to some well-hidden facility in the snow-capped mountains of the Pacific Northwest. "Soon, and I know they're looking for answers too, but I don't believe they know the right questions to ask. That's why it has to start here. It needs to come from practical research first, grounding us on what to set as our objectives. Otherwise we're blind mice sniffing around empty cupboards. Wasting time."

"Time we don't have," Rashi agreed.

Caleb leaned back, studying the other members, then looking past them to the scrolls laid out on the work area. To the banks of servers storing all the scanned documents.

The other two Keepers were looking solemn, palms flat on the table. Caleb had taken a seat next to Alexander. He leaned forward. "Tell me what you've found. About the Tablet, about... the Spear."

Rashi closed her eyes, and began to talk. "The first thing we found wasn't from the Library, it was something much more recent. We looked into Robert Gregory's files, decrypting his locked folders and accessing what he'd been studying in secret."

"So basically," Hideki said, "he had already done the research."

"Knew what he was looking for," Caleb said.

"But some of it wasn't even from what you found under the Pharos. He had access to other books, private collections, heretical texts acquired from individuals with powerful connections, to say the least."

Alexander was listening to all of this, confused. He kept focusing on the Zodiac images painted above, on the azure-background of the dome, imagining the animals taking form, moving around. He thought of the shapes in Genghis Khan's tomb, thought of how much he had seen in the past few weeks. How much death, but in the midst of all that life. His eyes settled on the constellation of Gemini, the twins. And he realized couldn't stop thinking about them, his new brothers. Where were they now?

"…revelations that seemed far too fanciful for us at first," Hideki continued.

"But," said Rashi, "now we've been reconsidering. In light of other insights. Now that the majority of the Pharos' documents have been scanned and uploaded, and everything that could be translated has been, we have been able to search for keywords and phrases."

"'*Tablet of Destiny*' being one," Hideki said.

Caleb's lips felt parched. His stomach grumbled. And he thought of Alexander and how neither of them had eaten in more than a day. He looked toward the door set back in a side room off the main domed chamber where they kept supplies, enough food and water for months. Beds, a shower. He thought about getting up and telling Rashi and Hideki to wait until he got a snack, but that was when he felt something.

A rumbling.

The table rattled. The microscope in the other room shook, toppled. The lights overhead dimmed.

Caleb blinked, and across his eyelids flashed an image, a vision in stark clarity:

A snowy field beset by enormous mountains ringed by an emerald aurora. Almost two hundred radar arrays, glowing, sparking with errant electrical discharge. And zooming in closer… through the walls of the main facility, lightning-quick through hallways and down elevator shafts to a control room… and a man in uniform holding a phone to his ear, saying: "Yes, Senator. It's been done…"

The very chamber shook now, dust fell from the dome, and the barest hint of a crack split through the constellations, ripping apart Pisces and splitting the Twins.

Rashi stood up, eyes wide. "No… They can't… They wouldn't dare!"

Hideki screamed and pointed to Alexander, who when he stood, leaned forward so the necklace with the three charms slipped out.

"The Keys!" she shouted. "They're after the Keys!"

Caleb got up, reaching for his son—but suddenly the room pitched and buckled and the table rocked into his side and thrust him backwards while Alexander stood there, helplessly.

"Dad!"

Caleb climbed over the table, and was about to leap and swoop him up when a huge section of the ceiling collapsed, masonry crashed between them, and everything turned black.

He stayed on his knees, arms outstretched toward the mass of debris: layers of twisted concrete, metal and girders. And all he could think of was: *this can't be happening!*

Robert and Lydia and all the Keepers had given their assurances that this library was built to withstand the ages, time and especially, earthquakes. Not only were the upper levels built upon shifting, standalone foundations that should have been impervious to ground fault tectonic shifts, but this sub-level especially was reinforced. A veritable bunker. Even if the unthinkable were to happen up above, the most treasured documents should have been safe down here.

Safe…

The rumbling subsided, the vibrations died down. But now what replaced it was infinitely worse:

Silence.

It was as all-pervasive. One set of flickering lights above remained, highlighting the cracked forms of the lower half of the Zodiac.

"Alexander?"

He held his breath, listening for anything. Studying the wall of debris, trying not to think the worst. Keeping it out of his mind, just as he kept away the horrors of what must be happening on the surface, up in Alexandria. What kind of devastation…?

A glimpse, a curse rewarding his lack of willpower: *A birds-eye view from two hundred feet up... The slanting glass roof destroyed, just a jagged semi-circular foundation left in the earth. Great chunks of glass and twisted metal girders strewn about an area that looked like a meteor had struck a direct hit. Centered perfectly on the library.*

Not possible, Caleb thought. Pausing now in his search. Going with the vision, the power that wanted, needed him to see.

Show me, he whispered, and mentally stepped back a few moments...

The domed library, scintillating in the sun, through the transparent windows hundreds of patrons could be seen strolling the aisles, reading at tables, looking at exhibits, while outside tourists took in the gardens, the fountains, or marveled at the planetarium.

Then, without warning, without even a flash of light, nothing but a faint ripple in the air, as if an invisible wave had just disrupted the fabric of the atmosphere—the dome imploded, shelves and floor were slammed down and met the exploding ground levels. Chunks of metal, concrete and earth rending and splitting, thrusting up and out and slamming down again, pulverized into Alexandria's foundation.

The force of a meteor, just like—

He'd seen this before. Something Orlando had shown him...

Caleb shook his head, gagging on the visualization of the complete destruction of such a grand monument, not to mention the instant death of all those people. And only minutes after his arrival!

There could be no natural event. Just like he now believed Tunguska, Siberia was anything but natural. That place by the snowy mountains... Calderon...

He hung his head, fighting the tears, the guilt threatening to rend his heart of its last remaining strength. Willing it all away. He had to get to Alexander.

As much as it might be the final nail in his heart, he had to *see*...

But before he even looked, he knew what he'd find. Alexander was okay. He just had to be.

If Calderon did this, he would only have gone so far if he knew of the vault down here. Knew they'd be here. Calderon gave them enough time to get settled in, then he brought the world down upon them, sealing them in.

Keeping Caleb and Alexander—and the other Keepers—from the worst of the destruction.

But Alexander had the keys.

That was the one thought that kept Caleb going.

If Calderon still wanted that translation, he needed the keys. Sure he could mount an excavation in the guise of a rescue, and dig up the lower vault to find the keys, but that could take months, especially given the level of response and world attention that would be starting even now.

No, something told Caleb that Calderon knew that there would be an easier way.

One that would only be possible if he knew about the other exit from the vault, and if he knew that Alexander might actually be okay. Or at least reachable quickly.

Caleb knew it had to be true. After all, Mason Calderon was not without his own resources. Resources that could see, most likely, as well as anyone on the Morpheus Initiative.

Caleb's other boys.

12.

Cairo

Mason Calderon put away his cell phone, slipped it inside his suit coat pocket, and turned back to the twins, standing on either side of their mother.

"It's done. If your visions were right, your brother is now buried under the sadly short-lived *Bibliotheca Alexandrina*."

Isaac shrugged. "We no more doubt our visions than you doubt when you look up into the sky and say it's blue."

Mason took a moment. "A shame really, about their library. Such noble endeavors for the sons of Thoth, but in the end, what is it I always tell you boys?"

Jacob looked at his brother, and they both intoned the mantra at once: "Nothing ever lasts, least of all knowledge."

Calderon smiled, a grin that lingered despite the concern he saw on Nina's face. "Don't worry, my dear. I'm sure you're old lover has managed to survive. Although what he's feeling right now, I can hardly guess. To actually be witness to the destruction of the great library on both occasions, and with his fondness for wisdom..."

Nina's lips curled up at the edges. "I still have a score to settle with him. So, are we going?"

The boys looked up at her with something like flashing respect. She was all business, a quality they understood.

Calderon nodded, motioning the soldiers to carry up the heavy chest and prepare to take it away. He addressed the senior guard. "Seal the door when we're gone. I want no evidence of this entrance, and no further questions. Tell the press the situation is controlled. The bomb threat was a false alarm."

Nina followed, lost in her thoughts amid confusion about her feelings for Caleb. Feelings now that seemed mired in shifting sands. Caleb and Nina shared something now, a connection to a line of heredity. Their genes, their individuality merged in these two living beings. She never imagined she'd feel this responsibility, this curiosity, or this stake in the future of other beings. Halfway up the stairs, she realized that Jacob was holding her hand, as naturally as if he'd been with her all his life.

Two more steps, and Isaac noticed. Scowling at his brother, he took Nina's other hand and led her up the last few steps impatiently.

"Come on," he said, manic glee in his voice. "I want to meet my father. Let's go dig them out."

"And get those keys," Calderon said over his shoulder as he headed for the helicopter. "And then..." He held the briefcase in a tight grip, feeling the handle tremble with the power of the Emerald Tablet inside. Another step and he paused and looked around the perimeter to the armada of jeeps, soldiers and onlookers. Then, back to the imposing sight of the Great Pyramid rising from beyond the Sphinx's back.

The Shepherd's tool was blunted, useless. But a new one was operational, halfway around the world. His gaze shifted and he looked up, beyond the pyramid's hulking outline, to the shining half-moon.

Soon... His destiny was just a translation away.

BOOK TWO
Seeing Is Believing

1.

Washington State

Phoebe woke with a start. Something wasn't right.

She stifled a yawn then lifted up the window shade, expecting to see they were still over the desert. Instead she was greeted with a majestic view of snow-peaked mountains, one in particular: a massive peak, level with their plane, appearing to be their destination.

Someone was in the seat next to her, and it took a moment for Phoebe to clear out the debris of her cluttered dreams and remember the events of the last day. The girl, the Hummingbird. Aria was sitting on her knees beside her, big blue eyes wide open and trembling.

"Don't be afraid," she whispered, laying a hand on Phoebe's arm. Behind her, Orlando's neck was bent awkwardly, his forehead pressed into a flight pillow and a little blanket bunched up around his ear.

"What's wrong?" Phoebe's heart fluttered. Pieces of the dream came back to her: *The night sky was falling, the stars tumbling down upon her. And books, thousands of books, millions, crying out in pain...*

"Your brother is safe."

Phoebe put a finger to her lips. "Alexander too?"

Aria nodded, just as the cabin door opened and Temple emerged. His ashen face told a story Phoebe didn't want to read.

He reached for the TV's power button. "No easy way to say this." On the screen emerged a scene of devastation. Phoebe leaned over and shook Orlando, who only grunted and pressed his face farther into the pillow.

"Alexandria was hit today with a seismic event."

"An earthquake?" Phoebe whispered.

"Seven-point-three magnitude. But..." Temple muted the TV as the camera zoomed in on a section of twisted iron framework that had once supported part of the glass dome. "...it only hit the library complex. Concentrated in that one area... Destroying it completely."

"Oh my God."

"Over a hundred dead, so far. Three hundred more injured. Some buried and calling for help. Some..."

"...farther down." Phoebe was only dimly aware that Aria was holding her hand, squeezing it and whispering, "They're okay."

"We need to RV them, see if Caleb and Alexander were there!"

"Already done," Temple said. "As soon as we got the news. My team relayed information quickly back here that they saw the vault. It's damaged badly. And several of the Keepers are dead, but your brother and your nephew appear   to   be   unhurt. Although trapped."

"We've got to get to them." She scowled over at Orlando, who still hadn't stirred.

Temple shook his head. "Won't make it before *they* do."

"What? Why not? Can't you get the Egyptian authorities to control the site, keep out Calderon's people?"

"Sorry, Calderon's inserted himself and his people into high-level positions at major disaster-relief agencies. We'd been puzzled by that for several months, trying to work out his motives. But now it's obvious. If they're testing some sort of weapon, then they need to have control, feet on the ground so to speak. Believe me, if this was him, and we're ninety-nine percent sure, then it's too late. They're already tunneling down there. They've got their own psychics–"

"The twins."

"–who will tell them where to dig, and how to retrieve the artifacts they need." Temple let the news run a few more seconds, before the feed shifted from scenes of destruction and tragedy to interviews with survivors.

Phoebe squeezed the girl's hand gently. "So there's no hope?"

Aria squeezed back and answered first. "Always hope."

"She's right," Temple agreed. "And right now, I hate to say it, but we need you focused on the bigger picture."

"Which is?"

"Mars," said another voice. Orlando, his eyes still closed, but flickering rapidly. "And... something else..." His eyes flashed open and he sat up straight. And Phoebe realized he hadn't been sleeping, not exactly. Dreaming, deep in a trance, focusing his inner sight on what Temple intended for them.

"Damn," said the colonel. "This is why it's so hard to work with psychics. I can never do things according to my own timeline."

"Stow it," Orlando said, almost under his breath. "We need to know what this is about, *now*. What's up there? How much do you guys really know, and why is it you need us to remote-view something on..." he cocked his head, squinting, trying to recapture the vision.

"...the dark side of the Moon?"

2.

After wandering in the darkness, a black so pervasive he couldn't see anything in front of his face, not even knowing which direction was up, Alexander shifted his perspective. Looking in a direction he at first insisted was down, his brain finally perceived the tiny lights above as stars and not reflective coins in the depths of some bottomless sea. A moment later, realization set in and he understood he was either dreaming or remote viewing.

This wasn't the vault in Alexandria, where he was surely still pinned beneath that table and the body of one of the Keepers—Rashi, who had thrown herself over him at the last instant before the ceiling collapsed.

This was *somewhere else*. A vast, black surface that suddenly wasn't so perfectly dark, as if his eyes were adjusting, filtering and refining the starlight so he could see...

He was standing inside a shallow crater. Impossibly shallow, and more like a trench ripped through the shale, and in every direction he could see the rough outlines of bizarre geology: ridges sharply-protruding peaks, rocky hills thrust out of the land, dust and debris laying in their ancient poses, and suddenly...

His consciousness shot upward, and then skidded around the horizon, until the darkness abruptly merged with light, and around the lip of the orb—the familiar cratered surface—he was greeted with the gleaming blue-green hues of the Earth.

"Alexander..."

His dad's voice. Weak, like it was spoken from the other end of a massive tunnel. Alexander shook his head, and was relieved to find he could do it. *No broken neck or spine at least.* But everything was dark, so dark...

He tried to sit up, but found someone was laying on top of him.

At first, with a choking sob, he thought: *Mom?* But then memories flitted back, descending into their respective pockets where they belonged, and everything fit right once again. The cave-in. The earthquake or whatever it was. Rashi... *oh, Rashi...*

He felt around her back, but could only move his hands so far before reaching something hard and cold like steel. Then he felt something wet and warm over her back.

"Rashi?"

Nothing.

Then again he thought he heard his father calling his name, but he shut it out for a minute, trying to see, really *see.* He relaxed, willed his mind to focus, and slipped back-

-*to this very room, only minutes ago. Rashi looking up, alarm on her face as dust fell. Dad yelling, reaching for him, and then the ceiling dropping, the dome shattering down the middle. Huge chunks of masonry shorn into pieces, tumbling, crashing onto the table, pummeling the servers, an enormous beam, trailing sparks, slamming toward him. Then Rashi was there, throwing herself onto him just as she grunted and the lights went out.*

But Alexander could still see, this time from a higher vantage point, in the gaping crater's hole, looking down as the walls crumbled and car-sized boulders tumbled free, raining into the hole, piling onto the carnage. But somehow, the beam and several larger pieces of bedrock formed a jutting triangular incline that protected part of the chamber from total destruction. Just enough, he saw in a hazy night-vision light, to crawl out and be able to stand, maybe reach the terminals. But his father...

His vision skirted over the barrier, the wall of debris in the center of the Keeper sanctuary. There was Caleb, trying to lift an enormous slab with a metal bar. Sparks were flying from the ceiling, dancing around the alcoves where the scrolls hid like frightened children behind cracked windows.

"Dad," Alexander whispered, ending the vision and returning to darkness. Then louder: *"Dad!"* He shifted, reached up and felt Rashi's neck.

No pulse, nothing.

Revulsion gave way to utter fear as the darkness reclaimed him. Shifting sounds in the room. The floor shuddering, beams groaning still. *Please no aftershocks.*

"Hideki? Belarus? Anyone? Can anyone hear me?"

"Alexander?" again, his father. A little stronger.

"Dad, I hear you!"

Silence, then: "Oh, thank God. Are you hurt?"

"I don't know. I'm trapped." *Under poor, poor Rashi.*

"I know," he said. "I saw. Rashi protected you. I saw you were pinned and not moving, but I didn't know…"

"I'm okay." He squirmed and was grateful for his natural skinniness when he found he could pull away gradually and slide out from under her. The beam shifted and dust and pebbles fell onto his face. Covering his eyes, he waited, not moving. *Feel like I'm playing 'Operation'. One wrong move and it's game over.*

"Can you see anything?"

"No," Alexander shouted back. "At least, not with my normal eyes. But I RV'd and saw... I know I can't get out of here on my own. I'm sorry, I can't even get to you."

He heard the metal bar drop. "I know, Alexander. I'm sorry. I saw that the floor collapsed, but the good news is that a lot of material ejected out of the crater."

"How's that good news?"

"Well, the stuff above you isn't solid, and air's getting in."

Alexander took a deep breath, relishing the taste, however dusty. "So I won't suffocate." He pulled himself out farther, until only his left leg was still caught. Then it was free, and it felt good to be out. He stretched his legs, wiggled his toes. Then tried to sit up.

"Alexander?"

"Fine!" he shouted back, wincing through the effort. "Although everything feels bruised. I'm glad it's dark, Dad. I don't want to see-"

"Don't think about it, not now Alexander."

He nodded. *Once again, face to face with death, but asked not to face it.*

"Listen, son. You have to be strong, and you have to do something for me."

Alexander got to his knees and reached above him, trying to see how much room there was, and whether he could stand.

"Are you listening?"

"Yes, Dad. And I know what you're going to say."

"You do?"

"Yeah. I've seen it. The computer terminal, the servers."

"That's right. Now, there should be a flashlight somewhere, in the computer desk if it's still in one piece.

After a long minute of fumbling and searching, scraping his fingers on sharp rocks and jagged pieces of masonry, banging his head on something, he touched a flat metal surface. Followed it around to locate a cold handle. Pulled it, reached inside, among a stack of papers, staplers, magnifying glasses.

"There it is."

The light was painful and almost surreal, bringing into focus a twisted scene of incomprehensible shapes, angles and obstacles. Nothing that Alexander could recognize immediately; it was as if he'd been teleported to some alien prison cell.

"Alexander, do you have it? Can you see?"

"Yep, got it. Now what?"

"The computer . Is it...?"

"Here..."   Alexander found the laptop, on its side, the top dented. He opened it and was relieved to see the screen saver functioning. Moved the mouse, and the password prompt appeared. "Working!"

"Okay, you remember the password?"

"Yeah." Alexander smiled. He secured the flashlight under his chin, and angled his head so it was pointing at the screen. "Sostratus."

He typed it in and he gained access.

"Good," said his father. His voice seemed weaker, tired.

Resigned. "Now, listen carefully. They're going to be here soon. And they're going to get what they really want-"

Alexander touched the charms around his neck. "The Keys. But maybe I could…"

"Save your energy. Your brothers will just RV the keys, and there's no place you can hide them where they won't be seen."

Alexander sighed. He set the flashlight down, pointing straight up and casting freakish shadows around the crushed alcoves, revealing the shattered scroll casings, the shredded documents and tablets. He forced his attention back to the computer screen, where there were six icons, and an open file.

"But you can still help."

"How?"

"Rashi was on to something. She wouldn't tell me everything, but I knew… The Keepers found clues in the ancient documents. Something that could help. Hideki was working on it too, scanning portions into the computer. There should be a file, or a series of files, excerpts translated from the original sources."

Alexander called up the first open file, scrolled down past the scanned cuneiform script and glanced at the translation. "I see it. This first one has something about…"

"Just read it," Caleb called. "And remember what you can. Read everything she saved out there—then, before they come for you, delete it all. And smash the computer."

Alexander smiled. "That'll be fun."

"Remember it, and you'll get a chance to tell me—or Phoebe, soon. And hopefully it'll be enough to stop this."

"What about you?" Alexander shined the light back to the wall of debris over the smashed conference table, waving the beam back and forth, looking for even a slight crack to look through and see him. But no, if that was possible, he could fit the keystones through and Caleb could try to protect them.

"There's a hidden exit back this way. Robert showed it to me once, after I said I was concerned about escape if the surface was compromised. A descending passageway that turns at a right angle and tunnels to the harbor. A huge bank-safe kind of door, opened only from the inside, one that then leads down to the harbor. Of course, there's scuba gear…"

"Oh." Alexander thought of how his dad didn't have the best experiences with scuba, and nearly died in that harbor while searching for the Pharos. "I'm sorry."

"Yeah, well, it's got to be done. I'll get out, and get help. I'll find a way to save you. But you... Alexander, listen to me. You have to be strong. You're a Keeper now."

"But..." Alexander looked around at the shattered walls, the broken alcoves. "All the scrolls..."

"We'll save what we can," Caleb said solemnly. "But remember, all of it—the whole collection—was scanned and uploaded to remote servers."

Alexander had asked his mother about those servers one day, while they were at a café outside the library. He still recalled the glint in her green eyes as she leaned in and whispered: "A lot of places. A cave system in the Himalayas. Another in the Andes. A bunker in Mount Shasta, Washington."

"It's all still there," his father's voice now. "If only in a different form. The scrolls wouldn't have lasted forever anyway."

Alexander knew he was right, but still—the original copies. So priceless. To have averted the doom Sostratus originally foresaw for them, only to be destroyed only a few years after rediscovery...

"I've got to go now, they're coming soon. Remember..."

"Yes, I know. I'm a Keeper now. I'll do what has to be done." A little hesitation. "I'll see you soon?"

"That's a promise. I'm proud of you, Alexander. Goodbye."

Alexander stood and raised his head, shining the light into the crevices and nooks, surveying what was left of his domain, the vault that had been built to survive for millennia. He allowed himself a moment to grieve for all this, for Rashi and Hideki. And for his mother.

And then he sat down and got to work.

3.

Xavier Montross waited alone in the limousine and didn't bother trying the doors. He knew they'd be locked. In the back trunk rested an iron box more than five thousand years old that potentially held the greatest of secrets. And somewhere down there in that monstrous fissure, were the only keys that could open the box.

The keys *and my nephew,* he thought, imagining the boy's terror, his sudden thrust into responsibility. *We're not so different. I was even a little younger when it happened to me.*

Out the tinted windows he could see the crowd of fire engines, ambulances, vans and relief workers. Three helicopters overhead. People surging around the perimeter, spectators pushed back by armed police, keeping everyone at a distance from ground zero.

Xavier closed his eyes and for a moment, pictured his childhood room as it was for years, up until the accident that killed his mother and his foster father: the bedroom walls covered with drawings, visions that made the transition from mind to paper. He recalled one in particular: *a deep hole bored into the earth, with tiny forms clinging to the sides, smoke rising from below.*

He had seen this all before. Didn't know what it was at the time, but now there was no mistaking it.

Just like there was no mistaking what he'd have to do next. He knew it was coming. Dreaded it, but at the same time found himself intensely curious. But first he allowed himself a moment.

A moment to think. About her.

A soaring flight over sandstone towers, deep ravines and striated cliff walls. Her breath on his neck, her arms fiercely encircling his chest. The intensity of adventure, the thrill of discovery...

And then he was back, and her scent left his lungs with the next breath, replaced by the stinging heat and flavor of death.

Mason Calderon slid into the seat facing Xavier, then shut the door. He had on a lavender silk shirt, sleeves rolled up, his white tie slightly loosened around his collar. A slight cough was his only indication of experiencing anything personally from the destruction outside. He brushed off his pant legs, then combed his fingers through his wavy gray hair.

"So, Xavier. We finally get to chat." Calderon held a thin leather briefcase on his lap, tapping it gently.

Xavier's head felt lighter suddenly, and the car seemed to spin. "The Tablet."

Calderon smiled, his palms now flat against the leather case. "I know you can feel it too." His eyes were large, Xavier thought, the pupils expanded like a focused cat's. They blinked, then glanced out the window. His smile never wavered as he shook his head. "Such loss. But still, it was a valuable test. And a warning."

"A warning to whom?"

Calderon's gaze swept back to Xavier. "Don't you know?"

"I know a lot of things. Maybe you should be more specific." If this was how it was going to be, Xavier was going to have to figure a way to just get in position to kick the senator in the face and shut him up. He knew the next minutes were going to be crucial. Everything he believed in was going to be put to the test. Something was coming, some revelation he hadn't accounted for. This was the grand meeting between dramatic adversaries, and Xavier, believing himself now thrust completely into the hero's role, wasn't going to be fooled.

But then again, maybe he needed a radical change in direction, because so far nothing had been altered. All his visions were still of the same thing: complete final destruction. His death, and everyone's death at the hands of this man sitting before him so calmly.

Calderon leaned in slightly. "Do you know why the Nazis sent elite missions out to remote corners of the earth? Tibet, the North Pole, Antarctica?"

Xavier stared at him.

"These were hardly positions of strategic importance to the war," Calderon continued. "And Himmler and other select SS members continued to expend vast resources seeking out areas where there were caves and tunnels penetrating deep into the earth. What were they looking for?"

Xavier shrugged, pretending not to care, although a sinking feeling was forming in his gut. "Treasure?"

"Not exactly. Hitler and the other members of what they called The Thule Society were following up on legends—or possibly if one source is to be believed—*remote visions* of a certain psychic named Trevor Ravenscroft. The belief in a pre-diluvian civilization, an advanced race, possibly coinciding with Atlantis or else even its predecessor. A race of supermen with advanced intelligence, physical strength and especially, mental powers. Powers and abilities that made them godlike."

Xavier nodded. "Yeah, so Hitler was insane. Easily manipulated by whackos with god-complexes. Aryan master race. Sure. If they could prove they were descendants of these Thulians or what-ever, then they'd what—justify genocide and lordship over the Earth?"

Calderon grinned. "Not only that, although certainly that was a big part of the justification for their quest. No, what Hitler intended was to discover where the remnant of this great super race went during the last cataclysm. Where they hid. And, he believed, where they continue to reside, deep in the earth, watching. Waiting…"

"For what?"

Calderon shrugged. "Hitler thought maybe they were waiting for him. Waiting for a ruler to step up and take the mantle of succession. To build an army capable of overwhelming the lesser races. All at the behest of a ruling class with advanced powers."

Xavier wriggled against his bonds, wishing he could have hidden a knife in his sleeve to give himself a chance at escape. A chance at ending this here and now. Instead, he had to think of another way. "So, forgive me Senator. What the hell does this have to do with anything? Hitler's gone, and us 'lesser races' smashed his superman dreams and dismantled his aspirations."

"Gone, yes. But the Custodians are not."

"The who? Oh, the Thule people. The master race. They're still there, hiding under rocks?"

"Deep in the earth. Deep underground." Calderon rubbed his hands together slowly, again looking out the window at the devastation. "And now, Xavier, we finally have a way to get to them." He patted the briefcase, his eyes glowing with excitement.

And then Xavier got it. He understood his visions. Understood why nothing could stop the coming devastation. And at last, he understood what they were doing up in Alaska.

"Oh dear god," he whispered. "HAARP. I guessed you used it to cause this localized earthquake. Modulating an ELF vibrational wave, using a billion watts of power, all in the same cadence and frequency into this one spot..."

Calderon waved his hand to move him along. "Yes yes, that was child's play. Technology we've had for decades, but enhanced only recently in the last upgrade to the antenna arrays. All thanks to Tesla's vision. But still, it wasn't enough. The Custodians are deep. Deeper than we could ever probe, deeper than we could reach, even with HAARP."

Xavier motioned with his chin to the briefcase. "But this is the game-changer."

"It is," said Calderon. "And I think they've been after it for millennia. Two sides, forever at war. It started up there." He looked up at the roof. "Among the planets. The myths, decoded, tell the story. The gods of the sky and their squabbles, their bloody and earth-shaking battles. Marduk and Tiamat. Thoth and Set, Odin and Loki... So often repeated, so often recalled, if only in fables by our small minds. But there were always those who knew the truth, those who sought for dominance—or if nothing else, at least détente."

Xavier tried to put the pieces together. "The Emerald Tablet gave the possessor what... a way to tap into greater destructive powers?"

Calderon nodded.

"But the Tablet does more." Xavier thought quickly. "And now you have the translation. So, what do you need me for?"

Calderon was silent for a moment. "The boys are untested and rash, while you... you have a strength they'll never attain, at least not in time to be of use.

And Nina… well you know her."

Xavier shrugged. "Does anyone really know her? I thought I did."

"Regardless, you have an affinity for the power in the Tablet. A power that needs to be wielded by someone who can already do what you can."

"So it was designed by one of *them?*"

"If you mean the Custodians, the early race, then yes. I believe so. We have certain evidence, scrolls and traditions that speak of a time when these artifacts were created by the greatest of the 'gods', used and coveted by their brethren. But like the hammer of Thor, only one of their own could access its true power."

"So, fine. You need me. But you already know I'm sworn to stop you. All I've seen my whole life is you destroying the world. At first I thought it was to exact some sort of fiery revenge for Marduk's ancient loss, but now…"

Calderon bent his neck. A moment of doubt crossed his expression. "I am not the destroyer," he whispered. "They—these Custodians, forever aloof but forever jealous and stewing, dreaming only of their return, like some slumbering Lovecraftian deities—they are the true enemy. As long as they exist, mankind can never be free." He spread out his arms. "I'm the world's savior. And you, Xavier Montross, can help me."

Xavier merely stared at him, dumbfounded. He'd known something was coming, but this?

"Join me," Calderon said in a voice just above the rumble of the bulldozers, helicopters and rescue equipment. "Stop the Custodians. Together with your remote-viewing, with your ability to spirit-walk or whatever it is you do, and my resources, we can find them. Seek out their hiding places, penetrate their shields, and with this…" He gripped the case in both hands. "With this… we will wipe them out, bury them under a billion tons of earth like the cowardly moles they are. Wipe them out and reclaim this world for ourselves."

Xavier felt dizzy. Tugged in two directions. "No," he whispered.

"Xavier, don't be a fool. They see what's happening. They're tracking evolution. We're changing, transforming… into what they can't abide."

"What?"

"Changing into *them.*" Calderon grit his teeth. "Use your viewing powers later to confirm all this, but trust me. They are the ones that have constantly interfered in humanity's path. The Flood. The Tower of Babel… Anytime we got too close, started working together, started evolving toward something, unlocking genes they had tried to deactivate. Custodians indeed!" He made an expression of disgust. "Custodians of their own perverse lordship perhaps. If you look, you'll see their bloody fingerprints stamped across history. Since Babylon and since crushing the last great human civilizations, like those Indus Valley, Peru, Egypt and Cambodia, China—wherever man dared to advance and reach for their true destiny—we believe they've opted for the subtle approach. Fostering wars and disunity. Corrupting religion so humanity is always at each other's throats."

"Fighting ourselves so we can't see the real enemy?" Xavier had to smile. "Reagan made the same speech at the UN in 1985. Thought maybe if aliens threatened us, we'd find common ground and unite against them."

"Yes, you have it! And yes, I've had predecessors who have sought to change the status quo. But none with the access to the knowledge or power that I possess. They fear people like you, like my twins. Like the Morpheus Initiative. And they've dreaded the rediscovery of The Emerald Tablet."

"But if it could hurt them, surely they would have found it first. Being as powerful as you claim. They could have done what Caleb did and found it first."

Calderon shook his head, his eyes twinkling. "For some reason, they couldn't. Maybe they've forgotten how, or else they misjudged and believed it was destroyed or if not, that at least no one would be able to retrieve it."

Xavier frowned. Something didn't make sense there. "But…"

"Xavier, stop thinking with your head. Use your heart. Your gut. You know I'm right."

"But HAARP… if it can do what you believe it can, then these Custodians would have infiltrated it. Sabotaged it, destroyed the potential tool of their own destruction. You can't sneak something like that past them." He glanced outside. "Especially after this."

"We're well defended," Calderon insisted.

"I found you, RV'd it quite easily. I just couldn't physically access the site, not without help."

Calderon shrugged. "I admit I was worried, but we're being protected. The legacy of Marduk perhaps. Either way, it's our fate. Our mission is crucial, and it's not going to be stopped. We will root them out, and with those keys..." He pointed out the window. "We'll translate this Tablet fully, and then their worst fears will come true."

"What do you think that's going to tell you?"

"Only how to reactivate the genetic material the Custodians blocked in our developing species." His eyes blazed. "We're going to do it, wholesale, across the globe. All at once, transforming the world."

Xavier trembled. He thought of Alexander, and the boy's love for that Pixar movie, *The Incredibles*. "And when everyone's super..."

Calderon got the connection immediately and laughed, then finished the line: "...*no one* will be."

After a pause, Xavier shook his head. "But something's not right. You're going to make a mistake. Enhancing your technology with the power of the Emerald Tablet will create a level of power beyond your control. You'll do something wrong. Maybe..." He had a flash of a vision: *rocks and magma blasting out of a hole, something with massive force drilling into the depths, layer after layer until cutting through a massive hollow cavity. A gleaming city of marble spires and citadels, suddenly pulverized by an invisible wave of energy which then continues deeper, deeper toward a churning crimson mass.*

Xavier's eyes shot open. "You won't be able to control the depth. It'll go too far, causing chain reactions, magnifying the initial vibrations into something unstoppable. It'll smash into the core, disrupt the earth's axis..." He felt a rush of heat, heard nine billion souls cry out at once, and then...

"You'll kill us all," he said as he collapsed.

Treading carefully over the massive fragments of the library's shattered glass dome, Nina followed the boys toward the smoldering pit. At the precipitous edge, she looked down. Hundreds of feet, past the crumbling masonry, the twisted metal posts, the smoking husks of several taxis that had been unloading passengers, the fused layers of iron and drywall, the sparking wires, the jagged bookshelves thrust like spears into the sides. Huge chunks of the library's outer wall—the rounded

Aswan Granite carved with scripts from 120 different languages—littered the ledges and were scattered about the pond, the highway, and even lodged in the walls of nearby buildings. Several boats in the harbor had been crushed with exploding debris. In the pit, a host of pages fluttered about, still whirling, descending into the darkness.

In the wreckage, Isaac found a large leather-bound book, its cover sheared in half, spine dented. Smiling, he picked it up, dusted it off and then flung it, Frisbee-style, into the void.

Nina lowered her head. *So unlike his father.*

Jacob stood farther back, a little wary of heights, still shaken from the last minor aftershock that had rescue crews and spectators running for safety. He edged closer to Nina, started to reach for her hand again, but then saw his brother glaring at him; so he withdrew, shambling over to Isaac.

"Keep back," Nina ordered. "You had your look. That should be enough."

Isaac shrugged like he hadn't a care in the world. "No problem, not for us. Just wanted to see the carnage, we did. See what daddy Calderon can do when he sets his mind to it."

"And when we help him," Jacob added, the excitement in his voice faltering as he surveyed the damage once more.

"Come along then." Nina led them around the barrier, care-fully stepping over blocks and gaping fissures. They made their way to the makeshift command center that had been set up inside the planetarium. Rising from a reflecting pool on the outskirts of the main library, the planetarium had been miraculously spared, along with several other ancillary buildings, research centers and administrative offices. The waters of its reflecting pool however, displayed only a pall of lingering smoke, occasionally bisected by roving news helicopters.

Nina and the twins walked around shell-shocked workers, numb-faced police standing beside army members and rescue workers who looked dumbfounded at the totality of the destruction, so much so that they had nothing to do and no one to save. Anyone down in that hole, they reasoned, was beyond hope.

But Nina knew otherwise. After flashing her credentials to a pair of soldiers, she entered the planetarium lobby.

She strode into the main command center, through members of UNESCO, who gave her a wide berth, barely registering the presence of the two out of place boys at her heels; she headed for the center terminal where a man in khakis was bent over a flat screen monitor. He adjusted the Bluetooth device at his ear and then tapped a section of the display—the output of the ground-penetrating radar, showing ridges, clumps of debris and hollow sections.

"Yes sir," he said. "We've pinpointed three such cavities directly under the impact site that could contain survivors. We can get drilling teams started, but without any other information, we're going to have to guess..."

"You don't have to guess," Nina said.

The man turned. Typical retired general sort, Nina thought. Stocky, a little pot-bellied. Neck like an elephant's leg and a hair as white as a tusk. He stood up straight and let his eyes wander over her body. "Yes senator. She's here now. With... a couple kids."

Nina saw Isaac stick out his tongue.

"All right, all right. Your call." He tapped his ear, ending the conversation. "So, your boss says to dig where these rugrats tell me to dig."

Nina smiled. "He's your boss too. And these rugrats are our only chance."

The man shrugged. Looked her over again, his gaze lingering around her chest. Then he stuck out his hand. "I'm-"

"I don't care," Nina said, brushing past him and letting the boys take two vacant chairs around the screen. "We don't have time to get acquainted."

Jacob glanced up at her with a smile of admiration at the way she handled the general, then settled his attention on the screen.

The commander tried to move in closer. "This, I gotta see."

"Give us some space," Nina ordered. "Go assess something. Now, boys. You know the target, and we know he's alive. So I need you to focus. Think about these three air pockets down there. Think hard, and try to *see*. Where is he? Where is-?"

"-our brother," they both said in unison, after closing their eyes.

But Isaac peeked, and nudged Jacob's arm. "Wanna race?"

"Shut up. I've already won."

"Boys," Nina began. They were rushing, clouding the reading. This wasn't the way.

But then, aware that the commander was still at her back, watching all this, both boys reached out at the same time, as if they were playing Rock, Paper, Scissors, and both pointed to the middle cavity, under the thickest section of collapsed concrete, earth and debris.

"Shit," said the commander. "Had a bad feeling they'd pick that one."

Just to be sure, Nina thought, she joined her hands to theirs, squeezed and let the information jolt up her arms like two pythons coiling and slithering up to strike at her skull.

Two visions, both almost identical:

Near darkness. A feeble beam of light, dancing around the wreckage, highlighting broken scrolls and broken bodies crushed under huge blocks. The light shining up... and the vision scuttling up the beam with it, through the gap in the cracked ceiling, up past huge blocks, broken metal beams, another body impaled on broken glass, and then out, looking straight up from the center of the crater...

She let go. "Good job, boys."

"Of course, mother." Isaac beamed at her, although she couldn't help notice the sarcasm in his voice. Jacob lowered his eyes. "How soon can we get down there?"

"About six hours, I'd say." The commander picked up a CB and started barking orders in Egyptian.

"So what do we do while we wait?" Jacob asked, glancing around at the exhibits, the huge photographs taken from the Hubble Telescope, the models of lunar modules and landers. Nina saw his curiosity and wondered again what kind of childhood they'd had with Calderon. School? Friends? Regular boy stuff like playing with rockets and digging for worms? Or had they bypassed all that, being groomed instead for a grander destiny?

"I've got new objectives for you all," said Mason Calderon, striding inside, then leaning on his cane. "And another set of eyes."

He moved aside, and pointed the cane like a stage magician—and there stood Xavier.

"Why," asked Nina, "is he out of handcuffs?"

Xavier shrugged. "Bondage was never my thing."

"Xavier has seen the wisdom of our mission, and that really there is no other choice. Isn't that right?"

Xavier kept his eyes on Nina. He seemed pale, shrunken, like he'd lost a couple years. She remembered how she'd reacted when Calderon first showed her what was at stake, who the real enemy was. It was a lot to digest, almost too incredible to comprehend.

"We've been working the same side all along, just from different angles. All that's important is stopping them."

"And your recurring visions of doom?" Nina asked, barely moving her lips.

Xavier gave a slight nod, a tell she knew all too well. *And one he knows I'll see*, she thought. *What was he up to?*

"If they're behind it, then this is where I need to be."

With his cane under his arm, Calderon clapped his hands. "Well spoken. But still, Nina please keep an eye on him." he sighed. "Now, anyone with the ability to see things that aren't right in front of them, please follow me into the theater of the stars. General McAdams, proceed with the rescue, with all haste."

"Yes sir," McAdams said, obviously annoyed at being told to do what he was already working on.

The boys skipped and ran ahead of Calderon who didn't even look back to see if Nina and Xavier were following. She stood her ground as Xavier calmly walked by. Without looking at her, he whispered: "We need to talk…"

"Talk?"

He glanced back, and in his eyes she saw a fear that almost stopped her in her tracks. "Actually, you need to see for yourself." He shot a look ahead toward Calderon, then hesitated. Suddenly, his hand was out, reaching for hers.

What's he got to show me? She found herself reaching to him, longing to meet his hand. To clench it, squeeze him, pull him to her. A rush of emotions, her brain a mess. First Caleb, then her boys. Now Montross. Her emotions were in flux, she wasn't thinking clearly. For a moment, she had the intense desire to be out somewhere in a dark alley, stalking her target with a machine pistol. Something violent, practical and with purpose.

But this…

Inches away, and Calderon's voice interrupted them.

"Hurry along, these visions aren't going to see themselves!"

Xavier pulled his arm back, then wheeled around, presenting a calm face once more. In his shadow, Nina followed. Her arms trembled and her hands opened and closed again, feeling nothing but the chance that slipped away.

What did he have to show me?

Somehow, she knew she was going to find out, but by then it would be too late.

4.

Caleb used the waterproof pouch to hold his clothes, then secured it around his waist, over the swimsuit. Tight-fitting and too European, Caleb thought, groaning and wondering which of the male keepers would have been able to fit in this one.

He tried not to think of the others. How many were left? Hideki and Rashi gone. Robert and Lydia. Four of the seventeen. The others had to be up above, or traveling to Alexandria to survey the damage. Or, Caleb thought, if they had some sense they were getting to their safe sites, communicating by untraceable phones and waiting to be sure they weren't being targeted again. When this was over, he would have to reunite the Keepers and rebuild a sanctuary somewhere else. They still had plenty of work to do, made more difficult by the destruction of so many original copies of the early documents. But everything they had scanned was still intact, waiting for their interpretation, secrets awaiting revelation.

At this moment, Caleb rued that he hadn't spent more time with the ancient scrolls; and now, when he most needed the lost wisdom, it was going to be up to his underprepared son to find out what he could, to find something to save them.

After donning his mask and strapping on the air tank, he closed and secured the supply cabinet, then punched in the code to open the hydraulic door set in the floor. It was built into the end of this reinforced tunnel, which extended for nearly a mile under the city, and another two hundred yards under the harbor. He stood on the edge and waited for it to slide all the way open, revealing a staircase below. He descended, and in the small concrete chamber below, he pulled a red lever, which closed the door above him and released the clamps on the far wall, raising it slowly, letting in the waters of Alexandria Bay.

Caleb braced himself, feeling the rushing wave over his shins. He held his arms outstretched at his sides, and imagined he was back under the Pharos Lighthouse, in the testing chamber, secured by chains and waiting for the flood that would prove him worthy to pass the second test. He thought of Lydia. He thought of his mother, of the early members of the Morpheus Initiative who had lost their lives down there.

This was nothing as intense, but he still had to keep his footing as the waters rose up past his waist. He kept his focus on the door, halfway up and rising. Bits of seaweed floated, along with a grey-eyed carp, swimming against the pull. The water rose up to his chin, and then he put in the regulator, took a deep breath, prayed Alexander was okay, then dove under and swam for the exit.

The door would close three minutes later, and the chamber would slowly drain. But by then, Caleb would be fifty yards farther away, heading toward the Ras-El-Ten peninsula. Heading for the edge, where Qaitbey's fortress stood guard over the foundation of the ancient Pharos.

He swam slowly, maintaining a depth of about forty feet. For the most part, he kept his attention upwards, counting the dark hulls of the boats, but mindful of the ropes and chains that anchored them. He gradually ascended. Thirty feet. Twenty. Closing in on one boat in particular. The closest one to the fortress.

Odd that there weren't more boats in the vicinity, as it was always a popular spot for tourists to come and snap pictures. A lot of them still remembered the incident eight years ago when a treasure-seeking team of Americans went diving, searching for an entrance to a mythical lost chamber under the original Pharos Lighthouse—only to encounter some sort of deadly fate, leaving their bodies to wash up, in pieces. The government subsequently outlawed scuba diving in a fifty-yard radius of the fortress, a law that Caleb was now flagrantly violating.

But he didn't have time to waste. He needed a boat. And with the tragedy and the destruction consuming the city's attention, Caleb felt he stood a good chance of being able to commandeer this boat from its owners and put it to better use.

As he surfaced at the back of the boat, which turned out to be a 26-foot Inboard Cruiser, bright red, he started fighting a queasy feeling. Maybe it was just the color, but Caleb had a sudden sense of danger, as if he had just stepped onto a street without bothering to look for traffic. His head spun as he took out the regulator and breathed normally, reaching for the ladder. *Should have RV'd this-*

He debated dropping back down under the waves and searching for another vessel, but then he heard something clicking from above. Something that sounded familiar to him after being around so many soldiers and military types in the past week.

It was the sound of someone chambering a round.

Even the way it was done sounded familiar, just as familiar as the sound this particular gun made. *A Beretta.*

Her weapon of choice.

"Damn," Caleb said, looking up into the brilliant blue sky a moment before a silhouette obscured his view.

She looked like just another sexy sunbather, wearing a thin bikini that matched the color of the boat. She even smelled like tanning oil; and her hair was pulled back in a tail that whipped from side to side in the wind.

Nina Osseni held the gun steadily aimed at Caleb's head. "Hi honey. I was wondering when you'd bother to show up."

He reached a hand up for her to take, but she just backed up, keeping the gun on him. "Sorry, but given our history, I'm not about to touch you right now. Just come on up here and have a seat."

Caleb hung on the ladder, his mask up on his forehead. He was calculating his chances of diving and getting under the boat, then descending out of her reach. "If I say no?"

She sweetly smiled and shook her head. "You're not that quick, lover."

"Don't call me that."

"Move. We have things to talk about. Our boys saw that you'd try to make for the fort."

After a wistful look down into the suddenly clearing water, and a yearning glance to the fortress, he climbed. Slid off his air tank, peeled off his mask and kicked free of his fins; then he stood there, dripping onto the boat as she sized him up.

She whistled, almost giggling. "I'm guessing you had to borrow a suit for the swim."

Caleb narrowed his eyes at her. "You're making jokes?" He pointed over his shoulder to the mainland, where helicopters roamed over the ruins of the *Bibliotheca Alexandrina*. "Right after *that* just happened?" His hand clenched into fists. "Nina, what have you done?"

Her grin evaporated. Her eyes darted to the disaster site, then back to her prisoner. "I… I'm still sorting it out. Still figuring…"

"Your place in Calderon's world?"

"My place," she said through clenched teeth, "is with my boys."

"Our boys." Caleb leaned toward her. "Nina, listen. If I had only–"

"Looked? If you had bothered, or if Lydia hadn't completely distracted you?"

"I know. I would have seen you, but I had no idea. I wasn't even thinking of questioning it. You were dead, I thought. Why would I want to relive that? Why would I look for you, only to see you die again?" His eyes pleaded, and this time, at last he really meant it. "I would have, Nina. I would have gone to the ends of the earth to save you."

She snickered. "Touching. But we both know that once you found out I was working for Waxman, you were glad I was gone."

"I'm not going to argue anymore. If you're not going to let me go, then shoot me if it'll make you feel better."

"Oh it would, Caleb. It really would. But I think Jacob and Isaac really want to meet their daddy, and I can't deny them such a simple pleasure." She took a seat opposite him on the deck, crossing her silky tan legs slowly while she leaned forward, casually holding the .45. "But first, there's the matter of Giza's subterranean labyrinth. Senator Calderon tasked me to find out exactly what you learned down there."

Caleb cocked his head. "Why? Couldn't he get the boys to RV it?"

Nina didn't move. "Their minds are... a little OCD, I'd say. Getting them to focus is like teaching a golden retriever to play chess in a park full of kids throwing balls." She absently tapped the gun's barrel against her front teeth. "Now, why don't you tell me what you're up to? What is it you and Xavier thought you could do to stop Calderon? Stop a man who could do..." she motioned to the devastation on the shore "...that?"

Caleb smoothed back his thick wet hair, and his eyes locked on hers. She didn't need the gun to make him feel like he was at her mercy. Just like when they had first met, he felt out of her league, humbled by her beauty. Only now, he could see something else behind her eyes: the calculating, catlike fury and selfishness that

Nina possessed in abundance. But he held onto a hope that just as Caleb had changed after he had discovered he had a son, maybe some grand lycanthropic transformation would work her over, reforming her. But it didn't seem likely.

"Go to hell," he whispered. "You want to find out, you know what you have to do."

"Oh," Nina said, tracing her lips with the gun's barrel, "you'd like that, wouldn't you?"

Caleb stood up. "Again, I'm not here to talk, and I'm not here to help you. Do what you need to do, but I won't be a willing subject."

Nina stood beside him, taking the bait without realizing she'd just been hooked. Smiling, she reached for him and said, "Just the way I like it."

He felt a burning rush as she grabbed his wrist, and then she was turning him towards her, and the sun was behind her, blazing through her hair, and her face disappeared into the blackest shadow as she leaned in.

And then her lips were on his, her tongue opening his mouth, her lungs sucking in his breath. He squirmed in her grasp, even as he felt the electric chill of her curves against his wet chest, her legs encircling his calves, pinning him in place as she took his thoughts. His memories, his essence.

But this time, he was prepared. His mind was focused.

She may have thought she was taking from him, but this time, he was the one giving.

She saw it all, just as he had mentally prepped it, as if he had loaded the projector in his mind, and had it playing in an infinite loop so that anyone that poked their head in for a look, would see...

A massive ripple of energy, nearly invisible but sparking as if roiling with electromagnetic charges at war within the ether, a wave tearing through New York City, blasting the skyline apart, cutting a swath through the island, tearing across the harbor and splitting the waters, causing mirror-image tsunamis, parting before the Statue of Liberty which seemed to wince before being struck. It shatters, arm, torso and crown tossed in separate directions, caught up in the flux and separately pulverized.

Then—ascent, and a satellite's view. The ripple tears across the globe, leaving a path of destruction from an origin point somewhere in eastern Alaska. But then... the clouds are massing, swirling over the northern hemisphere, lighting up from within, periodically bursting with intense flashes. Massive auroras are appearing in the upper atmosphere, as if an unseen hand works with vibrant watercolors, splashing them in broad brushstrokes over the world's skies. Breathtaking. Beautiful.

The earth trembles. Wobbles unsteadily. In breaks of the clouds, the land masses seem to be shifting. Major sections tearing free. Waters spilling over entire countries. The globe shifts the wrong way. The poles reverse. Flipping, as if something has completely unsettled the core, scrambled it and shut off the dynamo at the center of Earth's molten center, then jump-started it again.

The vision draws sideways so that the Earth is out of the frame, and its companion pulls near. The Moon. Silvery, lustrous, complacent. So bright...

...on one side. But we're nearing, soaring around, towards the darkness. Towards...

The vision ended in a searing ball of light. Intense white that turned to yellow, then dimmed... and dimmed. She couldn't get her bearings, but

Nina felt as if she were weightless. Still in space. Still...

Then it dawned on her. She couldn't see, not yet. Not with the glare of the sun still tearing at her eyes, but she knew all the same. She was in the water. In the damn harbor. With... a vest on? And—a regulator stuffed into her mouth. She was breathing the tasteless but pure air from a scuba tank.

That meant...

Shit!

She tried to spin around, awkwardly lashing out with her hands. Where was he? How did she get out here?

But then she realized it.

He had been ready for her. He knew she'd try to pry the truth from his mind, and he was ready.

But with what?

What the hell was that?

She floated, and her vision gradually returned along with the sound of a motor, a familiar motor, departing swiftly.

Damn Caleb.

Lucky, he thought, steering the boat the last few yards, coasting into the dock, where two youths waited with ropes to reel and tether him in. *I got lucky.* Nina had her guard down, and never considered that Caleb could show her anything that would literally send her reeling.

Let her stew on that, he thought as he disembarked and gave the boat-hands a tip out of the purse Nina had left behind. He took that with him, wrapped in a towel that he tucked under his arm.

Happily, she had also left her cell phone on the seat. He quickly made his way into the shadow of Qaitbey's Fortress and took it out, preparing to dial Phoebe. But first he glanced out into the harbor, where far out there he thought he could make out Nina, starting to swim for the rocky shore. He knew it was probably   a mistake to let her live. But he wasn't a killer. He could no more strap weights to her chest and dump her, unconscious, into the harbor, than he could strangle a sleeping cat. Not to mention the newfound connection they shared. But while he couldn't kill her, only incapacitate her for a time, neither did he believe they could work together.

Hopefully what he had shown her would cause her to second-guess what she had been told. Or at least, to start to question whose side she was really on. But he wouldn't count on it.

He had work to do.

On the second ring, Phoebe picked up and once she heard his voice, relief flooded hers. "Big brother! Glad my vision wasn't wrong, and you're still alive. How's Alexander?"

"Safe, for now. But listen, we need to move fast. And I don't want them tracking this call. I need your help. Can you get me out of here? Where are you, I tried looking, but only–"

"Saw something blue?" Phoebe's voice was giddy, like she had just opened a favorite present. "We got ourselves one of those shields!"

"A what? And who's we?"

"You won't believe me. Orlando and I, we're on a plane, nearing…"

Caleb heard an unfamiliar voice yell out and cut her off: "Don't say where we're going!"

"Oh right," said Phoebe. "Kind of defeats the purpose of a shield. Anyway, we're with some others with similar *interests*. Been recruited, you might say. We'll find a way to get you here discreetly."

"Phoebe, listen. That can wait. If you've got access to discreet transportation—and I can only cringe and guess why—then have your new friends have a jet waiting for me at the Alexandrian airstrip. I need to go to New York City. I'll explain later."

"Oh, I bet it's something to do with the statue!"

Caleb held out his hand for a cab, as soon as he reached the end of the promontory and back toward the street.

"You wouldn't believe what we've seen," Phoebe continued. "And we're about to learn a lot more, I'm guessing, but already it's *out of this world* stuff."

Caleb caught her emphasis, and immediately thought of the artwork down under the pyramids, the strange remnant technology, and his and Xavier's visions.

"Okay, just tell me you can get the plane."

"I think so. Go, and we'll have it ready. Just for you?"

"Yeah, Xavier's let himself get captured."

"What? Why?"

"Said it was to buy us our escape, but I know he's got something else in mind. He needs to get into Calderon's camp, probably has to do with something he's seen. But all that's out of my hands. I need to get the one thing I know can help us."

"All right, big brother. Get to the airport, do your thing. We'll see you when we see you. In the meantime..."

"You're in charge of the Morpheus Initiative, Phoebe. I trust you. And if you trust these new friends, then you have my confidence to bring them in on what we know. Pool your resources. If I fail..."

"Yeah, yeah. If you fail, it's up to me. *Again.*"

Caleb hung up, then dropped the phone on the street as he entered the cab. As soon as they realized Nina was gone, they'd be looking for him. And with the twins' ability to find him, he didn't want to make it any easier by letting them track her phone. He told the driver where to go, then settled back, hoping to close his eyes, rest and let his visions seek out some possible solutions.

5.

Alexander tried hard to focus, to do everything his father had told him. To just think about the computer and his responsibility, but it was difficult. So hard to concentrate down here in the dark. With the priceless books and scrolls and tablets, most of them ruined. With the darkness and the shadows.

With the dead.

He couldn't keep his mind on the task of sorting through the computer files. Clicking on folder after folder, trying to find something useful without even knowing what he was looking for. Worse than a needle in a haystack, because half the time these files just opened scanned photos of the original texts, which then had notes written in Greek or Coptic—languages Alexander was still not proficient with to say the least.

He was beginning to panic. The air felt thinner after every minute. The shadows deeper. The flashlight light a little fainter. Finally he turned it off and just focused on the computer screen, and tried to imagine he was home in his room in the dark. Nothing else but his familiar bed and books around him in the dark. Just those, and his computer.

And it worked, and he relaxed and started to make some progress.

-Until he heard the rumbling from above.

Oh no. He trembled and his mouth went completely dry. *The drill.*

He was going to have to kick this into gear. *Come on, you're a Keeper now.* He had to find the answer, finish his mission. For his father. For the Morpheus Initiative, for the memory of all the Keepers lost today. He couldn't let them down. But he needed to improvise. The computer search route wasn't working. It was time for another tactic. One that had to work, and fast.

They're coming.

He shut the laptop's cover and sat in darkness with his eyes closed. Ignoring the rumbling from above, ignoring the dust filtering through the gaps in the ceiling and coating his head like falling snow, he focused on the target. It was a vague objective, but hopefully something his subconscious could latch onto if it went fishing around in a murky pond with a hook the size of a bazooka.

Think! Rashi had found something in the recovered library. Something big, something she shared with the others. All of them except Dad.

Think!

And suddenly, a nibble. Something jerked in his mind, a vibration rattling his mind. And then he saw–

Lydia. His mother, hunched over the central table, looking through a large magnifying lens at an intact rectangular stone slab with odd writing all over it. Keepers Rashi and Hideki standing behind her, anticipating her reaction.

"This is it," Lydia whispers. "The Rongo-Rongo script. Its first translation into Sumerian. This is..." Her face pulls back from the glass, and her eyes are beaming, her expression numinous. "This is everything."

"Yes," Rashi says, "we now have a cipher we can use to decipher the writings at Harrapan and Mohenjo-Daro."

"And these others," Hideki adds, motioning toward a table full of rough-edged tablets, some looking incredibly ancient.

Lydia's smile matches theirs. "Robert will be so pleased!"

Rashi nods. "He's been searching for this translation for years."

"He hoped it would be in the collection," Lydia says. "You know Robert, he believes in all that pre-historical civilization stuff, that some great race was wiped out or went into hiding before our current recorded history, and that maybe this script was their only legacy."

"If we could only translate it," Rashi muses with a smile. "Which is now possible. So, are you going to tell Caleb?"

Lydia glances to the pile of waiting tablets. "Not yet. Let's see what we learn. He's not coming back for another four months. Let's see what we can translate first. And if there's anything he needs to know, we'll decide at that point. For all we know, this will just be gibberish, or maybe a list of holidays and crop yields or something."

"You don't believe that," Hideki says. "If that were the case, these pieces wouldn't have been safeguarded in the most secret vault on the planet."

Lydia sighs. "True. But still, let's be extra careful about what we translate. This could be the biggest revelation yet, in all these texts. Explosive knowledge that could have damning results for the whole planet."

A bitter blackness suddenly replaced everything, leaving Alexander in a near whimper, longing to stay by his mother's side. At once he crumpled over, nearing tears, reaching with his mind to get back there. To see her again, to see—

- her typing furiously at the computer. Alone in the chamber. The packed alcoves surrounding her on the rounded walls, all those priceless scrolls and texts crafted by ancient hands while her own fingers deftly move across the keyboard. Her lips silently spell out the words as she translates from the latest tablet and types.

The view moves closer and Lydia pauses, trembling, glancing around.

"Caleb?"

She backs up in the chair, moves her head back and forth, her eyes closed, as if seeking a scent. Then she shakes her head and returns to the screen. "Sometimes I get these feelings... Like you're looking in on me from another time and place. Maybe I'm just being paranoid."

She sighs, opens her eyes and looks intently around the room. Up at the ceiling, around the silent and deep alcoves. "If it is you," she whispers, "just know that I did this for you, and for Alexander. I'm hiding what we've found, because if you discovered it you'd mobilize your little group and go out hunting these... people. I know you would. And you're not ready, oh god Caleb... what I've learned..."

Her shoulders tremble. "Don't... just don't go after them. Don't even look for them. Because they'll know. Please, for Alexander's sake. For all our sakes. If you somehow find this, just leave them alone. If you can. Unless... it's unavoidable."

She moves the mouse to close out the file she's been working on—and just before it disappears, the name is visible:

"Custodians." Alexander opened his eyes and in the darkness he fumbled for the flashlight switch, found it and in the burning brilliance, he returned to the computer.

"Okay," he said, over the increasing volume of the drills coming closer. "Let's find where mom's hidden you, and what all the fuss is about."

6.

Mount Shasta, Washington State

They landed at the small airport outside of McCloud, near the base of the majestic, snow-capped Mount Shasta, then assembled into two jeeps that proceeded through the picturesque town at speeds Phoebe thought bordered on criminal, not to mention obviously attention-grabbing, at a time when she expected they'd want to keep a low profile. The lovely town instantly tugged at her heart, and she squeezed Orlando's hand. He was smiling at the scenery, the quaint shops, restaurants and inns at this resort town, reminiscent of the old gold rush period, and she wondered if he was thinking the same thing: that when this was all over, maybe they could get away and come out here for a romantic vacation.

Aria sat in the back with her father, who seemed to be recovering nicely, but was still in and out of consciousness. She watched with wide eyes, taking in the lush forests of pine, the variety in the colors of the leaves, the grass and brush. But always her attention was drawn to the great mountain, the ice and snow covering most of its surface up to the dazzling white peak. Phoebe could only imagine what the girl was experiencing, having lived her whole life in the dry desert.

With the town behind them, the road narrowed and they traveled for a while in silence, with Colonel Temple at the wheel, his mirrored sunglasses covering any sign of emotion. A few more minutes and they turned onto a bumpier trail where the alpine woods closed in and scraped against their windows as they moved into Shasta's shadow. Soon, NO TRESSPASSING signs began to appear, and their ears popped as they began to climb.

But it wasn't much longer before they stopped, coming to a high metal fence manned by two camouflaged men with heavy rifles. A nod from Temple, who showed them a pass, and they were through.

A rectangular two-story windowless building stood under a canopy of trees against the base of a steep rocky incline. A half-dozen satellite dishes of various sizes pointed through one clear section to the blue sky.

"That's it?" Orlando asked, stepping out of the jeep and stretching.

Temple chuckled. "Give us a little credit. We may not have unlimited funds, but we've got enough for a little luxury. This is just one of our redundant communication sites." He was smiling as he reached into his suit coat pocket and pulled out a small transmitter. He pointed it at a flat wall of the mountainside, and moments later a doorway appeared. Two sides split open and parted, revealing a tunnel, and a globe-shaped silver car on a set of tracks.

Temple removed his sunglasses And said, in a business-like tone, "Welcome to Stargate."

After the doors closed and they were all situated around the surprisingly roomy interior, the tram moved them along at a more-than-leisurely pace that made Orlando compare it to the New York subway system. Except the view out the convex windows was less interesting: just occasional dull lamps revealing little beyond what one would expect inside a tunnel burrowed into a mountain.

"Alexander would love this," he said to Phoebe. "Reminds me of the villain's secret lair inside that volcano in *The Incredibles*."

Temple heard him and smiled. "Not the vibe we were going for, but secrecy is vital. And anyway…"

Aria's eyes widened. "You didn't build this tunnel! You found it here." She was sitting on her father's lap, his arms around her waist protectively.

"What?" Phoebe stared at the girl. "You saw that?"

Aria pressed her little fingers against the glass window. "They found it, using their psychics."

"Following up on native American legends about a race living within the mountain," Temple added. "And... rather sensational reports through the years. Prospectors, climbers, explorers... tall tales of robed men and women appearing from the caverns, speaking enigmatically and then disappearing. Strange lights at night. Weird craft-shaped objects coming and going..."

"A regular UFO hotspot," Orlando said, then shrugged. "At least according to *Coast to Coast AM Radio.*"

Phoebe leaned across the aisle toward Aria, and looked out the window at the lights passing in the darkness. "What else did you see?"

The girl closed her eyes. "I saw... I see... that where we're going... it's one big hollowed out cavern that they've made into their headquarters. But there's something, some place they can't get into. They wanted to get further, but there's a door of some kind."

Temple nodded. "A barrier, black, solid and thick. The Dove had been having visions of it for years."

"But never," Aria added, "seeing anything behind it. Only blue."

"Correct. Apparently they let us get this far, but no further."

The tram was slowing, and brighter lights appeared.

Orlando frowned. "So there's a door. Couldn't you bust through? Or drill around it?"

Temple smiled. "Course we tried. But any machinery that got within twenty feet suddenly died. EMP field of some kind, protecting it. Tried manually digging around, but whoever we sent to do it came back... the only word I can say is... 'befuddled'. As if their brains were temporarily scrambled. They had no idea what they were there to do, or even where they were, and it took hours for the memories to clear. So no, we can't get through."

"Hmmm," said Phoebe. "Sounds like you were invited to a party, but then denied entrance at the front door."

"That's about the way we saw it," Temple replied. "But we didn't take offense. Instead, I'm thinking maybe this is their way of testing us, observing us first. Seeing if we're worthy to get inside to the big dance."

"How long has it been?" Orlando asked. "That you've been tested?"

"Four years, give or take."

Phoebe whistled. "Maybe it's not a test."

"What do you mean?" Temple cocked his head. And for the first time, his voice didn't sound so confident.

She shrugged. "Maybe you're just meant to be close. All of us in one spot…"

"So it's easier to wipe us out," Orlando finished.

Temple was about to say something when the interior sud-denly got a lot brighter. The walls of the tunnel gave way and their tram hurtled above an enormous open space. They hugged the stalactite-covered roof, racing along a monorail track that circled the mile-wide facility, looking down on a complex of rectangular buildings, pathways and plains. Pipes and wires ran along the sides of the elliptical cavern, with pathways laid out in concentric circular grids. Giant floodlights stood at regular intervals, and the track angled toward one pyramid-shaped glass building that stood fifty feet above the others.

"Central command," Temple pointed. "Where we're headed. Where you'll meet the team."

"And the diabolical super villain in charge," Orlando mused.

"That would be me," Temple said with a grin as they began to slow down. "Now, get ready for some revelations that are really going to blow your mind."

Inside the sparkling glass-walled command center, the tram stopped at a level lit up by major lights diffusing through the windows. Looking up, the walls converged at a point where another huge circular light hung, giving the whole area a feel of being inside the luxurious lobby of an ostentatious hotel. There were three fountains and a waterfall, nestled inside a park-like area with large palm trees and lush flowering bushes. Multicolored birds flew about, chirping and singing. There were rounded picnic tables, benches set alone in shaded areas where people sat and appeared to be meditation, or just sleeping.

"You'll have time to enjoy the scenery later," Temple said, urging them along. He headed toward an elevator set in a rectangular, ivy-covered central pillar. "We're needed down below."

They followed, Aria and Phoebe first, then Orlando who pushed Aria's father in a wheelchair. The doors closed and they descended quickly in a sealed car. "I'd have expected glass walls," Orlando said. "No view?"

Temple shook his head. "These levels are largely private. We have twenty-seven psychics at work down here, along with a staff of sixty to maintain the complex, cook the food, run information searches and gather real-world intelligence. That all happens on levels four and five. The psychics, they're down on six."

"In the basement," Orlando commented. "Where we belong."

Phoebe jabbed him. "Okay, so what's the plan? We meet everyone, and then what? We've got to help Caleb and Alexander, and stop..."

"The end of the world, yes. All in time." The doors opened and Temple led them out into a much different setting. Soft lights, mahogany walls, dark carpeting. Leather couches, gold-framed maps on the walls: ancient-looking maps of the world, depictions of the stars and planets from the Middle Ages.

Orlando whistled as he rolled Brian Greenmeyer forward.

"Leave me here," the man whispered. "Tired, and this looks like a good place to rest."

"Dad?" Aria turned around. She still held Phoebe's hand.

"I'm not worried," he said. "You're with good people."

A thin, matronly woman stood up from a desk in the dark corner and took the wheelchair handles from Orlando. "I'll watch over him now, get him a drink and some food."

"Thanks, Laurie," Temple said. He gripped the doorknobs and opened the two large oak doors, and then they were passing through a long hallway lit by what looked like turn-of-the-century gaslights set in bronze gargoyle sconces.

"What's behind all these doors?" Phoebe wondered, looking ahead and losing count until the distant end of the corridor.

Temple paused at the first one. "Okay, a little off the main tour, but I'll show you. These are our 'contemplation chambers.' Each a little different. Décor suited to the objective."

"What objective?" Orlando asked.

Temple put a finger to his lips and quietly pushed open the door.

Inside were three people sitting in large bean bags, each a different color. They wore sleeping masks and seemed to be dozing... except for the pads of paper and pencils in their hands. Around the walls were hung photographs—aerial maps of mountain ranges and coastal regions, geological studies that seemed to center around fault lines running across the ocean beds and highlighting volcanic areas.

Temple eased the door shut. "We have them solely focused on natural disasters. Trying to predict the next ones, probing likely hot spots."

"And if you get a credible hit?" Orlando asked.

"We quietly leak it to the geological community and do what we can do evacuate ahead of the event. But…"

"You haven't had much luck yet?" Phoebe asked.

"Not as such. Close, but timing's always a bit off. Sometimes they can't tell whether it's weeks or days, or in a couple regrettable instances, only minutes away. We're working on refining the techniques. And we hope, maybe with your help, to improve our results. But first things first, or there won't be any need for any of this."

"What's in here?" Orlando asked, reaching for the next door.

Temple grasped his wrist just as he turned the knob and the door opened a crack. "Leave that one alone." He closed it gently, but not before Orlando got a glimpse of two older women, dressed as gypsies, standing before a glowing globe with their hands out and their eyes closed.

"Was that the moon?"

Temple sighed. "Yes, but the less you see of that, the better. We try to keep them alone and what they're working on secret. We even have a shield permanently blocking that room, since it could cause the most alarm if certain elements determined what they were looking for."

"Which is?" Orlando clenched his hands into fists. "Let's get on with it. Get to the good stuff." He pointed to the door. "I want in there."

"Soon." Temple ushered them along, speaking as a tour guide without opening any more doors. "In here we've got a rather gifted, if unfocused, talent looking for other candidates across the world who have demonstrated precognitive abilities. In this next room we've got four siblings, ages twelve through twenty seven, who together seem to share the same visions. We've got them probing certain historical events, trying to piece together what really happened to colonies—or whole cities—that went missing. Roanoke. Mayan centers, Pueblo towns... We have a list." He slowed near the end of the corridor, passing two more doors. "Here we've got our largest room, a testing facility for new members. We put them through a series of blind objectives and gauge what they seem to be best at."

They kept walking, with Aria and Phoebe glancing at each door, and Orlando itching to get inside and dig in. "This is just the kind of place I told Caleb we needed. More psychics, more objectives. Cool stuff to figure out! Damn, Temple, unless you're jerking our chains, I love this place! Where do I sign up?"

Temple held up a hand before one more door on their left. "One thing more to show you before we enter the main conference center. In here, you'll meet-"

"-The Dove," whispered Aria with an odd smile on her face. They opened the door.

He was, to put it mildly, a little different than Orlando or Phoebe expected. He sat in an enormous leather reclining chair. Enormous because it had to be in order to fit his frame. Easily four hundred pounds, the Dove was in his late fifties. Balding, multiple chins, arms and legs the size of small redwood trunks. He went shoeless, and his big feet were up, presenting a grotesque view. Cheetos crumbs and pizza crusts littered the front of his extra sized Worlds of Warcraft t-shirt—the same kind Orlando had been sporting, until the incident with the eels.

Phoebe gave his arm a squeeze as if to say, *look—there's you in a few years.*

"Hey there," the Dove said, waving a big hand in their direction. "Just taking a break, boss. These the newbies?"

"New to you, maybe," Phoebe quipped. "I've been at this since before I could talk."

"I stand corrected." He slapped away the crusts from his shirt. "I'd get up and meet you, but I don't get up much. Not when these good people can bring me anything I want. If I didn't have to piss and... well, I'd never get up. Too busy anyway." He spun his chair around slowly, groaning with the effort. And Orlando took a step in, wrinkling his nose at the smell, noting the air fresheners working in the corners, overtime apparently.

Why is he called the Dove? he wanted to ask, and would as soon as they were alone.

The room was small, with maroon-painted walls supporting large bookshelves crammed full like the shelves of a used book store. On the walls were movie posters—specifically ones of a certain genre. *Invasion of the Body Snatchers. Close Encounters. The Day the Earth Stood Still. War of the Worlds.*

Orlando nodded. "So in here, you're studying film classics?"

The Dove made an un-dovelike sound. "Ha, good one. Nope, in here I do the important stuff, looking in on our 'friends'. As much as I can, sneaking around their defenses, mostly seeing the footprints rather than the feet—or tentacles—that made them." He grinned and chuckled, wiping his greasy hands on his dirty pants. "Hey Temple, you show 'em the NASA chick's highlight reel yet?"

Temple shook his head. "Heading there next."

"Highlight reel?" Phoebe asked.

"NASA chick?" Orlando followed up with.

The Dove grinned. "Oh, it'll be a hoot, believe me. I'd join you, but..."

"Right," Orlando said. "You'd prefer not to get up."

Making a gun out of his fingers, the Dove pointed and grinned. "You got it, Orlando Natch. And by the way, good work out there in Bamian. I took a little time off the hunt to check you guys out."

"And thank you," Temple said, "for your timely intelligence when we needed it."

The Dove gave a half-hearted bow from his seat. "Now, if that's all, gentlemen and ladies, I have some more snooping to do. And you have a lot of catching up to do if you're going to be anything but dead weight, which I have my doubts about."

"We'll try not to disappoint", Phoebe said, leaving quickly, eager to breathe the fresh air out in the hall.

"Toodles!" called the Dove as the door closed behind them.

"There," Temple said. "That went better than expected. He can be... a little less than charming sometimes."

"Please," said Orlando, "tell me he wasn't a skinny geek like me when you found him."

"He's actually on a diet," Temple said, "and doing quite well at it. We saved him from an extended stint at a rehab center where his chances were not very good. Gave him purpose and now he's actually trying." He made a face. "Just not entirely motivated."

He moved forward to the end of the hall, toward a gold-plated two-door exit. Smiling to his three guests, Temple opened the doors and led them into a room that gave Orlando the immediate impression of stepping into Mission Control at NASA. Two rows of tables with comfortable leather seats before a central conference table and a main wall covered with projection screens of various sizes, including one immense screen currently split into eight smaller rectangles. Different scenes were presented on each one, and Orlando recognized a view of some jungle temples in Belize, while another had a distant view of the Taj Mahal, another the Great Wall of China, one had the Pyramids, and another, Stonehenge, and another–

"The Moon. And that," Orlando pointed to a center screen where a reddish, rocky desert image stood eerily silent. "First I thought it was the Southwest, a random desert somewhere. But I've seen that before, from the rover's camera. It's…"

"Mars," said a new voice. A woman stood up from behind a large-screen computer monitor in the second row. She was thin and shapely, with long auburn hair and blue eyes that were haggard and weak, and yet sparking with a twinge of excitement that only came from discovery after long hours of searching. She wore jeans and a loose white t-shirt with the words: ROCK CLIMBERS DO IT HAND OVER HAND.

Nodding to Temple, she came around the table and extended her hand in greeting to the newcomers. "My name's Diana Montgomery. And I'm…" she glanced at Temple questioningly. "Well, I've only been brought on two months ago, but I guess you can say I'm a consultant."

Temple stepped inside, shutting the door behind them. "Sure, we'll keep that title. Diana was a consultant for NASA most recently, until certain illicit behavior was discovered."

Diana raised her hands. "Caught with my hands in the cookie jar, downloading some evidence they preferred remain classified."

"Before that," Temple continued, "she served as assistant to the Director of the Smithsonian."

Diana smiled at Orlando. "Before being kindly asked to resign after I once again…"

"Got your hand caught in the cookie jar?" Phoebe supplied, pulling Orlando back a little and sending a signal at the same time.

"More like their restricted archives."

"But not before she first found some rather interesting things," Temple said.

"Artifacts. Certain relics that didn't fit with the modern historical consensus. Things that made me question everything about our evolution, our discoveries and technology." She turned and walked back to the main wall, where she eyed the scenes of Mars. "And that sent me searching for answers in the one logical place where it made the most sense. The one place," she said, "that terrified the hell out of me."

"Up there?" Aria asked.

Diana nodded. "I used my connections and a little blackmail, I'm not afraid to admit, to get a job as a consultant to NASA. Then worked my way into a position to gain access to material off limits to most everyone except a few higher-ups. I took what I could, and confirmed in my own mind everything, all my worst fears."

"And then," said Temple, trying to hurry her along. "She got caught. Or would have, if the Dove hadn't glimpsed what she was doing. We acted quickly, scooping her up just before a team was prepared to take her out… permanently."

Diana looked down. "And I've pretty much been here in exile ever since." Her expression brightened. "But it's not so bad. Every once in a while I get a break and can go outside and do what I really love."

"Rock climbing?" suggested Phoebe.

Diana nodded. "Ever since I was a teenager. Me and my dad." Her face fell. "Until he died investigating something strange at a cave in the Grand Canyon."

Orlando gasped. "Kinkaid's cave?"

Diana smiled. "Figured you might have heard about it."

"I remember that," Phoebe said. "The news conference. That was you?"

She nodded. "I broke the story. Or tried to. Later, after my resignation, the Smithsonian retracted it all and said there was a huge mistake, that items had been misclassified in the archives. Forgeries, all of them. They said that I had acted rashly without their consent, blah blah blah."

"But you knew the truth," Orlando said wistfully. "Egyptian artifacts in a cave, thousands of years old. In the damn Grand Canyon. That must have been an adventure, finding those!"

"Well, I had help."

Temple grinned, looking from Phoebe back to Orlando.

"Help?" Phoebe asked.

"One of you," Diana replied. "A remote viewer. He came to me in the desert, saved my life, and then helped me find the hidden chamber. He showed me everything, and he... we..." Her eyes turned glassy and wistful. "Well, I haven't seen him since, but he had these drawings, and..."

"What was his name?" Phoebe asked, her mouth dry. Fearing she knew the answer already.

"Xavier," Diana said quietly, her voice cracking with emotion. "Xavier Montross."

7.

When the first rocks started falling, Alexander had just finished rereading his mother's file for the second time. His head swam with scanned images, rough drawings made by the other keepers. Ancient maps that looked like the inside of anthills, crude sketches and strange symbols, a timeline with notations in his mother's hand. He was still putting all the pieces together, trying to decide whether all this was some fanciful early myth or if it could it possibly actual history, when rubble crashed through behind him.

Chunks of stone, fused metal and pieces of glass tumbled free and slammed into a bank of shelves. Alexander jumped up, snatched the laptop and retreated to the far edge of the chamber, shrinking into a corner where a section of the wall had collapsed. He thought momentarily about throwing the laptop on the ground, picking up a sharp hunk of concrete, and bashing it in, rather than let them get its secrets too. But that file... something his mother had been working on, something Dad had never seen... And what could hold the answer to everything. He couldn't let it go.

He had to save something from down here.

A shaft of light stabbed inside as if a giant had just poked its finger through the top of a cave and let in the sun. In the uncomfortable brilliance, Alexander could see two ropes descending, followed quickly by dark-clad men.

Surprisingly, he discovered he was experiencing relief as much as fright. *At least I won't suffocate to death, alone in the dark.*

Two flashlight beams struck out in opposite directions, spraying the walls and the rubble. One hesitated on the face of the dead Rashi, then joined the other, converging, moving as one to the farthest corner. Both of them froze, highlighting their prey.

"We have him," said a voice.

The two lights blazed in his eyes, and Alexander couldn't make out anything but vague outlines of the men standing over him. He heard a familiar voice, but it came from a speaker, crackling.

"Does he have the keys?"

"Boy," said the man behind the closer light. "Where are they?"

Raising his hands before his eyes, Alexander said, "What if I told you they were under that pile of wreckage over there, and good luck finding them?"

A moment of quiet, and then the man chuckled. "I'd say you were bluffing. Your brothers seem to think you've kept them around your neck."

The other one coughed. "Care to show us?"

"All right, all right, I've got them here." Alexander reached under his dusty shirt and withdrew the cord. The three pyramid-shaped keys reflected in the light, sparkling green.

"We'll take those."

"Let him keep it on. Calderon said we're taking him with us."

"Fine. Okay kid, rescue time. Get up."

Alexander rose, still half-blinded. He bent down, reaching for the laptop, but suddenly one of the men snatched it up first.

"I'll take this too. Since you were keen on protecting it."

"Move it, kid."

Alexander let himself be led back to the ropes. Strong arms scooped him up under his armpits, something was clasped into the man's belt, and then—they were rising. About halfway out of the crater, Alexander's eyes adjusted—and he wished they hadn't. What he saw bore no resemblance to the place he had spent most of his young life. The world's largest library, a wonder of the modern age, gone in an instant.

His eyes welled up and tears cut through the layers of dust on his cheeks and fell back into the pit, to the vault still filled with the broken dreams of the ancients.

Something at eye-level caught his attention, and as the crane swung them over the drilling equipment and to a makeshift platform, he saw two boys standing on the edge, impatiently waiting to greet their brother.

"He doesn't look like he's all that special," one boy said, circling Alexander. "Does he, Jacob?"

Hugging his shoulders, he tried not to stare at the boys. Jacob stood right in front of him, looking at him like he was a sideshow exhibit, and Isaac moved around, inspecting him from all angles. But Alexander tried to stay strong. "Didn't say I was."

His two rescuers had moved to a position back near the black Hummer waiting at the other side of the platform. Alexander squinted and tried to see in there, but was too distracted.

"Ah but you're the promised one," Isaac said.

"The one who opened the door first," Jacob added.

"Found the great old box you did," Isaac sneered. "Just didn't open it. Now we have you. Got the box, the secret books, and the keys."

"Keys to the universe," Jacob said.

Alexander's hand went to his necklace. He held the three stones, immediately feeling a twinge of something vibrating into his fingers and up his arm. "It won't help you. Not after what I just learned."

"And what," said a new voice, "did you learn down there?"   Mason Calderon had come around from the side, behind a line of rescue vehicles, their lights flashing. Further in that direction, barricades held back a surging crowd growing larger by the minute, a sea of desperate faces.

Calderon came strolling forward, leaning only slightly on his cane. His suit coat waved in the wind around his back as he moved. His face, Alexander thought, was smoother, glossy and wax-like, as if he'd just been rejuvenated. His eyes sparkled as he came right up to Alexander, then stopped and looked at all three of the boys.

"A family reunion! Isn't this just grand. Boys? Did you introduce yourself to your long-lost brother?"

"He knows," Isaac said bluntly.

"Obviously," Jacob added.

Alexander resisted his curiosity at studying these kids and   instead turned his glare to Calderon. "My uncle Xavier thinks you're going to destroy the world. So if these keys are going to help you, then forget it. I won't help."

"Then what?" Calderon spread out his arms, with the cane's dragon head pointing up to the clouds. "Are you going to jump back into the hole? We'll just fish out your body and get those keys your family worked so hard to obtain. And as for destroying the world..." He shook his head. "Don't be silly. I intend to save it."

"But Xavier *saw*..."

"I believe he saw what would happen if I didn't succeed. If he didn't join me and help me unlock the secrets of the Emerald Tablet. To annihilate the true, secret enemy of mankind."

"He's joined you?" Alexander felt the energy leaving his voice. The keys now felt like heavy iron chunks. Calderon stepped to the side and Alexander could see a man with red hair standing by the back of the Hummer, opening the trunk. The two soldiers were with him.

"Come on," Calderon said as he turned his back to the boys. "Let's get this damn box open and see what we've won."

"But-"

"Move it," Isaac said as he jabbed his elbow into Alexander's side. "And give me those!" He reached out like he was going to strangle Alexander, then snatched at the pendants, caught a hold of the cord and yanked it free.

"Hey!"

Isaac skipped ahead, twirling around, holding the keys high. After a moment's hesitation, Jacob followed, glancing back once to Alexander. "Come on," he said in a low voice, and waved his hand.

Sorry, Dad. Hanging his head, Alexander followed, and the only thing keeping him going was the belief that maybe Xavier knew what he was doing. He was always a step ahead of everyone. Maybe this time, he had Calderon right where he wanted him.

But when Alexander made it to the Hummer and saw Xavier shoved aside by the guards, his head down in resignation, all hope fled.

"The Keys," said Calderon, and took a step back. "You boys do the honors."

Isaac quickly stepped up. He slid the stones off the cord and held them all in his hand, gazing at them longingly. Alexander wondered if he even appreciated who had held those objects. Cyrus the Great, Genghis Khan, Alexander... The greatest leaders and conquerors in history; and now, this kid was handling them, roughly inserting one into the slot.

"What about me?" Jacob asked, moving in.

"Snooze you lose," Isaac replied, fitting in the second.

"Hope it zaps you," Alexander said.

Isaac glanced back before inserting the third. "Right... Hmmm, why don't you do the last one?" He held out his hand.

Alexander glanced over at Xavier, who had raised his head and was watching Alexander. He gave a nod, indicating he'd be safe, as Alexander thought. There was no danger at this point to anything other than the contents of the box. But his visions had shown that the three keys alone would do it.

The hand bobbled. "Come on, brother. Honor's all yours."

"Somebody just do it," Calderon snapped.

Alexander sighed. "Let Jacob do it. I'm tired."

Jacob flashed his eyes at him—whether in anger or gratitude Alexander wasn't sure. But then he snatched up the key from his brother and slipped it into the slot. The twins jumped back with a cry as a flash of light erupted from around the crack in the lid. A hiss of steam shot out in all directions, and then the cover propped up an inch.

Calderon stepped through them, put the cane under his arms, and with the brazen confidence of a man fulfilling his believed-in-destiny, he lifted the lid up and off.

He peered inside and smiled.

Alexander couldn't see at this angle, and then the twins were climbing up, gathering around and looking inside.

"Just a bunch of clay tablets," said Jacob.

"Goofy writing," Isaac added. "Boring!"

"Have some respect, boys." Calderon lifted one tablet out, holding it up. The script was familiar in places, Alexander saw. With alternating lines of ancient Greek and then the familiar script that was on the Emerald Tablet—which

Alexander realized now was slightly reminiscent of the Rongo-Rongo carvings his mother had translated, the ones at that Mohenjo-Daro place, and Easter Island.

"Hey," Alexander said. "That-"

But then the scene melted away and he was on an island, standing on a flat grassy hilltop under a pure blue sky. Below, miles from the waves that caressed the rocky shore, a hundred workers toiled in a quarry, hacking at the black granite chunks. Molding them into giant Moai *that would be aligned into sacred patterns and stand guard, warding off the annihilation that comes for men when they become too advanced.*

"We will be safe here?" someone asks. And there is a woman, beautiful and shapely. Tall, with long black hair blowing in the breezes around her face, obscuring her eyes. She holds a smooth piece of driftwood in her hands. On it is written that script in alternating rows, front and back.

Instructions set to animalistic myth. Instructions on how to hide. To live simply and to protect themselves.

And wait.

Wait for salvation.

"Will it be long?" she asks, her voice cracking in the wind.

"Undoubtedly," the chief replies. "Many, many generations."

He looks to the sky, to the defiant moon hanging high and triumphant, stubbornly refusing to yield to the rising sun. And he trembles, recalling the legends.

She notices his gaze.

"How can we think to hide?"

"We just do as we were brought up. Just as there is evil, there is good. Darkness and Light. We must hope the light will protect us." He sighs and reaches for her hand. "But come, enough of this melancholy. We have much living to do before we pass on."

Alexander blinked and it was gone. Xavier's bushy red hair was centered in his vision, the wide blue eyes searching his. "You okay? Lost you there for a minute."

"Yeah, I'm…"

Xavier was shoved aside by the cane, and Calderon stooped down. "Tell me you didn't go looking anywhere you weren't invited."

"What do you mean?" Alexander stammered, still woozy, still smelling the salty ocean breezes and mistaking the sound of hammering and digging of the rescue attempt with the construction of the giant heads on Easter Island. "I don't have much control over what I see. I just saw that writing and-"

"And did you see anything... blue? A wall of blue, or a congregation of people, like monks in white robes?"

"What?"

Calderon continued staring at Alexander, searching his eyes for a fear that wasn't there. "Never mind. You're okay." He shot a glance at Xavier. "You too, watch yourself. We're in dangerous territory now. Now that we have this..." He motioned to the box, the tablets.

"What are you afraid of?" Alexander asked, his voice meek.

"Nothing you need to worry about."

"Does it have to do with the... Custodians?"

Calderon made a sharp breath. He spun and gripped Alexander's shoulder, tightly. "Where did you hear that name?"

"Stop it, that hurts."

Xavier's hand settled on Calderon's wrist, squeezed and pulled it back—and for a moment both men stared at each other in a contest of wills. Until the barrel of an MP5 was shoved against Xavier's temple.

"Take it away," Calderon whispered.

"You first," Xavier replied, squeezing harder. "You don't touch him."

Calderon opened his fingers. And the gun pulled away. "Fine." He slapped at Xavier's hand, then turned back to Alexander. "Tell me. What do you know?"

"Oooh," said Isaac, moving in close to Calderon's side. "Our brother's in trouble. Learned secrets he shouldn't have."

"Shut up," Calderon hissed. "This is serious shit. Up until now I've had the luxury of operating without their interference, mainly because the Morpheus Initiative have drawn their attention with their plunder of the Tablet."

"But they want it too," Alexander said. "It's why it was hidden so well. I learned the Custodians can see, but not as well as us. They've lost focus over the long years, and they've lost touch." He snapped his head to Xavier. And it all spilled out of him as if he now believed it to be pure fact, never any doubt. "They're underground, most of them. The survivors of the last age, the ones with the powers to see the damage the wars would do to the planet. Claimed to be the shepherds of the next race, the ones without any psychic abilities."

"The grunts," Isaac said, "as me and Jacob call 'em."

Jacob moved into view, looking pale, as if this was a subject he had heard once and didn't care to revisit.

"What else?" Calderon urged.

Alexander hunched his shoulders, trying to appear thinner and less consequential. "I don't know. My mom and some of the Keepers deciphered some ancient document from the Pharos vault that had these legends."

"About what?" Calderon prodded.

"Wars. Ancient wars," Alexander said. "Myths like a lot of the others. The gods in the sky battling it out. Good and evil." Excitement started building in his voice. "But they used great lightning bolts and blasted the planets. And there were two of those power things—the Tablets of Destiny. Each side had one and let loose on each other, first in small targeted ways and only to the warriors. But then it got worse, and more desperate and the one side—who based their weapon on Mars, attacked and flipped the Earth…"

"Flipped its magnetic pole," Xavier whispered.

"…and the Earth's forces retaliated with a weapon shot from a great pyramid that wiped out life on Mars, and then something else happened. Someone managed to steal the bad guys' tablet and break it with a lance."

"Marduk," Calderon whispered, nodding and caressing the slain dragon on his cane.

"And then-"

"All right, that's enough." He stood. "You've read the same legends I have, which I'm guessing is what Robert Gregory saw as well and conveyed to me. Just proof of what our leaders have always known."

"But," said Alexander. "It's true?" He waited, and after no response, said, "But if they're still here, waiting, and there's only one tablet left…" Alexander made the realization. "It should have been destroyed, too, if Thoth had not been so cautious."

"Maybe," said Xavier, "he kept it around in case mankind had need of it again someday. In case the threat wasn't gone for good."

Calderon nodded in agreement. "In case the enemy regrouped and was determined to claim its revenge. Well, thanks to that foresight, we now have it and can finish the job. Pack this up," he ordered the guards. "And we all ride together. We'll scan the tablets on the way to the airport, then send the data to my translation team standing by."

"Standing by where?" Alexander asked as he followed Xavier into the Hummer.

Jacob and Isaac moved in front of him and both turned at the same time and answered:

"Alaska."

8.

New York

The ferry to Ellis Island was nearly full, surprisingly so for a weekday. But Caleb quickly worked his way past the gift shop, where he bought a liter of orange Gatorade, then up two levels to the roof where he found an open seat on a bench near the back. He had bought a classic Yankees hat on the street outside, so now he looked like another tourist.

He sat and waited for the ferry to leave, and was grateful for the cloud cover, even if darker storm clouds seemed to be massing along the skyline. After all the days of heat and direct sun, he'd welcome the shower. From this vantage point he could keep an eye on the line outside, watching for anyone suspicious who might have been following him since he'd come back into the country. Watching, especially for Nina.

For all he knew, she may have recovered, learned where he was going and beat him here. In a minute he'd try to remote-view her, but he had other objectives weighing on his mind, vying for his attention.

An Asian family sat in front of him, parents and grandparents, while their kids—two boys and a girl—scooted into his row and sat on the bench beside him, grinning.

"First trip to the statue!" the girl said, waving a large foam finger at him. She had a pink crown on her head, contrasting with the green spiked crowns worn by her brothers.

Caleb smiled and nodded. "Going to the top?"

"I am!" one of her brothers boasted.

"Are not," said the girl. "I heard it's too hot in there, and too hard to climb."

"And," said the father, turning around. "We didn't get enough tickets."

"Tickets..." Caleb rubbed his head. "I forgot we need a separate ticket for the crown." The one he held only granted access to the museum and the lower pedestal.

"Sold out," the man said. "Months in advance, since they reopened it. Eight years after the attacks, it's been off-limits."

Caleb nodded, wondering... *What else is up there? What else are they protecting?* Mason Calderon knew something was there, but his boys weren't skilled enough at finding it. And whoever hid it there kept the knowledge to very few people.

Caleb would have to view it, and would have little time for trial and error, little time to spend getting the questions right. He took a deep breath, trying to relax. And then, even if he found it...

"Excuse me," he said to the man in front of him. "I heard that your children might not be interested in the long, hot climb. Might you have an extra ticket for the access to the crown?"

Halfway to their destination, as Lady Liberty appeared to grow in size, becoming the colossus that can only be appreciated from up close, the kids got out of their seats for photo opportunities along the railing. Caleb, pretending to sleep, now had some time to really concentrate. He put out of his mind all the things he could no longer influence: Alexander's situation, Phoebe and Orlando, the twins, Nina, Lydia... Everything.

At first, none of them would relent, and the weight of responsibility—as leader, father and husband—put up a brazen resistance. But finally, after gently pushing, he created space. Sent his other concerns drifting, out far but not out of sight. And for a time, he let go. And let his mind seek out the answers to a question he kept posing, focusing the words, preparing his thoughts. He felt his spine tingle, the back of his head break out in a sweat under the hat, and then-

The first vision rises up: *A great workshop. Enormous sheets of bronzed copper rest on tables. A giant's shoulder, partially completed, and*

an arm gripping an enormous tablet in its huge hand. A dozen men stride through the chaos, barking orders, assisting at different stations; hammering the copper sheets into the wooden framework.

Another glimpse: *a different warehouse floor, this time with the enormous head resting on the floor, two men standing before her melancholy eyes, admiring the workmanship. They're pointing to the crown of spikes, whispering and nodding their heads...*

Is that it? Caleb wondered, briefly returning to the world of light and wind and sound. The ferry rocked gently on the waves as it sailed toward Liberty Island. *Is it inside one of the spikes?* Signifying the seven continents and seven seas, maybe there was a riddle to solve, a way to determine which held the treasure by the location of its designated continent? Then he cringed, imagining having to crawl up onto the head and fight the winds and the view almost three hundred feet above the base.

Keep looking, he urged. He had to consider everything, and this was free-viewing, a brainstorming session. Next, he saw *a huge fairground, great crowds dressed in late-1800 fashions. Women with umbrellas and long dresses, men in top hats and canes, all strolling the grounds despite the heat and humidity, the flies and the refuse bins overflowing with trash faster than the workers could empty them. A long banner reads: 1876 Centennial—Philadelphia. Past the tents and display stands, invention stands and horticulture exhibits, to a line snaking around and around, where people wait to pay their fifty cents to enter the immense outstretched right arm and ascend into a huge copper torch. Along the balcony around the torch's simulated flame, people are crammed in, waving to their friends below and marveling at the sights.*

"Just another month," says the promoter at the tent's entrance. He spins a cane up and down, pointing at the gaping spectators as the sweat pours down his face and soaks his black suit. *"Before this engineering wonder will make its way to New York, to Madison Square Garden, before it'll be shipped back to France, and then... You'll see the whole thing, the new colossus—Lady Liberty—assembled in a few short years in New York's Harbor. But here, and only right here, you get to climb inside what will be the highest point. Imagine the view, imagine the spectacle! Just fifty cents! Get inside and see for*

yourself this marvel of the modern world!"

The vision swells, money changes hands, then a blur and now the interior appears. A winding staircase, a tight fit cramped with people on every side, going up and coming down. Then, up on the balcony. Others looking out at the scene, but the vision continues to study the flame. Moving around the torch from all angles, looking for any obvious seams or compartment entrances, not finding anything, but still...

Makes sense, Caleb thought dimly, part of his mind still lucid. Just like at the Pharos... which the Statue of Liberty was modeled after, in part. The treasure, the wisdom, was secured in the light, or in actuality, its mirror reflection below...

As above so below...

Caleb's eyes snapped open. They were very close now, circling around Liberty Island and veering toward the docking point. But the statue was there, rising like a giant in all her splendor. Caleb immediately focused on the pedestal and again had to marvel at how closely it resembled the Pharos' structure as he had seen it in his visions. If not for Liberty standing upon it, this could be the Pharos itself, it was that similar. Instead of a small statue of Poseidon gracing the top of the Pharos, this monument had the massive goddess of wisdom and justice—originally intended by Bartholdi to be a representation of Isis.

But in all other senses, both were beacons of truth and hope. And, Caleb recalled, both were lighthouses. The Statue of Lib-erty's torch had been meant to provide illumination for the harbor, to guide ships in during the darkest of nights. But...

Show me, he thought. Maybe that was the direction to search.

New York harbor, filled with ships. Spectators and business vessels alike. Anchored and watching the dedication. The scaffolding removed, the gleaming statue stood revealed in all her towering splendor. Fireworks blasting into the sky, exploding in brilliant reds and blues with showers of white stars pinwheeling over her crown. But the lights on the torch, eight lamps around the base, barely provide enough illumination to compete with the pyrotechnics display in the sky.

A flash, and later... Engineers are working on the torch, cutting into the flame, creating two rows of portholes and inserting lamps. Below, a steam-powered electric generator powers the lamps, but... Shift to Manhattan Island, and a gray-bearded man with an armful of designs stares out at the statue and mutters, "It's the light of a mere glowworm."

Another shift... A cool fall day, and again several engineers are at work along the torch's balcony... A thick belt of glass replaces the portholes, and an octagonal pyramid-shaped skylight is fitted as a skylight on top. An oil-powered generator replaces the old one. From the crown, the same bearded man looks up through the windows and frowns at the fractured, mutilated light that still fails to perform as expected.

Again a shift ahead... And a man in a brown suit stands on the deck of a yacht, with American flags waving around him, and a crowd of reporters and aides. It's night, and the harbor is dark, with stars blinking overhead, and a fleet of ships all around. Ahead, the black shape of the enormous goddess stands mutely in the dark. "President Wilson," says an aide. "You may now light it."

Grinning, he gives the signal.

And from high above, the torch springs to life. Different again, now fitted with six hundred small windows of yellow-tinted glass and fifteen gas-filled electric lamps.

The reaction is anything but spectacular. Wilson bites his lips and listens to the muted applause before turning around and heading down below.

It never quite worked as a lighthouse, Caleb knew. Even though it was retrofitted along with technology advances every couple decades. But certainly the torch was now hollow and could serve as a hiding spot. But technicians who changed the bulbs would surely have discovered anything like a slender ancient blade hidden inside. Wouldn't they?

Caleb shook his head. They were approaching the dock. People were getting up, heading down the stairs to get in line to get off the ferry.

He still had time.

Time to keep looking. To go back to something else he had seen. The dedication day. The ceremony...

A small group of men in full Masonic garb stand before the base while behind them, a great procession approaches, led by the Grand Master, all in attendance for the rite. A pastor gives a benediction, speaking of this statue as a symbol of freedom... And then the dedication. A copper box set into a space in the cornerstone and overlaid with a plaque. The box... containing among other items a copy of the Constitution, bronze medals earned by the Presidents, city newspapers, a portrait of Bartholdi and a list of Grand Lodge officers.

The box...

Caleb shivered with excitement. Was it possible? It could have been opened up, the spear placed inside, then reset into the cornerstone, guarded and most importantly, hidden in plain sight.

He stood up, feeling the rocking of the boat as it was finally secured. He was alone on the top deck, and felt the first sprinkles of rain. The heavy clouds now swirled over the statue, as if they'd followed him. It seemed the torch was in danger of being devoured by the ominous weather.

The cornerstone... If the Spear was there, how would he get at it? He started heading for the stairs, but then caught a glimpse of the base of the statue. The walls of the star-shaped foundation. And he recalled that this site, once called Bedloe's Island after a British Admiral who owned the land as a summer home, had later been occupied by the military where they built a star-shaped fort, with massive twenty-foot high walls and cannons at every point, ready to defend the harbor. Fort Wood was later chosen as the base for the Statue, perfect in its complimentary design and symbolism, and yet...

Something bothered Caleb, and on the way down the stairs and passing the gift shop, with all the dangling trinkets and miniatures of the Statue and base, he realized what it was. The orientation didn't make sense.

It could have been that General Patton was driven more by practicality and less by symbolism, and therefore didn't care about where the object of America's power rested, only that it was secure, but Caleb would have imagined that, like Sostratus, he would have hidden it either at the 'Above' or 'Below' points signifying light and wisdom. It should have been in the torch, or at its diametrical opposite, as in the Pharos' vault.

Somewhere equally below the level of the torch.

Caleb looked out the window, and first grimly imagined a

descent under the earth, three hundred and five feet to the mirror reflection of the torch. But geologically that would be challenging. The earth here in the harbor was soft and lacking in a suitable foundation for carving out tunnels or chambers. But with modern technology it wasn't out of the question. Maybe somewhere in the old Fort Wood there had been a vault, a storage area beneath the earth, something that could have been expanded. A shaft drilled and reinforced.

He leaned against the railing as the ferry rocked with a wave. A rumble of thunder groaned over the chatter of tourists, some of them now retreating into the safety of the ferry, not wanting to brave an imminent downpour.

But Caleb pushed through. He was distracted, his mind swimming with alternatives.

He had to get inside the pedestal, find someplace quiet. Some place of inspiration where he could finish the viewing, peer deeper and focus his vision. Too many competing possibilities. He had to narrow them down.

Pushing through the jarring, smelly tourists, past the Asian family gamely trying to get out, he made it down the ramp and through the crowd sheltered under the docks' rooftop waiting area, and just as the storm let loose, perfectly timed with a huge bolt of lightning to the right of the statue, Caleb ran out into the rain, heading for the main entrance.

Halfway there, something made him pause and look back. Another ferry was coming, tossed from side to side but chugging along, rounding the bend toward the docks.

And on the second level railing, he could just make out a flash of a red windbreaker alone in a sea of dark colors. A brunette leaning over, scouring the crowd, looking for someone.

It's her, Caleb thought, turning and running faster. He was out of time.

Nina had found him. And he was sure she hadn't come alone.

9.

Mount Shasta

"Montross," Phoebe whispered. "He…"

Diana nodded, blushing. "He opened my eyes. To so many things, in such a short time. And, well he promised to see me again soon. I haven't seen him in years. But I know he had a larger mission."

"Which," Orlando said bitterly, "involved ripping us off and killing a lot of people—and kidnapping a kid, don't forget that. And bringing back that Nina psycho."

"He would never–"

"Guys." Temple held up his hands, officiating. "Now's not the time to debate Mr. Montross's villainy."

"But it is," Phoebe insisted. "If Diana believes him, if she's holding a torch for him or something."

"I'm not!"

"Sounds like you are," Phoebe snapped. "When did all this happen?"

"Six years ago."

"Soon after he walked out on the Morpheus Initiative." Phoebe was fuming. "He saw the danger before the team ventured under the Pharos, and he saved himself without warning the others. Then he up and went halfway across the world to help you?"

Diana looked down at her boots. "There was something he said he needed. An artifact. Something he saw in the archives. He needed me to help him get inside to find it."

"So he used you."

"No. Well…"

"What was this artifact?"

Diana sighed, and her eyes clouded over.

And suddenly Phoebe gasped. Her body twitched and she saw…

A lonely farmland, a rusty weathervane. A few cows grazing. A red barn in the distance. And a backhoe with its shovel in the air, releasing a torrent of dirt beside a deep hole. The earthen sides are striated with deeply hued layers.

The engine stalls, sputters and stops as a man in dirty overalls jumps out. He has an election button on his grimy t-shirt: FDR '32. His shadow falls on the pile of dirt—and a gleaming fossilized skull. Enormous. Horned, with a wide-plated crania.

The man looks back into the hole. Bends down and peers closer at the rounded bones peeking through the earth. A ribcage.

And inside…

Something that looks like a soccer ball. Spherical

Shiny.

He jumps down, slides his fingers through the gaps between the bones. Touches the thing, brushing away the dirt and dust…

Revealing a gold surface. Thick plating. And–

–symbols.

Lettering. A script.

The farmer backs up, holding his head and wincing as if he's suffering the sudden onslaught of a migraine…

A flash, and the same site, except black cars are parked around the backhoe and men wearing dark suits, fedoras and sunglasses are standing around the hole. Diggers wearing what look like deep sea diving gear pull up the dinosaur ribcage, intact, with that spherical object still inside. They place the orb inside an open, lead-lined chest, slam and lock the cover. Money changes hands and the farmer signs some multi-paged document, then stands there, mute as the cars all drive away and he's left with a deep hole and a fistful of money.

"Oh my god." Phoebe had her hands on the table's edge, trying to steady herself. "I saw it… was that real?"

"What?" asked Orlando.

Diana leaned in. "What did you see? The archives at the Smithsonian where Xavier found the item?"

Phoebe glanced up. "The Smithsonian? No, but... the men I saw at the farm, in black suits and cars with matching paint jobs..."

"The farm," Diana whispered. "Wyoming. In 1931 a cattle farmer dug up a fossilized Triceratops, with something in its belly that should not—could not—have been there. An artificial object inside the gut of a sixty million year old dinosaur."

"So," Orlando said, "your old employer hushed it up. Like I've heard they did with a lot of stuff they found in America, things of obvious European, Asian and even Egyptian origin. Things that didn't fit with conventional theories."

"At the time, I convinced myself it was a hoax. That the Smithsonian hushed it up because there was no other logical assumption, other than that the farmer himself—or someone close to him—found the bones, then fabricated this sphere, put it inside, then reburied it to be discovered later."

"But now you don't think so," Orlando said.

"Not after everything else I found in those restricted archives. After researching literally thousands of other anomalies that never made the light of day because conventional scientists—whose duty should have been to objectively analyze all the data before making conclusions—instead buried or simply destroyed evidence that didn't corroborate existing theories of man's comparatively recent evolution. Or the Diffusion Hypothesis. Or the belief that Sumer was the first main civilization, or that the Americas were only populated by savages who had traveled across the Siberian Ice Bridge ten thousand years ago."

She took a breath. "While I had access to the secret archives in the Smithsonian, I catalogued thousands of man-made artifacts discovered in geological layers indicating great antiquity. Skulls and bones indicating that modern humans had coexisted alongside lesser developed species that we supposedly evolved from. Coexisted even with dinosaurs..."

Temple sat back, sipping his coffee, but unable to hide his smile as he watched Phoebe and Orlando's reaction. Aria how-ever, just seemed bored with the conversation, instead glancing around the screens with the awe of a kid watching Saturday morning cartoons on a big screen.

"I can't believe you just saw that," Diana said as she stared at Phoebe. "I mean, I shouldn't be surprised, especially here, but sometimes… I admit I often wondered if Xavier was just a good con man. If he cooked up everything and made his inside knowledge appear like psychic ability."

"Well, now you know," Orlando said.

"Although," Phoebe added, "I'd say Xavier's still a con man. Don't trust him. Ever." She turned her glare at Colonel Temple. "Whatever that sphere is, I'm thinking that it's something that can shield his presence from remote-viewers."

"Why do you think that?" Temple asked.

"Because I sat in on a lot of sessions where George Waxman and the Morpheus team searched the world over for Xavier, and never found a thing. I think he needed it to block his activities, to hide from us so he could break Nina out of her confinement and go about his mission."

"If he did all that," Diana said, "he must have had a larger reason. He must have known…" She waved her hand to the screens. "About this. About what's going to happen unless we stop it."

"And that," said Temple, "ends this uncomfortable discussion. Diana, if you please… the presentation. Tell our guests about your evidence. What you've confirmed, what we've been looking for."

"Maybe you should start," said Diana, who seemed winded as if she'd just run a race in the hottest part of the day. "I need a breather, and I'm guessing that our guests might not listen with an open mind if I start out."

"We might," Orlando started, then shut his mouth after a look from Phoebe.

They all took their seats, with Diana moving to the front and sitting by herself. She shot Temple a look and said under her breath. "You could have warned me about this."

Temple just shrugged. He poured himself a glass of water, then passed the pitcher around. "Okay, we're going to start with a little Theology 101."

"Ugh," said Orlando. "If I wanted to go to Church…"

"Listen. You all know the first verse of the Bible." Temple stared at them, and when no one spoke up, he said, "*In the beginning, God created the heavens and the earth.*"

Orlando raised his hand. "Ooh, I know! What is: Genesis, chapter one, verse one?" He tapped himself on the back. "Do I win a Lexus?"

"Nope. Listen, the word used for God is *Elohim*, which is plural—*gods,* or more precisely, *'beings from the sky'*. And get this, the Hebrew word for 'in the beginning' can have two meanings. Either the literal 'in the beginning', or it could mean *with the beginning*. Or put another way: *'with what*

remained of the past.'"

He let that digest. "So what Genesis could be saying is the same as what a lot of other creation myths the world over speak of: Advanced beings—or planets representing gods, or both—battled in the heavens, and their warfare resulted in massive cosmic destruction, reordered the heavens and created new worlds, our own included."

Diana cleared her throat. *"With what remained, the gods created the sky and the earth."* She took a sip of water. "So many creation myths the world over. And so many similar beliefs about a savior as well—one who dies violently and is reborn. And whose blood and body are then consumed by the survivors to either sustain life or to grant eternal life. The Mali tribe has Nommo, who is continually crucified to a tree, his body and blood taken into the earth, creating seeds that feed the people the next spring. There are so many more—Tammuz, Odin, Mithras, Quetzalcoatl, and of course, the original savior-god, Osiris, who was murdered, cut into pieces and sent to the underworld before he rose up and is now situated in heaven—not coincidentally at the destination point for the worthy in the afterlife."

Temple nodded, but saw that his guests' eyes were glazing over. "Okay, flash forward a couple billion years—or a half million, depending on how radical you want to take all this. In the more distant history, a huge planet— we'll call it Tiamat—collided with another body out beyond Mars, and the collision created the Earth and also the asteroid belt between Mars and Jupiter. The moon—one of Tiamat's satellites, remained with the Earth, basically forming a dual planetary system. Tell them Diana, about the moon."

She stood up, took a deep breath.

But Orlando cut her off. "You're not going to tell us that we never went there, are you? All that Hanger 18 crap? Because, I'll tell you—I RV'd a lunar mission once. And it was real, not filmed on any stage."

"Oh, we went there all right," Diana said. "But I'm guessing you didn't see much more than that—a visit and a landing, or you wouldn't be talking so calmly about this."

"Maybe..." Orlando said, glancing at Phoebe. "I didn't ask the right questions, those kinds of questions."

"It's okay," Temple said. "If you had, you would have either gotten the shield or some unwanted visions, things that have made other psychics give up ever working for us again."

"Okay... I'm not sure if you're joking or not, but sorry, continue. What's wrong with our moon?"

Diana took a breath, then started. "Our moon, by all theories, shouldn't be there. It's a celestial freak of nature. It's too large—the ratio between satellite and master the largest in the system, and dynamically impossible to explain. It's one-quarter the diameter of Earth. The next largest satellite circling a planet is Titan, but it's only one-eightieth of Jupiter's diameter." Diana took a breath. "No theory explains how it could have been 'captured'. Also its orbit should be elliptical like most captured satellites, not perfectly circular. And for that matter, it shouldn't be in a perfectly synchronous rotation."

"A what?" Phoebe asked.

"Our moon is at the perfect distance and rotational speed so that it always shows us the same face. That's a near impossibility to achieve through chance."

"So..." Orlando left the question out there. But Diana ignored it.

"For centuries astronomers and stargazers have been reporting unusual things up there—just on the side that we can see. Strange lights, pulses. Objects that seem... geometrical and show up where nothing existed before, like a twelve-mile 'bridge' over the Sea of Crisis viewed in 1958. Other strange anomalies include seven obelisk-shaped spires six-hundred feet tall near a gigantic rectangular depression in the Sea of Tranquility." She took a sip of water. "The seas themselves, the enormous dark areas you can see with the naked eye, are plains of fused soil requiring temperatures greater than forty-five hundred degrees to produce. NASA speculated that ancient cosmic bombardment must have occurred, the equivalent of billions of H bombs." She rubbed her hands together, continuing without focusing on anything but the table top.

"There have been unusual radio signals coming from the moon, reported early on by Marconi. Nicolas Tesla—more on him later—speculated that someone was up there, and we should be prepared. And the craters themselves—they often defy theoretical models."

"Like how?" Orlando asked. "I've seen pics, they seem normal to me."

"From down here, maybe. But their depth is wrong. For example, a one-hundred-fifty mile wide crater was found to be only three miles deep. Something that huge, causing such an impact, would have gone much deeper, unless the mantle was some kind of tougher material than anything we could expect. And... the bottom of the crater was found to be convex, instead of the other way around." Diana shook her head. "So many anomalies, and I've barely started."

Temple refilled her water. "Go on, quickly. Get to the good stuff."

She stared at her glass, the swirling liquid. "Since the beginning of the lunar program, there have been miscalculations, problems and... unusual missteps. The first few missions overshot the moon as mission control discovered to their surprise that they had miscalculated the moon's gravitational pull, expecting a much greater mass, given the moon's size. After adjusting again, early landings struck harder and faster than planned—and created a metallic ringing upon impact. And speaking of landing, the original craft and crew were prepared to be caught in a deep sea of dust, as should have been the case, given the moon's extreme age, its lack of atmosphere and its direct exposure to dust-producing solar rays. But there was relatively little dust, less than an inch."

Diana pushed a button and all the main screens went black, then started up with a presentation. "What I'm about to show you," she said, "are photographs captured by the early Apollo missions. There are a lot of these pictures, and they tend to be overwhelming after a while. None of these have been seen before by anyone outside of NASA—and only there to a select few." She tapped a key on her laptop and the screens went black as she talked. "From the beginning," she said, "there have always existed *two* space programs."

10.

Liberty Island

After breezing through the shortened security checkpoint, where the crowd impatiently waited out the rain, Caleb bypassed the museum entrance and opted for the stairs up to the top of the fort section and base. He ran through puddles, his face turned against the driving rain. Before the entrance, he glanced up at the dizzying height of the pedestal, and again had a flashback to Alexandria, a vision two thousand years old, with Roman galleys assailing the structure's base under churning storm clouds, a brazier of fire lit high above, and the huge mirror blasting a light through the gloom.

Inside, he emerged directly into the center of the structure, with metal mesh floors and a steep staircase bending around the central shaft supporting Liberty's frame. He had a moment of vertigo and had to grab a railing.

"Tough climb," said one of the park attendants, sitting at this ground level station and working on the newspaper's crossword section. He was in his sixties with a gray mustache and spindly fingers. "Take the elevator if you like, gets you to her feet at least. Then you still gotta climb. You have crown access?"

Caleb flashed him his pass. "Yeah, I think I will travel in style as long as I can. But first, tell me. What do you know about the cornerstone?"

"Masonic dedication, all that Dan Brown stuff? Why, you think there's some secret treasure stashed inside there?"

Caleb choked on a laugh. "Um, actually I'm a professor at Columbia. Just thought I'd do some research for a history class."

"Yeah, it's down there at the base. Hard to get to, especially in a storm."

"And the box?"

"Sealed up good, from what I heard. But I'm sure there's a way into it. I'd have to check with the director. Don't get much questions about it, actually."

"Is he here? The director?"

"At the administration office you passed on the way off the ferry. You should've probably set up an appointment."

"Yeah, this was kind of last minute." Caleb stood there, dripping, trying to decide what to do.

"So, you wanna go up, get your money's worth? Least it's not too stifling hot up there like normally. Usually a couple people fainting every day. Keeps me busy."

Caleb started for the elevator, deciding to at least check out the crown while he had the chance. And he didn't know how close Nina was. She might not have recognized him in his tourist disguise, but she would know where he was going. "Oh," he called back. "One more thing. What's below the base?"

"Under the old fort, you mean?"

"Yeah, ever been down there? I'm wondering about how far down it goes."

"Just a storage level. Nothing else I've seen anyways or heard about. Why, you think maybe there's some Nazi base down there or a secret government lab?"

"No, sorry."

"Maybe the lair for the true shadow government!" The attendant was really playing it up, and becoming annoying.

Caleb wiped the rainwater from his face. "You really need to get out more."

The guard shrugged. "A lot of time for thought in here. Time to wonder about all sorts of things."

"Wondering's not a bad pastime." Caleb entered the elevator and let the attendant send it on its way.

"See you on the way down," the guard called. "Unless the government assassins get you first and make it look like an accident!"

During the ascent, as Caleb marveled at the precision of the supporting interior structure of Batholdi's design, he had a moment to think. He tried to find a way to refine the search, but kept coming back to the one thing that had stifled him before.

Find out what Patton had done with it.

He knew the general had secured it from among the treasures found defended by the Nazis in Nuremburg, knew that he had recognized it as something special, something powerful. And after researching it, he'd petitioned Eisenhower to keep it as a tool for America, but had his request denied. It was ordered back to Vienna to be displayed at its national museum. That was a request Patton refused, and secretly had a replica made of the lance, and that copy substituted in its place while the original found its way here. Somewhere…

Where? That's when the visions broke down and he couldn't find the right questions to probe. He had been asking what Patton had done with it, and that only led to visions of a ferry not unlike the one he had just taken, to Liberty Island   where   Patton remained on the boat, just nodding confidently at the results of his efforts.

Where was it? Caleb probed again, thinking. It had to have been handed off to someone he trusted. Someone who had access to the Statue. An administrator, an attendant, a worker… An engineer? Caleb thought again of the men he had seen working on the torch. Still, it seemed more likely that the cornerstone and secret box contained the prize, but not only was that too obvious, but discovery was too likely. If anyone decided to open it up for study, the anomalous weapon would cry out for explanation.

That tended to rule out the cornerstone, which left the crown or the torch, or some secret passageway to an underground complex, something unknown to the conspiracy-minded security guard downstairs.

The elevator finally slowed, then the doors opened and he emerged at the top of the monument's base. Looking up at the winding staircase shaped like a double helix, he got dizzy all over again. *Now comes the hard part.* He really wished he knew if it was up there, or if this was all a waste of time. Time he didn't have.

He looked down. People were starting to climb, a few who had braved the drenching rain. He lingered for a moment, and was about to turn away when he saw a flash of red, way down there.

She's coming.

Before taking the stairs, Caleb glanced out the side exit to the viewing balcony. The day had turned a dismal shade of gray, with sheets of silvery rain pelting the platform, dripping down the exit's frame and flooding in rivulets to overflowing drainage vents.

Up the stairs now. Ascending through the skeleton with its crisscrossing metal beams, Caleb marveled at the interior of the garment, the incredibly thin copper sheets joined by iron bars. Two stairs at a time he climbed, while he heard others coming down the other side of the helix, seemingly less taxed with the descent. Caleb ran, pulling himself along using the railing. He slipped as his sloshing sneakers lost traction at one point, painfully banged his right shin, then got up and kept moving.

Come on, he urged, trying to stimulate his powers during the physical exertion, and he was again reminded of that night in Alexandria when Nina had taxed him fully, exhausting his body to the point his mind broke free and soared.

Gasping for oxygen now, feeling the air thinning, his temperature rising, the muscles in his legs and arms taxed to the extreme. He dared to look up and saw he was only halfway to the top.

He tripped again, hammering his elbow on the cool metal and nearly banging his head against the side railing. And then he lay there, heart thundering and the back of his neck pulsing.

Groaning, he opened his eyes…

And looked down at himself… wearing dark blue coveralls. A tool belt… and holding a leather satchel, with something inside wrapped in several layers of leather padding. Ascending these very stairs. Nervously gripping the satchel tight.

A flash and a rumble of thunder. Caleb felt the statue sway in the storm winds. He held both railings to steady himself, then pushed himself upward. One glance down sent him to hugging the far side of the stairwell, and for a second he again felt like Demetrius, the first librarian of Alexandria, during his tour of the Pharos. *Keep going, almost there.* He thought about his other boys, the twins he'd never seen. They were up here just a day ago. Searching for the same thing. Searching for the spear, to keep it out of his hands.

So they knew, or at least had the same sense that it wasn't in the cornerstone or somewhere underground.

It had to be up there. The certainty fueled his muscles and he climbed again. Rounding another bend, then another. One more tentative glance down, and his heart leapt. Nina emerged from the pedestal entrance, flanked by three men in dark suits. All of them looked up at once.

And Caleb's breath fled in a rush. This was it. He could still make it, assuming he could find and extract the spear quickly, then make it back to the descending staircase when it split at the crown and then get back down before they saw him. He rushed up the remaining flights, calling on every ounce of energy. Finally, he reached the last bend and then he was into another separate staircase leading up to the crown.

Now completely gassed, he joined a half-dozen people under the white ridged interior of her skull. Several viewers had climbed to the walkway and were gazing out the windows over the harbor and looking up to the torch. The temperature up here was twenty degrees hotter even than the interior at the base. Sweltering and oppressive, the sweat was dripping off him. He flung off the hat, figuring it was useless now. And he turned his attention to the crown, the spikes especially–

-and had a glimpse of men standing outside in bowler hats, wresting a new spike in place, replacing a damaged section.

Too early, he thought. But it showed him that they could be hollow, and easily contain something. *Where did that worker hide it? Come on, show me!*

A few other people were looking at him funny. Someone asked if he was okay, another told him to sit and rest. But their voices had faded, along with their images, and he had shifted back, back… almost seventy years.

The man in coveralls…

Heading up a ladder, with the heavy satchel over his shoulder. Climbing the narrow, tight rungs, climbing…

Into the arm!

Caleb pushed away from the concerned person bending over him. "It's in the torch," he muttered. "I'm in the wrong place. Damn it!"

"This is the crown," said the man, and Caleb focused and was surprised to see it was the Asian tourist from the ferry. "Hi there, you bought that extra ticket. Sorry it was such a bad climb, but you're here. You made it!"

"No," Caleb whispered, trying to stand. "Have to get to the torch."

"The torch? No way, wish we could, the view would be sweet, but it's been closed to the public since 1916. Some kind of attack on munitions plant nearby. The explosion damaged the arm and the torch, and no one's been allowed in since."

Caleb shook his head. "Doesn't matter. Where's the ladder?"

"Back down a bit, I guess. I saw it and took some neat pictures. You have to cross over a narrow walkway, then climb up through the arm. It looks really tight. And dangerous."

Nodding, Caleb patted the man's shoulder. "Wouldn't expect otherwise. Thanks." He stumbled for the descending stairs.

"But there's no way you'll get in," called the tourist. "If you need to see the torch so bad, why not just go to the museum lobby? The original one's down there..."

Caleb froze. The pounding of steps below, on the ascending stairs, was getting louder. Nina was closing in. His head snapped back. "*The original? How long ago was it moved?*" He cursed himself for being so careless. A quick review of the history on the statue's website might have told him all this.

The man scratched his head and looked at his wife, who had just now come down from the observation area. She met his questioning eyes. "The original torch? I remember—the changes made to it by that sculptor—the one who designed Mount Rushmore..."

"Gutzman," Caleb said, recalling the man working on the torch, retrofitting the windows with amber.

"Yeah, him. The glass windows he put in? I guess they leaked or something. Water and snow got in and corroded the torch and parts of the arm over time, so they decided to replace the whole thing. What's up there now is a gold-plated, solid structure facsimile."

"Right," said the husband. "And they shine the huge spotlights on it from the base, and it lights up nice now. No need for interior lamps."

Caleb's head throbbed. "What year? When did they move it?" *Was it after*

Patton's man came up here?

"Oh," said the woman, "not too long ago. I think during Reagan's term. Part of his public works improvement project, and…"

But Caleb didn't stay to listen any longer. He was racing down, heading for the lobby.

The narrow steps made it difficult, but after first checking to make sure he couldn't see Nina anywhere down there, he went as fast as he could, but quickly caught up with other people moving very slowly. He squeezed around them wherever possible, but other times had to complain that he was about to be sick and they had to move aside or face the consequences. Soon he was back at the pedestal. Outside, the rain was still falling in torrents and the sky had darkened. The elevator was nowhere to be seen.

But he wasn't waiting for it anyway. He made his way to the stairs and flew down, finding his energy getting better as the heat and altitude decreased. These stairs were much wider, with plenty of room to race by stragglers. He wondered how far back Nina was. Surely they had found he had slipped by them. Hopefully she may have been sidetracked at the torch, and had gone up there to check.

He could imagine a Hitchcockian scene if he had stuck to his original plan. If it hadn't been for that couple and their information, the torch might have been his last stand—or more likely—fall.

Now he had a chance. He was almost there. Rounding the last bend, then onto the main floor, past the attendant still sitting with his crossword puzzle. He looked up, recognition in his eyes. "Oh, it's you! A pretty lady was down here a short time ago, looking for you. Figured you wouldn't mind, so I told her."

"Thanks," Caleb said in a muffled voice. "No time to chat, but if she comes back this way, can you stall her for a few minutes?"

"What? Why?"

"Assassin," Caleb said, running for the next stairs, heading to the museum.

He burst through the lobby doors, emerging on the second level. A walled railing overlooked the floor and entrance to the museum…

Where the original torch stood in the center of the foyer.

A circular bronze railing set it off from public access, and a park attendant leaned against the railing by the main entrance, ready to answer questions or point tourists in the right direction.

Caleb stopped for a moment at the upper railing, studying the torch. He let his gaze quickly take in the details: the oxidized copper lattice-work, an intricate pattern making up the torch support; the weather-worn cylinder supporting the brilliant amber window-set flame, appearing windblown and magnificent, glowing with a comfortable internal radiance. It rested on a four-legged stand, keeping it several feet off the ground.

Caleb shut his eyes, trying to pick up the vision where he had left it. The worker, ascending the ladder...

Nothing but the doors opening, a mingling of voices. Then–

He's out, emerging through the cylinder, taking a moment to glance over the side, down to the enormous head and crown, and further down to the other arm, cradling the tablet...

And then he kneels and chooses a spot, selecting one section of the artistic railing design, one of the metal bars interspersed between the curved trellises. And he begins to unscrew it, using a heavy wrench from his tool belt. When it's free, he carefully places it in his satchel and removes something of a similar size. Unravels it from its leather garment, and holds aloft an almost identical bar, down to the knobs at the ends and in the middle. He unscrews the top and looks inside, verifying that the hollow cavity is filled with its prize... and then he screws it back in and sets it in place. When he's done, his eyes focus and the great Tablet held in Liberty's other arm is in direct sight, a straight line almost, to the object he just placed in the torch.

It was symbolic and fitting, Caleb realized, coming out of the vision, clearing his head. He wasn't sure if Patton or this aide understood the spear's true potential, but it may have worked on their minds, setting up the symbolic relationship. But they hadn't counted on technology advancements, and the bad luck of leaky craftsmanship.

Caleb moved down the steps quickly, then walked around the torch, studying it.

"Can I help you?" asked the attendant, noticing his interest. "This is the original–"

"Torch, yes I know. I'm just looking for something…" He stopped, studying the layout of the windowed flame, recalling how it looked in his vision. Then he took two steps to his right and looked straight ahead. The bar in front of him…

That was it. But how could he get it?

The attendant shifted, and was now talking to a group of wet newcomers who were complaining about their treatment in the security line and the fact that they didn't know they needed to reserve crown tickets ahead of time.

Seeing his chance, Caleb bent down, reached over the railing and gripped the bar. As the argument heated up, he twisted. One direction, then the next. It barely budged. He glanced at the door to the statue's interior climb, expecting it to burst open any minute with his pursuers, then looked over to the crowd at the door, and now a line behind them, shouting to move so they could get out of the rain.

Screw it, Caleb thought. He vaulted the railing. Balancing on his left foot, he raised his right and aimed. Then sent his heel down, kicking hard at the top of the bar. It broke free with a piercing *Crack!*

The attendant spun around just as Caleb wrenched it free, and without checking inside the shaft, he ran for it. Hurdled the railing and raced for the stairs. He'd never make it through that crowd and back past security. His only chance was to run into the museum or back into the monument, ditch the bar and hide the lance under his clothes and then try to blend in with the crowd and get out the back stairs. Up and to the door.

"Hey!" the guard gave chase while shouting something into his walkie-talkie.

Caleb reached for the door, flung it open—and stopped short.

Nina was there, alone and out of breath. Sweat caked on her glistening skin. She reached into her purse and pulled out a gun, aiming at his head.

"Stop right th-" the attendant flew around the corner, only to be stopped by a bullet into his shoulder. He spun around and fell back down the stairs. And only then did the gun's retort sound in Caleb's ears. She was using a silencer, but it was still loud enough. Maybe not to draw a crowd, and if the guard hadn't alerted security yet...

Caleb's eyes widened. He held the bar in both hands like a weapon, and as he trembled he could feel something rattling around inside the hollow space.

Nina cocked her head, staring at it. "Congratulations. Just like old times, wouldn't you say?"

"So now what?" Caleb asked. He looked behind him, waiting. "Why didn't you shoot me?"

The pounding of feet on stairs, and then three men in suits rounded the corner. Nina held up her free hand in a fist. "Under control," she said. "Fan out into the lobby. Stop anyone from following us."

"But-" one of them started, only to be silenced by a deadly look. They passed by, and then Caleb found she had grasped his hand and was pulling him back, back up the stairs.

"What the hell are you doing?"

"Shut up, and follow me. We've got no time to argue."

"I'm not going anywhere with you. This..." He raised the bar, "Isn't going anywhere."

Nina stopped after taking one step up the next flight. Her grip was fierce, and yet intimate. "Caleb. You touched me, and I saw..." Her eyes faltered, the cold melting away.

"What?"

"I'm probably going to get killed for this, but I'm going to help you. Because I believe what I saw in your vision."

Caleb narrowed his eyes. "Yeah, well I still don't trust you."

"And also, because if that bastard thinks he can keep my—our kids—from me for all those years, and then act like a hero for reuniting us, he's got another thing coming. I was only biding my time until I could shoot him in the back of the head, but you've shown me that if he gets his hands on this thing, then it's all over and I won't have my chance."

Caleb squeezed back. "Okay, but..."

"Shut up and stop thinking for a minute. Come on, they're coming."

He chased after her, still dragged along by the hand. "Where are we going?"

They burst out into the now familiar floor, the start of the climb. *Not again,* he thought, rushing up the steps behind her. He glanced back and saw the crossword-loving Dan Brown fan smiling up at them, nodding his appreciation of their reunion. Nina let his hand go and tapped at a device set in her ear. She muttered something lost in the pounding of their feet on the stairs.

Up two more flights, and then–

Gunfire roared and echoed back and forth inside the stairwell. Something struck the underside of the platform below his running feet. Another shot punched through the wall to his left. Nina squeezed off two blind rounds, hoping to slow them down.

"Calderon's men," she yelled back. "My escorts. Must've realized I turned on them."

"Or maybe," Caleb said, wheezing. "They got new intel. From the twins."

"Cocky kids, Caleb." She flashed him the start of a smile. "And creepy. Definitely missed out on years of discipline."

"Something to remedy if we make it out alive." He leapt up three stairs to catch up. They were nearing the pedestal top, and he could hear the rain and rumbling thunder, broken by another gunshot that went wild. "And how exactly are we getting out?" He stopped at the top of the stairs, doubled over and feeling the start of a cramp.

But his attention remained fixed on the view out of the tunnel to the exterior, where he saw something that wasn't there before.

"Is that a ladder?"

Nina turned back and hauled him up by his sleeve. "Helicopter. Pilot's loyal to me. Had him circling. Then just told him where we'd be coming out."

"Wait. I am *not–*"

Another gunshot, one that cracked the glass around the elevator cage. Calderon's men were right around the bend.

He took off, passing Nina who had dropped to a knee and squeezed off three more rounds, one striking home as the first man ran into view.

Heading for that shaking ladder, he couldn't tell if it was on this side of the balustrade or outside, with one hundred and fifty feet separating it from the base. He started to slow down just as he hit the rain, but then felt a hand on the back of his shirt, drawing him backwards, slowing his momentum, and then she was sling-shotting past him. She had hooked her gun under her belt, and like a gymnast, used her hands to vault up onto the slick stone wall and still in a crouch, she pushed off.

Nina launched, swan-like, into the air just as a lightning bolt ripped across the gray-black clouds. She caught the ladder, swung all the way out and then back, gripping it with one hand and using her weight and momentum to propel it back, right to the edge of the wall…

Where Caleb, seeing her intention and realizing he only had one chance at this, vaulted up as she did—and then just reached out and grabbed the rungs beneath her. He hooked an elbow around one rung, and his knees around another, leaving his left hand free to grip the bar and his prize.

Two gunshots roared in his ears, Nina firing on the men who darted into the passage. But Caleb couldn't look to see the result. The helicopter swung away, and he was soaring out into space, pelted with stinging missiles of rain, completely drenched and hanging precipitously to a slippery ladder far above the ground. Then they were over the churning waves.

And only later did he realize he was laughing, his emotions overwhelmed. He looked up, seeing Nina climb into the helicopter, and then he raised the metal shaft, shaking it victoriously in defiance of the lightning-rippled storm.

11.

Mount Shasta—Stargate Facility

"Two space programs?" Orlando asked. "You mean us and the Russians?"

"No, I mean a public one and a secret program. The Russians," Diana said, "were in on it. We may have been Cold War enemies to all other purposes, but once the early probes got out there, once the Russians shared with us what they found on the far side, well... after that point we were really all on the same side."

"Just not as far as the public knew," Temple said. "Tell them about the Brookings Report."

Diana nodded. "The Brookings Institution, a Washington DC think-tank, put together a report entitled *The Proposed Studies on the Implications of Peaceful Space Activities for Human Affairs,* commissioned by NASA and delivered to Congress in 1961. It talks about the need for research into a lot of areas of space exploration, but the explosive section that has gained the most attention is the part called *Implications of a discovery of extraterrestrial life."* She took a breath, then turned to her notebook and read a passage. "Page two-fifteen. *While face-to-face meetings with intelligent extraterrestrial life will not occur within the next 20 years (unless its technology is more advanced than ours, qualifying it to visit Earth), artifacts left at some point in time by these life forms might possibly be discovered through our space activities on the moon, Mars, or Venus."*

"Cool," said Orlando. "How did I miss that?"

"Too busy with video games?" Phoebe quipped.

"Page two-fifteen and two-sixteen," Diana continued, "go on to talk about the consequences of such discoveries. They cite cultures that have disintegrated when faced with unfamiliar and more advanced societies, resulting in a breakdown of values, and sometimes complete destruction of the people itself."

"And," urged Temple, "what was the recommendation of this section, on the question of such a discovery and its implications?"

Diana smiled. "The only logical one. They posed a question that might shape policy. *How might such information, under what circumstances, be presented to or withheld from the public for what ends?*"

"*Withheld*," Temple said, "being the key word."

Orlando nodded. "So they were scared shitless out of what they found up there, and for our own good decided to hush it up."

Diana clicked the button and started the presentation. "After seeing these images, I can't say as I blame them. Not sure I wouldn't have done the same thing."

Photos started playing across the screens. And Phoebe and Orlando moved to the edge of their seats, open mouthed. "And you got these…"

"Through great difficulty, and danger," Diana said.

Orlando was rapt with interest, barely taking a breath as he watched the images—impossible sights of things that looked like domes set in the sides of craters, then long, straight walls that went on for miles, casting enormous shadows. Tall, glass-like spires, transparent, set in groups around octagon-shaped structures. Something that looked like a castle, gleaming half-covered in the shadow of a lunar crater. A glass-like tunnel stretching many miles, connecting the rims of two craters.

Diana continued, "Astronaut Gordon Cooper went on record, and then recanted, that all the missions had been followed by UFOs, discreetly, and the astronauts had instructions on how to react, what to say as to alert Mission Control, and yet not alarm anybody. They had code phrase, little jokes like 'There's a Santa Claus sighting out our port window.'"

"Nice," Orlando said in a whisper, still gazing at the pictures. "So if I tried to RV these things, could you give me coordinates?"

Diana shook her head. "You don't want to try that. Colonel Temple will tell you why in a moment. Just let me wrap up, as you're looking at all this… All these things that if they got out—and some of them have, the less obvious ones that they didn't censor in time—NASA would just claim they were tricks of light and shadow. Sunspots."

"Swamp gas," Orlando offered with a grin. When Phoebe frowned at him he said, "It's what UFO debunkers here have been offering as an excuse for UFO witnesses for years. Kind of a running joke."

"Anyway," Diana continued. "The timeline, and real history of the space program kind of goes like this. We had a pretty good idea, before we sent humans up there, that they'd find something. There was enough visual confirmation from probe flybys that there would be evidence. It didn't look like a full-fledged civilization or anything, but possibly as the Brookings Report theorized, we'd find remnants of a lost civilization, and possibly something that would explain the moon's mysteries and the unanswered questions about our own evolution and history."

Phoebe scratched at the goosebumps on her arms. She offered a wan smile to Aria who still seemed lost and bored, playing now with her water glass.

"So we went there," Diana continued, "but found it wasn't quite… deserted. Something kept tabs on our mission. Followed, observed. But refused to acknowledge repeated attempts at communication. Radio signals didn't work. Then we tried light. That was the deal with the mirrors. Light pulses aimed with larger mirror arrays. Kind of a Morse Code. But no response. Imagine the buildup, the suspense, and then… to be ignored."

"Like a nerd trying to get the attention of the head cheerleader," Orlando said, trying to smile at Phoebe and lighten the mood. "Disheartening."

"Next, in following missions, NASA had their team try to investigate some of these unusual sites up close. My guess is they hoped to discover something, some leftover technology perhaps that could be used. A lot of areas could be accessed, where we got to explore ancient walls, towers and cathedral-like ruins, all empty. But some areas, it seemed, were off limits. Especially in areas where there were entrances. Tunnels, caves, openings in the deeper craters. The lunar modules would break down, equipment would just stop when they got to a certain distance. Nothing worked. Cameras included."

"Just like…" Phoebe pointed back behind them. "The door?"

Temple nodded. "Go on, Diana."

She took another sip of water. "So we were left with the conclusion that there is a remnant of an advanced race out there, either living as some suggest, or possibly artificial..."

"Robots?" Orlando asked. "Makes sense. Ruled by logic commands. Maybe only to observe and document, but not interact?"

Diana nodded. "That's a thought. Or else it's a small contingent of the former civilization, staying behind to protect something. And apparently... to watch. NASA even took to calling them the Watchers. They're observing us, that much is clear... but not much else. Possibly, if the anecdotal evidence is to be believed, they may abduct our citizens covertly, experiment on them..."

"And on cows," Orlando added. "Don't forget the poor cows."

"And monitor our technological advances," Diana said. "Strange lights and un-trackable objects have been seen in greater abundance over military installations and nuclear facilities."

"As if," said Temple, "they're gauging our strength, growing more interested as we come closer to the ability to destroy ourselves and our world."

Phoebe scratched her head. "Ok, I'm still not sure I believe all this, but what's the status quo? That a secret group among our leaders really know and are keeping the truth from the rest of us? That ETs are here, but their motives are totally unknown, and they don't seem hostile, that they're just a bunch of voyeurs?"

Diana smiled. "Not far off. We know we can't touch them technologically yet. But that has only fueled research like you wouldn't believe. Look at all the advances in technology and weaponry since the sixties. SDI—Star Wars— being the latest."

"I thought we all learned Star Wars was a big waste of money," Orlando said. "That it couldn't shoot down any missiles effectively."

"What if," asked Diana, "its name was actually spot-on? What if its purpose wasn't as defense against a terrestrial enemy?"

Orlando blinked at her, then nodded. "So what, the Russians pretended to be all angry about it, but really they were on board, trying to help create some sort of defense?"

"Against an inscrutable and unpredictable enemy that could attack and wipe us out at any moment. Yes."

"But it was scrapped..." Orlando said.

Temple smiled. "More like replaced. And in secret, with a new technology." Then his face fell. "A technology that we recently learned, may have been subverted to other uses."

He let that hang in the air. Orlando was rubbing his temples, trying to massage away the confusion. "Wait, back on Star Wars, if I recall correctly, many of the scientists who worked on it wound up dying mysteriously."

"That," said Temple, "was when we learned of the Black Lodge. Of Senator Calderon and his Marduk cult."

"How do they fit in?" Phoebe asked.

"In Nazi Germany, Hitler sought out legends of an advanced race living inside the earth, a race of supermen with great longevity and heightened psychic abilities. Missions were sent to the Arctic and Antarctica looking for a way inside the earth at the poles. Teams went to Tibet, trying to find the mystical home of these... Custodians."

Phoebe gasped. "I heard that name. In Afghanistan, the tunnels. I saw... I thought I saw a city. And a robed man who called it..."

Temple's eyes widened. "Shamballa?"

Phoebe nodded. "What does all that have to do with the Moon, and ETs and..."

"And Mars," Orlando said. "This all started with Mars, or have we all forgotten that? What about the Face? I'm assuming NASA did some cover-up job there too, and wasn't too happy about all the attention."

Diana smiled. "That almost blew everything wide open. Fortunately they were able to airbrush and doctor later photos to try to dissuade everyone, but still... there were too many other anomalous structures in the Cydonia vicinity. Pyramids, walls, geometric angles and ratios between the enormous constructions."

"So what's there?" Phoebe asked. "Same deal as the moon—ancient ruins, nobody home?"

Diana shook her head. "Oh no, it's a little more complicated than that. Whatever's there is different. More aggressive and defensive. We've lost probe after probe. The Russians had their mission blown out of orbit as it neared the moon, Phobos. A craft-like object was seen streaking out of a crater and heading for the probe right before it was lost." She sighed. "Investigators have repeatedly asked why we don't just send a lander down to Cydonia to answer the question of the Face and pyramids once and for all, and NASA has cleverly dodged such requests by stressing their process, and looking for water in other areas, and throwing off attention by all that fuss about microbes in a Martian meteorite, but the truth is—we can't go back to the Cydonia region because *they* won't let us."

Temple stood up, looking grim. "And this is where it all comes together. Where you fit in, why we need you. Calderon and his team... they're the inheritors of Hitler's Black Lodge. They found what Hitler had been looking for. Made contact with these Custodians—or one branch of them. What appears to have happened is that whatever great war raged in the heavens millions of years ago, the most recent was waged between bases on the Moon and Mars."

"Thoth and Marduk," Phoebe said. "The moon was Thoth's..."

Temple nodded. "And Mars belonged to Azazel, Marduk, Apollo. Call him what you will. What we're talking about here is more likely a group of beings rather than an individual. Factions with a common purpose. But yet, that was our conclusion too, that the faction most concerned with humanity, the ones who believed—according to all the myths—that we could aspire to their level, they're the ones on the Moon. And some are here, apparently, in Tibet and possibly we hope, here in Shasta. They're the Watchers. Watching over us but not really getting involved."

"The Custodians," Phoebe whispered. "But... the one I saw... he said they needed us. To save them."

"The war has begun again," Temple said. "If it ever really ended. Many times before, Marduk's followers have attempted to wipe out humanity. The Flood. The Tower of Babel. I'm sure if we keep looking, other disasters might be pinned to them."

"The Black Plague," said Orlando, then shrugged. "Just a thought."

Temple nodded. "And each time, apparently at the last moment, these Watchers intervened. Giving Noah warning, saving a select few here and there. Secreting away knowledge of the world—astronomy, farming, maybe even genetic material. All so they would be able to restart civilization in new places after the devastation had subsided."

"Which," Phoebe said, "explains a lot of the sudden appear-ances of civilization in areas like Egypt and Peru and others."

"So how does the Tablet fit in?" Orlando asked. "And why does Calderon need it?"

"That," said Temple, "is your objective number one. Probe the Emerald Tablet and question its relationship with Cydonia. There's something there. What it is, we're entirely in the dark about."

Diana cleared her throat. "We know Mars once had a thriving ecosystem, a habitable environment, before its devastation. And now, knowing what we know about the real history of Earth, I believe we're in a position to answer one of the great mysteries of evolution. Where we came from, and how we 'evolved' so fast, without a discoverable missing link."

"How?" Orlando said, then trembled.

"Wait," said Phoebe. "A cataclysm on Mars. The red land that sunk. Out beyond the Pillars of Hercules." Phoebe looked at Diana and saw the agreement in her eyes. "That's where Plato put it."

"Put what?" asked Orlando

Diana smiled. "Atlantis. I believe Mars was Atlantis, and it's why no one has ever found it."

"Looking in the wrong spot," Phoebe said. "But so many legends speak of it. Mayans, the Phoenicians, a lot of cultures, not only associated Mars and the color red with war and violence, but with their origins. Egypt, with its 'upper' and 'lower' land. The lower world, or the Underworld being red... The place where they came from. The place..." She gasped.

"The place where they would go again. Once they died."

She stared at Orlando. "Oh my god."

"What?"

Temple frowned. "What are you thinking?"

Phoebe closed her eyes. "I'm thinking I'm nuts to say this, but it might explain it all, especially what Calderon is after."

"What?" Orlando asked again, insistent.

"What's   the   great   mystery   of   many   religions,   and especially Christianity?"

Orlando shrugged. "The resurrection?"

"Close," Phoebe said. "How about this—that in order to receive eternal life, what do you have to do first?"

"Besides all that, do good deeds, give to the poor and believe in Him?"

"Think more obvious," Phoebe said. "First, before your soul can live forever, you have to die."

"Die..." Orlando's eyes clouded. "Oh, I get it."

"Explain please," Diana said, leaning forward. "Does this have to do with the Emerald Tablet?"

"Oh yes," Temple said. "If it's truly the Tablet of Destiny, like in the Babylonian creation epic, then it has the power of the universe. A power to harness energy and create a weapon. Maybe it's been used in the past like upon Mohenjo-Daro."

"And in the Great Pyramid," Phoebe said at once. "I think Thoth had it, and used it as a retaliation or preemptive strike, maybe on the remnants on Mars, or somewhere else here, as the two sides squared off over our fate."

"But the Tablet has another power," Orlando said.

Phoebe nodded. "For eternal life, you need to die first... but I'm guessing that first, you need to be prepared. Ready, like all those instructions on the walls of the Pharaoh's tombs. They were trying to give the soul directions, a way to get somewhere and be reborn. But to do that..."

"You had to have control over your soul." Orlando's eyes flashed. "The Emerald Tablet—it somehow acts to free your consciousness from your body. And keep it under your control."

"I know," said Phoebe, "my dad could do it. Even after he died, he kept appearing to us. And Xavier... it seems he learned how to leave his body for a time."

"And now," said Temple, "Calderon's got it. Maybe he plans to use it just for himself, but my guess is that he'll extend that ability to people in his cabal, his lodge or whatever. And then, with HAARP as his tool and the Tablet's power to enhance its ionizing beams..."

"He'll destroy the Earth," Orlando whispered. "I wondered why he would just commit suicide, just for revenge—and wipe us all out. But now I know."

Phoebe nodded. "Wow, just like those Heaven's Gate cultists back some years. They killed themselves and hoped their spirits would hop aboard some passing spaceship on a comet."

"Looks like they may have gleamed a bit of the truth," Orlando said.

"Or at least, what Calderon believes is the truth."

"So we've got to stop them," Phoebe said. "But how? He's got the Tablet. Probably the keys and the translation as well. They could be on their way to Alaska now. We're out of time."

"Not necessarily," Temple said. "There's still Mars. If you can find out what's there, maybe it's something we can use or threaten Calderon with."

"And if we can't?" asked Phoebe. "Don't they have shields there? I'm guessing they do."

"Yes," Temple said. "But you've shown you can get past them by looking for creative end-arounds. I trust you."

"Not to sound like a broken record here, but what if we can't?" Orlando asked.

Temple's expression turned rock-hard. "Then we can only hope for aid from an unlikely source. That the Watchers get off the sidelines and rejoin the fray."

12.

Gacona, Alaska

Alexander awoke with a start and a popping in his ears. Yawning, he looked out the window, taking several moments for the vast expanse of white to register as snow and ice.

"We're over the Yukon," one of the twins said. Alexander let his vision linger on the sprawling ice-capped mountains draped in wispy clouds. The sky was a stark but dull metallic blue; the sun somewhere low beyond the range of jagged peaks. Finally he turned his face away and looked at the boy standing in front of him.

They were on some kind of fancy Learjet. Alexander hadn't really paid attention when they'd boarded. He just knew it was sleek and narrow, with wide leather seats and TVs and a lot of leg room. But he'd had little time to appreciate any of it, as they lifted off quickly from Alexandria, and then someone gave him a drink of water that tasted funny, and as the twins looked on from across the aisle, giggling, he dozed right off, unable to even hang onto any coherent thoughts.

All he knew now was that he was alive. Safe for the moment, but everything had changed. Their enemies had the Books of Thoth and the Emerald Tablet— the ancient relics he had sworn to protect. Some Keeper he turned out to be. Probably the shortest tenure of any of them throughout history. And now, he very likely was going to preside over their extermination.

But then he had a more sobering thought. That it wasn't just going to be the Keepers. What was done to the Library—as awful as it was—that was just a taste of what would happen if Calderon and his followers succeeded.

Sleep was troubling and anything but restful, full of fiery cataclysmic nightmares, shifting earth, exploding volcanoes and rivers of lava. Clouds of ash hung low in the sky, huge fissures opened in the ground, swallowing up entire cities; seas boiled and monster waves crashed over the world.

He shook the visions away, then yawned again, popping his ears. "We're descending?"

"Yep," said the twin stood in front of him, just standing there like a bemused spectator at a zoo. He was nibbling on a Snickers bar.

Alexander frowned at him. "Jacob?" It wasn't easy to tell them apart, especially when they dressed the same. Now they wore baggy jeans, hi-top Nikes and long-sleeve navy-blue shirts. But Alexander had spent some time studying the twins. Jacob seemed to be a little neater, his shirt tucked in, his hair combed back, while his brother's appearance was more ruffled. Isaac sat in his seat, playing a Nintendo DS, grinning as he energetically twisted his arms and mashed the buttons with his fingers.

Calderon was in the back, sitting opposite from Xavier Montross, who seemed to be fast asleep. *Or drugged,* Alexander thought. Two of Calderon's goons sat on either side of Xavier, arms crossed, eyes straight ahead.

Alexander craned his neck to see what Calderon was holding, and he let out a gasp.

"The Emerald Tablet," said Jacob. "Yeah, he's been studying it, meditating and stuff for about two hours." It was resting on the senator's lap, and he seemed to be in a trance. His palms gently rubbed the Tablet's outer surface, fingertips moving slowly, tracing unseen words and signs. Tiny flickers of green sparked off his skin and fizzled in the air.

"My brother and I are next," Jacob continued.

Alexander turned his attention away. "Next?"

Jacob took a seat beside him, crossing his legs and leaning forward. "Our dad—stepdad, obviously—said we need to learn its secrets after he's done. Us, and the other members of…" He trailed off suddenly, catching himself.

"Members of what?" Alexander asked. "Oh, your special cult that wants to destroy the world?"

A light shined in Jacob's deep brown eyes. "More like remake the world."

"And how are you going to do that? By first killing everyone else?"

Jacob smiled. He glanced over to Isaac, who was still deeply involved in his game, the headphones crackling with explosions and violence. "You're special, Alexander. Maybe when you see what we can become, what we're meant to be, you'll accept that. And then maybe we'll accept you. You'll be one of the saved."

Alexander shook his head. "I don't understand any of this. And I don't think you do, either. You're just being used. And that Tablet..." He glanced back at Calderon.

"Come on, Alexander. Don't be like that. We're brothers, the three of us. Part of an ancient prophecy. Even you have to see that we're special. Chosen."

Alexander glanced out the window, seeing the mountains in clearer detail. "If that's true," he said. "I wish we were never born."

Jacob eyes hardened. "How can you say that?"

"Let him whine," said another voice. The headphones were off, and Isaac was sitting up, stretching. "Our little brother doesn't have any sense of purpose. He can't dream big, like you and me, Jacob."

Alexander turned away again, flushing.

"Doesn't even have any real talent, I bet." Isaac leaned forward, his coal-black hair flipping over his eyes. "Didn't see us coming, did you brother? Didn't see your lighthouse burning up. Or," he said, chuckling, "your mom..."

"Shut up," Alexander said. It was just above a whisper. He was gripping the chair's armrests. Legs tensing.

"Or what?"

Jacob held up a hand. "Isaac, leave him alone. I think he's had a bad week."

"Awww." Isaac leaned back and put his feet on his twin's chair. "Suck it up, little brother. It only gets worse from here."

Alexander gave them both a glare, full of hate. "Stop it. Don't talk to me anymore."

His grin widening, Isaac shrugged at Jacob. "Another threat, brother. I don't think we like his tone."

Alexander leaned forward. "I've already killed a man during this 'bad week'. Don't push me."

Jacob and Isaac both stared at him. "You?" Isaac cut off his laugh when he saw Alexander wasn't backing down.

"Shot him in the head," Alexander continued. He never blinked.

Jacob's mouth hung open until Isaac slapped him on the shoulder. "Huh. Maybe we should give that a look-see. Make sure the brat's not lying."

Jacob nodded.

"Besides," said Isaac, "it would be cool to see someone get shot in the skull." He gave Alexander a begrudging look of modest respect.

"You ever killed anyone?" Alexander asked, still feeling cocky even though his heart was thundering. His ears popped again, and he winced with the sharp pain.

Jacob looked down, but Isaac smiled and rubbed his hands together. "May 5th, last year. Seattle. Check it out while we're checking you out."

Alexander met Jacob's eyes, and the silent twin gave a slight shake of his head in warning. His lips moved, forming the word "Don't…"

Alexander trembled, tried to listen to the advice but it was too late.

Some kind of ceremony, people with robes and holding candles. A dark, shadowy chamber, with a circular—or octagonal—rim of marble pillars and some kind of black altar in the center. A man wearing silver shackles and a white robe with lunar designs on it topples over as the crowd of ram-headed spectators cheer.

Two boys stand over the gagged man who's bleeding from his skull as the boy—a leering, dancing youth dressed in red and wearing a horned mask— dances on his feet; he's holding a gold-tipped spear, preparing for another jab.

The captive tries to wriggle away, but there's some kind of barbed-wire netting caught around his legs and pinning back his arms. A thrust, and the golden point comes back red after puncturing the man's lungs, between two ribs.

Another cheer, and then a man with a familiar cane steps out of the shadows. "Very good. Now it's your brother's turn to finish the battle."

The boy lowers his head and grudgingly hands the lance over to the other boy, who reluctantly takes it.

"Finish the re-enactment," Calderon urges, raising his cane as the multitude begins to hum and chant incomprehensible syllables.

Feeling the eyes of everyone upon him—especially those of his brother—the boy steps up, raising the spear with both trembling hands. He meets the agonized eyes of the sacrifice. Chooses his spot, hoping for a clean kill, and closes his eyes before he wills his arms to strike.

A gasp and a shrieking cry of pain.

Laughter.

Isaac's mask is off, and he's barely able to contain his glee, pointing...

The spear point is stuck in the captive's breastplate, just under the throat. He's missed the heart completely.

Jacob lets go, turns and drops to his knees. Bile rushes up out of his mouth, soaking the floor. Calderon shakes his head, then nods to Isaac who moves in. He puts his foot on the captive's chest, pulls out the lance, then quickly drives it in, lower and to the right, spearing the heart and ending the man's cries.

Jacob crawls away, into the shadows where he curls up, safe in the darkness.

Alexander lurched back in his seat with a sudden jolt. Turbulence.

Isaac was back in his seat, cross-legged. Eyes closed. Remote-viewing with a smile on his face. But Jacob looked ashen, staring at Alexander. "You saw...?"

Nodding, Alexander glanced away, out the window to the snowy terrain rising up to meet them. "Why... what was that?"

"A re-enactment," Jacob whispered. "Marduk and Tiamat. The whole planetary war thing. Everyone has to do it, our stepdad said. And... it was supposed to prepare us for what we needed to do."

"What—to kill a lot of people?"

Jacob gave a weak nod.

"But you... you're not like your brother." Alexander took a breath, and with it, found some hope. "This doesn't have to happen. You can help us."

Jacob shook his head. "It's already done. It's over."

"No," said Alexander. "Our dad's still out there. He'll figure out a way. He'll stop this."

Jacob looked down, then back to where Calderon had just now opened his eyes. He was exhaling calmly, but his eyes shone with an emerald tint. "I'm not sure I want to. You don't understand what we can become..."

"What?"

"Don't you get it? It's what we were meant to be. It's what we were promised."

Alexander frowned, trying to remember his dad's lessons. The stories and myths.

With a little enthusiasm returning to his voice, Jacob said: "We'll be gods."

"I'm a kid," Alexander said quietly, fixing Jacob with a cold stare. "That's all I want to be."

Calderon slipped the tablet back in the leather case on top of the translation tablets, then raised his cane and nudged Xavier, who didn't move. His eyelids were rapidly flickering.

"Look sharp, boys!" Calderon called. "The HAARP facility is standing ready for us. We're landing in ten minutes. And then…" He turned his gaze out the window, looking out of over the expanse of the polar realm, and Alexander imagined he considered himself observing the whole world.

A grunt, then a familiar voice filled the cabin.

"Don't celebrate yet," said Xavier. He was blinking, rubbing his eyes. "I just popped in on my half-brother."

Alexander saw Calderon's shoulders tense. He gripped the cane with both hands. "And?"

Xavier flashed Alexander a smile of reassurance. "And it seems, dear Caleb has found it."

"No… Nina should have stopped him by now."

A shake of his head, and then Xavier gave a light chuckle. "Seems old flames have been rekindled. And Lady Liberty has given up her deepest secret."

"The spear…" Calderon almost choked on the word, then reached for his cell phone.

Xavier nodded. "Yes, call in your troops. Alert Homeland Security, and hope he hasn't already booked a flight. Because he's got it."

Alexander's heart was pounding, his throat tight with excitement and hope.

"And," Xavier continued, "he's coming for you."

BOOK THREE
Myth and Marvel

1.

Caleb didn't relax until they were over the Rocky Mountains and the majestic range loomed out the windows, presenting an imposing sight, rising tall and proud. Finding comfort in their strength, as if they offered protection from any pursuers, he leaned back, clutching the satchel to his chest as he exhaled.

On the seat across from him, Nina smiled. She hadn't taken her eyes off him since they'd sat down, making him nervous. He wondered what those cat-like jade eyes were seeing. Was she regretting her decision to come with him, to turn against Calderon and their boys? *And was she even sincere?* That was the bigger question, and Caleb had spent the past six hours nervously looking over his shoulder.

Back in New York City, Caleb had called Phoebe and had their new friends provide transportation, a jet fueled and piloted by one of Temple's trusted men. Despite fears of a last-minute assault on the runway, they took off and traveled quickly and without interruption.

Refusing to speak to her just yet, Caleb closed his eyes.

"Rest," he heard her say. "You'll need it."

He gave a nod, but that was all. His mind was already drifting, losing its grip on reality, bumping and shifting visions with the turbulence.

A flash of city streets, mobbed with cheering people as a familiar man stands on a balcony, framed by huge red banners, displaying the Nazi swastika. He's shouting, raising his fists defiantly to the churning clouds above, while down by his legs, out of sight, rests a narrow case, open, revealing a gleaming metallic shard inside.

Another rumble, the jet dipped.

Caleb's eyes stayed closed. And dimly, he nudged his consciousness along... *Show me what they were planning.*

And the theater in his mind dissolved, replaced with: *a vast tunnel, a yawning cavern. Frosted, gleaming with enormous icicles. A team of twenty men in parkas and heavy woolen hoods, brandishing flashlights as well as sub-machine guns, red armbands proudly displaying the same swastika. They advance slowly, toward a smooth wall with a similar design, much larger and carved with deep precision. The rectangular wall section is guarded by a pair of ram-headed sphinxes that stand crookedly on the uneven ground.*

One man steps forward and unwraps something long and narrow from a cloth bundle.

"Our fuehrer will be pleased," he whispers to the nearest man, who merely snorts.

"We don't do this for him. But for us, for the true masters of this world."

"You think they will notice us?"

"With the spear in our possession? They must. Everything we've learned, what the mystics told us... They've been seeking this, and now it is ours to offer up to them."

The man with the lance nods, lowers his head and raises it up toward the door. "This then will be the key that opens their realm—their secrets—to us."

The others bow their heads and drop to one knee.

And they wait.

And wait.

Until the man's arms get tired and he can barely hold up the artifact any longer.

"What are they waiting for?" he whispers to his companion.

The other man, his eyes narrowed under ice-flecked eyebrows, shakes his head. "Maybe we're not yet worthy."

The spear lowers. "We did not yet come as victors."

"The war goes badly."

"We must win first. Conquer."

"Purify."

Both men stand, and as the spear again is wrapped in its cloth, they turn their eyes from the door, from the ram-headed guardians.

"We will return when we've succeeded."

Caleb stirred. Something was happening. Not there in the vision, but-

"F-18s!" the pilot's voice shouted over the intercom. "Claiming we're violating FAA directives. Forcing us to land."

Caleb looked outside. They were over water.

"Where are we?"

"You slept long enough," Nina snapped. "We circled Seattle, and are flying up the coast. Thought it best to avoid complications, but apparently that didn't work."

"Get Temple," Caleb yelled. "Ask him to–"

"Already tried. He's working it, but his orders are being countermanded."

Calderon.

"He knows," Nina said, gripping the back of the chair in front of her. She shot Caleb a worried look. "The boys… I'm a liability right now. They can latch onto me easily, find me anywhere."

"We have to land," the pilot called back. "Or they're promising to shoot us out of the sky."

"He'll do it," Nina said.

"But the Spear-?"

"He must know you have it. Even if the explosion doesn't destroy it, it's likely that no one will find it in this wilderness. At least not until Calderon's done what he plans to do."

Caleb nodded. "So what do we do?"

"I think I can get you over the border," the pilot called back, veering sharply then, skimming low over the rugged ice-capped hills. "Then the Canadians will move to intercept. I doubt they'll take kindly to our boys zipping over there, terrorist threat or not."

"Then what?" Nina asked.

The speakers crackled. "Then I'll be forced to turn back and I'll be escorted to the nearest base. But maybe there's another way." Caleb saw that the pilot was leaning to his left, staring down, then checking something on the radar.

"What is it?" Nina asked, then moved into the cockpit to take a look. Movement on his right: another plane dropped into view, close enough that Caleb could see the helmeted pilot inside, turning toward him. He could see the missiles locked under the wing.

Nina came back with a mischievous grin on her face. "We have to act fast."

Caleb stared at her as he stood up and tried to balance as the plane tipped,   banked   then   dipped   away   from   their uninvited guest.

"What?" He had a sinking feeling in his gut, and not just from the sudden drop in altitude.

Nina went to a compartment, reaching inside. "The pilot assures us he can get us right above it."

"Above what?" Caleb shook his head before he even found what she was looking for. "No..."

Nina   got   up   unsteadily   and   slipped   something   around her shoulders.

Caleb said, "No, please tell me we're not..."

"Yes," Nina said, heading toward the cabin after strapping in the parachute. "We're going to jump out of a perfectly good airplane."

They dove out together, with Caleb hugging onto Nina for dear life. He was facing her, arms and legs wrapped tightly around her slender body, fingers interlocked under her parachute. He hoped he wasn't screaming during the descent, but even hours later, he couldn't recall. It was all a terrifying blur, with nothing but the terrifying certainty that the chute wouldn't going to open and that he would die with his former lover, slamming into the ocean without even seeing it rise up to meet him.

He had a view of their jet, banking around and heading back—just as something streaked out of the blue, and the cockpit erupted with a fire that split the plane down the middle, scattering its skeleton in all directions. Something soared over the falling debris, and then Nina angled her body, spread her arms and seemed to fly sideways, floating on air currents, spinning...

Caleb nearly passed out when he glimpsed a huge piece of the smoking wing drop past where they had just been. He looked up into Nina's eyes, where he saw a touch of amusement.

"You're enjoying this!" he yelled, but if she heard, she didn't respond. Her eyes were focused on something else. And when Caleb turned his head, he couldn't see anything except the stretch of blue, capped with streaks of white, and then just miles and miles of shoreline.

"We're looking good!" Nina shouted, and pointed straight down to something Caleb at first couldn't make out. Just the act of turning his head and trying to get his bearings during free fall made his stomach lurch, and he wondered how revolted she would be if he was sick all over her right now.

Then he saw it: a rectangular shape below them, white against the Pacific blue. It was getting bigger and bigger. In moments, he could make out other shapes and colors on the rectangle: sections of green, white and smaller bluish rectangles.

"You're kidding me!"

Nina shifted her weight and took them on a trajectory ahead of the object, which was now expanding in his vision. He could see orange along the sides, and tiny forms strolling on the deck.

"Yes honey," said Nina as she ripped the cord. "We're taking a cruise."

It wasn't a bad landing, all things considered. After the chute opened Caleb felt as if he'd tear through the straps and go plummeting away from Nina on his own, but he held on, and he saw she was steering—with two straps and handles. Bearing them one direction, then the other, riding the winds, circling around and coming down fast toward the cruise ship. He kept silent, heart in his throat until it looked as if they were way off target and would miss the stern or at best, land on the smokestack, but then an updraft caught them, Nina tugged hard on the left strap and banked them around. They circled over the chimney, then shot over the heads of tourists wearing sweaters and scarves, a few brave souls in the hot pool shielding their eyes to watch what they believed was a cruise-publicity stunt.

And then they set down, right in the middle of the putting green. They scrambled, and Caleb teetered off balance, taking Nina with him, tumbling and getting tangled up in the ropes and the chute—until the fake rock wall stopped their progress with a jarring halt.

"Where... did you learn that?" Caleb asked as they extricated themselves from the mess of fabric and ropes and tethers.

"Montross," she replied. "He insisted I train with him. Hang gliding, parachuting, steering. Said you never knew when you might need to leap out of a plane and land on something."

"Sounds like he might have *seen* this."

"Exactly, which is why I went along with it. Now, come on. I'm sure security's on its way."

They stood up to the cheers of a large crowd below, surrounding the pool. People were snapping pictures, filming with camcorders and phones. Nina raised her hand and did a mock bow. "Play along," she whispered to Caleb. Then, kicking off the last of the ropes and smoothing back her hair, she leapt over the side, tugging Caleb along behind her.

He jumped too, and just as he caught a glimpse of men in blue running up the far stairs, he landed and dove into the crowd with Nina, high-fiving a few people, then pushing through and making for a side door. They were through, and into a cafeteria teeming with people in line and at their tables, gorging on lunch. Nina took Caleb's hand and he felt a sudden surge of power, a tugging of a vision, but urgency squashed any connection. Under his shirt, strapped to his back, the shard of strange metal –the spear—seemed to vibrate and thrum. It felt warm, almost hot. Itchy, and for a desperate moment he feared he'd have to strip off his shirt and rip it free, giving away their location; but as soon as she pulled her hand away, it subsided and again felt cool.

He glanced back, but saw that the security men were whipping their heads around, trying to see anyone out of place. The rest of the crowd had moved on, back to their sightseeing and roaming the decks, lining up for the driving range or the rock climbing station, the previous excitement forgotten.

A dish was thrust in his hand, and then he and Nina were on the far side of the buffet line, nodding to an older couple and heaping fruit onto their plates beside their cold cuts.

"We're safe," she whispered.

"For now," Caleb said. "But we could just let them take us to the captain, then call Colonel Temple."

"Not yet," Nina said. "Better to blend in. If my guess is correct, this ship just set sail from Vancouver on the first leg of the popular Alaskan Inside Passage tour. Next stop, tomorrow morning, will be Juneau where we can get out on the shore excursion. Rent a jeep and head overland to Gacona."

"Tomorrow," Caleb said, looking at the line of food as his stomach grumbled. Mimosas, coffee, heaps of scrambled eggs and sausage and fresh-baked rolls. "What do we do until then?"

Nina piled food onto her plate. "Why darling, we enjoy the cruise."

2.

Mount Shasta

After Temple had finished up the presentation, he had Diana take Aria aside to debrief her. Then he turned to his other guests. Phoebe and Orlando had moved in closer to the wall-length screens, studying the pictures of Mars.

"Okay then," Phoebe said after tearing her eyes away and blinking as if to rid her irises of the grainy Martian sands. "I guess we know our objective."

Orlando grinned at the screen. "Big Red. The God of War, Ares to the Greeks, Mars for the Romans, and..."

"Knock it off," Phoebe quipped. "You're not my brother."

"No," Temple said, "but you'll do just fine. Orlando, I'd like you to go and assist the Dove in his search. Both of you together should be able to crack this thing, get around those shields and see what's really down there."

"You mean Google Mars isn't accurate?"

Temple rolled his eyes. "Please." He turned to Phoebe. "I won't even get into the layers of disinformation and out-right data manipulation, but in all honesty, despite a few badly eroded surface monuments, what's really of interest is, I believe, *under the surface.*" He turned to Phoebe. "I'd ask you to go too, but I'd spare you what could be rather... awkward company."

Phoebe nodded. "Thanks. I gather he doesn't see many girls on a day to day basis."

"Not in the flesh, no."

Orlando clapped his hands. "All right, I'm off to see the Dove. Or as I would have called him–"

"Please don't say it," Phoebe begged, shaking her head.

"-Big Bird."

Orlando chuckled to himself and headed out, while Phoebe rolled her eyes at Temple. "See what I have to live with?"

Temple managed a smile. "Now, for you. I'd like you to-"

His phone chirped. "Hang on a sec."

But as he reached for it, Phoebe swooned and had to grab the nearest table edge. She looked up sharply just as his eyes met hers and he spoke into the phone. "Talk to me."

He nodded, then again. Then said: "When was this? Okay, get me a secure channel to Eielson Air Force base. Commander Maxwell. Have him call me back in three minutes."

When Temple disconnected the call, Phoebe searched his eyes. "My brother! I saw him!"

He studied her carefully. "Where?'

Phoebe almost choked on the word. "Falling." She swallowed hard. "From a plane."

Temple nodded, his face grim. "They were shot down just north of Vancouver Island."

"And...?" Phoebe's heart was racing. "What else did you hear? Because I saw nothing! They were falling towards something below, on the water, something..." She rubbed her head. "I don't know! Then it all just went blue again!"

"Blue? You're sure?"

"Do I look like I'm kidding?"

"No, but that I don't understand."

"What?"

"I believe they fell together, or they jumped out of the plane before it was attacked."

"They? Who do you mean?" Phoebe blinked, then winced as she eyes closed for a second. "Nina! It was her I saw falling before him."

"Yes, it was her plane. She may have been taking him to HAARP."

Phoebe frowned. "I... don't think so. That's not the sense I had. Plus, they were shot down, and not by your guys, right?"

"Right, which I suppose indicates that Nina may have had a change of heart."

Phoebe looked down. "Still don't trust that bitch." Her eyes lifted. "But you think they survived?"

"If you can't see them, then it might mean something else is acting in their vicinity. Something that's clouding your sight."

Phoebe blinked, then glanced over Temple's shoulder, to the side area where Aria sat talking to Diana.

"Something," Phoebe said, focusing on the NASA scientist, "that might be powerful enough to keep them hidden—and maybe even safe."

Orlando knocked, softly at first, then a little louder. Shrugged, then pushed his way inside. After a moment, his eyes adjusted to the darkness, and then... a squeaking, and the great bulk that was the Dove turned in his massive ergonomic chair.

"Ah, so it's to be babysitting duty, is it?"

"Uh," Orlando stammered. "That colonel guy said I'm supposed to help out here."

The Dove let out a belch. His eyes, serious and dark, focused on Orlando for an uncomfortable moment. Then he brushed crumbs off his bulging gut, grinned and pointed to a plain-looking metal chair in the corner. "Pull up a seat, amigo. Let's see what we can see."

Orlando nodded, wrinkling his nose at the smell of Cheezits, and stepped over a collection of Hostess Twinkie wrappers. "Okay, so it must be the maid's day off?"

"Cute." The Dove clicked some buttons on the arm of his chair and the giant screen on the far wall flickered to life. And The Face came into focus, stopping Orlando in his tracks. "Never seen it that big, have you?"

"Or in that much detail. I thought we didn't have these kind of images. And the last one was all kinds of fuzzy. Looked like crap."

"Exactly like some weather-eroded three hundred million year old mountain would expect to look, right?"

Orlando nodded. He reached the chair and started dragging it back as The Dove clicked and moved a joystick, and the image zoomed in on the Face's left eye. "Of course they don't show you the good stuff, the stuff they can't understand. Everything else—everything released out to the world and to Google—all clever manipulations. Like you've probably heard from now, certain people in certain positions have known for years that something was out there long ago. Something that apparently hasn't stuck around."

"Or else it got blown up long ago."

The Dove's huge head nodded. Beads of sweat cascaded down his cheeks like he'd just come in out of a rainstorm. "That's the thought, except we all know that just like when you try to wipe out a bees' nest, you never get them all. Some are out gathering stuff or just buzzing around, and they're the ones that then go into hiding, waiting out the eons."

Orlando sat down and looked at his empty hands, then glanced around the room. "Got a spare Tablet?"

"Nope."

"Pad of paper?"

"Negative."

"Napkin and crayons?"

Another shake of the massive head. "Just take a deep breath, focus on the eye there, and go to work."

Orlando sighed. "So it's going to be that kind of day. Demoted to the Dark Ages." He crossed his arms, lowered his head and tried not to breathe through his nose. One last peek at the rounded dark cavity on the screen, and then he closed his eyes.

And...

Nothing.

Sighing, he kept focusing, thinking about Mars, about all that red stone, about the dust, and the winds. But something kept interfering. At first he expected the blue screen, even felt it converging a few times as his mind's eye attempted to descend into the Face's eye. Then he'd pull back and try another angle, another route. He tried focusing on recent lunar missions. *The Martian Pathfinder, the Rover. The probes...*

All that technology, he zeroed in on each one in turn, but in turn he was shot down by the screen of blue.

"Not doing so hot, are you?" Came the Dove's voice. Orlando ignored him. Kept focusing, but the Dove's heavy breathing and raspy, almost snore-like breaths were breaking his focus.

"Trying, but can't get in through the eye. Are you sure-?"

"Keep at it, amigo." A raspy snort. "I assure you, something wicked-cool is down there. It'll blow your mind."

A few more minutes, then… Finally, Orlando shook his head. He was about to open his eyes when another particularly obnoxious grunt from the Dove sent Orlando's thoughts on a tangent.

His mind reached out tangentially to the sound, locked onto the Dove for a second and was sent spiraling off in a new direction, and all Orlando could do was hang on for dear life.

Flying around Mt. *Shasta, the snow-capped peaks, the dizzying precipices and sharp cliffs. Day turns to night, stars burn fiercely in the black night, then spin as the point of view circles the mountain, faster and faster.*

Then: angelic lights sparkle below, snapshotting shadows past the icy ridges. Orbs that start off as golden spheres, then transform through the color chart, turning silver, crimson, turquoise, violet... The spinning stops and the lights flicker, then form a line and blast through the mountain wall, all except the last one, the violet-shimmering globe that sweeps past and collects the vision-

- and draws it inside, then propels forward. Straight at, and through the ice-blocked mountain wall.

A brief shimmer of Blue, a protective shield that closes, then scatters in the wake of the violet ball.

And Orlando's in.

He's done it: found a back way inside, past the great unbreakable door, to the very heart of the mystery.

The Dove licked the vanilla icing off his fingers, then turned to regard his guest. Orlando's head lolled to one side, his body slumped almost to the point of falling off the chair. His eyelids flickered rapidly.

Wiping his hands on the front of his shirt, then on his pant legs, The Dove reached down under the right armrest. His fingers moved around, searching, searching. All the while, his attention didn't leave Orlando.

Under the chair's arm, he finally found it—a section of duct tape securing a .357 Magnum.

Inside the mountain.

The viewpoint magnifies, roars through crystalline tunnels. Gleaming walls of quartz and topaz, pillars of emerald, into a vast a chamber where the other colored orbs settle into alcoves, sparkle, fizzle, then fade into the surrounding shadows, revealing singular riders—*robed, bald men and women who, heads bowed, retreat into tunnel-like structures.*

Viewpoint shifts.

This orb's parking space. After the light fades, a robed man (or woman?) exits. His/her bald head from behind is indeterminate, and the shadowy quartz walls do little to illuminate any features.

Follow.

In darkness, a long corridor, finally emerging into a chamber, plain walled...

Empty, but for a single machine. A reclining seat not unlike the one Orlando has just left, except more elaborate. More... comfortable. It's on a track, a track leading forward into another glittering tunnel.

The figure moves to a wall, touches it and presses her (it's definitely a her) forehead against the smooth quartz surface. As if activated by her mind, an image appears. It's the Stargate complex interior. Phoebe and Temple are talking quietly in the main room.

Viewpoint changes: back to that lone chair. Moving in, closer.

Closer

Something out of place.

Something... left on the floor.

A piece of crumpled plastic. Lettering on the outside.
A wrapper.
With an unmistakable imprint.

"Twinkies!" Orlando shouted, his eyes flying open.

He leapt out of the chair—then froze, staring at the hefty gun gripped in the Dove's unwavering hand, and pointed right at his heart.

The huge head shook slowly back and forth as beads of sweat fell unnoticed off the chin. The Dove made a clucking sound with his tongue.

"They said you were good, so I didn't really have any choice."

"You're working with them?" Orlando was still trying to process everything. "They've taken you beyond the wall."

"What can I say? Apparently I'm the chosen one."

"Or the fool." Orlando cleared his throat while inching ahead. "Or maybe the *tool* is more like it. What do they want you for?"

The head continued to shake. "Uh-huh. No, don't think I'll blab about it, not while others could snoop. Sorry, but you'll die without answers."

Orlando lunged just as the gun fired.

In their suite, spacious as far as cruise accommodations went, Nina sprawled out on the bed, kicked off her shoes and pulled up a map on her smartphone.

"Okay, the next stop is at Juneau. We can charter a plane from there and–"

"No more planes," Caleb said, groaning. He was at the desk, bent over the spear point. Two lamps trained their lights on its surface, and Caleb reverently lifted it, one side up at a time, studying the markings. Every nick and scratch, every line of etched markings.

"Fine," Nina said. "Although parachuting out over HAARP would be a hell of a lot easier than the driving close and then having to ditch the vehicle and hoof it through the ice and snow."

"Stealthy approach is what we need."

"But we've got *that.* Surely-"

"Surely it can't stop the whole arsenal available to such a heavily guarded installation."

Nina shrugged. Turned over and arched her back in a long stretch. "Have it your way. I'm starting to think you just want to spend more time with me."

Caleb gave her an acid stare.

"Come on," Nina chided. "Now that you know we've created life? Brought not one, but two children into the world?"

Caleb stared at the spear, shaking his head.

"Come on," Nina repeated. "I know that's what did it for you and Lydia."

Caleb's eyes closed.

"She backstabbed you just as good and hard as I did, yet you took her back with open arms once she showed you pictures of little Alexander, the son you never knew you had."

"That was different."

"Was it?" She rolled onto her stomach now, then pivoted on the bed so she was facing him, chin cradled in her hands. "She was following orders from her Keeper father, following the rules. Playing you to get what they wanted. How was I any different?"

Caleb's right hand settled on the lower edge of the spear; his fingers curled around it in a tight grasp and his lips trembled. He was about to turn when—

KNOCK.

They both froze, met each others' eyes, then looked to the door. Another knock.

Nina was up in a flash, digging into her purse and retrieving her silver-plated Beretta. Finger to her lips, she approached the door. Caleb followed at a distance, the spear still in his shaking hand.

I don't feel anything, he thought, imagining there should have been a magnetic sensation, a vibrational interface. Something like Frodo's dagger glowing in the presence of goblins.

"What is it?" Nina called out, while eying the viewing hole.

From the other side of the door came a gruff young voice. "Delivery."

Nina frowned, glancing back to Caleb, who was shaking his head. He whispered: "No one knew we were here, and this room was vacant. Don't open it."

But Nina was already unlocking the door. She slid the gun into her waistband behind her back and opened the door partway. Caleb saw the young man outside, dressed as a ship's bellhop, holding a square box, which Nina promptly snatched out of his hands.

She dug into her pockets, but the bellhop backed away. "No need for a tip, just doing my job. And frankly, we're all a little relieved down in the mail room."

"What for?" she asked.

The bellhop looked around nervously. "Well, strange thing about this delivery…"

Caleb noticed now that the box was wrapped up tight with non-descript brown delivery paper, but covered excessively with yellow wrapping tape.

"…it was dropped off at our cruise director's office three years ago. Addressed to this here room number, but—and here's where it got really weird—instructions were that it wasn't to be delivered until this date, which was, as I said—"

"Three years later," Nina robotically answered. She gently shook the box, eyeing it from different angles.

"Yup," said the bellhop, edging out of sight. "Apparently paid quite a sum for the instructions to be followed directly, and claimed he'd know if we didn't do as he said. And he'd know if we opened the box."

Nina looked at him. And the bellhop shifted back into view, eyeing the box, then Nina. "I uh, well... some of us, we wondered what's in there. And well, the fact that this room only today got sold was weird enough, and well..."

Nina slammed the door on him. Locked it and turned around, facing Caleb. She hefted the box.

Caleb raised the spear. "Need a box cutter?"

They sat on the bed, the box between them.

"Is this smart?" Caleb asked, spear point poised over a seam.

"What, using a priceless ancient artifact to open a delivery box, or just the fact that we're even considering opening it at all?

"Yes," Caleb said, trying to be confidently humorless. "And you know as well as I, that we're far too curious as to who sent this, and what it is."

"Go ahead," Nina said, nodding. "Although I think we can already guess as to *who* sent it."

Caleb started sawing, gently slicing through tape and cardboard, freeing one side, then the next. "You're thinking it's from Montross."

Nina smiled. "And if so, it can only mean that he saw something. Saw that-"

"We'd be here at this time."

"And," Nina continued as Caleb set down the spear, parted the cardboard and paper folds and reached inside with both hands, "that we'd need whatever it is that's inside there."

With some effort, Caleb lifted the object, just about the size of a bowling ball, and held it up to the light. Held it up so both he and Nina could admire its intricate gold and silver inlays, its detailed carved symbols unlike any language they'd ever seen.

He turned it around and around, open-mouthed until finally, he set it on the bed.

"Apparently it's a wedding gift," Nina said. "Otherwise, I have no idea."

"I was wrong before," Caleb whispered. "About the Spear being the most ancient, priceless artifact in the world. Hell, it doesn't even fit that description for this room."

"So you're saying...?"

"Whatever this is, I glimpsed two things while I was holding it."

Nina met his eyes, then suddenly reached forward and grasped his hand. Caleb moaned, fell forward towards her and suddenly her lips were there, pressing fiercely against his. His mind was rocked, his senses flattened. Something passed quickly from his mind to hers, and just as quick–the kiss, the connection–was severed.

She was on her feet, holding her head, shaking it.

"A ranch in Montana. A beat up old tractor hauling up the fossilized bones of a triceratops..." She rubbed her eyes, even as Caleb, through his reddened ones, watched her with begrudging admiration. "Men in suits taking away that... thing... that had been inside the dinosaur's ribcage. Took it... to the Smithsonian..."

"Where," Caleb said, continuing the vision, "it languished in the forbidden archives until one Xavier Montross conned a beautiful employee to grant him access."

"He stole it," Nina whispered. "And the girl... I've seen her before. Xavier's never quite forgotten her." A smile formed. "He still... loves her. This... Diana. Diana Montgomery."

Caleb picked up the globe. "Yes, well that may be. But he's done us one solid favor here. No one will find us now, no matter how hard they look."

"Why? What does that thing do?"

Caleb looked up at her. "The Morpheus Initiative spent years searching for Montross after he disappeared from Alexandria, but could never find him. Not even a trace, despite having the best psychics in the world."

Nina just gave him a blank stare until Caleb palmed the globe in his hand like a basketball.

"He's given us a *shield.*"

4.

HAARP Facility - Gacona, Alaska

Alexander waited until his eyes adjusted to the darker interior of the control room before he allowed himself to take a breath. What-ever he was expecting, their entrance to the HAARP facility hadn't been at all as he thought. It was rushed, just a quick ride down a descending ramp, past barbed wire fences beyond which the storming clouds obscured the sky and the mountains, leaving only glimpses of the sentinel-like radar arrays massed upon a field of unyielding ice.

The storm erupted just as they neared the facility, and Alexander had the impression that the station was alive, brimming with its own weather system, occluding itself with a mantle of impenetrable snow and ice. The winds swirled cyclonically, and the snowflakes seemed to be the size of baby rabbits, racing hell-bent around in a maelstrom.

And as much as the exterior was obscured, the interior was excessively bright. White walls, stainless steel doors and railings. Powerful lamps at every turn and glaring overhead bulbs seared at his eyes, eliciting smirks from his half-brothers, gliding ahead on their skateboards.

Isaac circled around and glided up on the other side of Alexander. "Don't worry yourself about the tour," he said in almost a gleeful whisper. "We won't be here long enough to enjoy it, not us. Not you. Right, brother?"

Jacob's skateboard slowed to a crawl, letting Alexander catch up. "Leave him be," Jacob said. "Had a hard day, he has."

"A hard couple of days, I'd say," Isaac said. "Wandering in lost mausoleums and catacombs, getting shot at, avoiding deadly traps. Oh, and nearly buried alive under the ruins of the twice ruined Library of Alexandria!"

Alexander winced, looked down at his feet and clenched his fists.

"How tired you must be!" Isaac taunted, now from the other side, still riding circles around him. And even Jacob broke down, joining his twin in a little chuckle.

"Boys!" Calderon's voice cut through the laughter. "Knock it off, we're almost at the control room."

"Just having a little fun, righto?"

Calderon leaned heavily on his cane, stamping it hard on the floor with every new step. And in his shadow, proceeding the two armed guards, Xavier Montross followed, head down. His red hair was in tangles over his face, still with the dust from the Cheops' labyrinth trapped in the curls. He looked up once while Alexander glanced back, and they shared a mutual exchange: *Hang in there,* Montross seemed to say.

But when Alexander turned, he saw the two twins gliding together, making figure eights down around each other, across a huge circular floor and toward the waiting guards at a set of double steel reinforced doors, and his hopes fled.

This is it. And Alexandria was just the beginning. Montross is going to help them achieve his vision of the world's destruction, and Dad –

He stopped, closed his eyes and *focused.* Drove his mind like a spike through time and space. *Dad!*

An arm on his shoulder pulled his vision away from a swirling pool of turquoise, complete blue in all directions. Alexander turned, and the hooded, owl-like eyes of Mason Calderon bored into his brain, and for a heart-stopping moment, Alexander feared Calderon could slip inside his mind and see what he himself couldn't. That he could find Alexander's father, and then it would all be over. His one, last chance. The only hope.

For all of us.

"What'd you go looking for, boy?"

Jacob and Isaac braked their skateboards, then kicked them up together, ending the ride. Alexander saw them out of the corner of his eye, but couldn't pull away from Calderon's gaze. "I…"

"Oh, leave him alone," Montross' voice came from the side, soft as a welcome breeze on a humid day. "Of course he's looking for his father."

Calderon blinked. "And? Did you see him?"

Alexander shook his head slowly. "Nope. I felt… blocked, like a wall was in the way."

Something grumbled in Calderon's throat. "Or a shield?" His eyes darted away, landing on Montross, who just shrugged.

"Doesn't matter, does it?" Montross waved his hand toward the doors, and then pointed to the satchel over Calderon's shoulder. "You have what you need. Caleb and Nina are too far away to be of consequence, your enemies cower in their tunnels, realizing there are no safe havens. The prophecy's fulfillment is mere hours away." He smiled broadly, stretching out his arms. "And you've got me at your side."

Calderon thought for a moment, then gave a slight bow of his head. "True." His grip loosened on Alexander's shoulder, and a gentle push turned him around and sent him toward the doors.

"Inside, now. Time to see what this facility is truly capable of."

Struggling to stay on his feet, still fighting the recurring splotches of blue walls in his mind's vision, Alexander stumbled on ahead after his laughing brothers. Never feeling more alone, or lost. In a daze, he looked up, past the blinding lights, to a railing where armed military personnel patrolled the hallways outside the offices.

And for just a gleaming, hopeful moment, he thought he saw the afterimage of a woman, not unlike his mother, leaning over, smiling at him…

And he clung to that hope with all his strength. That maybe he wasn't so alone after all.

Keeping an eye on Alexander, but feeling at least he was safe for now, Montross entered the control room and found it just as he had envisioned.

"Been here before, I take it?" Calderon was watching Montross' reaction as the doors closed and the great chamber lit up.

"Never in the flesh."

Montross let his eyes roam about, following the thousands of wires, ventilation tubes and piping snaking around the corners, connecting to various refrigerator-sized servers and computer banks. A glass-walled office overlooked the main floor, reached by a platform elevator.

"Of course," Calderon said. "I assumed as much. And we never had the luxury of the Afghans and their Shield. Or, I presume, our friends in the revived Stargate Program, with theirs."

Montross gave him a quick look, then continued his visual tour of the chamber. He took in the apexed ceiling, a hundred feet above, the sheer metal walls inclining to a point, leaving a gap straight above a device on the floor–a massive throne-like contraption that looked like it could fit a person after they had ascended the nine steps into the machine's 'seat'. The arm rests were enormous, and the one on the right supported a pedestal–with a slot wide enough to insert something the size of the Emerald Tablet.

"There it is," Calderon whispered, leaning forward with both hands on his cane. At his back, the twins had gathered, at last showing some reverence. They had left their skateboards outside and now stood, heads bowed as if in prayer.

Isaac glanced sideways, first at Jacob, then past him and behind Montross, where Alexander seemed to be shrinking, trying to find a shadow. "Magnificent, eh brother?"

Jacob couldn't help himself, he was grinning ear to ear. "Think we'll get to try it out?"

"Could be fun," Isaac said. "Me first though. I got me a list of cities I'd like to crush. Like Godzilla, Tokyo will be first. Then, I never liked Paris, so snotty. And..."

Alexander felt a lump in his throat. "No. This has to stop."

Jacob shot him a confused glance, while Isaac merely chuckled. "The sad, motherless crow wants to fight destiny."

"Not destiny," Alexander said softly. "Insanity."

Isaac took a step toward him, hands balling into fists. But Jacob was there in an instant, restraining his twin.

"Boys," snapped Calderon. "Stand aside, and be quiet until you're needed."

After glaring at Alexander, who refused to back down, Isaac turned away and grumbled, "*If* we're needed."

"Now," said Calderon, pivoting on his cane and facing Montross. "To work, my friend. We have an ancient enemy to eradicate. One that has slumbered too long in the glow of false superiority."

Montross kept his attention on the central device, even as he noticed the workers above; through the windows, he could see them getting ready, industriously running about preparing the equipment and calibrating the arrays. "And just how do I fit in? And Alexander? The boys?"

Calderon gave a wolfish smile. "Alexander's here just as insurance. So you don't get any funny ideas of being a hero. My boys... well, if they're needed, if you can't do what we need, then they may step in."

Montross gave a little laugh. "They didn't do so well at Liberty Island, if I recall."

Calderon shrugged. "They came through when needed at Cairo."

"But Alexander succeeded first." Montross sent an admiring look to his nephew, where the boy still looked hopeless and lost by himself, keeping his distance from the central machine.

"So let me guess," Montross continued. "You need me to access the machine and interface with the Emerald Tablet and use its power to enhance this facility's weaponry."

"In a nutshell," Calderon said, stroking his cane's dragon tip. He pointed up at the windows. "First, my team is cracking the code, translating the instructions on the Tablet from the cipher we retrieved, thanks to Thoth and his box of secrets."

Montross sighed, looking up at all that activity. "Then you'll feed the instructions into the machine?"

Calderon shook his head. "Actually, I think we already know what needs to be done. You already know."

"I do?" Montross didn't. Sure, he had seen this facility, seen what the aftermath of this day would cause: the cataclysmic devastation, the eradication of all life on the planet, but he didn't know how. Didn't know exactly how the Tablet would be used. He stared at the machine, at the chair-like structure, suitably fitted to one individual and one Tablet.

Calderon watched his eyes. "You *know*. The Tablet has already worked on you. And on Alexander. You can separate from yourself. And it's in that *phase,* and only in that phase, that the Tablet's true power can be accessed. Tuned to your own astral body, melded and amplified."

Montross nodded slowly, the truth settling in. "So in the spiritual form, someone sits in the chair, and releases the dogs of war. So to speak."

"So to speak." Calderon stretched his arms, and held the cane tight lengthwise. "And then we finish what the Dragon started."

Montross thought for a moment, a hundred questions surging to be let out, but it was Alexander, coming up behind him, that spoke what was foremost on his mind. "What about Mars?"

Calderon rubbed the silver dragon's head, tracing the jagged horns and scaled jaws. "It's all about angles, my dear boy. All about angles." And with that, he approached the machine.

Alexander watched the guy with the white lab coat step off the elevator and come running over to Mason Calderon. He whispered something into the senator's ear, and then showed some numbers and figures on his handheld PDA, a stream of symbols and text.

Calderon nodded rapidly, and then patted the man on his shoulder before sending him back to the elevator. "Ready the array, Dr. Phelps. We'll have a target shortly."

Montross approached the chair. "I don't know about you, but I have no idea how to work this yet. We're not ready."

"That's all right. We have a test scenario first."

Montross raised an eyebrow. He glanced at Alexander, then at the twins, who were smirking to themselves. "I can only guess."

"Why guess?" Calderon asked. "Surely you can figure it out. Or Alexander can see it."

"Your target?" Alexander shot back. "You mean the next place you want to destroy. More buildings to crush, people to kill?"

Isaac made a chuckling sound in his throat. "Just coming attractions."

"Before the main event," said Jacob, with a little less enthusiasm.

"We should have the actual coordinates momentarily from our feathered accomplice in the nest of our woefully under-matched adversaries."

Montross perked up. "You've got a mole in Stargate?"

Calderon smiled. "We have followers everywhere. We could have struck and leveled them much earlier, but we've found it useful to have a viewpoint into our enemy's activities."

"Staying one step ahead," Isaac said. "Righto, father?"

"Righto, as you say." Calderon approached the back of the chair, where there was an LCD screen set on an angled post, and a keyboard. He tapped a few keys, grinning to himself. "Translation is done, my friends. And our scientists are working on calibrating the device, feeding in the new data. Simply… astounding." His eyes rapidly skimmed over the data and the schematics, the formulae. "It's all here!"

"Congratulations," Montross said from the other side. His fingertips traced the armrests, caressing the smooth metal contours, all the way up to the rectangular slot for the Emerald Tablet. "So now you'll have the power of the ancients."

Calderon looked around the side. Met Montross's eyes. "The power of Tiamat and Marduk."

"The power of the universe."

"You're like me, Montross. You can't pass up this chance. You were born special, and now you've been given a chance to rise above the mass of humanity. To become like Marduk, like Thoth even, if you must compare yourself to him."

Montross closed his eyes. "A god."

"Leave your body. Leave this world, travel to a new one."

Montross's eyes opened. "Mars?"

And Calderon smiled. "It's all there, waiting for us. Where the ancients left it."

Montross swooned. There was a flash in his mind—*a desert of blue that suddenly cracked down the middle. Revealing: a glimpse of a monument in the sands, a giant face, and a tunnel-structure below it; a vast complex supported by reinforced pillars. Within the walls: flashing lights, tubes and wires, humming machinery.*

He held his head, shaking it until Alexander came to his side. "Was it—?"

Montross kept his eyes on Calderon, who now appeared very interested.

"Tell me, did you just get a look at our little secret?"

"I saw something down there below the Face. A facility."

"The sacred texts are clear," Calderon said, barely above a whisper. "The caretakers, just a few of them, remained after the War. Maintaining the banks of DNA, the memory tanks and flesh pods. When we need to be corporeal again, bodies will be ready for our arrival."

Calderon had the Emerald Tablet out now, and its glow was fierce. Pulsing, bathing the three brothers in its light, making Montross giddy with anticipation.

"At first," Calderon continued, "it was simply a safeguard. Redundancy in case something happened on the Earth. And there was a precedent, apparently. The meteor, what did in the dinosaurs..."

Montross nodded, but was barely listening. "It's clear now. Wipe out the earth, get rid of the competition. Just like the Tower of Babel or the Flood."

"Except we'll do it right this time. And this time, we—the Gods now—will be reborn anew on the planet that is our birthright."

"Yeah," said Alexander, brazen now, "but then what? It's a desert. No atmosphere, no water. No Fun."

Isaac smirked at him and Jacob just licked his lips.

"Good question," Montross said. "But I don't think Mars is their ultimate destination."

"True." Calderon moved up, then placed the Emerald Tablet over the slot. "It's just a bouncing off point. The stars await—the true birthplace of our race, and we will venture out there, immortal, timeless. Sending out our astral bodies, to which there are no time and space limitations. But first, there is something we must do. One more loose end."

Isaac grinned. "About time. We strike at the lunar base."

"The what?" Alexander asked.

"The far side of the moon," Calderon answered as he lowered the tablet gently into the slot and the machine began to hum "Where the last remnants of Thoth's guard have lingered. Just as a few of Marduk's custodians stayed behind on Mars, so did Thoth leave his faithful on the lunar colony."

"On the far side," Montross whispered.

"Always with its face turned away from Earth," Calderon said. "Protected from telescopes and other prying eyes."

"And from your reach with the HAARP weapon."

Calderon nodded, as he finished inserting the tablet. He stepped back. "But now that we know the formula we have the power to separate from matter and can travel to the Mars facility—"

Alexander got it first. "—Where you can aim from there and strike at the lunar base!"

Isaac jabbed his brother. "God, he's slow. Must've been home-schooled."

Alexander took a step back as the Emerald Tablet disappeared into the slot and the machine trembled, sending vibrations through the floor. Then, it started to glow.

His skin prickled, and he swooned as a shooting pain tore through his skull.

Just as quickly as it came on, the pain was gone.

And he was standing over his body.

Oh my god, oh my god, oh my—

A flash of green light, then *pain,* and he was back.

Phew! Back inside.

On the floor, holding his head. Relieved to be back, but just as certain that he'd just been given an opportunity to save the day—

—and blown it.

5.

Mount Shasta

Phoebe raced out of the control center and rushed down the hall. She thought she'd get there first, but there was already an alarm sounding. Guards raced ahead of her, guns drawn. They took their positions on either side of the door.

"Orlando!" Phoebe shouted, just as Temple and Diana rounded the corner. "I saw a flash back there of a gun. Someone firing at him."

"He was in the room?"

"I don't know, I don't know!" She couldn't think, couldn't focus. Could barely breathe.

They reached the door together, and when Temple tried it and found it locked, he nodded to the larger guard, who promptly entered an override code on the keypad, then threw the door open.

Phoebe pushed inside, wriggling in ahead of the guards, just slipping past Temple's reach as he tried to hold her back.

"Orlando!" Emotions raging as she ran inside, her heart nearly gave out as soon as she saw him on the ground, face down beside the empty chair.

"Phoebe, wait!" Temple called, desperation in his voice. Dimly Phoebe thought he was trying to save her from the worst, but it was too late.

"Damn it, Orlando, don't you be dead, don't die on me here." She dropped to her knees beside him, hands shaking. Touched his shoulder, squeezed it. Then, reached for a pulse.

"I'm sorry," Temple whispered, even as his men spread out, searching the room.

"Sir!" one of them called. "A section of the wall here—it's gone!"

Phoebe whimpered as she touched Orlando's neck. Her fingers shook so badly she couldn't tell if he had a pulse or not. Instead, she smoothed back his hair, leaned down and gave him a kiss. *Works in the Disney movies*, she thought. She bent down. Closed her eyes, heard scrambling feet, men rushing out the room through the newly-discovered exit. She caught a strange but familiar smell: of a cavern underground and a fresh stream, clear and pure air.

Ready to feel his cold skin against her lips, instead she gasped as, with a grunt and a rush of motion, Orlando turned and sat up.

"Where'd they go!?"

Phoebe opened her eyes and as she grabbed Orlando's shoulders she scanned his chest, looking for blood stains and bullet holes.

"I'm fine, I'm fine. Now where's the Dove?" Orlando stood up, taking great heaving breaths as his head whipped about in confusion. He caught sight of Temple, at the strange, arched doorway that had materialized at the side wall beside the view screen. The edges of the arch looked as though they'd been cauterized, blasted through the metal and concrete and seared right through the bedrock into the waiting tunnel.

Temple cleared his throat. "Good to see you still up and about, soldier. Now, before we go blundering in after the Dove, why don't you tell us what happened here?

Orlando scratched his head, and only now noticed Phoebe gaping at him with a mix of relief and anger. "Wait, are those tears?"

"Shut up." She wiped at her eyes. "Saw you get shot, so if you're from Krypton you better start explaining."

Orlando swallowed hard. "All right, but I'm not sure you'll believe me."

"You kidding?" Temple asked. "After what you guys have been through, what we've seen? About the only thing I don't believe in is the Tooth Fairy. But even that, I remain open-minded about."

"The Dove had me scanning Mars, looking for an end-around to the shield that's blocking us up there around the Cydonia region."

Phoebe looked closer at him. "And you got it, didn't you?"

Orlando grinned sheepishly. "I got something. I questioned whether I could view someone or something else who knew what was up there. And I saw him."

"The Tooth Fairy?"

"The Dove."

"So he knew," Temple said through gritted teeth, drawing the conclusion ahead of Orlando's schedule. "Son of a bitch."

"Knew, and apparently had been dealing with your friends behind the door."

"What?!" Both Phoebe and Temple said it at once.

"Yeah," Orlando said hurriedly, as he stepped over to the chair and picked up a Twinkie. "Breakfast of champions. Saw a wrapper in my vision, inside Mt. Shasta. I followed one of those glowing orb-UFO-like deals inside."

"Foo fighters, we call 'em," Temple said. "Track 'em sporadi-cally, couple times a year they come out, but they never make contact, and before we can engage, they're either gone or back in the mountain."

Orlando nodded. "Anyway, I saw another one of these chairs. The Dove's been down there, a special guest apparently. That's when I came out of the vision, and that's when he pulled a gun and shot me."

"I knew it!" Phoebe said, and again looked at his undamaged chest. "You are from Krypton."

"No, but apparently the Dove overestimated his allies."

"What do you mean? And hurry," Temple urged. "My men are itching to go after him, and I'm itching to see what's down this tunnel."

"He shot me," Orlando said, "but I don't know how to describe it except to say that time just stopped. The bullet hung in the air a foot from my chest. I couldn't move, I was stuck in mid lunge for the Dove, and he was frozen with this crap-eating grin on his big face as he pulled the trigger. But then..."

"Then," Phoebe whispered, "you saw one of them. The Custodians."

"Yeah, them." Orlando took a deep breath. "A bald guy with deep black eyes. Unnerving as hell. His head was huge, and at first I thought, holy crap it's an alien. But he was tall, and wore a brown robe like some Franciscan monk. And he moved. Damn, did he move. Fast and jerky, like in one spot then the next without even taking a step. Like stop-motion film. I noticed the wall, disintegrated. And then this bald dude with big black eyes like I said, he was there. Staring into the Dove's eyes and shaking his head sadly."

"Then what?" Temple said, still trying to hurry him.

"Then..." Orlando closed his eyes and shuddered. "And this is why there's no hurry looking for the Dove."

"Oh God," Phoebe whispered, and then she saw it too:

The Custodian, from behind. Standing between Orlando and the Dove. First, he plucks the bullet from the air and flicks it with one motion of his finger, sending it sputtering across the room. Then he turns and lays his large palm with its long spindly fingers on the Dove's forehead, covering his eyes. "We gave you insights, opened your mind. Chose you to be the messenger, but instead you traded our secrets to the Great Enemy and worse, you sold out your own kind. And somehow you thought your actions beyond our sight?" The great bald head shook, and—from another shifting viewpoint—the almond-sized eyes turned even darker.

"All those things we would allow, as you are a pure spirit of free will. But we cannot allow the death of this one by your hands. So now we must act."

The hand moved back and the fingers turned inward slowly, as if squeezing a grapefruit, and formed a fist. And the Dove shook, rose off the floor in an outline of fire, then... imploded. His body was rent to shreds, but all self-contained in a central implosion that swallowed up his entire exploding bulk.

And then it was gone, and the Custodian turned. "You have work to do." He placed a finger on Orlando's forehead and said: "Resume."

Phoebe took in a huge gulp of air and returned just as Orlando finished telling the story to Temple.

"... blew him right up in front of me. And then touched my forehead and told me to get back to work. Like I was some slacker."

"Knows you too well," Phoebe said. "But apparently they have plans for you too."

"For both of us."

Phoebe and Orlando stared at each other in wonder, until a returning guard yelled: "Nothing there! Ends in a solid rock wall."

"Of course," Temple said. "So what now?"

Just then, a tiny form entered the room from the hallway.

"Aria?" Phoebe said, immediately turning at the sound.

"Glad you're okay, Orlando," the Hummingbird said. But she was pale, shaking. And Diana appeared behind her momentarily, pushing the wheelchair with her father.

"What's up?" Temple asked, immediately concerned by Diana's expression.

"She got a vision," Diana said. "And it's a doozy."

"We have to get out," Aria said quietly. "Now!"

"What?" Temple's eyes widened.

"They know. The place in Alaska. They're getting ready. The Dove, he told them about us. Told them to strike now."

"Sir," said one of the guards, a walkie-talkie to his ear. "Reports from the watch desk. The lights, the orbs—they're leaving the mountain. *All of them!*"

Aria was shaking, her eyes white. "We have to go, have to go, have to—"

But Phoebe, Orlando and Temple were already running for the door.

6.

HAARP

Xavier Montross knew he only had one shot at this. What that one shot was, however, he had no idea.

He saw that Mason Calderon had entered the machine. A helmet, full of tube-like wires, sensors and goggles, was lowered over his face, and Calderon stretched out his arms to grip the hand rests. The Emerald Tablet flickered and pulsed, the chair vibrated like some expensive mall store novelty for the rich and lazy, and the senator's dragon-head cane, which had been leaning against the chair, slid and fell, then rolled—

—only to be snatched up by Isaac, who raised it up to his face and locked eyes with the dragon.

Montross saw all this in a distracted, yet hyper-aware state. He noted the technicians in the room above, scrambling, entering coordinates. Saw Calderon's lips moving, communicating with the techs, barking orders.

Then Montross saw—or more explicitly—*saw* outside. Through the walls, into the blinding snowstorm where the hulking shadows of the array devices turned, angled, pointed. *Aimed.*

Then, a thousand miles away: a lonely, majestic mountain enjoying its last few moments of peace; multi-colored orbs of light blasting out from invisible pockets in the snowy peaks, hurtling towards elsewhere.

Within: a young girl, asleep. This one, the Shield, and now it's down, with none to take its place. But there, in the next room, a sandy-haired woman, staring at screens and astronomical information on the red planet. Diana! She stops momentarily, looking up, then around as if...

Do you sense me? I'm here, I'm here! But you have to go, have to run. Hear me! Little girl, hummingbird! Tell them, warn them!

She wakes. It's done. And hopefully there's time.

Surging back now, closer. On the ice-swept dunes, roads barely cleared, a black Jeep Cherokee rumbles at full speed, tearing ahead toward Gacona. Inside: two familiar faces. Nina, Caleb. Hurry—

—Montross urged as his mind returned. He glanced up.

There was Calderon, furiously concentrating, aiming, wielding the device as if it was a part of himself, a hideous grin on his face.

Can they stop it? Montross wondered. *Those occupants of the lights? Could they make it here in time, stop the firing sequence?* He doubted it. If they could, surely they would have intervened by now.

Perhaps they weren't powerful enough.

Or perhaps they are, Montross thought. *But they just won't get involved. Instead acting the part of gods wholeheartedly, letting those they watch over truly live or die according to their free will.*

A blur, and Alexander was in motion. But Montross knew his intent, saw it first. The boy, his nephew, was going to attempt to knock Isaac down, take the cane and charge Calderon. Only, it wouldn't work.

An abrupt, shocking image:

Alexander on his back, choking on his own blood, hands over his chest. A look of complete confusion and loss on his face.

Montross wasn't sure if Isaac killed him or if one of the guards intervened to protect the senator, but it didn't matter. Nothing mattered.

Montross might not be able to save the world, but he could at least save one person, someone he had come to care about more than he ever imagined.

He moved, stepping in Alexander's path, then he rushed Calderon.

Three steps away, Montross was sure he'd do it, he'd get in there and twist Calderon's head, snap his neck, rip the Emerald Tablet free and then—

But that was when he felt a sharp prick, and at first thought he got stung by something. With the next step, however, just as Calderon's eyes flashed in surprise, Montross felt a warm splash of liquid. And his left side went numb.

"No!" It was Alexander's voice.

Then a chuckle, and Isaac moved into focus. Holding the cane with a sword point dripping red from its tip. Isaac's grinning face angled down on him as Montross slipped on his own blood, fell to his knees.

Calderon's voice: "Damn fool kid! We need him alive. Alive!"

"He is, dear father. He is."

"Pull through, he will," said Jacob at his other side. But his voice wasn't as confident.

Alexander moved into view, his eyes pleading. "Stay with me, uncle Xavier! Stay."

But Montross could only shake his head. Leaned forward and whispered: "Don't give up. Your father's coming."

And then, as the machine rumbled and sparkled with emerald energy, as Calderon roared uncontrollably with the power he sent out as a conduit, a power surging on a path of destruction toward Mt. Shasta, Montross collapsed.

7.

Outside of Gacona—Twilight

Caleb lowered the binoculars. He shifted on his belly, crept backwards and stood back up when he was out of sight of the HAARP facility. "Can't see anything through the snowfall."

"Not with those eyes," Nina said, watching with amusement as he brushed the snow off his chest. "Try your other skills."

"Try yours. You should be able to zero in on your kids."

"*Our* kids. Plus one of yours." She leaned back against the Jeep Cherokee. "You've got better odds."

"And skill, apparently. Even with my drawbacks."

"Guilt. Self-oppression." Nina snickered. "Do you slap yourself for fun or just wallow in your own loathing?"

"Knock it off and try to help. We've got to get in there, and undetected long enough to use this spear and destroy the Emerald Table before it's used."

"Hopefully they haven't already done it. Those arrays are in motion, from what I can see through the storm."

"Either way, let's go." He started back for the Jeep. "Maybe we just try the brazen frontal assault and see what happens. Maybe the spear will protect us."

Nina laughed. "What's the quote? 'Heaven looks after fools, drunks and the United States'?"

Caleb sighed. "At least with the Spear on our soil, it seems the latter's been pretty much true. Not sure about fools and drunks, but I'm not seeing an alternative to a foolish act at this point. And besides, with this snowstorm, we might get close without attracting attention."

Shrugging, Nina followed, then set a hand on his shoulder as he was about to get in. Caleb turned, surprised, about to shrug away to avoid any psychic intrusion her touch might elicit, but instead, he found she had other plans.

Her other hand, fast as a bullet, whipped around the back of his neck, and before he could struggle, she pulled his face close and locked her lips on his.

And as the storm seemed to take note and surge in their direction, the ferocity of the icy wind was dulled by the heat in her touch. Caleb moaned, his legs went weak and his mind evaporated into her insistent caress, supplying visions of complete clarity, plucked from a short distance away.

A face in the snowstorm, only a face as the body is covered in a gossamer gown the color of the snow. Her hair, untouched by the flakes, and her eyes: deep green, lush like a forest of sweet-smelling pine.

Lydia.

It's like she's watching, but there's no hint of jealousy. Closer and closer she comes, and now her breath exudes crystalline steam, so close as her eyes melt with emotion, with a mix of pity and urgency, as she speaks.

"Let go, Caleb."

The viewpoint shudders. Flickers, and Nina's appearance superimposes over Lydia's.

The response floats over the howling wind. "I can't."

"Let go, and forgive."

"Forgive her? Never!"

A hand raises and soft, warm fingers touch his frozen cheek. "Not just her."

Another shudder, Nina and Lydia joining, two sets of matching green eyes boring into his mind. "Forgive..."

"... myself?"

Lydia-Nina smile. Fingertips linger on his cheek, brush his lips... Eyes shine once more as they retreat... then are lost in the swirling, screaming storm.

And the kiss is broken.

Nina pulled away, fighting a look of shock and dismay. "What was that?"

But Caleb closed the gap, not thinking, reacting only on gut emotion.

Forgive, forgive. Accept what's been there all along.

He locked his numb hands around the back of Nina's head, dropped one to her side, and pulled her close. Before she could react, other than to say "What the f—", he pressed his lips hard against hers.

Their eyes closed, bodies pressed tight and suddenly becoming rigid, locked in an unbreakable embrace as the visions unraveled, then coagulated and shot through them both simultaneously:

An ancient battlefield, something out of an expensive CGI movie: war machines squaring off amid hundreds of thousands of foot soldiers. Cannons firing energy particle shells of some kind, ripping up the earth, decimating entire battalions. A purple-crimson sky, roiling with smoke scattered by brutal winds. Mushroom clouds appear painted on the horizon in a grotesque caricature of Armageddon.

On one of the futuristic tank-like vehicles: a man with a jackal-headed Egyptian-like helmet roars a battle cry and raises a long-handled weapon with a familiar spear point at its tip. A lance that dazzles with its own light, as if reflecting the brilliance of an unseen star. Lightning rips from its tip, scattering the enemy soldiers ahead, as they roar forward—

—toward a huge pyramid set amidst a burning jungle.

Caleb winced, tried to pull away, but now Nina was latched on tight, her mouth open, tongue entwined with his, two snakes hungrily devouring and sharing each other's every thought.

The stars...

And the small green and blue neighbor, just clearing the eastern rim of this lunar landscape. Cratered, desolate. Except for a structure. A ziggurat shape, bordered with massive columns and an arched entrance. The hint of emerald stairs leading up into mystery. Somber Ibis-headed statues on either side, welcoming the elusive, non-corporeal visitors.

—who move forward, reverently bowing, then ascending.

At the stairs' apex, a near-blinding light. Then, features that resolve into enormous shelves. Stacks upon stacks of metallic-looking scrolls with oddly-familiar symbols forming titles. Shelves that stretch on and on into the darkness.

All this fades as the light explodes, pinwheeling into kaleidoscopic swirls.

And then they're back on a snowy field. The white dims, forms appear: giant beams of metal on stands, like giant fans. Turning, aiming into the sky.

Exploding light, pinwheels.

And now, a red clay surface. A desert stretching, unbroken until a large cliff, and what appear to be a series of triangular structures aligned before it. The cliff shakes, shedding boulders and the dust from millennia. The pyramids tremble, then shatter like toy clay pieces. A side of the cliff collapses, turns this way, revealing a giant EYE, cracking, splitting, tumbling a mile down into a pile of rubble.

Another explosion of light and then a single chair appears. A machine. Wires and tubes and consoles hooked to it.

And three young boys stand before it. The youngest is hesitant, but he moves forward on trembling legs as if this is his destiny.

But the other takes a weapon from behind his back. A familiar ancient spear point. Raises it above the younger one's head—

And then, finally, the vision ripped apart.

And Caleb pulled away from Nina.

The wind and the stinging snow slapped at their faces, but still the heat between them refused to waver.

"What the hell?" Nina shouted.

"I don't know!" Caleb looked down and saw that their hands were still together, holding each other the way kids used to at a sixth grade dance.

"A library on the Moon? Some ancient battle with the Spear?" Nina tried to shake the images from her head. "And was that Isaac, with the spear?"

Caleb nodded grimly. "He was going to kill Alexander."

Nina's eyes darkened. "Then let's stop him. The hell with the subtle plan. We go in fast and hard."

Inside the Jeep, Caleb found himself in the passenger seat, trying to warm up as Nina started the engine. He thought of something. "That's a good plan, but we can improve our odds a bit."

"How?"

"Still got your untraceable satellite phone?"

"Yeah, back there. Next to the half-a-billion-year-old snow globe."

Caleb turned and looked down, where they'd secured the

ancient gift from Montross, the thing that had been obscuring their location from all psychics, his sister included. He reached back and picked up the phone.

"What are you thinking?" Nina asked as she revved the engine, then tore ahead.

"Thinking we could get Temple to supply a little distraction. Some air support, or at least a fly-by to distract them while we come in fast through the back door."

Nina grinned at him, then licked her lips as if re-tasting him. "Good idea."

Caleb dialed, keeping his eyes on Nina. *Forgive her?*

She glanced at him as she sped the Jeep over the ridge and into the air before it struck ground and dug in. He turned away, phone to his ear; and in the windshield's reflection, against the nearly impenetrable blanket of snow, he saw his own face staring back at him.

First things first.

8.

Mount Shasta

Phoebe held on for dear life as the tram raced at top speed. Still, at the halfway point, she managed to free a hand and reach out to Orlando's, clasping it tight. They shared a look of fear and confusion. She knew he was as blind as she was. Too much adrenaline, too much shouting, yelling and chaos. And... fear for the girl.

The Hummingbird, strapped in beside her father, clutching him tight. And Diana, on the other side, eyes wide, glancing out the windows as if expecting to observe a half-remembered face from her past somewhere in the darkness and flashing lights.

Temple yelled over the screeching metal, "Do you see anything? Any psychic intel? How close is it?"

"You mean, are we going to make it?" Phoebe asked, focusing the question.

Orlando shook his head, lost, unable to concentrate. "Can't see a thing!"

Suddenly, something rocked the tram. Everyone jolted in their seats. Windows shattered, rocks pounded the ceiling. The mountain trembled. Aria screamed. Out the windows, the tunnel's lights blinked off, then on, then off.

And they plunged into darkness.

Orlando tightened his grip on Phoebe and held onto one thought. *That bald dude didn't save me down there just so I could get flattened in this tin can on the way out.* "I think we're going to make it."

"You *think?*" Temple shouted from the front, looking out over the driver's shoulder. "Or you *know?*"

Orlando shrugged. "Just a—"

"Don't say 'hunch'."

"—hunch."

Temple shook his head.

"Just the same," Diana called out from the back, "I hope the others made it out."

Temple nodded. "One tram evacuated before us, and there were two teams of psychics in the field, and one in town on a training mission. At least they'll be okay."

"Yeah," Orlando said dryly. "Stargate will live on!"

"No one will live on," Phoebe countered. "Unless Caleb can find and stop Calderon."

She dug her nails into Orlando's hand. He was about to tell her to chill and enjoy the ride when the tram rocked violently. The driver screamed just before they impacted something and the car jumped the tracks.

"Oh, shi—"

It flipped, slammed off the walls, then careened forward, sparks roaring like the Fourth of July behind them, bounced again, and then, like in an underground rollercoaster, it simply *dropped.*

Down a huge incline where the rock floor had been, gliding on its belly until finally, slamming head-first into a barrier, punching through rocks and grinding to a stop.

"Everyone ok?" Orlando helped Phoebe up. He wanted to make sure neither of them had any broken bones before verifying the condition of the others, but she was already up and rushing for Aria.

"She's okay," Diana said, stepping in the way. Orlando couldn't see around her in the blinking overhead lights and the sparks still flying from the smashed equipment, but he thought he saw the little girl leaning over her father.

"Give her a minute," Diana whispered, shaking her head sadly.

Phoebe squeezed Orlando's hand tighter. "Oh no..."

Someone behind them cleared his throat. Temple, limping, bleeding from half-dozen cuts on his face and neck. "Sorry, and I know this is no place for something like this, but we don't have a minute."

"Sir," Diana pleaded. "She saw him die. She—"

"She'll be fine," Aria said, and they all turned to see her form in the shadows. Aria laid a gentle kiss on her father's forehead, then backed away, head bowed. Then she turned and with eyes brimming with tears, she nodded. "And I know, we can't take him with us."

Phoebe gasped. "There's got to be a way."

"No," said Aria, climbing over wrecked seats and broken glass. "There isn't. Just like there isn't time to climb back up and run to the exit."

Temple let her pass, but shielded her from the cockpit, where another casualty lay impaled under a pile of granite. "Then?"

"We need to go ahead."

Phoebe looked ahead, following the beam of light that Temple just turned on.

Aria's little feet crunched as she moved ahead. "Into *their* place."

Orlando swallowed with anticipation, and after another step he realized the hand he was holding was now smaller. Aria was between them, holding Phoebe's hand as well as his, urging them forward.

Orlando blinked as she squeezed his fingers and he gasped, the same time as Phoebe.

"How did you do that?" She whispered, then looked over to Orlando. "Did you see it?"

He nodded, just as the flashlight beam fanned back to them, highlighting Aria's grim but determined expression.

"See what?" Temple asked as Diana moved around and took the beam from him, then turned it off. And their eyes immediately picked up the local lighting, soft and ambient, revealing a widening chamber, largely undamaged except for a few cracks in the ceiling and walls.

"Oh," Temple said. "This."

Aria nodded, still leading Phoebe and Orlando, heading toward a rounded marble staircase that ascended to a second level. "I've seen this before," Orlando said. "It's where the UFO-things returned from outside."

Temple looked doubtful. "But they all left, hightailed it out of here."

"They did," Phoebe agreed, "but not all their crafts left with them."

"There," Diana pointed, toward the second alcove from the right on the upper level. Something multi-hued, transparent. And inside...

"Room for four?" Orlando wondered, but Diana was already running up the stairs, leading Temple and Aria.

"Let's hope," she called back. "And let's hope I can figure out how to fly it!"

"If anyone can," Temple said. "It's you."

Orlando was about to race up after them when Phoebe held him back. He stopped and saw that her attention was riveted on the side wall. "What is that? Artwork? A mural?"

"A map, I'd say" Phoebe's eyes bounced around from the colored circles to the elliptical lines drawn around the center object—a bright orange sun.

"There's Saturn," Orlando said, pointed to a striped, ringed circle. "But what's that symbol over the smaller dot next to it? And there, the same thing on other dots."

"They're moons, idiot." Phoebe smiled, looking at them all, taking in the whole scope. She was aware of Aria on the second level, watching them with interest while Diana and Temple tinkered with the craft's controls. She hoped they could gain some insight without psychic intervention, and in time. But for now, she was engrossed with the map.

"Tell me," said Orlando, "it's not another Pharos-like door. Some kind of devilish test or code to break."

Phoebe shook her head, her eyes shining, even as the room shook again and dust fell on them. "No code. No test. Just a map."

"Of what?"

"Look closer at the symbols on those moons, Orlando." She stepped closer as well, just to be certain her theory was correct. "Oh, if I'm right, big brother is going to be so jealous I figured this out without him."

Orlando grinned, then peered closer under the ringed planet. "So, if I remember my astronomy class, this would be Saturn's largest moon. Almost the size of the Earth itself. Titan." Looked even closer, and brushed away some dust from the raised symbol. "A book?"

Phoebe nodded, tracing the same symbol not only on the Earth itself, but on its satellite. Specifically on the shaded side. "Wisdom," she whispered, and closed her eyes.

"What does it mean?" Orlando frowned. He noted the book symbol elsewhere. "It's also on Pluto's moon. What was that one, Charon? And here, closer, on Phobos, for Mars."

"And look out beyond Pluto," Phoebe said. "At the edge of the wall."

"Another one?" Orlando scampered there, then looked back on the five feet of emptiness, just black tiles. "What the hell's out here? And this is one big ass book, twice as large as the others. And it's just one dark planet."

Phoebe shook her head slowly, still staring at the Earth and the Moon. "I can only guess about that, but for those closer to home, I'd say everything is a *learning plan.*"

"A what?"

Another rumble, and the floor cracked. The stairway split and three steps crumbled.

"Hurry, people!" Temple shouted. "Get up here."

"Not ready yet!" Diana yelled back, sounding like she was in a tight position, perhaps trying to jump start the craft.

"On our way!" Orlando yelled, glancing at Phoebe. "We are, aren't we?"

Phoebe nodded, giving the map a long last look, memorizing it. "We are."

"Learning plan?" Orlando said as they ran for the stairs.

"Libraries," she said. "It has to be. Repositories of wisdom, starting with the one on Earth."

"In the Pharos Vault."

"Originally, yes." They gingerly took the steps, careful where they placed their feet. "And maybe the others are similar, just copies of everything we—our ancestors—once knew."

"Ancestors, or aliens?"

"Half-dozen of one, six of the other."

"Okay," Orlando said, jumping over a gap, then helping Phoebe. "I guess. But you think it's more?"

"Just by the sequence and distance." She caught her breath before the second level. "I'm sure the other lunar locations—probably well-fortified like the Pharos—contain similar wisdom so that if anything should happen on Earth..."

3.

Grand Princess Cruise Liner

"Room 2311," Nina whispered, looking up from the terminal. They were in the business office, and Caleb stood by the door, nodding to passing guests, keeping an eye out for security—or suspicious parties.

"You sure?" he called back.

"Sure. Easy to hack into their reservation system. A lot of unsold rooms, bad economy and all, but this one's the most out of the way, yet convenient to stairwells for an easy getaway."

Caleb looked back and met her stone-cold eyes. "If there's an abundance of rooms, we can each get one." He smiled. "On different floors."

Nina smiled back, a catlike grin. She picked up a card, swiped it on a nearby imprinter and held it up. "Sorry, darling. Only one key. And we've got to keep up appearances." In a flash she was up, slipping her arm in his and leaning her head against his shoulder.

"Bring me back to our honeymoon suite, darling."

Caleb rolled his eyes. "Honeymoon? Seriously?" His free hand tapped the object strapped to his ribs. "I've got the most powerful object, potentially, in the world under my shirt, and you want to–"

"I want to live," Nina whispered. "Long enough for us to use that thing and save the damn world." She tugged him toward the elevators. "Now, let's move."

"Like what happened to the dinosaurs."

"Right, then if there were time and some of humanity made it out safely, they could start again."

"But on another planet or moon? Without oxygen, or hell, even an atmosphere?"

"That's not necessarily true," Diana's voice interrupted Phoebe's response. They approached the end of the walkway where Diana was standing beside Temple, just behind the spherical violet field. Behind them, rounded seating zones, capable of holding a dozen of them.

"Tell them on the way," Temple snapped, motioning Phoebe and Orlando inside. But it wasn't until Aria ran through the sparkling field and grabbed their hands that they overcame their fear and passed through, inside the UFO.

"It tickles," Orlando said, and then he was through and taking a seat beside Phoebe, next to Aria.

"No seat belts?" Phoebe asked, but Diana only shrugged as she stood in front of a pedestal and what looked like a flat podium-style presenter.

"That'll be the least of my violations, right after driving one of these without a license. Or a clue."

The mountain rumbled again, the floor pitched and gave way, cracking into chunks that fell out of sight. But the sphere remained, even as the rocks crumbled around them, bouncing off the field.

"If you're going to try something," Temple urged, "now would be a good time."

Aria sighed, leaning against Orlando. She looked down and whispered, "Goodbye, Daddy."

And Diana touched something on the screen, then sent her index finger sliding outward against the surface.

The craft moved instantly, and lurched them all forward, through the disintegrating layers of rock—

—and out into the night sky.

While behind them, the mountainside fell in chunks, pulverized and blasted outward by an invisible drill that bore deeper and deeper, annihilating everything in its path.

"I can't control it much longer," Diana whispered, sweating, leaning over the screen.

"You're doing great," said Temple. "Just try to take us down."

"Gently," Orlando offered, gripping Phoebe and Aria a little too tightly.

"Yeah," said Phoebe. "What he said. And then, when we land, how about telling us what you know, or think you know, about the lunar sites."

"That whole 'not exactly' comment about oxygen up there."

Temple made a throaty sound. "I can answer that. What she means is that there have been reports, scientific analysis of trace oxygen levels given off on the Moon and on Mars and Phobos, around certain locations, that indicate the venting of breathable air. Somewhere down there. Most likely a contained facility, a habitat structure."

"Damn," Orlando said. "So..."

"So that's what they're planning," Phoebe said, eyes wide. "Calderon and his Marduk cult. Destroy the earth, but save themselves by jumping to the next station. A community all ready for them."

"And all the wisdom they'd need to keep going."

"And build on that knowledge," Phoebe said. "That's what I suspect. That, as you get farther out in the solar system, you're rewarded for your skill in reaching those places by receiving better information, more knowledge."

Orlando closed his eyes, seeing that last dark planet and the huge book. "Until the ultimate prize."

She nodded just as her stomach did a back flip and they dropped precipitously fast.

"Sorry!" Diana yelled over Aria's cry of surprise, which then turned to a giggle as she realized they were on the ground, and the sphere was rolling around them, yet keeping them upright inside it.

"Stop, stop," Diana hissed, sliding her finger backwards repeatedly. "Brake?"

Finally, they ground to a stop, lurching against one another. Diana tapped a section of the pad.

And the sphere vanished and she fell out on the soft earth in the middle of a pine forest. Behind them, trees were smoking, scattered in their wake.

Phoebe glanced back, gasping at the shadowy, stooped form of Mt. Shasta, looking grotesquely mutated, half-formed and still losing cohesion. The sound was building, near deafening. So much so that she didn't hear Orlando crying out until several moments later.

And then, it was just to hear a recap of his vision.

"The shield! It's gone!"

"What shield?" Temple asked, righting himself from the dirt. His voice was barely audible.

"Mars!" Orlando yelled. "The Martian shield is gone. Well, not yet, but it's their whole facility... bodies in tanks. Robotic-looking caretakers." His wide eyes fixed on Phoebe. "It's being attacked!"

"What? Who's doing it?" Temple yelled over the rumbling destruction, even as a cloud of dust rolling from the mountain obscured the stars and the bright red speck of light in the eastern sky.

Orlando shook his head, but Aria started clapping.

She fixed her bright blue eyes on Temple, then on Diana, and smiled.

9.

HAARP

As Calderon stood up and smugly left the chamber, his work done and Stargate destroyed, Alexander briefly shut his eyes and tried to picture his father.

Repelled by an undulating, unscalable wall of blue, more powerful and unyielding than anything he had encountered before, Alexander withdrew, feeling like he bounced off entirely. And landed—

Inside of a huge snow-capped mountain, Phoebe and Orlando race into what looks like a floating globe, then soar outside in an exhilarating rush before half the mountain col-lapses around them.

And then he returned, wiping the grin off his face just as Jacob noticed, and Isaac turned around sharply. "What do you think he saw, brother?"

Jacob shrugged. "A happy childhood memory?"

Isaac laughed. "Couldn't have been happier than ours. What with the hunting, the remote-viewing, the killing."

"Everything we ever wanted," Jacob said glumly.

Alexander shook his head. "You aren't my brothers. I don't care anymore. You're nothing like my father."

"And you," Isaac spat, "are too much like your mother." He grinned and raised his hand for a high-five with Jacob, who let it hang there.

Alexander felt his blood boiling. Fists clenched, he was about to advance on Isaac when he saw the boy still carried the sword-cane in his other hand behind his back. And Alexander noted the body laying beside the chair. Montross, bleeding out still, his blood pooling onto the polished floor.

Bleeding. That means he's still alive.

"Isaac. Jacob," Calderon stepped between them. Reached over and held out his hand. "Ah, there it is. My cane, please."

Isaac handed it over with a slight bow, never taking his eyes off Alexander.

Jacob cleared his throat sheepishly as he glanced up to the engineers. "So, is it over?"

Calderon spun his cane, keeping his eye on Alexander. "Why don't you boys tell me? I know I brought the mountain down around those Stargate fools, but I don't know if any are still alive under all that rubble."

"Let's get us a look-see then," said Isaac. "Seems to be all we're good for."

Jacob managed a grin. "Found us our brother in Alexander, we did."

"And wait a sec. Hold the phone, he never thanked us for that, did he?"

"Boys!" Calderon snapped. "Enough. Now we have to pre-pare. It's time."

Jacob and Isaac smiled and closed their eyes, their training kicking in. "Time," they both whispered.

"Time to shed these skins. Leave our bodies and travel the path of the Great Ones to the Red Land..."

"...where we'll be reborn," Isaac and Jacob said in unison.

"...and from our new home, with new eyes, we'll observe the death throes of this planet and imagine the suffering as the world is purged. First, I will follow the instructions on the Tablet, and I will let it guide me from this flesh and into the machine, where only pure matter can interact with the Emerald Tablet's true form."

Isaac clapped his hands slowly, picturing it.

"We'll set the target as the earth's very core, and send the scalar energy waves at a direct path through the pole..."

Calderon approached the device, about to retrieve the Emerald Tablet, when a call came in over the speakers from the techs upstairs. He glanced up, and two men in lab coats rushed out of the room and leaned over the railing.

"What is it now?" Calderon snapped. "You should be powering down and resetting the arrays before we—"

"But that's it, sir. We can't power down!"

"What?"

Alexander perked up. His attention turned to the chair-device, where for just a moment he thought he saw an outline, like an afterimage of Calderon sitting there.

Except, that wasn't Calderon.

"We can't power down! It's not letting us, not responding."

Same build and posture, but one thing different...

Calderon fumed. "Then what's it doing?"

...red hair!

"It's firing, Sir."

Calderon fumed. *Firing without my guidance?* "All right, so it's still blasting Mount Shasta. Just turn the damn thing off already, that's taken care of."

"It's not aimed at Mount Shasta anymore."

Swearing, Calderon started toward the chair. *I can't wait until we're free of this damned world. Just a few more hours.* "All right, then where is it aiming?"

The technicians looked at each other, whispering, then pointing back. One of them ran inside the control room as the other raised up a hand to wait.

"Oh for heaven's sake." Calderon took another step toward the machine, which was still humming, still throwing off waves of photo luminescent energy, then stopped as one of the boys wasn't standing still any longer.

Alexander had slipped by on the right, and was kneeling by Montross. Leaning over, whispering something as he tried to apply pressure to the stab wound.

Montross?

Calderon spun his head back around to the device, and for a glimmering instant, saw him: the flaming red hair, the shining blue eyes. Everything scintillating in an emerald radiance.

Montross! Sitting like an emperor on his throne. Like Loki after usurping Odin. Like Lucifer on the throne of Heaven, or just like Thoth, imagining he could usurp the rule of Marduk.

"Where is it aiming!?"

"Sir," came the voice from above. "Nowhere right now. Just up in a straight line towards the east." The tech's voice cracked. "But in three hours and twelve minutes, after the scalar wave of destruction has traveled a distance of two hundred and fifty million miles..."

Calderon closed his eyes. "No."

"...entering into the path, will be the planet Mars."

"I assume," Calderon said in a dull voice, "You've calculated the precise point on the surface that will be affected?"

"We have." Another pause. "Cydonia."

Throwing down his cane in frustration, Calderon dropped to his knees. Basking before the Emerald Tablet's glow, he prepared himself.

"He's got you," Alexander whispered, glaring at him from his uncle's side.

"Shut up."

"Tricked you good."

"Shut him up!" Calderon pointed and the guards moved in, past Isaac and Jacob, who were still standing, open-jawed, unsure of what just happened. "And if the dead man stirs, shoot him!"

"Father?" Isaac was at his side.

"Be quiet, and be ready. I'm going to stop the traitor. Beat him at his own game."

"But has the pulse already fired?"

"Not long enough," shouted the tech above. "Another thirty seconds and the power level of the scalar wave will be sufficient to penetrate the depth of the Cydonia installation, smash the barriers and reinforced supports, and—"

But Calderon had tuned him out. Or, more appropriately, he no longer had ears with which to hear.

He stood on gossamer legs, his form shimmering with plasma-like sparks.

Everything was as he had foreseen.

Freed from flesh, he was power.

Freed from all restrictions, he was invincible.

He was a god.

And his enemy sat before him, startled at his sudden appearance. And unable to extract himself from the machine. Unable to defend himself.

Thirty seconds, Calderon thought.

Plenty of time.

10.

Ten minutes earlier, while three F-16 Fighting Falcons roared overhead, dispatched from Eielson Air Force Base, the Jeep Cherokee rammed through the chain wire fence at the southwest edge of the facility.

"Think it'll work?" Caleb shouted over the tortured metal-on-metal collision that sent them rocketing off-road for a moment. The tires dug into the fresh snow, spun, then Nina got the Jeep back on the old service road and accelerated for the dimly-visible supply center, adjacent to the office buildings.

"Well, we heard the jets but I'm sure their security people picked them up on radar long before that. Their attention has got to be on the sky."

"Temple said he ordered radio silence, too. So if they tried contact, they'd get nothing. Which would have to scare them a bit."

"And the scalar weapon, I imagine, isn't good for knocking out fast-moving aircraft, only motionless enemy sites."

Caleb cringed, thinking about the Library of Alexandria, the devastation and loss of life, not to mention the original copies of all that wisdom.

As the snow and ice slapped the windshield, keeping the wipers working in hyperspeed, Nina shifted and threw caution out the window. "Wish our boys weren't in there, otherwise we could have had them just level the damn place. Napalm it up."

Caleb gripped the shrouded Spear in both hands, hefting it, feeling the rough rounded edge, just enough of a hilt-like handle, wishing he had a long staff to fit on it to truly make it a lance-like weapon instead of what it was now: a glorified dagger. He thought of his last vision, that of Alexander about to be attacked by Isaac.

"They're hardly out of danger."

"I know." She shot him a quick look. "And I'm sorry. I wasn't there, I didn't know."

"We'll get there in time," Caleb said, staring ahead, seeing the dark shape approaching. "We'll get there."

"Now that's some confidence even I don't have." Nina slowed, seeing two smaller shapes peel away from the building. "Especially since we've got company."

"Of course they've guarded the back." Caleb unraveled the Spear point. "But they're woefully unprepared."

"No idea what's going to hit them."

The men, visible now in the brutal maelstrom, raised their guns.

Caleb responded, raising the Spear, pointing it at them through the windshield. "Confident or not, I have no idea how this works."

Nina shrugged. "Then I'd suggest ducking."

The windshield cracked just as Nina lowered her head and peeked around the steering wheel, aiming for the pair of defenders. But Caleb merely sat still, Spear held out before him like a narrow shield. Two more cracks in the windshield. A bullet whizzed past and then—SLAM—one of the guards went flying over the roof, while the other just managed to dodge out of the way.

"No chance to shut him up," Nina said, sitting upright. "They know we're here, but with any luck, they think we've got a whole army with us to go along with the air support. We've still got some element of surprise and distraction. Time to use it."

The Jeep picked up speed as the building loomed in their view. Two double doors were no match for the head on greeting they provided at eighty miles an hour. The Jeep smashed through a metal railing and launched down into the warehouse floor. It slid and then Nina braked hard and spun it in a one-eighty, slamming Caleb's side into two more astonished guards and pinning them against a rack of steel replacement girders.

One, still alive, managed to raise his MP5 and before Nina could recover and reach for her Beretta, he fired.

But Caleb was directly in his path. He instinctively held out the Spear tip and closed his eyes. Heard the gunshots, then what sounded like his own cut-off scream, but felt no pain.

"Holy crap," came Nina's voice. Caleb blinked and opened his eyes, registering the fate of the shooter: the MP5 had exploded as it fired, sending shrapnel backwards; his face was blackened and bloody, and the ruined gun fell from his limp fingers.

"I guess no instruction manual needed," Nina commented as she unhooked her belt and withdrew her Beretta. "Now let's move. Out my side, on three."

Caleb looked past her, seeing several dark-clad forms running from shelter and hiding behind crates and piles of equipment.

She counted to three, kicked open the door and went out low, rolling, then shooting at two guards who came charging out of cover. By the time Caleb was out, she had fired three more times, and there were four bodies on the floor.

She ran to the edge of a stack of piping, aimed through it and fired again, taking out someone hiding on the other side. Reloading, she glanced back. "Move it, darling. Or else just stroll out there and draw their fire. We'll see how well it protects you."

Caleb crouched and moved to her side. "I think I'll err on the side of caution for now."

Nina shrugged. "You know, anything happens to you, I promise to take the Spear and do what has to be done."

"I appreciate that. Just come back and give me a proper burial after you save the world."

"No problem."

Caleb winced as gunfire erupted from the back of the warehouse, and impacts ripped through the canisters and sparked off the floor. He looked to where the dead guard's operable MP5 had fallen beside the broken one.

"Just the same, I'm adding to my arsenal." He slid the spear point-down under his belt, hooking an edge, then scampered back for the weapon.

When he returned, keeping his head low in the barrage of incoming fire, Nina said: "You, a gun? Ever actually use one?"

"Yes."

"Other than a BB gun?"

"Yes, one of these in fact."

Nina gave him a disbelieving look after another burst of gunfire, which she answered. "And did you actually hit anything?"

Caleb peered around the edge, sighting. "Now you're just being mean."

"Oh just pull the trigger and aim that way." She nodded to the left as she crouched and took off to the right.

Darting out of cover, he aimed and fired. A momentary panic as two black-clad guards stood up and leveled guns at him from twenty yards away, but then red splotches exploded on their foreheads and they went down, just as fast.

Caleb held down the trigger, struggling to maintain control against the recoil. He sent a long burst that took out lights, shattered crates and ricocheted off metal girders and frames. Two screams as the bullets punched through soft cover, and another as a guard took off and Caleb's uncontrolled sweep happened to catch him in the shoulder.

Three more guard-soldiers ran out, charging him. Two fell to Nina's expert marksmanship before they could take aim, the third ducked for cover. Caleb could hear him slinking around the side of a massive crate. He aimed for the far side, then saw a flash in his mind.

Behind his position: men had circled around outside. A team of six, guns drawn, running fast.

Crap! He thought. No time. He dropped to his knees, spun and let loose a screaming volley of fire out the open doors into the swirling snow that obscured the men running inside. All four, bunched together, caught the slugs square on and spun back, falling. One made it inside only a few steps before the last few rounds stopped his progress.

Now he'd hit something, Caleb thought. But he knew it was all for nothing. The last soldier, hiding behind the crate, would have sensed his opportunity. He's out, aiming, and Nina's not in position.

Caleb dropped the gun and reached for the spear the instant he heard the gunshot. He winced and dropped into a ball. The bullet sailed overhead, striking the pillar beside him. Then he turned, raising the Spear point as another gunshot went off. The Spear shook in his grasp, and then lit up as if struck by lightning. Electric charges crackled along its outline and darted outward.

The guard froze, so mesmerized by the light show that he didn't see the sleek form pulling out of the shadows behind him; the figure that raised then lowered something at his head. A *thwump* and he went down, out cold.

"Quit screwing around," Nina quipped. "We're almost out of time. And reinforcements are coming."

More bullets. More chunks of debris exploding around them. Caleb cringed and rushed to her side, where her back was up against a large section of concrete piping. "Do you have another option?"

She grinned as she leaned across him and squeezed off two shots. "Honey, you must know better than to ask that. Don't forget, Montross obsessed about this facility for half his life. He and I went through a hundred different scenarios of how we could get in here. Studied every diagram, blueprint and schematic of this place. Someone takes a shit on level two, I can tell you which pipe flushes it out."

Caleb made a face. "I'll keep that in mind. So, anything that will actually help us?"

She fired again, then turned back around and shot straight ahead, seemingly at the wall. Sparks flew as the bullet impacted metal; then she grabbed Caleb's arm. "Come on. Air duct, ventilation shaft 24B. It'll take us right through to the central weaponry lab."

She hauled him forward toward the broken grate that was now swinging open.

Caleb had to shake his head. "I'm suitably impressed."

Just inside the grate, after closing it behind them and retreating into the shadows, Nina turned him around and planted a firm kiss on his lips.

This time he didn't fight it, except a quick pullback to ask, "Now what? I have nothing else to show you."

She locked her eyes on his. "No, but there's something I've held back that *you* need to see."

"Really, we don't have the time."

"Just take a sec." And she pulled him close, closed her eyes and as soon as their lips touched, he saw it.

A jungle in Mexico, a touristy hacienda at the edge of a cliff overlooking a jungle of trees and vines. Inside: a young girl, auburn hair, green eyes, maybe nine years old. Sitting on a floor of blood amidst two decapitated bodies: a man and a woman. Staring, numb and unable to cry, as the two drug hitmen sling her parents' heads into the bag and prepare the ransom letter.

A flash: and she's escaping, darting out a window while one of the hitmen chokes on his own blood, a dinner knife stuck through his trachea. She runs...

...arriving at the American embassy the next morning, where she promptly draws them a map, and includes sketches not only of the remaining killer, but his boss. And the location of the drug kingpin's hideout.

The DEA agents brought in to interview her ask how she got her information, if she ever left the hacienda, but she merely replies: "I just saw it."

And then, after the operation concludes and the kingpin and his henchmen are dead, their supply confiscated, the agent makes a call. When he hangs up, he sees what the little girl has drawn now.

It's the symbol of the CIA: the Eagle and the Star. Only, she wrote the word 'Stargate' underneath.

Smiling for the first time in a week, she asks when they'll be flying back to Washington.

Caleb rocked out of the vision to find that the kiss had ended, and Nina, with but a somber nod back to him, was crawling ahead. "Now you know," she whispered. "We've always had a lot more in common than you'd figured."

Wordlessly, he followed.

11.

Alexander, crouching over Montross, trying to protect him from the two goons with guns pointed at his body, had few options left.

Calderon, kneeling on the floor, seemed to have gone into a trance; and for a moment it looked like something wispy, spectral and green passed out of his body, hurtling toward the chair where Alexander had seen that brief outline of Montross at the controls.

Then, he had to keep an eye on his 'brothers'. Jacob and Isaac had taken up flanking positions on either side of Calderon, defending him. The sword-cane, previously at the senator's knees, had been snapped up again by Isaac, who was glaring back at Alexander now, almost urging him to try something.

Helpless, Alexander turned toward the chair again, wishing he could see what was happening. Whatever it was, it had to happen soon. Calderon had been told he only had thirty seconds, or else their plan was finished.

At least knowing what question to ask, Alexander was poised to try to see if remote-viewing could see into the astral dimension; but his regular vision first snagged on an air vent at ground level twenty feet away. And his heart leapt in surprise.

Two faces inside, an unlikely pair. But definitely his father, a finger to his lips.

"Take out the guards," Caleb whispered, pointing to the two over Montross.

"I could," Nina said, "but there are six more at the back. In the shadows."

Caleb looked. "Damn. Good eyes." He sighed, watching

his son, sizing up Jacob and Isaac, Montross bleeding and lying still; and then Calderon. And finally, the chair and the power unit.

The Emerald Tablet!

He closed his eyes and projected outward, willing to see...

Calderon was there, a blur like a green-tinged ghost. Arms out, reaching for Montross, sitting like a statue in the chair, like a man possessed or in a deep slumber. Xavier's eyelids flickered and his lips moved as if voicing commands in an alien tongue.

Calderon launched himself and wrapped his hands around Montross' throat. Sparks flew, the machine shuddered.

And Xavier's mortal body rocked with convulsions just as his astral body thrashed under Calderon's vicious assault.

"No time to wait," Caleb shouted, kicking out the grate. "We're going now!"

"Damn it!" Nina hissed, and her Beretta spat fire twice, knocking back both guards over Montross.

Staying in the grate was suicide, so she launched herself out, somersaulting and firing back toward the wall, even as shots came back at her.

But Caleb was there, holding the Spear aloft in both hands. Bullets slammed into something and for a moment a nearly invisible curved aperture appeared. The bullets struck and then evaporated like water droplets on a hot pan.

Caleb moved ahead and reached out for Alexander, to encase him in the shield as well. Nina's shots apparently still went through from this side, as another grunt of pain sounded and another guard fell.

The machine continued to spark and rumble. The conduits shook, wires exploded. More guards appeared, now from above on the landing.

Caleb shouted out a warning, but too late. Nina had rolled to the side and from behind, a shot found its mark. She spun around, blood spurting from her thigh. On the ground, she aimed up, squeezed off two shots and then rolled around to fire two more at those at the bottom level. Behind her, two bodies slumped over the rail and hit the floor.

"Mom!" Jacob ran to her side, and for a moment, the gunfire stopped as the soldiers couldn't get a clear shot. And in the respite, Caleb turned to the machine. Saw the slot on the right arm holding the Tablet.

Now or never.

He raised the spear. Briefly considered stabbing Calderon in the back, but apart from the moral disgust at the thought of attacking a defenseless human, no matter how evil, he knew the target was straight ahead. And he only had one shot at it.

Stepping around Calderon, he brought his arm back. Three steps, that was all, and strike!

But a chilling voice made him freeze.

"Stop or Alexander dies!"

Caleb turned, and saw the boy, Isaac, standing behind Alexander. Just like his vision. Isaac had him gripped by the hair, the sword tip of the cane pointed right at his son's skull.

Montross gagged, choking for a breath. He never imagined such non-local sensations of agony could be experienced even without a body. Couldn't even defend himself, couldn't move his arms or else the procedure wouldn't finish.

He was almost there. Interfacing with the machine had been surprisingly easy in this form. It was just as Calderon had expected. The Emerald Tablet was of both worlds and when he had 'sat' in the chair and reached through the slot, it fit like a glove. A glove that tightened and sent immediate sensations flooding through his consciousness. Numbers and equations, distances and measurements, a river of calculations. Weights and compositions of everything from massive stars to the smallest particle. It was too much, sifting through all the data. Took too long to focus, discard and graciously decline any more knowledge—things that he knew would be fleeting anyway, should he return to his body. Knowledge a physical brain just couldn't retain and would only fade like the details of a complex dream.

So he focused. On Mars. On trajectories and lines of sight, traversing vast expanse of space, plotting a course, and then he focused on charging the power of this facility. Channeling it, building up the power levels.

It was taking too long. Taking all of his focus. He hadn't even kept tabs on the players in the room, assuming no one could see him. Especially if they weren't looking. His dying body was the perfect distraction.

And dying he was. He knew this here was a one way trip. Never imagined he'd be a martyr, but at the same time, he had also never seen a way to survive this day. Could he live with being the only one not to live through it?

So be it.

He thought fleetingly of Diana, and for a brief moment, he was back at the Grand Canyon, soaring over the sandstone monuments on a hang glider, with her clutching to his back in fear and excitement. And then he peeked in on her again, and there she was, piloting some unbelievable orb-like contraption, like something out of a Spielberg movie.

I'll miss you.

He pulled his attention away momentarily, as the machine rumbled and throbbed and the arrays were charging. Glanced at his body. Alexander leaning over it, sobbing.

Then he focused again and his world turned green, blasted with more scrolling lines of data, binary codes and more formu-laic text, symbols of every language, numbers and code, all whizzing past in a blur.

And the power multiplied exponentially.

And surged through the conduits and roared up through the thousands of arrays. Still building in intensity. *Can't release it all at once. Start small, then rising, each pulse a little stronger. Another minute, and the full strength will be reached. Full strength to pound the Cydonia surface. And goodbye escape route.*

Sorry Calderon. Sorry—

But then the icy hands of the senator's astral form locked around his throat, interrupting the sequence and jumbling the equations.

Montross struggled, resisting the option to remove the symbiotic connection to the Tablet. His viewpoint shifted from Calderon's wild and crazed visage, to beyond: to see Isaac with a blade point an inch from Alexander's skull; Nina on the floor, bleeding, and Caleb...

Caleb standing there, indecisive. In his hands, something glowing intensely bright. A long triangular object that shone like the sun emerging from an eclipse.

The Spear. The Lance. You've got it... Now use it!

Montross was fading, couldn't hold it any longer.

The gambit's failed. Cydonia will survive.

He wrenched his arm free, breaking the connection. Like ripping off a Band-Aid and losing your arm in the process.

But it doesn't mean this son of a bitch gets to see it.

Montross swung his fist as hard as he could, sitting up at the same time for leverage.

Calderon rocked back and loosened his hold. Another punch came at him like a wrecking ball. He staggered, leaned forward and caught a blur of green descending from the chair just before an uppercut launched into his midriff and lifted him three feet in the air.

He's stronger, more adept at using this form.

Wincing with another blow, he weakly raised his arms to defend himself as his crazed adversary continued the beating.

But I've succeeded. Broke the connection. Rejoicing inside, he saw an opening and shoved Montross backward. *And I've still won.* He glanced at the body lying on the ground.

Time to sever the cord, Montross. Set you free to linger in limbo forever.

Turning back to his own kneeling body, he was about to re-enter it when he saw the impossible: Caleb Crowe had a glowing weapon in hand, something that burned away all thought and reason.

No! The Lance!

Calderon rushed toward his body, driven by absolute rage. He willed himself back inside...

But at the moment of contact, something passed in front of him like a breath of cold air. He tried to enter, but was violently repelled, tossed across the room, spinning and floating uncontrollably. He spun and spun and finally righted himself. Rushed back toward his body, but froze.

There in front of him, Mason Calderon stood up and stretched, grinning from ear to ear.

Caleb had no choice.

"Drop the lance!" Isaac yelled, shifting the blade around and pressing it against Alexander's throat. "Drop it, you better, or see your boy's blood paint the floor."

Alexander stiffened, chin up above the cold steel point as if trying to stay afloat. "Dad, don't listen. You can't give it up."

"Do it, *'Dad'.*" Isaac sneered at him. "Prove you're just as worthless as we've always believed."

Caleb started to lower the weapon.

"There you go. Embarrassed, eh Jacob? Good thing we never saw daddy before now, righto? Got all we needed from mom, it seems."

Alexander's eyes flickered to Nina's side, to Jacob, the boy standing now. Slowly. Deliberately. Nina's arm was outstretched toward Jacob, but her hand was empty, as if she had just given him something. Then she laid her head down, eyes flickering with pain, exhaustion and blood loss overcoming her.

And then Alexander got it. What was missing...

But Jacob answered first. "Not righto, brother." And he aimed Nina's Beretta at his brother.

"Oh-ho!" Isaac chortled. "You're kidding me?"

Jacob shook his head. "No. And Mom's just showed me something."

"You let her touch you? After what Mr. Calderon warned you about?"

"She showed me you can't be strong without being vulnerable. And you can't be superior if you have no compassion."

Isaac made a face.

"A stupid trick."

"No, I saw it. Her life, what happened as a child, what made her how she is now. And then, her feelings for our father."

"Ridiculous." Isaac tugged Alexander's head back. "So after all we've done together, you're dismissing our destiny? You're taking their side?"

Jacob let out an exhausted sigh. "I was never on your side, brother." He sighted and pulled the trigger.

Isaac tried to slash Alexander at the same time, but it was useless; the bullet caught him under the collarbone and spun him away. The cane dropped as Isaac fell onto his side, choking on the pain, unbelievable pain that washed over everything, every glorious fate he had nurtured his entire life. He slipped in his blood, staggered, then lay on his side, vision blurring.

"Just like shooting a deer," said Jacob, who then stepped away, leaving an unobstructed view of his mother. Of Nina, lying in the same position, reaching out to him as they both slowly bled to death. She gave Jacob a look of three parts admiration and one part pity.

But then a shifting sound, and a hand came into view, a hand with a dragon seal ring on the ring finger.

Calderon.

He bent down and picked up the staff, then yelled for the guards to stop and back away, even as Caleb rushed him, lance up high.

"Dad, No!" Alexander yelled, and that stopped him, mid-swing.

Caleb froze, the spear point throbbing and pulsing in his grasp, just a few inches   from   Calderon's   smug   face,   pointing   right between his eyes. His eyes... something that seemed odd. Off-putting and weirdly familiar about them.

Calderon opened his mouth, cleared his throat and was about to speak when Alexander, holding his forehead, eyes clenched tight, yelled: "The Tablet! Do it now, before—"

The machine hummed again, roaring now. Surging with a new burst of power.

"—before it fires! He's changed the target, right at our feet now! Do it, do it, do it!"

Caleb   stared   from   his   boy,   who   was   obviously   in   the midst of a vision, to the machine. *Who was in there? Montross still? Someone—"*

And for a brief instant he saw it too. Like a transparent page flitted over the backdrop, this one with an afterimage superimposed on it, *an image of Mason Calderon seated like a god, head thrown back, mouth open, shouting out with all the power of the universe. The power that would rupture a world.*

"Now," right behind Caleb's shoulder, whispered Calderon-who-wasn't-Calderon.

And then, a flitting glimpse of a woman bathed in silver, just standing beside Alexander, as if her hand was on his shoulder; Lydia, here at the end when everything came down to Caleb, when all he had to do was trust.

But first, forgive and let go.

He closed his eyes. *I'm sorry, one last time, I'm sorry, but no more. I must accept.*

And act.

And four huge lunging steps brought him to the edge of the great chair, the machine whirling with plasma energy, trembling and shaking the foundations. He brought the Spear back, like an Olympic javelin thrower, and just as reality fluttered and Calderon appeared, roaring his protests in the other realm, Caleb thrust home the lance, slamming the point directly through the slot.

As it skewered the Emerald Tablet, a flash of light erupted and he was there, straddling both worlds. The dazzling golden spear thrust into the heart of the kaleidoscopically-shifting tablet, splitting it down the middle, through its multiple dimensions, then diagonally twice, forming a star shape.

All that knowledge, all the wisdom of millennia, the symbols, equations and mystic instructions... rending apart, shattering.

Caleb felt the wound as if he'd stabbed his own heart. *It had to be done.*

And besides, came a voice that wasn't his. *There are other routes to knowledge.* And a succession of majestic structures hurtled through his vision: great pillared repositories set in the unlikeliest of settings: lunar monasteries, crimson landscapes, frozen wastes under alien stars.

It's all out there, waiting for us.

Caleb shoved the spear in farther, twisted, then wrenched it free.

"NOOO!" Calderon shouted in his mind, and reached for him, but Caleb swung the spear free in a wide arc, slashing Calderon's ethereal form across the neck. A disembodied, glowing head went sailing into the gloom just as the tablet exploded with such force that Caleb was hurled ten feet back, just as the machine tore apart and pieces scattered in all directions.

Gasping, dropping the spear which was now too hot to hold, his fingers scalded, Caleb stood up, only to be surrounded by six soldiers pointing MP5s at his face.

"Stop!" yelled Senator Calderon, now leaning on his cane, standing over Isaac's body. "It's over," he said. Not to the guards, not to Jacob or Nina or Alexander, but to Caleb.

"It's over," he said again, and added a wink and a smile.

Alexander raced past him and slid by the guards to throw his arms around Caleb. "Dad!" Then, lower: "Don't worry, I saw it all."

Calderon's voice cracked then sounded more urgent as he addressed the guards. "Go, get medical help." He leaned down beside Nina, and curiously, took her hand in his. Through glazed eyes, she smiled at him. Jacob knelt beside his brother and bowed his head.

Caleb stood up warily. "What the hell is going on?"

Alexander pulled on his arm, and when Caleb bent down, Alexander whispered in his ear.

Then Calderon turned, reached over and closed Xavier Montross' eyelids. "Sleep tight, old friend." He stood, faced Caleb and spread out his arms, as if feeling for the fit of a new suit.

"I don't believe it." Caleb just stared, wide-eyed.

"He's right, my dear half-brother. Not a bad trade overall." Xavier Montross, speaking through his new flesh, grinned. "And now that I'm a powerful senator, things are going to go a little differently."

12.

Seattle, Washington - 12 Hours Later

When Caleb finally left the hospital room, it was only after a promise, doubly made, that he would not leave Nina this time. That he'd be back to check on her in a few hours.

"And besides," Caleb had said, leaning over and brushing her dark curls away from those penetrating eyes that for the first time displayed a sense of weakness, "Jacob wants to spend some time getting to know you."

He had backed up, and then let the boy come closer. Jacob pulled up a chair and leaned in, eager to hear more of his mother's stories, the ones she could tell just by touching him, with little effort.

Caleb eased the door shut behind him, and went to the conference room that Colonel Temple had secured for their use and debriefing. Temple had his arm in a sling, and the others were all in some form of recovery: bandages, tired eyes, covered in dust and filth.

"Looks like we could all use a good hosing down and a night's sleep at the Ritz," Temple said, "but that'll have to wait."

Phoebe came over and gave Caleb another big hug. "Good to have you back, big brother."

Caleb squeezed her tight, then let go and nodded to Orlando. He shook hands with Diana Montgomery and offered the same to the girl, Aria, but she merely high-fived him and went back to whispering and giggling to Alexander, who was blushing profusely.

"Alexander? Made a new friend, I see." Caleb took a seat across from his son, who just grinned sheepishly. "It's okay," Caleb said, "just stay where I can see the both of you. If you're out of my sight and I go looking and only see blue, I'm going to be mad."

Phoebe kicked him under the table.

Orlando, finishing his second Red Bull, licked his lips and grinned foolishly at Phoebe. "Still, I may have to borrow your talents, Miss Hummingbird, from time to time."

Phoebe glared at him. "Don't you dare try to hide from me. Or I'll go dig up that Spear—wherever you hid it, big brother. Seriously, I'll find it and—"

Just then, the door banged open.

And Senator Calderon walked in, closing the door behind him.

"Ah, good. You're all here." He walked inside, leaning slightly on a new cane, this one carved from a knobby pine. "Stupid limp. Guy should've taken better care of himself."

Smiling at Diana, he took a seat beside her, and after a moment she took his hand in hers.

"This is going to take some getting used to," she said.

"I'll get his body in better shape," Montross promised.

"I can wait," she whispered. "As long as I've got you back."

"So," Temple asked breaking the awkward moment. "Senator. What was their answer?"

Calderon-Montross smiled and took a moment to answer. "How could they refuse me? Apparently I've got half the country's leaders in my pocket, or dying to get there. Influence is too tame a word."

Caleb looked around, confused. "Sorry, I've been in seeing to Nina's recovery. What's going on?"

Temple sighed. "Only my retirement." He leaned back, rubbing his neck with his good hand. "From direct involvement, at least. Getting too old for this. Time for new blood."

Caleb blinked at him, then at Montross. Everyone else in the room seemed to be smiling at some inside joke.

"Congratulations," Montross said. "Caleb Crowe, you are now the new acting head of the Stargate Program."

Caleb nearly fell off his chair. "What? No, I couldn't, not after—"

"You can," said Temple.

"And you should," said Montross. "I know they royally screwed your dad, and Waxman did what he did, but you have a chance to do it your way."

Caleb looked at Phoebe and Orlando for help. "But the Morpheus Initiative—"

"—can still exist, just merge it in with Stargate."

"Bigger budget, more resources," Phoebe said.

"Better benefits," Orlando added, shaking his empty can. "Maybe get us a decent health plan?"

"Think about it," Temple said. "I'll stay on and help as an advisor. But you're the man with the skill. You, Phoebe, Orlando. Montross and Nina. Alexander. You guys were way ahead of us, and sure I've done okay with recruiting, but you... You can do this the way it should be done."

Caleb looked helplessly from Phoebe's smiling face to Montross, his eyes shining more and more like the true Montross.

"Do it," the senator said. "Because I'm going to need your skills very soon. Yours, and a lot of others'. We've got to build this big, because the threat's not over."

"What do you mean?" Caleb asked, his head still spinning.

"The threat," Montross said, "and the opportunity."

"The Custodians," Phoebe said. "They're still here. And what they are scares the beJesus out of us."

"I thought you said they saved you. Both here and in Afghanistan."

"I did. They did." Phoebe sighed, leaning in across the table. "But the one told me that they 'weren't what they seemed'."

"And some of us," Orlando said, "we got impressions, hits of different kinds of stuff. Scary impressions..."

Alexander added to the discussion: "Like maybe there are two sets of these beings lurking around."

"Some," said Montross, "that are watching out for us, maybe even encouraging us mere mortals on the path back to wisdom..."

"Others," said Phoebe, "more like the Old Testament nasty gods who want to keep us down. Divided, with our link to the eternal forever denied."

Caleb closed his eyes, then resisted the stirring, the call of visions that tempted. After a breath, he surveyed the room, stopping on Alexander. "So what can we do?"

"You know what to do," Montross said, standing up slowly. "Get back to work. Look, find, learn. You have more tools now, and will have much more resources at your disposal."

"A new headquarters?" Phoebe asked.

"With free parking?" Orlando added.

"Back in Sodus, New York?" Alexander insisted.

Montross shrugged. "If you wish."

Caleb sighed, then nodded to Temple. "I still don't know."

"I do," Montross said. "In fact, this whole conversation has been redundant. I've seen the outcome. I know how it ends."

"Crazy psychics," Temple said. "Before you go, Senator. And Ms. Montgomery. Tell them about the other phase of the investigation."

Diana stood up beside Montross, her hand still holding his. "That's where I come in. NASA's priorities will be changing."

"Again," said Montross, "my influence. Been a busy few hours, but I've lit some fires under some asses. Got the bug in their ears. Now that the shuttle missions are done, we need a few high profile wins. Targets..."

"Objectives," said Diana. "Things we already know are there, but will have our probes 'discover'. Things that will blow the lid off conventional wisdom."

Phoebe smiled at Caleb. "And you thought the books under the Pharos were explosive!"

Caleb felt his pulse rising, his palms sweating with excitement. Now there were flashes of visions behind his eyes.

Those temple-like buildings nestled in lunar craters. Geometric structures in sacred patterns on remote worlds, distant testaments to a former existence. Beacons promising greater and greater rewards.

But there were risks.

These Custodians. Watchers.

And most assuredly, defenses of the sort only members of The Morpheus Initiative could handle.

Caleb blinked, then nodded to Temple. To Montross and

Diana, to his friends, his sister and finally, to his son whose broad smile let him know he was doing the right thing. The only thing.

"All right," he said proudly. "I'm in."

THE END
?

AUTHOR'S NOTES

Thanks for coming along this incredible journey with me. Hopefully you've been entertained, and along the way, maybe had your mind stretched—or possibly batted around like a piñata. That was ultimately my intention. Our world (and indeed our universe) is a strange place, and to think we've got it figured out is just plain lunacy. We've come a long way, but any peek into the some of these enduring mysteries should just put us back in our humble chairs.

But in any case, the research for these books was an extension of my love for the unknown, beginning with shows like *In Search Of* as a child, and continuing with books, books and more books (my room looking a lot like Caleb's, growing up). And so, like a magician eager to reveal his tricks, I'd like to share some of the more 'incredulous' bits that came out of influences for this series, and particularly this novel. Obviously I don't believe everything I read, and there are a lot of debunkers out there for each and every one of these things, but there are a lot of compelling—and large, very large—ideas here, enough to make your brain hurt, and possibly I hope, give you pause and wonder, *what is the truth?* Is it really out there? And is it way more mind-boggling than we can imagine?

In no particular order, here you'll find some background on the novel's more intriguing concepts:

1)   *The Spear of Destiny*. It's been a major subject of a lot of thrillers, and yes—of great interest to Adolf and his pals. Also called the Holy Lance, this spear was the one that supposedly pierced Jesus's side as he hung on the cross in John's account of his death. Legend has it that whoever possesses the lance will rule the world. Richard Wagner's opera *Parsival* revolved around the Spear and clearly influenced Hitler's dreams of world supremacy. After obsessively studying the history of the Spear and learning that numerous emperors from Constantine to Frederick all claimed power deriving from its possession, he was determined to acquire it—which he did when he invaded Austria in 1938. And yes, the day the Americans took Nuremberg and the Spear changed hands, Hitler took his own life. History has it that Patton returned the spear to the Austrians; but of course, I've taken license here and asked, *What if he didn't?*

2)   Nazi interest in the occult. This is fairly well known (and a frequent source of speculation), with characters like Himmler, Ravenscroft and others fascinated with the legends of an ancient race of Supermen hiding away in the Himalayas or other remote areas. Expeditions were sent to the poles in search of entranceways to find these members of the Thule race, seeking legendary sources of power and hidden bases such as Shamballa.

3)   The Statue of Liberty. Its colorful history is as I've depicted here, including the base's similarity to the Pharos Lighthouse, and its original intention to serve as a lighthouse itself (although never quite achieving that purpose due to technological shortcomings). The original torch is on display as you walk in—but I wouldn't advise snooping around down there.

4)   The theories about the great antiquity of the Sphinx, the Great Pyramid as a weapon, and the labyrinth under the Giza plateau are also abundant, with Herodotus being a source for the legends about the Pyramid being built by a 'Shepherd King', and standing over an underground complex of great mystery and power. Many authors (such as Joseph P. Farrell and Zecharia Sitchin) have extensively decoded myths and researched the possibility that the Pyramid could have been used as a devastating weapon or source of power.

5)   The great statues of Bamian, Afghanistan ('The Imperishable Witnesses') were indeed destroyed by the Taliban, and hopefully will be rebuilt. And yes there are legends that the monks didn't actually build them—that they only modified what they had found already in place, statues that were incredibly ancient.

6)   The ruined cities of Mohenjo-Daro and Harrapan in Pakistan frequently make the list of baffling ancient locations. Residual radiation levels, a lack of historical detail about the cities (even their existence was unknown until

excavation), and the prominence of bodies found in various positions of sudden death, make these sites interesting choices to compare to the *Mahabarata's* chapters on the ancient wars between the gods, with descriptions of battles wiping out populations in the manner of neutron bombs—or some heretofore unknown weaponry.

7)   Mount Shasta has a colorful past, between Native Ameri-can legends, accounts of gold-rush era prospectors, and more recently, hikers and tourists who have claimed to see not only strange glowing lights, but cave entrances that appear and then disappear, on occasion revealing monk-like inhabitants…

8)   Remote-viewing (and Stargate)—see my notes after The Pharos Objective, but the intriguing bits I expanded on here involve the ability of some psychics to probe things on the Moon—and breaking out of their efforts, apparently scared that they were 'being observed' by something up there.

9)   The Moon. Plenty of Fortean phenomena here—and just plain facts that don't add up. Diana's descriptions of NASA's early surprises upon reaching the moon are valid, as we were continually confounded by the moon's mysteries. (The lack of dust, the inexplicable shape and depth of craters, the difference in expected gravity, the sound made on landing). And for decades before the first launch, amateur astronomers had been recording strange lights and structures that appeared, then changed, and recording radio signals emanating from up there. There have also been some revelations by astronauts in recent years of UFO sightings, and even a lost 'audio tape' that surfaced claiming to be of Armstrong's voice relaying the sighting of other ships on the lunar surface, watching us carefully but not engaging or responding.

10)   Mars, the 'Face' and Cydonia. Nearly 40 years after Viking first photographed the site it's still a matter of speculation. If it was just the appearance of a face in a desert, however muddled it looks now after further 'enhancements', it would have been discounted and we would have moved on; but numerous books and studies have come out, analyzing not only the enormous head-shaped structure, but a plethora of other incongruous shapes

and features in the Cydonia region, including a cluster of pyramid-shaped objects and a cliff wall many miles along and incredibly straight. Altogether— along with the tantalizing hint that Mars may have been quite Earth-like in its ancient past)—Cydonia still cries out more than a little for further investigation.

11)   Phobos and Deimos. Mars's moons. A lot of odd stuff about this pair, including the appearance of parallel surface lines, unusual orbital characteristics and generally porous interiors. All of which led Soviet and American scientists to   suggest   that   these   satellites   might   be   'artificial'.   In   the journal *Astronautics*, Fred   Singer,   then   science   advisor   to   U.S. President Dwight D. Eisenhower, said: *if the satellite is indeed spiraling inward as deduced from astronomical observation, then there is little alternative to the hypothesis that it is hollow and therefore Martian made."* Oh, and one of the Russian probes (Phobos 2) was lost right after a shadowy missile-like figure was seen between it and the Martian surface. Make of that what you will.

12)   Finally, the *Brookings Report*. In collaboration with NASA, the Brookings Institute released to the House of Representatives on April 18, 1961 the *Proposed Studies on the Implications of Peaceful Space Activities for Human Affairs*. Page 215 is as I've had my characters quote in this book, basically suggesting that the logical course of action should alien artifacts be discovered in our solar system, would be to carefully consider keeping such knowledge from the general public in order to protect our cultural legacy, and indeed even keep our society from deconstructing, as has been the case in many other instances when less advanced societies have come in contact with ones far in advance of their own.

And I've just scratched the surface. There's so much more, if I can find the drive to get my team back in gear, back to probing the mysteries that will always be out there. I hope this isn't the end, but a new beginning.

Thanks for coming along—and hopefully staying—for the ride.

David Sakmyster

7/15/12

45736453R00162

Made in the USA
Lexington, KY
18 July 2019